INHERITANCE

INHERITANCE

TARA PALMER-TOMKINSON

ISIS
LARGE PRINT
Oxford

First published in Great Britain 2010
by
Pan Books
an imprint of Pan Macmillan Ltd.

Published in Large Print 2011 by ISIS Publishing Ltd.,
7 Centremead, Osney Mead, Oxford OX2 0ES
by arrangement with
Pan Macmillan Ltd.
a division of Macmillan Publishers Limited

British Library Cataloguing in Publication Data
Palmer-Tomkinson, Tara, 1971–
   Inheritance.
   1. Upper class women - - Great Britain - - Fiction.
   2. Drug addicts - - Rehabilitation - - Fiction.
   3. Large type books.
   I. Title
   823.9'2–dc22

ISBN 978–0–7531–8866–8 (hb)
ISBN 978–0–7531–8867–5 (pb)

Printed and bound in Great Britain by
T. J. International Ltd., Padstow, Cornwall

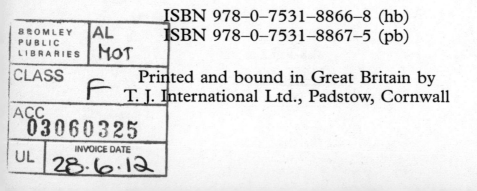

To my Mother

1st February

". . . and we should be arriving in approximately one hour. It's a crisp, dry day in Geneva, and with a high of six degrees it looks like being a lovely sunny afternoon for you both. Enjoy the flight."

Lyric Charlton smiled as Jean-Jacques, the Lear jet's regular pilot, finished his routine welcome from the cockpit. She wriggled her toes in her cream cashmere flight socks and marvelled at how perfectly they matched the leather upholstery. At this level of luxury, no detail was left unattended to, from the customized bar filled with her favourite tipple of Perrier to the monogrammed in-flight pillow. Not for the first time, she thanked her lucky stars. Because although she didn't wish to take any of this for granted or abuse her privilege, the most important thing to her right now was speed, and this private jet afforded her the luxury of it.

As she felt a squeeze on her hand, she turned to her right to smile at the man she loved. Here was something — some*one* — else she would never take for granted. The love of her life, her gorgeous, perfect, once-in-a-lifetime soulmate. He leaned across and kissed the top of her nose. She wiggled it delicately, breathing in the soft, musky, masculine scent of him.

"*Salade Niçoise*, Miss Charlton?"

Lyric pushed her thick, honey-coloured hair off her shoulders and smiled her acceptance as the air stewardess carefully placed the food in front of her on the linen-covered flight table. She looked the girl up and down appraisingly, taking in the demure bun holding back her shiny dark brown hair, the chiselled bone structure, her deep-set brown eyes and her pale, almost sallow complexion. Her fundamental beauty required no make-up other than black eyeliner and red lipstick, and she left behind the faintest aroma of hand soap, rather than scent. Eastern European, thought Lyric, without a shadow of a doubt, and all of twenty-two by the look of it. And what a sweet, innocent twenty-two she was, too. How different from herself at that age, Lyric thought wryly.

As the stewardess reached the dividing curtain, she knocked something off the work station behind it. "*Pizdets!*" she swore under her breath. Yep, thought Lyric, she was Russian all right . . .

Lyric restlessly pushed her salad to one side and turned her head to gaze out of the window as the jet progressed steadily through the clouds. She was feeling too keyed-up to eat — reflective, and nervous, too.

Leaning back, Lyric touched a button to recline the seat, stretched out her long, olive-skinned legs, crossed them at the ankle and rested them on the low-slung coffee table. She felt gloriously decadent. Madame Benoit, principal of Lyric's exclusive French finishing school, would be apoplectic if she could see her now, she thought with a smile — in Madame Benoit's view,

4

ladies should sit with legs together and folded demurely to one side at all times.

She smiled inwardly, thinking back to the Lyric of those days. It was only eight years ago, but it seemed a lifetime. How far she'd come from that would-be sophisticate — a born ringleader with a nose for mischief, fresh out of boarding school and en route to a pampered life among the upper classes. She'd thought she was invincible, but what a shock finishing school had been. Her own background, whilst undeniably privileged, was anything but spoilt, and the other girls' unselfconscious flaunting of their enormous wealth had totally floored her. They used private jets like buses, whereas the only previous experience Lyric had had of the Club cabin on a charter flight was the glimpse of it she'd got as she turned right to take her seat in Economy Class. With a giggle, Lyric remembered when a boyfriend had taken her on holiday and — oh joy! — instead of turning right on the plane into Economy, they'd *turned left*, into the hallowed environs of First Class. But instead of relaxing into the lie-flat seats, enjoying the free drink and making the most of the luxury available, Lyric had spent the whole eight-hour flight sitting bolt upright and starving hungry, loath to blow her super-cool cover. She hadn't dared ask how to recline the seat or extend the tray!

Sitting up to take a sip of her mineral water, Lyric felt a tug of nostalgia for the girl she'd been then. Finishing school and all its material competitiveness had been only her first step into the world of the super-rich. Since then, as It girl extraordinaire and the toast of international society, she'd become fully immersed in the surreal existence of the world's jet set. And whilst it had been a blast, and she'd revelled in the opportunities it had afforded her, at the same time every flamboyant display of wealth and every OTT extravagance had seemed to enhance her inner sense of unworthiness and the nagging feeling of emptiness.

Her story from then on was somewhat predictable, as she'd numbed her feelings of inadequacy and unfathomable loss with non-stop parties, drink and drugs — how predictable was that? But now, six months out of rehab and still clean, Lyric wasn't just on her way to restoring her own self-worth and repairing the damage her Class A addiction had done in her old life. She was on her way to solving the riddle that had troubled her since childhood and, in doing so, setting herself up for a whole new life.

Because now she had a purpose — a newly discovered raison d'être that for the past six months had defined her every waking moment. And finally, discovery after shocking discovery, revelation after earth-shattering revelation, the resolution she'd waited for all her life was within her grasp. But what she hadn't counted on was that others would be so desperately — and violently — opposed to her reaching it, and that her search would send her headlong into an international minefield of jealousy, deceit and betrayal. Right now, she needed to get to Geneva as soon as possible — before the forces working against her got there first . . .

As Lyric's thoughts turned to the unexpected opposition she'd come across as she solved the mystery of her life, she felt a chill run down her spine, and a familiar twitch in her left eye materialized. Absently, she reached up and scratched it. Funny that she'd never really questioned it until recently — it had always just been there, troubling her every now and again, a quirky part of the way she was made.

A muffled bang from the front of the plane snapped Lyric out of her reverie. Next to her she felt her companion sit up too, before a sudden thwack sent a shudder through his body and his strong, upright torso slumped wordlessly beside her. There was a soft click over her shoulder and, as she turned, she gasped involuntarily. Beside her seat, the air stewardess was staring at her intently. There was no sign of the meek expression and sweet good nature of earlier. Now the eyes were steely and the chiselled cheekbones had taken on a sinister appearance. A vein pulsing in her forehead showed her deadly intent. At the end of her confident and unwavering outstretched arm was a revolver. And it was pointing directly at Lyric's temple.

Three years earlier . . .

CHAPTER ONE

August

Crispin leaned forward and pulled the neckline of Lyric's dress further down her front.

"There you go, sweetie — if you've got it, flaunt it," he said, admiring the extra expanse of ample cleavage he'd revealed. "Isn't that what Madame What's-her-face would have told you?"

Lyric laughed and looked down at her generous all-natural cleavage. "She would have kittens if she could see me now."

"Puppies, if that pair is anything to go by," deadpanned Crispin. Pulling a white-tip Marlboro out of his silver cigarette case with a flourish, he leaned forward to ask the driver of their limousine for a light.

Lyric's stomach lurched as she looked down at her borrowed Antony Price couture gown. Old habits were hard to break. Although for the past few years she'd become as renowned for her outrageous outfits as for her sassy sound bites and party stamina, she could still hear Madame's mantras reverberate around her head every time she broke one of her rules of decorum. But this outfit, from the delicate crystal straps designed to look like drops of water to the sequins the colour of the deepest, darkest, loneliest ocean shimmering over the low-cut bodice and sexy slashed skirt, was perfect for the "shipwrecked" theme of the night. Not for nothing was the designer famous for giving you the body you'd always dreamed of — the hidden corsetry, although restrictive, had a miraculous effect and had shaped Lyric's lithe size ten curves into something out of Greek mythology. The colour of the dress drew out the natural highlights in her wild mane of thick, honey-coloured hair, and the sparkles enhanced her wide brown eyes. Lyric, as usual, wore little make-up — just a sweep of mascara on her long, dark lashes and a slick of lip gloss on her bee-stung lips. With Manolo Blahnik sharkskin sandals (he professed to having had the shark killed especially for Lyric), a conch-shell bag personally lent to her by the British Museum and — the *pièce de résistance* — a Philip Treacy reproduction of the *Cutty Sark* perched on her head, her look was sure to be the talking point of the evening. Or talking *points*, as Crispin had drily observed earlier, eyeing her boobs as they'd got ready together in her tiny Kensington mews house.

And what a night it promised to be. Of all the glamorous, extravagant, paparazzi-filled launch parties that had crammed her diary since she had taken on the mantra of London's favourite It girl, the best ones were still the exclusive private parties that her social set, rather than her social standing, guaranteed her an invitation to. With every month that passed, the parties seemed to get more and more decadent — and tonight's promised to be no exception. Thrown by

12

Thierry Langton, a merchant-banking colleague of the hedge-fund-manager husband of Lyric's best schoolfriend Laura, it was being held in his recently restored hunting lodge in the Wiltshire countryside, and anyone who was anyone had been invited. Except, of course, anyone with a flashbulb or an agenda.

The car turned off the B road into an unassuming entrance that opened on to a tree-lined gravel drive. As it crunched slowly through the overgrown woodland, the twilight threw shadows into the car and Lyric screwed up her nose.

"Ugh — spooky. He'd have been better off waiting until October and throwing a Halloween bash, wouldn't he?"

Crispin pressed his head to the window and tutted.

"O ye of little faith. Take a look at that, sweetie."

Lyric leaned over to his side and breathed a sigh of relief. "Now that's more like it . . ."

As the drive curved round to the left, the trees gave way to the house's main approach. The thirty-bedroom pile had been given a ten-million-pound makeover — and it showed. Set on the shore of a huge lake, within a thousand acres of rolling countryside and ancient woodland, the impressive ivy-clad building seemed to glow with pride under the glare of the hundreds of lights strung all around it. The gravel drive was packed with Ferraris, Porsches and limousines, and "man Friday" valets in loincloths (models from a top London agency) scurried about parking the guests' cars and directing the chauffeurs to the parking area.

As the car pulled up at the entrance, they could see the sea-green arrivals carpet and a glimpse of ancient beams dressed to look like driftwood. Lyric clapped her hands in delight. "I just *love* a theme done properly!" she cried. "It makes all the effort so much more worthwhile."

Crispin, whose sole contribution to the theme was to accessorize his Ralph Lauren slacks, just-too-tight Jean Paul Gaultier T-shirt and Gucci blazer with a seaweed-style scarf slung artlessly over his shoulder, ground his cigarette into the ashtray set into the arm of his seat and grabbed her hand. "So do I, darling, so do I. Now: party checklist. Lip gloss?"

Lyric patted her sequinned clutch. "Check!"

Crispin gave her a sidelong glance. "Not for you, darling — for me. Now, where were we . . . inability to breathe?"

Lyric wriggled in her dress and blew him an exaggerated kiss. "Check!"

"Headache from totally excruciating designer millinery?"

Lyric pulled a face and touched the ship on her head gingerly. It was definitely heavy.

"Check."

Crispin grinned. "Passport?"

"*Check!*" Lyric squealed. You simply never knew where you'd end up at these parties. For hosts with their own helipad, glamorous foreign after-party locations were literally through the conservatory and out the back door, but after a long night of partying, it was often those guests with private jets at conveniently

14

placed airfields who carried the party on to breakfast in a new exotic location.

Crispin leapt out of the car as a buffed-up "man Friday" appeared to open Lyric's door. Smiling graciously, she took Crispin's arm and the pair of them shimmied into the party.

Compared with the dim twilight outside, the lights spilling out of the huge front door were almost blinding, and it seemed even brighter inside. The high ceilings, ancient old beams and exquisite antique furniture made the "shipwrecked" theme seem strangely incongruous and somewhat Disneyfied. Everything was supersize — from the tall pyramids of glasses on the enormous bar set up along the length of the room to resemble the bow of a ship, to the wide, white, Hollywood-style smiles of the assembled guests. At one end of the room, a DJ was spinning track after track under a fairy-light-strung palm tree, whilst more man Fridays worked the room with silver trays groaning under the weight of fizzing champagne flutes or studded miniature treasure chests piled high with cocaine.

"Excellent, excellent," said Crispin, grabbing two glasses of champagne and gesturing to a treasure-chest waiter to come back later. He handed a glass to Lyric. "Dom Pérignon, without a doubt. Now we shan't want for anything."

Lyric smiled at him fondly. Despite her party-hard reputation, she still had a very low tolerance to alcohol and never touched drugs. She knew it was unfashionable, but she didn't see the point — she had no problem remaining fabulous company for hours on end without them, so why bother? She pulled herself up as she felt the all-too-familiar tug from deep inside her. A nagging, gnawing, unexplained emptiness that had plagued her all her life and simply refused to go away. Why, when she was about to enter a room full of people, did she often feel at her loneliest?

As she and Crispin walked into the drawing room, they were met with smiles of recognition and kisses from the people they knew well, along with many admiring glances, and Lyric felt her party adrenaline kick in. The guests, as always, had gone all out to reflect the theme, and the dress code ranged from theatrical Treasure Island-style costumes to "clever" interpretations. One woman had set off a monochrome outfit with a stunning set of black Tahitian pearls, another was wearing a diamond and sapphire sea-horse brooch, and yet another some conspicuous fishnet stockings. But none of the outfits came close to Lyric's. She was in her element when she had an adoring audience, and tonight's outfit would certainly ensure that, if nothing else.

"Look, darling, you're the centre of attention, despite crack-as-whack Tara Palmer-Tomkinson strutting her stuff in a bikini and snorkel," muttered Crispin into her ear as they passed another It girl holding court by the bar. Then, spotting a group standing around the fireplace, he waved delightedly.

"And thrice excellent!" he exclaimed. "There's Mindy Braithwaite and pals. They are an absolute hoot, darling — let's go and see them."

16

Lyric grimaced as she spotted a bloated, red-faced man in his seventies, wearing little more than an old piece of fishnet, standing beside a fifty-something blonde draped in a halter-neck Amanda Wakeley dress layered in different shades of blue crêpe. Half-naked, he was leering down her creased and mottled cleavage, shaking his netting and shouting repeatedly, "I'm still waiting to be caught." Spotting Crispin, the blonde waved flirtatiously. Lyric took one despairing glance at her, and her heart sank. Mindy was wearing rather too much make-up, which drew attention to her cheap surgery, and laughing loudly, all of which combined to give her a trashy look. Crispin, who had a weakness for rich middle-aged women, was drawn to her like a moth to a flame.

"Dear God, Crispin, never mind the ship, they all just look *wrecked*," Lyric murmured in his ear. She was about to protest further when she spotted in the group a tall, slightly-built man with sun-streaked brown hair, hooded aquamarine eyes and a louche air, wearing a dishevelled open-necked shirt under his black dinner jacket — YSL if she wasn't mistaken. But it was his unashamedly bored look that grabbed her — and the fact that he was possibly the fittest-looking man she'd ever seen. Well, since she'd sat next to Johnny Depp at a film premiere last year, anyway.

Lyric gave Crispin her most ravishing smile, tossed her hair back and raised her glass to him. Crispin, having followed her gaze, smirked and raised his in response.

"After you, then," said Lyric. "May the best girl win!"

Crispin laughed and, grabbing her hand, pulled her across the room. In a shower of air kisses he introduced Lyric to Mindy, her husband Anthony and the two women standing with them. Then, openly appraising the stranger, he held out his hand.

"And I don't think we've met. Crispin Nielson-Jones."

The stranger pulled himself away from the bookcase he'd been leaning against and held out a limp, unenthusiastic hand.

"Ralph Conway," he replied, pronouncing his name "Rafe" in a languid, plummy drawl. Lyric nearly melted. God, he was gorgeous. Even the usually blasé Crispin looked flustered.

"And *this* is Lyric Charlton."

Ralph looked her up and down slowly and deliberately. He sought her gaze and held it for a moment longer than was quite necessary. "Oh, I know who you are," he said, almost too low for anyone else to hear. Almost.

"Well, you'd have to have spent the past four years under a stone not to," sniffed Crispin, slightly put out that Lyric had robbed him of Ralph's attention quite so quickly. Lyric was speechless.

"You missed dinner," Ralph said, still in the same low tone. Lyric had to lean in to catch what he said, and caught a tantalizing whiff of his musky aftershave.

"We ate in. Why have steak out when you can have beans on toast at home?" said Crispin tartly to the

18

group, prompting gales of laughter from Mindy and friends.

"I had . . . an engagement," stammered Lyric.

What was wrong with her? Where was all her sparkling wit when she really needed it? Suddenly, she felt her left eye begin to tingle — the beginnings of an exaggerated but unexplained nervous twitch she'd had since childhood. It was extremely rare, her doctor had told her — just her luck! As if on cue, and before she could turn her head, her eye twitched and winked theatrically at Ralph. He raised an eyebrow in surprise, and Lyric cursed the affliction. As throughout her life, once again it had happened at exactly the wrong time.

"An engagement," repeated Ralph, slowly and deliberately, in a tone that was almost mocking. "That sounds very important. Well, too bad — dinner was spectacular. But at least you made it for the Champagne Surprise."

Lyric looked at him blankly. "Champagne Surprise?"

Ralph raised his nearly empty glass to her, drained it and tipped it upside down over the palm of his hand. From the bottom dropped a small, sparkling stone. He held it up delicately between his thumb and forefinger.

"That's your surprise — a diamond in every drink. Novel, isn't it?"

Lyric gasped in spite of herself. Despite their frequency on the party circuit, such extravagant displays of wealth still shocked her. She looked into her own glass, and, seeing nothing, drained it defiantly. As the bubbles coursed down her throat, she felt something else, too — something hard, something . . .

She choked loudly and messily as the tiny diamond became lodged in her throat. The barely swallowed champagne made to return and she burped — a quiet, ladylike burp, but one firmly within Ralph's earshot.

"There you go — there was one in yours, too," said Ralph in amusement.

Lyric inhaled sharply, eyes watering. Why did he make her feel so *gauche*?

Ralph grinned a stomach-churning, lopsided grin and turned his back slightly on the group, who had already tired of the frisson between the two and were excitedly checking their own glasses. He nodded at a waiter to top up his glass.

"Lyric?" he asked. Lyric shook her head. "Perhaps you'd prefer a fresh glass, so you can swallow another precious stone?" he teased. "Do I spy, with my little eye, something beginning with *spoilt*?"

"Not at all — I simply prefer my diamonds set in platinum," she said, trying to match his irony. She felt herself redden and got annoyed, which only made her blush deepen. He was really getting to her!

A "man Friday" passed with a stunning jewelled Fabergé egg on a tray and offered it to them. A delicate diamond-encrusted spoon lay by its side. Ralph picked it up and flipped opened the egg. There, inside, was another pile of fine white powder.

"Lyric, maybe I can tempt you with a little of this rather fine cocaine?" he said, still in the same teasing voice.

She shook her head confidently. "No thank you — not for me."

Ralph cocked his head to one side. "Oh, come on — don't tell me you don't do drugs? You're practically an endangered species!"

Lyric smiled back less certainly. Was she coming across as a real bore? She looked back at the group, where Crispin was standing next to a treasure chest doing his party trick, which consisted of throwing a scoop of cocaine up into the air as if it were scent and walking under it, sniffing and shrieking with laughter. Mindy was preparing to follow suit.

Ralph leaned in to Lyric again and whispered in her ear, his breath tickling her ear lobe and making the hairs on the back of her neck stand on end. "Don't look on it as deceptively altering your mind, but rather as increasing your party power. If you struggle with drinking too much, cocaine is your answer — it's the best leveller you'll ever come across." He pulled back and gave her a knowing look. "And if you're going to make it to Venice tonight, you'll need it."

Lyric looked straight at him quizzically. Was he propositioning her?

Ralph raised one eyebrow at her. "We're off for liqueurs at Harry's Bar. But later. *Much* later."

Lyric stared at him, butterflies fluttering in her tummy. She turned to the waiter and winked cheekily in an attempt to disguise the way her left eye had now started to twitch. "Well, I guess a girl's got to pass the time somehow."

Ralph allowed himself a condescending smile, and Lyric grinned bravely at the waiter. She might as well give it a try. After all, you only live once. And really, what harm could it possibly do? Just once.

Two hours later, at the same party, Lyric and Ralph were sitting barefoot on a sunbed by the side of the elaborate swimming pool, spotting constellations in the sky. Lyric had been chatting away for what seemed to her like hours, but Ralph didn't seem to mind. Groups of partygoers were dotted all around the edge, and the booming bass from inside was clearly audible, but Lyric felt, cliché though it might be, that she and Ralph were totally alone. Fire-torches cast a romantic glow across the water, and, sitting here in the open air, she could almost imagine they were shipwrecked together. Frankly, she couldn't think of anyone more wildly, sexily, intoxicatingly appropriate to be shipwrecked with. She was in love. In lust? No, in *love*. She realized she'd only known him for a short time, but she was sure of it. This was it. She'd finally found the gut-wrenching, all-consuming love she'd always hankered after. She loved Ralph. In fact, she was going to tell him —

Suddenly, from behind the sunbed, Crispin planted a noisy kiss on her shoulder. "There you are, darling! I've been looking everywhere for you. Shunt up, will you?" He squeezed on to the sunbed next to her, pulling out a Marlboro Light and completely ignoring Ralph. "I'm starting to tire of tonight. I mean, how many people do you know who have been shipwrecked in diamonds and couture?"

Lyric looked at Crispin, heart racing. He was right — this party could do with some livening up. And who better than herself to do it? She prided herself on being the life and soul, after all . . . With that, she leapt up and dived elegantly into the pool. There was a hush as Lyric resurfaced and pulled herself out. The crowd around the pool gasped and someone cheered.

"Now do I look shipwrecked?" she called out to Crispin and Ralph triumphantly. Her dress, always figure-hugging, now clung sexily to all her curves. Her eyes shone in the half light and her skin sparkled with the water dripping from it. Ralph shook his head in disbelief.

"No, but you look beautiful," Crispin called back, laughing. "You're off your face!"

Lyric held out her arms to the sky and twirled around gracefully. "No, I'm not — I'm off to Venice!"

She felt euphoric. Yes, she might be off her head — but she was happy. And one thing was certain — tonight had changed her life for ever.

Two years later . . .

CHAPTER
TWO

May

Lyric pulled on the handbrake of her Audi TT and gave a happy sigh. Despite nursing one hell of a champagne hangover, she'd made it. Broughton Hall, the family home, was her fortress, a haven away from the madness of her whirlwind existence, and the only place she could really relax. More importantly, it was the place she felt closest to filling the huge void that gnawed deep inside her. She just wished it hadn't turned into such a chore getting here. As if getting out of bed and getting anywhere after a big night wasn't bad enough, the prospect of the two-hour drive had caused her to cancel more weekends at home than she cared to remember in the past year — so much so that her mother now followed up her habitual mid-afternoon call to make sure the recently unreliable Lyric was still on for the visit (i.e. out of bed) with a second call: a "traffic update" (i.e. a check-up to make sure she was on the road). But it wasn't just the getting up and going. Once on the road, Lyric found the M4 to be a complete trial — those endless miles of tarmac and the relentless white lines in the middle, one after the other, racked up like thick lines of cocaine, mockingly reminding her of her narcotic-fuelled nightlife and what a mess she'd got herself into. And though it was a huge relief to pull off the motorway and on to the country roads that led to Broughton Hall, the relief at actually arriving was even more palpable.

This was a three-line-whip occasion — her father's birthday weekend, a date set in stone in the family calendar. She certainly couldn't wriggle out of it with a fictional flat tyre or sudden head cold. Grabbing her Louis Vuitton weekend bag from its place amidst the overflowing ashtray, unopened post and apple cores that littered the passenger seat, Lyric banged her elbow on the handbrake. Damn it! She rubbed her arm in frustration and noted with dismay that a bruise was already appearing. She had always been accident-prone, but she seemed to mark so easily these days. Ignoring the persistent ache, she leapt out of the car and waved excitedly as she saw Jeffries, the Charltons' ancient butler, standing between the pillars of the main entrance to greet her. Along with the rest of the staff, Jeffries was almost as old as some of the furniture and had probably had his suit longer than that. He still insisted on calling her *Miss* Lyric.

"Good evening, Miss Lyric," he said, with his characteristic bow of the head.

"Hello, Jeffries," replied Lyric, giving him an impromptu hug. He said nothing, but she was sure she detected a flush of pleasure creep over his face. Her natural effusiveness, total lack of affectation and innate sense of mischief had long made her a favourite with the staff.

28

She handed Jeffries her bag and looked around her with undisguised joy. Although stately, there was nothing intimidating about Broughton Hall. Carefully tended climbing shrubs softened the austere Grade-One-listed facade, and the interior decor was more about comfort than grandeur. Although her mother's exquisite taste and penchant for overseas travel — much of it with her best friend and Lyric's godmother, A-list actress Truly Stunning — was evident in the eclectic mix of Ming china, kilims and full-sized standard bay trees artfully dotted around the house, Broughton Hall was resolutely old money and the epitome of shabby chic. Most of the expensive ornaments, broken by children or dogs, had been superglued back together at some point over the years. Lyric breathed in deeply, relishing the familiar smell of wet dog, huge log fires and Jo Malone candles.

As if on cue, Stan, Lyric's beloved golden Labrador, came trotting down the hall and greeted her with adoring eyes, loud woofs and a big doggy smile. She knelt on the floor and enveloped him in a hug as he slobbered excitedly over her and thumped his tail heavily on the rug.

"You'll find your parents in the drawing room, Miss Lyric," said Jeffries with another little bow of the head, picking up her bag from the floor. "Will Mrs Gunners find your laundry in the back of your car?"

Lyric gave him a guilty look and nodded sheepishly. She had developed the habit of saving up her washing for weekends at home, and rather than spend her coke money on a maid, she was now doing this more frequently. She stood up, ran her fingers through her hair (blow-dried en route by the car heater) and straightened her Chloé blouse and Joseph trousers. A far cry from her flashy party clothes, but the appropriate choice for a weekend in the country. Thank goodness she'd thought to change for dinner before she left London. She was always *sooo* late, no matter what lengths of forward planning she went to. Her mother expected her to be punctual, and took a dim view if she wasn't.

A chorus of pleased hellos greeted Lyric as she bounced into the drawing room, and she happily embraced each of the family and friends gathered around the room.

First was her father, George, standing proudly in front of the fireplace, surrounded by photographs of the triumphs of the racing yard he'd established, and the horses he'd loved over the years, with a faraway look in his eyes. Lord Charlton was still handsome, his weather-beaten face tanned from years of hunting, shooting and fishing, his hair now showing more salt than pepper. Twinkly eyes and crinkly laugh lines gave away his permanent good humour and hinted at the caring nature that sometimes outweighed his balanced judgement.

"Hi, Daddy," she said warmly, and was rewarded with a loving kiss on the top of the head and a hug. Dear Daddy, in his ancient, faded country clothes, smelling faintly of cigars and Scotch and looking every bit as much a part of Broughton Hall as the ancient beams in the ceiling.

Next to him, cousin Jacob — thankfully without lecherous Uncle Quentin in tow — his classic good looks now slightly blurred around the edges from too many boozy Westminster lunches, was leaning on the grand piano as his latest girlfriend crucified Bach's *Prelude in B Minor*. Predictable Jacob, thought Lyric as she silently appraised the girl. Pretty, but not outstandingly so, well-brought-up, polite, with a pedigree to match — but sturdy, oh-so conservative and deadly *dull*. When was Jacob ever going to find someone who fitted his personality rather than his political aspirations?

"Hey, Jacob — still shaking up Whitehall?" she said fondly.

"I most certainly am," he said with an affectionate hug. "I just wish I could build my profile into a tenth of what yours is!"

Lyric grinned. "Well, notoriety seems to be a family trait."

A shadow flashed across Jacob's face, and Lyric suddenly wanted to kick herself. She'd been referring to herself, but she could quite equally have meant his father. Uncle Quentin was Daddy's younger brother and the errant black sheep of the Charlton family — but the fact that he had been his late father's favourite meant Daddy persisted in turning a continual blind eye to his gambling, debts and dodgy business arrangements. On the social scene, his reluctance to put his hand in his pocket for any of his extravagant tastes had earned him the nickname "Penguin", and even the society pages had started to refer openly to his less appealing side.

Across the room a couple of Daddy's birthday guests were admiring a Constable on the wall, one of the Charltons' many works of art hanging from heavy chains around the house. Then Lyric noted with delight that, standing behind a Sheraton sofa table, decked out head to toe in the latest Holland & Holland collection, was George's old school friend Sheik Haddad de Sattamin. His latest wife Carola was perched on a chair, self-conscious in elaborately coiffed hair, glitzy Versace dress and high heels — the ultimate no-no in a house with as many wooden floors as theirs. No doubt Lyric's mother would have one of the staff following her around buffing up the dents left by her stilettos — when they weren't getting stuck down the cracks between the old oak floorboards.

Lyric stifled a fond smile. Poor, gold-digging Carola. She tried so hard but always got it just that little bit wrong — proof that money didn't necessarily buy you style, and that too much could make the humblest person into an instant snob. The first time Carola had visited Broughton Hall, she'd complained that the bath water was brown. Brown! Lyric couldn't remember a time it had been *clear*! Didn't Carola realize that soft, slightly cloudy water was one of the ultimate signs of a classy, ancient home? Then Carola had set out on the next day's shoot in all the colours of the rainbow — Daddy had joked that she'd have been mistaken for a cock pheasant if the sight of her hadn't frightened them all away first. Yet the Sheik, in stark comparison to his fourth wife, was an unselfconscious, worldly, larger-than-life character — jovial, sociable and super-rich, and a regular on Lyric's jet-set party circuit. The Sheik was famed for his warmth and his generosity, and his own expensive attempts to fit into his social surroundings seemed endearing rather than try-hard.

And then, of course, flitting about the room putting everyone at ease — and studiously ignoring the calorie-laden canapés — was Lyric's mother, Lady Charlton. Ever the perfect hostess, Constance Charlton was the epitome of good taste, and legendary for both her sense of style and her exquisite entertaining, whether it was casual drinks before Sunday lunch, a formal dinner for twelve or a banquet or ball. Tonight she was resplendent in Indian silk bought on one of her many travels, the long tunic and flowing trousers emphasizing her whippet-thin figure, the ethnic jewellery setting off her cornflower-blue eyes and latest expensive facelift. Constance's easy-going demeanour and ready smile belied her neurotic nature — who would guess from the gracious way she made her guests feel so at home that Constance herself was a total neurotic who loathed hunting, shooting *and* fishing, and survived on pills and diet shakes?

Right now, Constance made a beeline for Lyric, stretching out her neck to air-kiss her daughter so that Lyric was enveloped in Fracas scent and a crêpey neck.

"Darling, you're here," she said to Lyric but also to the room in general. "We thought we would have to start without you." She gave her daughter a warm hug and then held up Lyric's chin and studied her face, taking in the pale, pinched skin and the huge dark circles under her eyes. "You look tired! Did you go to see the dermatologist I recommended to you?"

Lyric grimaced. "Yes, Mummy — he told me to drink more water and get more sleep and then tried to get me to spend my entire trust fund on a facelift," she said evenly. She smiled warmly as the Sheik approached and hugged her paternally.

"I think that your mother's dermatologist was wiser than you give him credit for," the Sheik said knowingly. "You *do* look tired, my dear. And so thin . . . Perhaps a weekend in the country — with your family — is just what you need?" Lyric pulled a face, all at once feeling about ten years old. "But that's you young people all over, isn't it?" the Sheik continued, looking over her shoulder at Constance. "You may be the nation's best-loved hostess, Constance, but your daughter, she continues to be the world's best-loved party guest. And so —" here he paused for dramatic effect — "I felt she might like the world's best party dress — as a little gift from an old family friend."

Lyric looked at him quizzically. The Sheik snapped his fingers, and seemingly out of nowhere, his manservant brought over a dress bag. From it, he produced a cocktail dress in claret crêpe, cut on the bias and delicately encrusted with Swarovski crystals and semi-precious stones. It glittered seductively and expensively, and seemed to epitomize refined, sexy sophistication.

Lyric gasped. "Oh my God! That's the most beautiful dress I've ever seen!"

34

The Sheik smiled. "Well, if you like the dress, why don't you put it on?"

Lyric stared at him, thinking of the thousands of pounds a dress like that must have cost. "But — I couldn't possibly . . ."

The Sheik's smile widened even further. "Yes, you could. And if it fits, Lyric, you can have it."

Lyric looked around the room and grinned impishly. "Well, I'll bloody well make it fit!"

She raced upstairs to her mother's bedroom — the closest — and, making a mental note to come back and raid her dressing table for a new stash of Valium later, tore off her clothes, heart racing. The dress had to fit! She'd always been sample size, and she certainly hadn't put weight on lately — if anything, she'd lost it.

Lyric touched the fabric reverently. It slipped softly through her fingers as she pulled it on and seemed to glow under the dressing-table lights. Lyric gazed into the mirror. She gasped at the sight of herself, and tears welled up in her eyes.

"Come on, Lyric, we're waiting!" called Jacob from the bottom of the staircase. "Have you got it on yet?"

Lyric stared at herself miserably. The dress hung limply as if it were hanging off a coat hanger. Her limbs stuck out in it like jagged corners, and where there should have been curves the material simply sagged. Panicking, Lyric opened her mother's tights drawer and, pulling out a pair of stockings, shoved them down her bra. But it was no good. It wasn't just her weight, it was the expanses of skin, too. All over her usually flawless skin were big, ugly, black bruises — on her arms, her shins, her legs: bruises *everywhere*. And not just where she'd bumped herself, but, it seemed, even where she'd slept. On her back, her collarbone, her thighs. What had happened to her once shapely figure? What had she done to herself?

One thing was certain — she couldn't go downstairs looking like this. Slowly, reluctantly, she slipped off the dress and pulled her own clothes back on. Carefully, she folded it over her arm and walked down the stairs.

Back in the drawing room, all eyes turned to her and jaws dropped in disappointment as they saw her return in her own clothes.

"Lyric, darling, don't tell me you couldn't fit into it?" Constance tutted. "How can you look so thin yet still not fit sample size?"

Lyric, ignoring another of her mother's habitual put-downs, smiled at the Sheik shyly, eyes downcast, scared to meet his gaze. "You know what, I can't accept this," she said. "But thank you — it was a very kind gesture." She looked up into his eyes, and with a shot of realization instantly knew that he was totally aware of just how deeply she'd got herself into trouble. And he was offering to help her. But how?

Just then, Jeffries appeared at the door. "Your Ladyship, dinner is served."

Lyric was now shaking from something other than her champagne hangover, and wished she'd had time for a drink to steady her nerves.

The guests took their seats around the table, and the cheese soufflé was served. Lyric, feeling conscious of both the Sheik's and her mother's eyes boring into her across the table, tried to please them both — Constance by appearing to have a healthy appetite, and the Sheik by playing delicately with her food with polite nonchalance. As usual, Constance had managed to spread her own tiny portion around her plate without actually consuming any of it. Trust Mummy to avoid eating any of what was really no more than Gruyère-flavoured air.

As the main course of roast grouse was served, Lyric caught her father's eye as he looked at her in fond amusement. They both knew she hated the pungent taste of game and would have preferred a breaded veal escalope. Her childhood favourite, the dish had been banned from Broughton Hall menus from the day she had taken one of her mother's "chicken fillet" bra pads, tossed it in oil and breadcrumbs and had it served up for dinner on a bed of rocket salad. Whilst Lyric and her father had been in hysterics, Constance had feigned amusement — but ever since, the dish had been absent from the Charlton dinner table.

The studious scraping of cutlery on china and cheery dinner chat was abruptly shattered by the tinny ringtone of Lyric's mobile.

"Does your phone ever stop ringing?" laughed Jacob, peering at her round the tall vase of Casablanca lilies in the middle of the table. "You're in more demand than I am!"

"Yes, well, dear, there's always been more politics at parties than in Parliament," quipped Constance. "But Lyric, you might have the decency to switch it off at dinner."

Lyric flushed and, fishing the phone from her clutch bag, rejected the call. She picked up her heavy silver knife and fork and returned to her food. She'd only managed one more mouthful when Jeffries appeared at the door.

"Miss Lyric, there is a telephone call for you. I explained you were dining, but the gentleman was most insistent."

Lyric looked up at him, perplexed.

"Dear God, does no one respect mealtimes any more?" sighed Constance, more to herself than anyone in particular. "Who is it, Jeffries? Don't tell me — it's that Conway boy."

Forgetting her inner turmoil for a moment, Lyric scowled at her mother. She never missed an opportunity to put Ralph down. Why was no one Lyric fell in love with ever good enough for Constance?

Jeffries cleared his throat. "The gentleman claims he is ringing from the *News of the World*."

A hush descended over the table, and concerned looks were exchanged. Lyric, suddenly and inexplicably fearing the worst, turned to Jeffries and held out her hand for the receiver.

"Please, excuse me — I think I should take this," she said quietly. Inadvertently, she caught the Sheik's eye. He looked about as worried as she felt.

Her concerns were wholly justified. Listening silently to the voice on the other end of the receiver, Lyric felt as though she was going to pass out. She sat, dumbstruck, head pounding. It couldn't be any worse. The public humiliation. The shame. She looked around her at the people she loved gathered at the dinner table, and felt physically sick. The hurt this was going to cause them . . .

"No comment," she said into the phone and hung up.

She paused for what seemed like for ever, then looked up, eyes full of fear. She almost couldn't speak.

"Daddy, Mummy." Her voice broke. The table now was deadly silent.

"That was —" she swallowed hard. "The *News of the World* have some pictures of me. Taking drugs. In a public loo. In Camden."

In the context of admitting she took drugs, the details of where and how hardly seemed important. But she knew that it was exactly this that would matter so much to the paper. It was so sordid. And so . . . so much of a one-off. She took drugs, yes. She had a problem, yes. But her habit had never been that . . . desperate. That *depraved*. If only Ralph hadn't been so insistent about going to that bar, the latest hang-out for super-cool rock types, if only they hadn't bumped into their dealer, if only . . .

If only.

There was a deadly silence.

"So what are you saying, darling? You've smoked some cannabis? Isn't simply everyone doing that again? God, you'd think this generation had invented it," sniffed Constance with a dismissive air.

The Sheik cleared his throat. "I think Lyric may be referring to something rather more serious. Rather more than a simple puff on a naughty cigarette?" He raised his voice questioningly at Lyric, inviting her to open up, to admit everything. "Something that, maybe, she'll need treatment for? And that's before we've dealt with the media backlash."

Again all eyes turned to Lyric. She hung her head.

"I have a drug habit," she mumbled. "I think I'm . . . addicted to cocaine."

There was another stunned silence.

"Oh, come on, now — a few days in the Four Seasons and a couple of algae wraps and you'll be back on your feet," said Constance matter-of-factly. "Truly's always going off somewhere or other to treat her exhaustion. I'm sure this is nothing different." She fixed Lyric with a stern glare that seemed to be saying, *I knew hanging about with that Conway boy was going to end in tears, Lyric — and now look.*

Lyric's father shook his head kindly, his eyes twinkling at his daughter. "Constance, I think she's better off staying put here. Some home cooking and fresh country air and she'll be as right as rain."

The Sheik clapped his hands authoritatively. "If I may be so bold? I think we might be underestimating the gravity of the situation here." He turned gently towards Lyric. "You see, it's not really about the newspaper story, is it, Lyric?"

Lyric shook her head miserably.

He turned back to her parents. "You see, George, Constance, this is more like having an illness. Lyric is very ill, and she needs to go and get better. But the newspaper story — well. That puts a whole new level of urgency into the situation. We have to get her on a plane before it hits the news-stands on Sunday."

"On a plane?" asked Constance stupidly.

"On a plane," repeated the Sheik gently.

"But where on earth to?" questioned Constance.

"I know of a very good place — extremely discreet — in the middle of the desert," said the Sheik. "I took the liberty of speaking to them some weeks ago. It is exceptionally exclusive, but it seems they would be happy to welcome an associate of mine."

Constance gulped, for once close to losing her legendary composure. Her eyes shone with unshed tears. George blew his nose noisily into his handkerchief, his brow furrowed as he wrestled with the bare truth. Jacob raised his eyebrows at his girlfriend and looked over at Lyric with concern. The rest of the table shuffled cutlery and wine glasses uncomfortably.

George, pulling himself together and looking meaningfully down the length of the table at his wife, cleared his throat and turned to the Sheik. "So, then, this place in the desert — tell me more."

"She'll have to give up that Conway boy once and for all," said Constance, almost to herself. "There's no way we shall ever condone that relationship now."

Lyric listened miserably as the assembled crowd discussed her future, numbly watching her family make the arrangements for her salvation. She was humiliated, she was embarrassed, and she was scared. The fact that they were all being so goddamn *understanding* almost made it worse.

But in her heart of hearts, Lyric felt sheer relief. It was her ugly secret no longer. Somebody understood how bad it had become and wanted to help her. Somebody had taken her under their wing and was going to make it better.

One thing still troubled her, though. Solving her drug addiction was one thing, but would she ever get to solve the real problem in her life — this nagging sense of debilitating loneliness?

CHAPTER
THREE

"Well, well, well — Lyric always did have a penchant for trouble," said Treeva Sinclair gleefully. She dropped the copy of the *News of the World* she'd been scanning on to the deck and held out her left hand to the white-linen-clad manicurist. At her feet, another nail technician was busy painting her toes a vivid pink. Treeva turned her attention back to the portable plasma screen in front of her, currently blaring out *MTV Cribs*.

"Still, I hope she's OK," she added, almost as an afterthought.

Her mother, Pamela Sinclair, looked at her over the top of her oversized Dior sunglasses.

"I just can't believe a well-brought-up girl like Lyric would get herself mixed up in something like this," she said. "I've known her since she was tiny! I remember when you first told me she was taking drugs, I refused to believe you. I mean, *why?* You'd *never* do that!"

Treeva smiled sweetly and pulled her baseball cap further down till it covered her face. "Of course I wouldn't. Don't be ridiculous, Mummy."

Blowing on her long, airbrushed acrylic nails, Treeva casually looked over the side of the luxury super-yacht at the sparkling azure sea. A perk of having Jed Sinclair, one of the most powerful men in music, as a father meant that she had grown up surrounded by not only the luxurious fruits of his success, but those of his wealthy friends too. This floating palace, all cognac marble, beige deep-pile carpets and mirrored ceilings, belonged to his Saudi business associate Nasser Al Haji and was a favourite bolthole for Treeva and her mother. She surveyed the waters surrounding the yacht disdainfully — a school of snorkellers and divers were bobbing up and down like porpoises.

"Haven't you found it yet?" called Treeva as one popped up and, seeing her peering over the edge, took off his face mask.

He shook his head emphatically, waving his torch aloft. "There's no sign," he called. "It's not easy trying to find a diamond in waters this deep."

"Well, it's in there somewhere — don't come back until you've found it," she replied dismissively and turned back to her nails. "It wouldn't surprise me if one of them had found it and pocketed it," she said out loud to no one in particular. "I knew I shouldn't have gone swimming in it. I mean, a solitaire ring like that could set one of them up for life." Her mother, head buried in a gossip magazine, murmured in agreement without looking up.

Picking up her glass, Treeva swirled the cocktail umbrella around and drained the rest of her Sex on the Beach. She held out the glass to a nail technician without turning away from the TV. "I'll have another of these. And some of those crunchy little crudités we had last night."

The nail technicians both looked around for a bartender or waiter, but, seeing no one, looked back at each other in confusion. The manicurist scowled and muttered something unintelligible under her breath, whilst the woman at Treeva's feet raised her eyebrows, downed tools and scurried off in search of the refreshments.

Treeva stroked her mahogany-brown shoulder thoughtfully, picked up the bottle of Piz Buin Classic Brown next to her and shook it. It was empty.

"Oh, look, I'm clean out of suncream," she said to the manicurist. "Get me some, will you?"

The woman hesitated a nanosecond as if waiting for something, but when no pleasantries were forthcoming stomped sulkily off below deck.

"I'm so glad I tan naturally like you, Mummy," Treeva said, stretching out one of her long legs, which had the deep orangey-brown look of fake tan, and contemplating it happily. "I couldn't stand to be all white like Laura."

Pamela looked over the top of her magazine. "Well, it's just as well you grew out of your own pale skin then, darling," she said pointedly. Treeva's insistence that she had naturally sun-kissed skin might fool most people, but her obsessively secret twice-daily applications of fake tan couldn't fool her own mother.

"Talk of the devil . . ." said Treeva, unabashed. As the latest grime track blared out tinnily from under her sunbed, she picked up her pimped-up BlackBerry, which sparkled with Swarovski crystals. "Yah, Laura — hi, sweetie."

"Hi, Tree," said her other best friend, Laura Hoffman. "Have you seen the papers?"

"Yah, sweetie," said Treeva, picking up her newspaper again and fanning herself with it nonchalantly. "Trust Lyric, eh?"

"Have you spoken to her yet?" asked Laura, her voice full of concern.

"No — I've tried a few times, though," lied Treeva. "Her phone's always turned off."

"That's weird. I've been trying to get through too, but it's always engaged," said Laura absently. "Poor thing! I just want to make sure she's OK. I wonder how it's gone down with Constance and George?"

Pretty mother-of-two Laura was a born worrier and natural do-gooder, and had spent the past twenty-three years picking up the pieces after whatever trouble Lyric had got into — usually having led a willing Treeva along with her. This episode, however, put Lyric's former loveable scrapes and high-spirited mischief in the shade. This was trouble with a capital T. Lyric's life was never going to be the same again.

"I would imagine she's more worried about how it's gone down with the Guess jeans campaign, her column and her adoring public — not to mention her record company," Treeva said bitterly, not bothering to disguise her jealousy at Lyric's successful career. "The papers say she's lost the lot — and if their tone is anything to go by, the public won't be far behind them."

46

Treeva's own career in the public eye had never quite got off the ground in the same way that Lyric's had. Her modelling career had started and finished when her disastrous debut on a London Fashion Week catwalk a decade ago had eclipsed the schoolfriend's first collection she was modelling. The collection — and Treeva — got the desired column inches, but for all the wrong reasons, as Treeva's "Playboy Bunny" image had jarred uncomfortably with the pared-down grungey minimalism of the early-Nineties styling. Since then, she'd tried her hand at singing (her girl band, Sugar Rush, was dropped by her father's record label after their first single bombed), and acting (her walk-on role as an extra in *Hollyoaks* was turned into a cameo when, despite all efforts to disguise her, Treeva Sinclair simply looked like — well — Treeva Sinclair). Her latest attempt at world domination — as a VJ presenter on a satellite music station — seemed similarly doomed.

"I heard they'd all dropped her, too," said Laura compassionately. "Poor, poor Lyric. It's just so unlike her. How on earth did she get herself into such a mess?"

"Well, Laura, think about it. Lyric's always had some weird kind of attraction to the world's lowlife. I mean, let's not forget that she is the only girl to go to an exclusive French finishing school and fall in love with the gardener's son, for God's sake!"

"Oh, Treeva, come on — that was a silly crush, that's all," cooed Laura soothingly. "Lust from afar. I don't think she ever even spoke to him!" It never paid to encourage Treeva when she was warming to her favourite activity — bitching.

"Well — OK, you're right," Treeva acknowledged grudgingly. "But the drugs thing, you know — it could happen to anyone in our position. Drugs are just so available, aren't they, and it takes a strong person to say no to them," she continued, her voice loaded with meaning.

Which was lost on Laura. "Yes, but surely you can just turn them down?" she said with genuine confusion. "I mean, it's not as though Lyric's ever had problems with her confidence, or had to resort to some kind of artificial high to be the life and soul of the party."

"Oh, Laura, we don't all have your strength of character or your constitution," snapped Treeva. "And people are not always what they seem. Maybe Lyric just wanted to do us all a favour and take a break from being a national treasure for five minutes."

There was a silence on the other end of the phone as Laura absorbed the rebuke and worked out how to respond to it. Throughout their years together at boarding school, she'd been the sensible, sturdy one of the trio — in looks as well as personality, for whilst leggy Lyric had the racing metabolism of someone of her restless disposition — not to mention the honed limbs of someone used to skiing for several months a year — and image-obsessed Treeva had shaped her model-thin limbs with years of working out and liposuction, five-foot-nothing Laura had spent her adolescence fighting a losing battle with puppy fat, not helped by stodgy school meals and generous helpings of her grandmother's lemon drizzle cakes during the holidays. But at some point during the final year of school, she'd shed all her excess weight, and ever since then her jet-black hair, alabaster skin and dark brown eyes had been set off by the appearance of some striking cheekbones and sexy 1950s contours. Her new sex-bomb status — not to mention social eligibility as the daughter of banking supremo Tiny Goldstein — had attracted the attentions of hot-shot hedge funder Robert Hoffman, and she now lived the society-wife dream, running charitable events and lunches for super-rich and super-bored ladies. But despite the fact that she had been first to achieve the next accepted rung of marriage and motherhood, it felt a world away from Lyric and Treeva's nocturnal existence, and in their company Laura often felt transported back to the days when she was the eternal singleton, dowdy in comparison with their glittering public personas.

"Well, Treeva, maybe you're content to go along with the superficial line the rest of the world will take, but as her best friend I'm a little more inclined to look beneath the surface for the *real* reason," said Laura calmly. "Now, tell me, how does the Med find you on this glorious June day?"

Treeva sighed disinterestedly. "Well, guess what, more bad news — I've dropped my solitaire in the sea and the service is all *mañana, mañana* — oh, *thank you*," she finished sarcastically as a steward brought her drink and some crisps. "I thought you must be growing the potatoes for them." She turned back to the phone.

"But you know, I needed the break. Filming just totally takes it out of me."

"I thought you were doing one show a week?" questioned Laura.

"Yes, sweetie, but filming is ten a.m. till two p.m.!" exclaimed Treeva. "And then there's hair and make-up on top of that. It's simply relentless."

There was a brief pause as Laura tried to formulate a response, which was shattered by the ear-piercing wail of her baby daughter. "Tree, I'm going to have to go — Kitty's just woken up," she said distractedly. The birth of Laura's son Max, now three, and her daughter had uncovered her inner earth mother, and despite her and her husband Robert's joint fortunes and traditional upbringings, she had resolutely refused to employ a full-time nanny, preferring instead a part-time mother's help to cover for her appearances at fund-raising charities. Robert had been unimpressed. However, the thing about Laura was that she didn't insist on much, but when she did, she really meant it — so in the end he'd had little say in the matter.

Treeva sighed again. God, children were so boring. And why was it that, having long decided that kids would do nothing but cramp her style, other people's had to come along and spoil all her fun anyway?

"OK, Lau, see ya! Wouldn't wanna be ya! Ciao-ciao, baby." Dropping her BlackBerry on to the deck, Treeva picked up the gold hand-mirror she'd pinched from one of the yacht's bathrooms — there were over thirty bathrooms throughout the yacht; who was going to miss one teeny mirror? — and checked her appearance.

She really needed to get her veneers done again — she was convinced one of them was going yellow. Baring her Hollywood-white teeth at herself, she idly rearranged the white-blonde strands of hair poking out from under her cap.

Her BlackBerry rang again, this time a sexy R&B ringtone. She smiled triumphantly as she recognized it and, throwing a surreptitious glance towards her mother, crossed her legs and snuggled further down on to her sunbed.

"Well, hello, handsome," she said coyly.

"Treeva," drawled a man's languid tones on the other end of the line. "I do hope I haven't interrupted anything important?"

Treeva giggled in a way that was meant to be both suggestive and seductive. "Oh, you know, just chilling. Lying on the deck in my tiny string bikini, rubbing oil over my sun-kissed limbs," she purred. "Nothing important. Nothing I wouldn't want you to distract me from."

She pictured the effect she hoped the image would have on him, and smiled softly to herself. Her face fell when he tutted at her.

"That's not the attitude I expect from someone whose best friend is splashed all over the nation's papers," the caller scolded. "You should be ashamed of yourself."

Treeva laughed again, this time more shrilly. "Well, I'm not the only one who should be, am I?" she retorted. "The question is, what are you going to do about it?"

There was a pause. "I'm going to do what I always do when you've been a bad girl," scolded the caller. "I'm going to make you pay for it. And you're going to love it."

Treeva smiled into the phone. "I'll look forward to it. Laters."

She shut the phone off and lay back on her sunbed, slathering on more oil from the bottle the manicurist had placed by her side. She smiled contentedly to herself. Why was it that one-upmanship was so addictive? And why was it that being bad, no matter what the consequences, or who got hurt in the process, always felt so *good*?

One thing was sure. If this particular indiscretion ever got out, someone was going to get very badly hurt.

CHAPTER
FOUR

August

"And I don't just mean thousands. I have millions — *millions* — of pounds to spend. On the right pieces, naturally."

"Naturally." Quentin Charlton sat back as the wine waiter topped up his glass of Château Lafite and pondered his good fortune. Just as his latest business venture — dealing fine art to the aristocracy — was about to go belly-up, what should land on his plate but a billionaire oligarch hell-bent on impressing the highest echelons of international society by splashing his cash on some paintings. Life was cruel by nature, and he'd had to deal with his own unfair share of misfortune — but every now and then it handed you a winner.

The waitress placed Quentin's choices from the well-stocked cheese board in front of him and he grunted with pleasure. He loved the reassuring waitresses in their black dresses and white aprons. You couldn't beat White's for a good lunch — and after potted shrimps, Welsh saddle of lamb and a couple of bottles of fine claret, Quentin was ruddy-cheeked and feeling on top of the world. However, in his dishevelled

Hackett shirt and jacket, bloodshot eyes bulging from a face disfigured by thread veins and a mottled complexion, he looked as if he'd crept out from under it. Across the table, in spite of his leathery, tanned skin, unkempt eyebrows and thick, fat fingers showcasing heavy gold signet rings, the Russian looked fresh-faced and fragrant by comparison.

As the waitress moved away, Quentin tutted mockingly. "Come, come, m'dear — haven't you forgotten something?"

The waitress politely hid her irritation at his familiarity and looked at him quizzically.

"Sir?"

"Branston Pickle, m'dear," barked Quentin, looking proudly over to Sergei Alexandrov, his lunch guest, and shaking his head in mock disgust. He raised his voice ostentatiously and looked around, hoping to expand his audience. "I've been coming here for over thirty years — thirty years, d'you hear — and I always have Branston Pickle with my cheese. Now, jump to it, m'dear, before I smack that pretty bottom of yours."

The waitress drew herself up in indignation but, too polite and respectful to respond, turned on her heel and made a dignified exit in search of the pickle.

Quentin patted his protruding paunch and, spearing a piece of Stilton, pointed it at Alexandrov. "The thing is, Sergio, my friend . . ."

"Sergei," corrected the Russian, without expression.

"The thing is, Sergio," Quentin continued without even drawing breath, "to create the kind of collection you're talking about, you'll not just need millions." He leaned across the table conspiratorially, wiping his upper lip free of the beads of sweat that had gathered there.

The Russian cocked his head questioningly. "Go on."

"You'll need the three Cs: Connections. Class. And — um — Kudos."

The Russian nodded solemnly.

"And that's what no other dealer can deliver," continued Quentin. "The old-boy network is something that does not come by chance. It is the product of generations of 'old school ties', if you see what I mean." He chuckled at the pun, which went straight over the Russian's head. "You can't buy them, you know," he added patronizingly, "and for good reason. They are the key to a myriad of exclusive worlds — the art world being only one of them — impenetrable to the average citizen, regardless of wealth or standing, unless, of course, you happen to be invited through the door by one of its existing members." He paused dramatically. "And I, as one of those very people, am offering you that very chance."

Sergei nodded graciously. "And this is something I am very pleased for," he said in halting English. "My daughter Rini, she was delighted with her birthday gift. And now I, Sergei, plan to fill my wife Olga's new home in Dubai with similar, but even better, works. Magnificent pieces of fine art that show not only that I, Sergei, am rich, but that I, Sergei, have great taste and great knowledge too."

A shadow passed over Quentin's face for a split second as he tucked into the rest of his cheese. He was

55

conveniently ignoring the fact that by sheer good fortune, the one piece he'd sold Sergei had actually been his, a Constable that his father had bequeathed him when the rest of the bloody Charlton estate and most of its treasures had been left to his older brother George. That Alexandrov wanted more of the same for his multimillion-dollar dacha on the outskirts of Moscow was going to pose its own problem, but he planned to address that later.

And who in their right mind bought their bratski teenage daughter fine art for her sweet sixteenth anyhow? Come to think of it, their strumpet of a trophy wife either, for that matter? How incongruous that priceless landscape must have looked to a young girl absorbed by her world of pop music and glitter. Alexandrov had presented it to her at the eight-million-pound extravaganza he had thrown for her at that hired stately home in Barnet. The location might have worked for the party's Bond theme, but even hapless Quentin could think of more cost-effective locations. Sergei had reportedly used hardly any of the antiques-filled interior, but had instead commissioned a glamorous casino set to be tacked on to the front of the building — a huge expense to cover up a building he'd paid a huge amount to hire. No ordinary party, that.

But then, Sergei was no ordinary father. The loo-roll king of Eastern Europe, Sergei Alexandrov had raised himself from his humble peasant upbringing in rural Russia to become one of the richest men in the world, an astute businessman with a killer instinct and a ruthless, iron will. Word had it that he kept his friends

56

close and his enemies closer — until such time as the latter could be adequately disposed of, that is.

But Quentin had no intention of becoming one of Sergei's enemies. Far from it. Rather, he had plans to become Alexandrov's right-hand man and provide him with one of the few things money couldn't buy — entry to the inner sanctum of the English aristocracy — and get rewarded handsomely for it. One day soon, Quentin vowed, he wouldn't be entertaining people like Alexandrov at his exclusive gentlemen's club, but at home, in his rightful place as lord and master of Broughton Hall.

Quentin shrugged off the irritation that always came over him at the thought of the familial injustice dealt to him at birth. The fact that he, as the second Charlton son, had missed out on inheriting the family estate had long rankled with him. Although his elder brother George had been a model son, devoting his life to the estate, and was therefore well placed to take over when his father died, Quentin had allowed his resentment to fester. Overindulged by his father from an early age — either through guilt or through favouritism, no one was quite sure — Quentin's many weaknesses, misdemeanours and failings had been overlooked and even tolerated over the years. He was now a seasoned gambler and functioning alcoholic, with a string of failed businesses behind him and a growing list of debts in front. The straw he had always clutched at was that, according to the ancient deed of covenant that governed the Charlton millions, only male heirs could inherit — which meant that as soon as George, who had just one daughter, was "gathered", as Quentin chose to put it, then his own son Jacob would take his place at the head of the family. With his father firmly in charge, of course. Luckily, no one knew the lengths to which Quentin had been prepared to go over the years to achieve his lifelong ambition. And now, finally, it was all within his grasp. Sooner — far, far sooner — than he ever could have hoped. And thanks to his lawyer's clever digging and the drug-fuelled lunacy of his only niece, Lyric, it would fall into place with Quentin having to do nothing at all. Well, almost nothing.

This thought cheered Quentin immediately and, pushing his plate away from him, he gestured for the wine waiter. "Sergio, you'll join me in a little mouthwash of brandy, won't you, my friend?"

Sergei clicked his tongue and shook his head as he rose from the table. "Regrettably no, Mr Charlton. Time is pressing on, and I, Sergei, have —"

"*Pas de problème, pas de problème,*" interrupted Quentin, breaking into French as he tended to do when fuelled by a fluid lunch. Delighted to be relieved of his networking duties, he stood up and walked over to settle the bill with the cashier. Smiling broadly, he greeted her by name, and was therefore more than unsettled when she said she had been instructed to accept nothing other than cash from him. Quentin protested, and, as his voice grew louder and the cashier's grew softer, Sergei came over, reached into his coat and, slapping Quentin on the back and loudly thanking him for lunch, slipped a wad of notes into the pocket of the scruffy Hackett jacket.

"This should clear your account as well, Mr Charlton. Have a pleasant afternoon."

"Good man, good man," boomed Quentin, recovering his bluster. "I have various matters to attend to and had planned to spend the rest of the afternoon here."

"So, Mr Charlton, I, Sergei, leave my wishes in your hands," the Russian said deliberately. "A generous advance will be wired into your account tomorrow to cover any interim expenses. I shall expect regular updates as to your progress — but my darling wife, she has her birthday in four months, and I expect my home to be filled with the finest of art by then. Agreed?"

Quentin laughed loudly and crudely. "My dear Sergio, you shall have enough fine art to fill a dacha and a half by then," he roared.

Some hours later, peering through the fog of his second Montecristo, Quentin was firmly ensconced in a leather armchair, conspicuously ignoring the club's non-smoking rule as he ruminated with self-satisfaction on the influx of Russian investment into the art world. He was a genius, he'd decided, to have discovered such rich pickings with so little effort. The fact that he actually had no contacts in the art world was no problem — after all, there were millions of pounds' worth of fine art just gathering cobwebs in rooms that were seldom used at Broughton Hall. All he needed to do was figure out how to get hold of them.

The lazy afternoon peace was suddenly shattered by a Nokia ringtone. Quentin looked around him in annoyance before realizing it was his own. He fumbled in the pockets of his jacket for a moment, then pulled out an oversized brick of a phone, a relic of the late Eighties, and stared at it drunkenly. Irritated at the interruption to his reverie, he sighed heavily and answered.

"Charlton."

"Quentin. It's Macintosh."

Quentin looked around him surreptitiously.

"What do you want?" Quentin slurred, in a deep, angry voice, with scant regard for the unspoken "no mobile phones" rule of the club. "And goddamn you, old boy, why use the phone? It could be tapped."

"I had no other choice," said the voice on the line.

Quentin laughed cruelly. "Don't tell me. Not more namby-pamby soul-searching for your very well-rewarded actions all those years ago?"

On the other end of the line the doctor hesitated, leaving only the rasping of Quentin's heavy breath in the air before replying in a soft, well-spoken, nervous voice: "No, Quentin. This is not about me. It's the Bulldog."

At the use of the all-too-familiar codeword, Quentin slapped the arm of his chair in irritation. "What about him?" he snapped. "And why should it concern me, anyway? Come to that, if you hadn't belatedly developed a conscience, it wouldn't concern you, either."

The doctor hesitated. "He's getting curious."

Quentin laughed a hard, brittle laugh. "Curious. Curious! Someone in his position shouldn't be getting curious — he can't afford it!"

The doctor cleared his throat. "He's asking questions," he said haltingly. "Lots of questions. Awkward questions."

Quentin spluttered down the phone. "Well, it's not his right to ask! Keep him in his place, man. How hard can it be?"

"It's not easy," said the doctor lamely. "He's very persistent."

"Well, shut him up, then!" hissed Quentin, more menacing now. "You've had plenty of practice, after all."

Again, a hesitation. "He's not asking me. He's asking a search agency."

There was silence now at both ends.

The doctor took his advantage. "It's not helpful, this stint in rehab — the publicity . . . If it should ever come out —" He left the consequences unspoken. "Well. We're both in deep, deep trouble."

"Goddammit, old boy, if it should ever come out it would tarnish the aristocratic bloodline for ever," Quentin barked cruelly. He tapped a few times on the arm of his chair before continuing decisively. "Well then, there's only one thing for it, isn't there? I'll need a photo. It's been thirty years, after all." He paused for a millisecond, then spoke in cold, hushed tones. "It's time to shut them both up. Him *and* the girl. For good . . ."

There was a gasp, and a click, and the conversation was over. Only Quentin's rasping breath remained as he tossed his phone across the room in anger.

CHAPTER
FIVE

Lyric flung open the French windows and let the mid-morning sunshine bouncing off the terrace pour into her suite in the east wing of the villa. As the soft late-summer breeze touched her cheek, she breathed in deeply as if to inhale the panoramic seascape, the gently bobbing yachts glowing white in the bright sunshine and the sheer, gorgeous, delightful space of it all.

Space. Something you barely noticed when you'd got it, but something you positively ached for when you hadn't. Like in London. Lyric shuddered as she remembered the media maelstrom that had greeted her return from rehab just a week ago, the frenzy of flashing bulbs and thrusting lenses as the hungry paparazzi jostled her through the airport and into her parents' waiting car. A few days staying with them in the country had settled her sufficiently to attempt the return to London. And then there was worse — a braying mob camped outside her house. Their high-speed shutters had caught her as she'd fumbled with the key on her front door, taking frame after frame of her looking hunted, harassed, *haunted* — anything but the sober, self-aware soul she'd felt she was on leaving the safe confines of rehab.

Funny how circumstances could change your perception so speedily. Overnight, it seemed, the cosy Kensington mews house had turned from her refuge to her prison. Unable to do so much as draw the curtains without making the front page of a newspaper somewhere, she'd felt like a recluse, a refugee from life — much more so than she had ever done in rehab.

There'd be no escape from it, either. She might have lived in the pretty mews house before she'd come into her trust fund, but she loved it and it was her home, so why, just because she could afford somewhere bigger, should she move?

Instead, she'd had to get out. And — lucky, lucky her — the perfect opportunity had presented itself, once again via Sheik Haddad de Sattamin and his lovely wife Carola. Installing Crispin as official housesitter in London — beside himself at the prospect of a few days' cat-and-mouse with the paps and all the related banter (not to mention a few deflected rays of the spotlight for himself) — Lyric had welcomed the offer of the Sheik's private jet and the sunny sanctuary of his sprawling Mediterranean villa nestled in the hilltops overlooking Monte Carlo bay. And not only the villa but, most importantly, a houseful of like-minded, trusted, gregarious guests, including some of her very favourite people: her hosts, the Charlton's nearest neighbours, Colonel Peter Leighton-Smythe, his wife Trinny and their two late-teen daughters, Fenella and Pru, and her best friends Laura and Treeva. (Treeva had only arrived by helicopter the previous night, "fresh" from an all-nighter in London.) Retail magnate Charlie

Bussman, his trophy girlfriend Claudia and their precocious, pre-pubescent daughter Tabitha had also flown in for a half-term holiday yesterday afternoon.

If ever an escape was designed to safely displace and distract her at the same time, then this was it. The last three days had been long and warm with late-summer sunshine, filled with idle conversation, poolside games with Laura's little boy Max and endless laid-back luxury. And tomorrow, her parents were due to join them too.

But today, she was looking forward to catching up with Treeva properly and finding out what everyone had been up to during her three months in rehab.

"Lyric! Are you there?" Treeva's shrill tones called up from the terrace. Lyric smiled. Since the 5a.m. starts in rehab, she'd become an early riser, but Treeva still loved the lengthy lie-ins they'd both indulged in during their party days. Today, Treeva had been conspicuous by her absence at breakfast time, her elaborately laid place at the table on the frangipani-lined terrace resolutely empty, but now that she'd finally surfaced, she was making sure everyone knew about it.

Lyric leaned over the balcony, her diaphanous maxi-dress swirling around the wrought-iron railings in a sherbet-coloured cloud. Standing by the villa's black-slate swimming pool, Treeva was a vision in Versace — fully made up, hair elaborately styled, her printed Atelier Versace micro-mini showcasing her uber-tanned legs.

"Yes, Tree! What's up?"

Treeva, looking straight into the sun, shielded her eyes with her hand and craned her neck to see Lyric. The action caught her off balance, and she tottered backwards slightly in her towering Gucci platforms.

"The first car is leaving for Carola's lunch reception in a minute," she yelled through a mouthful of chewing gum. "Are you coming? We don't want to miss those cocktails, do we?"

Lyric groaned inwardly. Now she was teetotal, the prospect of being surrounded by free-flowing champagne was galling, to put it mildly. But Chez Pipo was one of her favourite restaurants, idyllically tucked away at the top of a tiny, woody peninsula surrounded by breathtaking views of the Med. There were certainly worse places to spend an hour nursing a Perrier.

"Give me five!" she called down. "Where's Laura?"

"Oh, I don't know — feeding Kitty somewhere, I expect," said Treeva dismissively. She still couldn't understand why Laura had brought her babies with her. As far as Treeva was concerned, the only place for children on a girls' weekend was at home with the nanny. "I'm sure she'll catch us up."

Lyric waved and ducked back inside the room, pulling the doors closed behind her. Picking up her hairbrush, she ran it through her heavy mane of hair and slicked on some tinted lip balm. She looked at herself appraisingly in the mirror. A couple of days in the Mediterranean sunshine had already given her a light tan, and freckles dusted her nose and cheeks. Her eyes were bright and clear, and her honey-blonde hair was becoming naturally streaked by the sun. But next to Treeva's va-va-voom glamour, she felt rather plain.

"Lyric! Come *on*!"

Shaking herself out of her self-doubt, Lyric pulled on her Louis Vuitton rope wedges, grabbed the matching clutch and raced down the wide, expansive marble staircase and into the waiting SUV. Who cared about drink and drugs any more? She'd got the best friends and family in the world.

"Lyric, my dear, you look sensational," said the Sheik, beaming widely as he kissed her paternally on the head.

Flushed with adrenaline from playing his role as the flamboyant host, the Sheik was resplendent in flowing white robes of the finest silk and a mountain of ostentatious gold jewellery. Ostentatious, but somehow perfectly fitting, thought Lyric. Today he most definitely looked like a very chic Sheik. Behind him, wearing a showy one-shouldered coral dress with a skirt a couple of inches too short for her, his wife Carola was looking slightly out of her depth but smiling bravely regardless. With gym-toned legs a shade too pinky orange from her enthusiastic use of the fake tan, Carola had taken on the appearance of a king prawn.

Lyric smiled at the glimpses of ocean between the huge white weathered pillars on the grand restaurant terrace. "It's hard when you're competing with this kind of beauty," she said. "I'd forgotten quite how lovely it is here."

Indeed, the unassuming, somewhat distressed chic of Chez Pipo merged so seamlessly with its surroundings that, from the wrought-iron garden furniture to the bright splashes of begonia and bougainvillea gently creeping up the faded paintwork, it was charm personified. A selection of tax exiles and their trophy wives had joined the house guests for lunch, and the balcony resounded with a lively hubbub of chinking and chattering.

"Lyric, are you sure I can't tempt you with a glass of bubbly?" said Treeva, snatching a second flute from a tray as she appeared from the loo. "Just one little cheeky one for old times' sake? What's a girls' get-together without some shampoo, after all?"

Lyric looked at Laura standing next to her, all conservative glamour in a delicately patterned mid-length Temperley dress, her naturally bouncy dark-brown hair pulled back from her face in a Dior Alice band, and rolled her eyes.

"Well, I could do — but it would be the most expensive glass I'd ever had," she deadpanned, referring to the many thousands of pounds it had cost the Sheik to send her to rehab. Laura stifled a giggle, but Treeva frowned in confusion.

"I thought it was your drugs habit they got you out of — I didn't realize you had a drink problem, too!" she complained. As her voice rose, several heads turned in their direction and Lyric shifted uncomfortably from one foot to the other. This was hardly the time or the place to explain to Treeva the ins and outs of her treatment at Directions rehabilitation centre.

"I didn't," Lyric said quietly and firmly. "But it's all part of the bigger picture. And for the immediate future, at least, I'm laying off alcohol."

"Dear Lord," said Treeva, sighing heavily as if Lyric had just announced she had taken holy orders. "Anyone would have thought you really *had* been on heroin!"

A hush fell over the immediate group and Lyric stared at her friend, stunned that she should bring up that old story here, of all places. Lyric had had a blood test the morning before she'd flown out and had stupidly forgotten to remove the plaster on her arm before being papped at the airport. She'd had everyone from Perez Hilton to the *Daily Mail* speculating that she was on heroin, which was *so* far from the truth, and Treeva knew that. So why was her best friend bringing it up?

She took a deep breath and again looked to Laura for support. Laura shrugged helplessly. Her look said it all: Treeva's big mouth had been getting them all into trouble for as long as they could remember, and would probably continue to do so well into the future. Around them, guests tittered awkwardly and returned to their conversations, but Lyric was sure she saw one of the Colonel's teenage daughters whisper something behind her hand to her sister, and then look knowingly and disdainfully at Lyric.

Treeva took her gum from her mouth, stuck it on the side of her champagne flute and took a long swig. She pulled a face as she swilled it around her mouth. "Are you sure they haven't got any Cristal, Carola?" she called. "This tastes rank."

Carola blushed, adding yet another layer of crustacea to her look. Laura put a reassuring hand on Carola's arm and laughed as she took a delicate sip herself.

"Treeva, you are incorrigible. This is vintage Laurent-Perrier. Just because it doesn't come in a Swarovski-studded bottle with a firework display attached doesn't mean it isn't any good! Haven't we managed to instil any *savoir faire* in you at all over the years?"

Lyric smiled inwardly. Good for Laura — she always knew how to put Treeva back in her place. She noticed an all-too-familiar glint in Laura's eye and made a mental note not to be *too* grateful for her help. Her friend seemed convinced that the way to keep Lyric on the straight and narrow was to sign her up to the committees of as many charities as she could, and whilst Lyric was more than happy to take on more voluntary work, the thought of becoming a "lady who lunched" before she was forty filled her with dread.

"So, Tree, what's been going on while I've been away?" asked Lyric brightly, trying to steer the conversation away from herself.

"Oh, you know — it's just been party o'clock. Nothing different, really, sweetie. You know what it's like — everyone who's split up has got back together again, and everyone else is shagging everyone else. Same old same old." She laughed overenthusiastically, and the brittle sound echoed around the terrace.

Lyric sipped her Perrier thoughtfully. She had to ask. Now.

"And . . . how about Ralph?"

The words caught in her throat and came out sounding strangled. Since Ralph had failed to so much as phone her during her time in rehab, she'd run the whole gamut of emotions: hurt, confusion, despair, anger. Then, as her treatment had progressed and the rawness of his rejection had receded, a curious sense of inevitability had set in. After all, she couldn't remember a time when Ralph had been in her life and drugs hadn't. They went hand in hand, like coke and champagne, like uppers and downers, like addiction and danger. And when, during her treatment, she'd been instructed to burn the names and phone numbers of the people in her life connected to drugs (which, to her horror, she'd discovered was most of them), Ralph's name had, to her reluctance, been at the very top of the list. She'd been through all this a thousand times, told herself over and over that a boyfriend who had to be entrusted to your best friend's care while you went away to get better was hardly a boyfriend worth having. However, losing him still hurt. A lot.

Treeva's gaze wavered and she looked away uncomfortably for a split second. Lyric immediately felt awkward for putting her on the spot. Poor Tree. Keeping an eye on party-boy Ralph couldn't have been the easiest assignment, and must have left her feeling somewhat compromised when they'd split up.

"Well, you know," Treeva replied awkwardly, chewing on the corner of her finger. "He's coping. From what

70

I've seen of him, anyway. It can't have been easy for him, you know, when you just upped and left like that."

Lyric spluttered on her mineral water and she stared at her friend in amazement.

"Tree, I was *ill*!" she gasped. "If he was that upset, why didn't he at least send me a letter telling me so?"

Treeva shrugged non-committally. "Well, I guess that's just his way, isn't it?" she replied unhelpfully. "But you're over it now, right?"

"Right," said Lyric, feeling shocked. Laura squeezed her arm supportively.

"We're very proud of you, you know," Laura murmured with a reassuring smile. "After all you've been through, the last thing you needed was Ralph's dreadful treatment of you."

"Well, you know what — it was probably exactly what I needed," said Lyric with more vigour than she felt. "After all, Ralph and I have totally different priorities now. He's proved he's not interested in leading a life with the cleaned-up new me, and I can't be around people on drugs, so . . ." Her voice trailed off as she thought of how good they'd been together. She and Ralph, partners in crime, taking the party scene by storm, over and over. Funny how one little newspaper feature could change the direction of two different lives so irrevocably.

"Ooh, goodie — lunchtime," said Treeva, noticing that the rest of the party had started to filter into the airy dining room and swiping another glass of champagne from a passing waiter's tray. "You sure I can't tempt you, Lyric?"

As the group settled into their seats, Lyric found herself at the opposite end of the table to Treeva with the two Leighton-Smythe girls. She grinned to herself as she sat down between them, the pair of them all gangly legs, gauche teen giggles and shiny hair. Just what she needed — some light-hearted teen banter and gentle gossip. She smiled and leaned over towards Pru, smoothing her skirt under her legs. "I'm starving," she confided to her conspiratorially.

To her surprise, Pru smiled tightly and turned to her sister with raised eyebrows. Fenella giggled into her napkin and looked down the table furtively.

Lyric stared at her, stung into silence. Now she really wasn't imagining it. These girls weren't only talking about her behind her back, they were now being openly hostile. She could remember the days when they'd look up to her as their glamorous society friend. What had she done to upset them so?

Bewildered, and feeling isolated in her place at the head of the table, she looked around for another conversation to join. At the other end of the table, she spotted Treeva staring at her pointedly and gesturing theatrically for Lyric to wipe her nose. Confused, Lyric picked up her napkin and dabbed her top lip delicately. She hadn't yet touched her scallops so she couldn't be displaying any stray crumbs — could she be sweating or something?

Out of the corner of her eye she saw Pru give Fenella a knowing look as they both dissolved into uncontrollable giggles again.

Lyric looked back up at Treeva with a questioning look. Treeva made as if to wipe her nose again and shook her head as if giving up on her friend. She stood up and beckoned at Lyric to follow her to the ladies. Puzzled, Lyric stood up self-consciously and hurried along after her.

Once in the cool confines of the loo, Lyric checked her face for the offending mark and, finding none, turned on her friend.

"Tree? What on earth is going on?"

Treeva shrugged innocently. "I don't know what you're talking about, sweetie — I just wanted you to check my skirt for me. Are you sure it's not too short? I can feel Charlie's eyes all over me." She rolled her eyes dramatically.

Lyric shook her head disbelievingly.

"Look, Tree, can you please stop all this sign-language business," said Lyric, trying hard to remain composed. "It's sending out all the wrong signals. I wouldn't be surprised if half the party thinks I've relapsed and am fully back on the Class A after all this!"

Treeva clapped her hand over her mouth and stared at Lyric in wide-eyed horror. "Oh noooooo! Sweetie, I didn't mean it like that! I was just being silly! You don't think . . . ?"

Lyric nodded in frustration. "That's exactly what I think. Just engage your brain before you're 'silly' next time, OK?"

Treeva looked instantly crushed and Lyric immediately felt bad for snapping at her. People were bound to jump to conclusions — and she'd only got herself to blame for that, after all. It wasn't her dappy friend's fault.

"Tree, your dress looks fab — and you can't blame Mr Bussman for checking out those knockout legs, can you?"

They giggled like schoolchildren, and Lyric hugged Treeva with genuine warmth. Her friend was a nightmare, but she'd got used to her idiosyncrasies over the years, and loved her regardless.

"You go back — I'll be through in a minute," said Treeva airily, picking up her clutch and closing a cubicle door behind her.

On the way back to her seat, Lyric had to walk the length of the table again, and felt conspicuous and self-conscious — almost as if she were doing some hideous walk of shame. As she sat down, she saw Pru cast her another suspicious look.

Emboldened by the exchange with Treeva, Lyric put her hand on Pru's. "Pru, darling, do tell me what I've done to upset you. I can't stand the thought of going through the next few days with you treating me with such hostility every time I so much as sit next to you," she said kindly. "I've only come here for a bit of uncomplicated R and R after all!"

Pru went pink and pulled her hand away sulkily.

"That's not what we hear," said Fenella tartly, leaning forward in defence of her sister. Pru shushed her and kicked out under the table.

"Darling," her mother cautioned.

But Fenella ignored her. "Treeva reckons you're still bang on the coke," she said bluntly.

"Fenella!" gasped her mother, flicking her reproachfully with her napkin.

Lyric stared at her unseeingly as Fenella's words reverberated around her head.

Just then, Treeva re-emerged from the loo, stopping briefly in the narrow doorway as if she were a model stepping on to a catwalk. Lyric looked at her friend, all wide-eyed innocence, as if for the first time. So her instincts were right. Treeva had been spreading rumours. But why would Treeva betray her like that?

Unless . . . Something about Treeva's manner suddenly had Lyric on red alert. The wide eyes. The maniacal laughter. The persistent gum habit. Was Treeva trying to make out that Lyric still had a drug habit to cover up one of her own?

Lyric pushed away her untouched starter and forced a bright smile on to her face. She turned to Pru confidently.

"Well, Pru — you know, Treeva isn't used to expecting the best from people," she said levelly. "Luckily for her, I plan to surprise her."

The rest of the meal passed in a blur. The Leighton-Smythes continued to ignore her, but she rose above it. Lyric was lost in her own world, unable to shake the increasing feeling of pain as Treeva's betrayal sank in. She watched her friend, picking up on other subtle signs that not only was Treeva trying to insinuate that Lyric was still using, but she was actually using herself. Her constant trips to the loo, her non-stop banal chatter, her casual indifference to the food in front of her, all pointed to Lyric's theory having substance. The question was, what was she going to do about it?

On the way home, the answer presented itself to her. Unable to keep up her stoic facade in front of her friends, Lyric hung back and jumped into the blacked-out Merc with the Sheik and Carola.

Despite her self-imposed isolation, even Lyric could detect a frosty atmosphere in the SUV that had nothing to do with the overenthusiastic air conditioning. She flicked through her phone texts seeking solace in past messages — most of them pre-rehab. All she came across, however, were gossipy one-liners from Treeva and a few flirty texts from Ralph. She rested her head against the window dejectedly. What else could go wrong today?

She didn't have long to find out. As they were driving back along Monaco's main street, the Sheik, sitting in the seat in front of Lyric, let out a long sigh and turned around to face her.

"Lyric, my dear, I must confess to being rather disappointed in you," he said heavily.

Lyric looked up in shock. "Disappointed — in me?" she repeated stupidly.

To her right, Carola tutted and shook her head, turning dramatically to look out of the window.

The Sheik also shook his head slowly. "My dear," he said deliberately. "You know I have always looked upon you as family. As a daughter, even."

Lyric nodded, a lump in her throat. She had a sinking feeling that she knew where this was going.

"And so when we discovered you were, ahem, ill, my first thought was only how we could help you. It gave us great pleasure to be able to send you to the best possible place of recuperation. But I must say, your immediate relapse into addiction is testing even our love and devotion to the limit. What your dear mother and father will think, I can almost not bear to consider."

Lyric stared at him open-mouthed. "But . . . but —"

Carola turned in a flash of anger from the window. "Don't try to deny it, Lyric," she spat bitterly. "Treeva told us everything over lunch." She sneered nastily. "Thirty thousand pounds! That's what your treatment cost us. And this is how you repay it? I may not have your rarefied upbringing, but I would never have the bare face to do what you've done."

Lyric stared at them, mortified. Could these people, whom she looked on as extended family, who had spirited her away to safety not just once but, with this trip, twice, really feel that she would betray them like this? Her eye twitched and she touched her fingertip to it nervously, hurt to the quick.

"What exactly has Treeva told you?" Lyric said in a small voice.

"What *hasn't* she told us?" sneered Carola in disgust. "We know it all. How you've asked her to get drugs for you. How you begged her, pleaded with her. How she even had to ask the villa staff on your behalf! Honestly, Lyric, are there no levels to which you won't stoop?"

Lyric felt nothing could compound her misery any further. It was one thing for people she barely knew to think she was using again, but that friends such as these should show so little trust? Was this how low their expectations of her had really sunk?

She cleared her throat softly. "You know, Carola, even when the newspapers had photographic evidence that I was taking cocaine, they rang me and asked me to put my side of things. It's called a right to reply. Aren't either of you interested in my side of things?"

There was a long silence, broken by Carola snorting as she turned her head back to the window. Lyric turned to the Sheik and raised her eyebrows to him. She saw those familiar eyes soften and he nodded solemnly. "Go on."

"Well," Lyric began nervously. "I hate to say this — and I've got no other proof than gut instinct — but I believe the reason Treeva is doing and saying all this is to cover up her own cocaine habit."

There was another long, uncomfortable silence. As Lyric looked at the Sheik, she saw a shadow fall across his face. Her heart sank again.

But Carola was the first to speak. Shriek was closer to the truth.

"*You wicked, wicked girl! To turn on your own best friend this way!*" She turned to the Sheik. "You see! You didn't believe Treeva, but she was right!" Carola turned back to Lyric, her face contorted in anger. "Treeva told us you'd do this. Blame her. She even showed us the drugs you'd asked her to look after and said she feared you'd try and pass the blame on to her."

Lyric stared at her open-mouthed. "But — but they must have been *her* drugs! Think about it, Carola — why would I —"

"*Out!*" screamed Carola, stuffing her fingers in her ears. "Get out! I won't listen to your filthy lies a moment longer. Haddad! Get this girl *out* of the car!"

The Sheik sighed and tapped the driver lightly on the shoulder, indicating to him to pull over. He turned back to Lyric. His demeanour was almost apologetic, but his eyes were like flint and he slid open the passenger door purposefully.

"You've given us little choice, Lyric. I think you should do as Carola says."

Lyric stared at him wildly as a sob rose in the back of her throat. She wanted to throw herself on the floor and plead for mercy, but her indignation, and what was left of her pride, prevented her. Instead, she drew a deep breath and exited the car with as much dignity as she could muster.

As the SUV sped off in a cloud of dust, she felt her poise desert her. The heat of the day prickled the back of her neck like tiny needles, and she looked around her desolately. The street was lined with pavement tables spilling out from bustling restaurants, with diners stretching out the last moments of their long, boozy lunches. Others were falling out of the doors in colourful, glamorous heaps. Lyric tried to envisage the route back to the villa, up the steep road that led out of town. How was she going to get back there? She had no money with her, so a taxi was out of the question, even if she had known the address of the villa. Unless . . .

She delved in her clutch for her mobile phone. She'd call Laura. Scrabbling around in the silky interior, however, there *was* no phone. Lyric's heart sank yet again as she visualized it sitting on the car seat where she'd momentarily placed it earlier. She took a deep breath and looked regretfully at her towering wedges. They might be comfortable for a couple of hours at lunch, but not for the long, hot, sticky walk she had in front of her.

Three hours later, after a humiliating trawl through the streets of Monte Carlo, Lyric limped up to the imposing iron gates of Sheik Haddad's villa. Her trek had left her hot, tired and with a whole new impression of the so-called glamorous tax haven. Each restaurant she'd passed had seemed more vulgar and excessive than exclusive and luxurious, and the diners more drunk and disorderly than sophisticated and chic. The gold-paved streets had turned up more baking dog turds than bullion, and the smell had permeated even her damaged septum and was refusing to go away. What she needed even more than an instant flight home now was a hot shower and pair of bedroom slippers.

She pressed the buzzer with a mixed sense of relief and trepidation, and leaned her head against the cool railings as she waited for them to open.

"*C'est qui?*" came the tinny voice of the on-duty security guard down the intercom.

"*C'est Lyric Charlton!*" she replied eagerly into the receiver. "*Je suis invitée du Sheik Haddad de Sattamin.*"

There was a short crackly silence before the voice replied.

"*Désolé, mademoiselle, je ne suis pas permis de vous faire entrer.*"

Lyric stared at the gates. Not allowed to let her in? But — but at the very least she needed to get in to get her passport!

She buzzed back, at first insistently, then, panicking, in quick staccato buzzes. But there was no response.

Lyric kicked out at the gates in frustration. Why was this happening to her? She sank on to the road in front of the villa and started to cry. How long would she have to wait out here until someone let her in — if ever? What if even Laura believed Treeva's lies and refused to help her? After the events of this morning, anything was possible.

A passing car blared its horn at her and startled her out of her desolation. Lyric pictured herself — a pathetic crumpled heap — and shook herself. She'd spent her whole life getting in and out of scrapes — how was this any different?

She pulled herself up and studied the gates. They were at least twenty feet high, with aggressive-looking spikes at the top and narrow gaps between the bars. But there had to be a way in that didn't involve an unhelpful security guard. Gingerly, she placed one leg between two of the bars. She'd lost so much weight during the final months of her addiction that even after rehab she was still reed-thin. To her joy, her leg fitted. She turned sideways on and found that the rest of her body — hips, bum and boobs — could be squashed through too. She was in! Apart from . . . As she tried to pull her neck upwards through the crack, Lyric realized the flaw in her plan. She'd obviously lost no weight on her head, and it certainly wouldn't squish in the way her décolletage or derrière could. Try as she might, she simply couldn't get through.

Foiled, Lyric stepped back and reconsidered the huge obstacle. The gates had a fretwork of iron in the centre making up the Sheik's coat of arms. It was as naff as hell and typically new-money (he'd probably bought the insignia on the Internet), but right now, it was going to provide Lyric with the all-important footholds she needed to scale the gates. Hitching her skirt into her G-string, and shoving her clutch into her mouth, she started the climb to the top. Naturally agile, Lyric silently thanked the years of gymnastics at boarding school and the ballet classes at finishing school for the extra strength and dexterity they had given her.

She reached the top easily and was inwardly celebrating her success when she came nose to spike with the top of the railings. The point looked angry and dangerous, and Lyric momentarily paused. If she fell on that, the next interior she'd be experiencing could be her own coffin — at the very least, she could have to wave goodbye to ever having children. Somehow, she had to protect herself from it. Reluctantly, she looked down at her shoes. Louis Vuitton or her fertility? It was a tough one. They were the one decent pair of shoes she had with her. Still, she was planning to be home in a matter of hours. Seeing the ground waver below, Lyric became resolute. She simply had to get in, at whatever cost. And right now, that cost was going to have to be her designer wedges.

Leaning down to pull off her left shoe, she raised it above her head and slammed it firmly on to one of the spikes. Repeating the action with her right shoe, and then her matching clutch, she triumphantly surveyed her handiwork. Here was her safe passageway . . . albeit into the lion's den.

But as she straggled barefoot up the hot, dusty drive, leaving her shoes and bag impaled on the vulgar gates, a feeling of impending doom descended on her. It wasn't so much the hostile reception committee that was troubling her. It was Treeva. Because if rehab had taught Lyric one thing apart from how to get clean, it was to make amends with all the people she'd sold down the river during her addiction. But if Treeva ever managed to clean herself up of her own Class A habit, one thing was for sure. She was going to have to come up with a pretty convincing explanation to make up for this weekend's betrayal.

CHAPTER
SIX

September

Lyric groaned inwardly as she saw the straggle of paparazzi lined up along the pavement opposite the Ritz. There was no way they were here for her, she reminded herself. She just hadn't expected them to be out at this time in the afternoon — there must be someone high-profile staying at the hotel. Unless . . . She shook herself. She was here for a family conference, for goodness' sake — one of her nearest and dearest was hardly likely to have alerted the paps to her arrival!

But as the car pulled up at the entrance, two of the photographers surged forward expectantly. As she pulled herself up demurely from the car seat (during her addiction she'd been so scared of people finding out she was off her face that she'd taken extra care always to act with the utmost decorum wherever she was), one tried to slip his camera on to her car seat and the other stuck his leg out in front of her to trip her up. Trying not to show her panic, Lyric tutted at them and stepped delicately over the photographer's leg. She'd always had a good relationship with the press. What did they think — that now she was clean she'd all at once transform from a bit of a prude (albeit one who was often off her face) into a "knickers off" kind of girl? And why would they want to get that shot, anyhow — surely there were nicer parts of the body to photograph?

Head down, Lyric went for it and dashed across to the hotel entrance.

"Good afternoon, Miss Charlton."

Lyric smiled and nodded at the Ritz doorman as he opened the door for her with a sweeping flourish. Her heart was still racing at the close encounter, and she breathed a deep sigh of relief as she entered the familiar confines of the Ritz lobby. She wandered down the long passage, past the second sitting of guests enjoying afternoon tea towards the Wimborne Room.

She laughed as she thought back to the last time she'd been here, for her mother's fiftieth birthday party a few weeks before she'd gone into rehab. A long list of celebrities and minor royals had been invited, and the likes of *OK!* and *Hello!* had fought tooth and nail for the coverage — which was ridiculous, because frankly there had never been any chance of her parents agreeing to it. (In fact, when the final offer from *Hello!* had come in at a million pounds, her father had scoffed and told them he'd pay them three million just to stay away.) That afternoon, as the Charltons had got ready for the party, the Ritz had closed the Palm Court to outside guests, but of course even the hotel hadn't been able to prevent its own residents from taking the world-famous tea. And it hadn't gone unnoticed that all the "guests" were journalists from national newspapers.

Not that it had done them any good, of course — her father had ensured security was watertight. In the end, the papers had had to bribe one of the guests with a six-figure sum. Hmmm, she mused now — they'd never discovered who had sold them down the river. They'd all been so wrapped up in the party they'd never got around to working it out. Whoever it was, family or friend, she'd never really given it much thought before now.

Lyric's footsteps echoed round her ears as she quickened her pace across the Grand Hall. The intimidatingly cavernous space always made her feel so small, insignificant, and slightly edgy — unless it was filled with people, of course. At the other side, Lyric slipped gracefully through the door leading into the Wimborne Room, a bright, warm space that had been used for Charlton family gatherings for years. She looked around it in satisfaction, noting no changes — just as it should be. Beneath the gilded ceiling, the crystal chandelier lit up the yellow silken damask walls, and the beautiful inlaid mahogany table was set with place mats, glasses and notepaper, as if for a board meeting. In the centre of the table, tea and coffee pots sat in between platters groaning with biscuits and patisserie. Mummy's order, of course — not that Constance would ever touch them herself, but she loved to see other people eating their heads off.

"Goddammit, man, do I have to babysit you every step of the goddamn way?"

Lyric jumped — she had thought she was the first to arrive. But of course Uncle Quentin would already be here, hanging round the drinks table, first in line for the whisky. Lyric watched him pace angrily up and down the other side of the room, shouting into his mobile phone. She didn't even know he had a phone — though from the looks of it, he'd had it since the early Eighties. Uncle Quentin's cheek was famous in the family. And this was typical of him, calling a late-afternoon conference so he could start to get tanked up on single malt — on the family account, and at her father's expense — before sitting down for a well-lubricated dinner in the restaurant with one of his old cronies. Also probably on account, as would be the late-night drinks in the Rivoli Bar where he'd eye up late-night, scantily clad party-goers, she thought ruefully.

Quentin, unaware of Lyric's arrival, continued to rant into his phone. "This is your problem to sort — repeat, your problem! Do you understand? Stop the boy, and stop him NOW!" He slammed the phone down on the polished table and it span noisily across the shiny wood.

Lyric frowned. She'd never seen Uncle Quentin so angry.

"Hi, Uncle Quentin," she said brightly.

Quentin jumped visibly and grunted irritably. "How long have you been there, then, eh?" he snapped. "Sneaking around behind me."

Lyric smiled fondly. Crabby old Uncle Quentin — he never changed. Walking over to give him a warm hug, she tried not to recoil at his stale breath and unwashed hair. He hugged her back stiffly, and Lyric looked at him quizzically. This was odd — grumpy or not, her uncle was usually much more friendly and tactile than that. "How are you?" she asked.

"Fine, Lyric, fine," said Quentin, knocking back a whisky and pouring another immediately.

There was an unmistakeable sense of awkwardness in the air, and Lyric restlessly wandered around the table, trailing her hand along the back of the upholstered dining chairs. Uncharacteristically at a loss for something to say, she pulled her phone from her bag and texted Crispin to confirm their dinner plans for later that evening. Text sent, she looked up at Uncle Quentin, who appeared to be staring unseeingly at a blank spot on the wall. What on earth was up with him?

But before Lyric had time to wonder any longer, the rest of the family began to arrive — her mother and father first, her mother wrapped up in her favourite mink despite the mild September weather, and her father in his battered old city coat and red scarf, still managing to look distinguished, though with more than a touch of Rupert the Bear. She embraced both of them delightedly. It was only a few days since she'd last seen them — since she'd retreated to Broughton Hall full of horror at her treatment in Monaco — but these days, it seemed she couldn't get enough of the secure feeling that being with them gave her.

After them came dear Jacob, as dashing as ever, wearing his Westminster uniform of smart grey suit and silver tie.

"Where's Vera?" she said after kissing him hello.

"Verity," corrected Jacob.

"Ooops," mumbled Lyric. She had never been great with names, particularly those belonging to people who didn't interest her.

Jacob smiled at her conspiratorially and nodded towards the Palm Court. "She's having afternoon tea. Said I'll pick her up afterwards. Father said this was for family only."

"Ooh," said Lyric, eyes widening, her interest immediately awakened. What on earth was on the agenda that could be that private? Discretion wasn't like Uncle Quentin — he usually liked to swank about in front of Jacob's latest flames, especially the rich ones. Lyric moved towards the table to pour herself a cup of tea.

George cleared his throat and looked at his watch. "Well, Quentin, as this was your idea, maybe you'd better chair the meeting, eh, old chap?"

Not for the first time, Lyric marvelled at the difference between her father and his brother. Although there were only four years between them, going by appearances there might have been twenty-four. Where Quentin was bloated and overweight, George was fit and glowing with good health. Quentin's haphazard, crumpled image contrasted vividly with her father's neat, if slightly shabby, appearance. George's gentle, confident, calm manner was a world away from his brother's chaotic demeanour.

Quentin picked up his whisky glass and took two uncertain paces towards the centre of the room. Suddenly appearing to draw courage from somewhere, he slammed his glass down on the table purposefully and looked around the room.

"There's no easy way of saying this," he said falteringly. His eyes rested on Lyric and the sight of her seemed to spur him on — his voice grew stronger and louder. "But I have grave reason to believe that *you* —" he pointed at Lyric accusingly, and she dropped her teacup into its saucer with a clatter — "that *you* have severely damaged the Charlton family name."

Lyric and her parents stared at him in shock, and Jacob rubbed his forehead uncomfortably. Quentin took a deep gulp of his whisky and turned back to Lyric, eyes popping and veins bulging.

"This is a family, I need hardly remind you, that has held its place as one of England's foremost and most respected for centuries," droned on Quentin, warming to his theme. "We are known as honourable, upright, esteemed members of society. As least, we were — until recently. Thanks to you, Lyric."

Lyric shook her head in disbelief. If anyone had come close to sullying their reputation in recent years it was, surely, her uncle? The attack was unexpected, and as far as she was concerned, unfair. She looked at her father for support, and he held up his hand, indicating that her uncle should be allowed to continue.

"Quentin, old boy, I can't say I'm really following you on this one. Where is this headed?"

Quentin rounded on his brother, pink face deepening to an angry shade of puce.

"Where this is headed, George, *old boy*, is the effect that your drug-addled daughter and all her alcohol-fuelled antics have had on my reputation and the political prospects of my boy! Not that I'd expect you to realize it, stuck out there in your ivory tower in the country." Quentin shook his head bitterly, years of jealousy overcoming him. "But here in the city, where things actually happen — well. It is, shall we say, still a hot topic. One that seems hell-bent on sticking around. And while it does, it is doing untold damage not only to me and my network of business contacts —"

Lyric, outraged, looked at her father in exasperation. Uncle Quentin's business sense was legendarily bad, and so, she suspected, were his contacts. Certainly not the kind of "network" who'd let a family drug scandal affect them, anyhow. Her father shook his head almost imperceptibly, warning her to remain quiet.

"— but to my son Jacob's political aspirations too!"

Now almost boiling over with rage, Quentin slammed his fist on to the table.

"Jacob, unlike Lyric, hasn't had the Charlton millions to propel him through childhood, through school, through adolescence and into an overprivileged adulthood."

Lyric gasped audibly. Not only had Daddy personally paid for Jacob to board at the very best schools, but he'd fought the established rules and released funds to put in trust for her cousin. The sizeable amount had matured five years previously and had paid for a handsome pad in Belgravia and, Lyric suspected, at least one investment in a failed business interest in Quentin's lacklustre portfolio.

But Quentin was unstoppable. Now he rounded on Lyric.

"But you — you, young lady — not only basked in every privilege you could get your greedy little hands on, you wallowed in it while you partied away your twenties, then threw it all in our faces with a drug scandal as you approached your thirties! What's to come next, eh? An affair with a married man? High-class prostitution?"

It was Constance's turn to gasp, her hand clasping her mouth as she turned away from Quentin in disgust.

Lyric, blood boiling, could keep quiet no longer. "I'm clean, for God's sake!" she said, her voice quavering in anger. She cleared her throat, struggling to keep from losing her temper totally. "I made a mistake, yes! But I'm not the only one to get it wrong sometimes, am I? What happened to the principle of learning from your mistakes, rather than being judged by them for ever?"

Next to her, her father placed a cautionary hand on her arm. Lyric tutted, shrugging off her father sulkily, but quelling her protests nonetheless. She knew better than to disobey her father when he was rattled.

"Quentin, that's quite enough," said George firmly. "No one's denying that Lyric has made serious mistakes, but she has endeavoured to make the necessary amends, and we admire her for her courage. Constance and I support her wholeheartedly and will not listen to any more of this."

"But what about the rest of us?" persisted Quentin. "Unfortunately, Jacob can't take himself off to rehab at someone else's expense and come back with a clean slate. Once there's a drug slur on a politician, it never goes away. It'll be there, in black and white, brought up by the press every time he so much as sneezes. His formerly spotless character is now sullied, and his political career in ruins. Unless . . ."

Lyric, Jacob, and her mother and father stared at him in suspense. Lyric felt like she was seeing him properly for the first time ever. His ugly, grasping, conniving greed suddenly seemed not just faintly repulsive but frightening too. She thought back to Monaco and the calculating betrayal of her lifelong friend. Was there really no one you could trust other than your immediate family?

"Unless what, Quentin?" said her father in an exasperated tone.

"Unless you hand over Broughton Hall."

There was a deathly silence. Lyric and her mother stared at Quentin in horror.

Lyric felt a chill run through her veins. Her uncle was serious. "You're mental, Uncle Quentin," she said out loud. Too astounded by Quentin's demands, no one took any notice.

"That's preposterous!" spluttered George. "Get a grip of yourself, Quentin."

"Oh, I have, George," said Quentin smugly, pulling a crumpled sheet of paper from his jacket pocket and waving it aloft. "I have. You see, handing over Broughton Hall to us will not only be just the publicity

Jacob needs to distance himself from his cousin's cataclysmic fall from grace, it will provide him with the perfect family seat."

Quentin cleared his throat triumphantly.

"You know that covenant that had Broughton Hall passed over to you in the first place?" A stray fleck of spittle flew from his mouth and landed on a Viennese Whirl. Lyric made a mental note to avoid that one after the meeting.

George nodded as Lyric and her mother looked at him numbly. Jacob shifted his weight on to his other leg awkwardly.

"Well, it also states that the first-born should 'maintain and uphold the family honour'. Any whiff of scandal, and the house goes back into trust until the next in line can take over. As there's hardly any argument over my suitability, I fully expect I shall be ensconced at Broughton Hall before you can say 'rightful owner'."

Quentin pressed his hands together gleefully, his piggy eyes shining with greed.

"Broughton Hall, George. It's going to be mine. Get used to it."

CHAPTER
SEVEN

October

"It's a triumph, isn't it?"

"So wonderful to see you!"

"You look marvellous, darling."

As Lyric worked her way through the sea of people milling around on the grass in front of Laura's family home, it felt like she'd never reach the other side of the lawn.

The garden party she was hosting, held not only to celebrate the opening of the estate's newly landscaped formal gardens but also to double as a celebrity fundraiser for some of Laura's many charitable works, had attracted a multitude of stars from every walk of life, intrigued as much as anything by the unseasonal timing. But that was Laura's father all over. An unapologetic eccentric in the best English tradition, he had no thought for the season or any preconceptions about when things should happen and where. And so today, a sunny, unexpectedly warm day in early October, supermodels, diplomats, royalty and rockers were all gathered on the lawn, which was as weathered as the bark on the estate's ancient oak trees, all inappropriately dressed to the nines. What was it about garden parties that brought out the inner chav in even the upper classes and led people to dress to match the gardens? Lyric mused. Everywhere she looked, women dolled up in floral prints and a sartorial sugar-rush of frothy hats to match were fighting a losing battle as their spiky stilettos embedded themselves in the damp turf. Lyric checked herself and her criticism, reminding herself that some people here would find her simple cream linen shift dress and matching coat boring and clichéd rather than understated and comfortable. *Live and let live, Lyric*, she reminded herself.

She continued making her way slowly across the lawn, her cheeks aching from her permanent smile. Everyone she passed wanted to greet her, thank her, congratulate her. It was overwhelmingly heart-warming, but in truth she was finding the whole thing exhausting. She'd agreed to break her self-enforced rule of a new, low-profile existence and host the event as a favour to Laura. But whilst she was glad there was a public way of thanking her friend for her loyalty and support, she was secretly rueing the moment she'd said yes and longing for the crowds to disperse, leaving her alone with her closest friend and her family. She waved across the lawn at Laura's husband Robert wandering morosely around the edge and frowned. The Robert she knew loved a party. What on earth was the matter with him today?

"Lyric! Wait."

Lyric turned, smiling, as Laura approached with Kitty balanced on her right hip and Max clutching her left hand and looking at Lyric with a cheeky grin. Lyric felt a momentary flash of concern for her friend. Laura looked as lovely as ever, but underneath the flawless Estée Lauder face there was no hint of her normal, natural glow — her dark hair seemed lank and lifeless, and she looked puffy and bloated. Maybe Kitty was teething or something, thought Lyric — Laura did insist on doing all the hard mummy work herself, and a few sleepless nights in a row would take their toll on anyone's looks and their husband's good humour.

"Aunt Lyric — Mummy says you simply must come and meet Uncle Thomas," lisped Max. "He's very handsome and he's got the biggest yacht you've ever seen."

Lyric groaned inwardly. Another rich banker with a lot of zeros after his name — including, no doubt, zero personality and zero appeal. Sweet, innocent Laura was obsessed with finding Lyric "the perfect man", and there was no doubt she knew her fair share of eligible bachelors. But when was Laura ever going to realize that all these attributes that made them so — well, bankable — were exactly what turned Lyric off? And that, in her experience, the more wealthy a man, the stingier he tended to be — both materially and, more importantly, emotionally? The last thing she wanted was to be cosseted and controlled — to end up as a trophy wife, another asset on a long list of material achievements. She wondered where this Thomas was on Laura's "Richer Scale".

She bent down and ruffled Max's hair. "He sounds simply wonderful," she said, smiling. "But your Aunt Lyric has met so many people today already! Maybe we could go and meet Uncle Thomas later." She looked up at Laura sternly. "Or another day?"

"OK, Aunt Lyric!" said Max cheerfully, running off in the direction of the crèche and the irresistible appeal of the bouncy castle. "See you!"

Laura, busy persuading Kitty to wave goodbye to Max, turned to Lyric reproachfully.

"You know, it won't hurt just to meet Thomas," she said. "You can't hide away for ever. Not everyone is a shit like Ralph. And Thomas is a real catch — he's just your type."

Lyric sighed. "Laura, the very fact that you have to say those words instantly tells me he's *not* my type," she said. "But I promise I'll get myself back on to the dating scene soon. Just in my own time, OK?"

Laura smiled and hugged her friend with her free arm. Kitty cooed and reached out a dribbly hand to Lyric, leaving a damp gooey patch on her cheek. Something twanged inside and she felt an unexplainable lump forming in the back of her throat. There was that searing sense of emptiness again. It wasn't her biological clock, she was sure — it was an all-too-familiar feeling of loss, as if there was a fundamental part missing from her emotional being. She pulled away from Laura's embrace and kissed her lightly on the cheek.

"I was just on my way to the loo," she fibbed. "I'll be back in five minutes."

"OK, darling. We'll see you in a bit. Let's go and find Daddy, shall we, Kitty? And a glass of champagne for

Mummy!" Laura turned and sauntered off, bouncing her baby girl and chatting to her as she walked away.

Lyric watched her go for a moment. Laura's casual demeanour had put her mind at rest. Maybe she'd imagined there was something amiss with Laura, or Robert, or their marriage.

She turned and, seizing the opportunity of a few moments' solitude, hurried along the gravel path and round the side of the house, along the neatly tended lawns and through the orchard, heading for the tiny ancient folly on a grassy knoll overlooking the rest of the gardens. Buoyed by the feeling of freedom, she pulled off her coat and started to run, desperate to feel the wind in her hair.

All of a sudden, Lyric felt her toe stub on something and her foot gave underneath her. As she tripped on the gnarly old tree root, she fell, and sat up to rub her ankle, cursing the chic court shoes she'd not had the foresight to remove before running. Grabbing hold of a tree branch, she pulled herself up and hobbled the last few yards to the folly, sitting down on the rusty old bench in front of it.

In front of her, the sprawling grounds of Laura's childhood home spread out like a painting from a bygone age — the acres of neat, rolling lawns that led down to the lake, the shrubbery half hiding the walled vegetable garden, and now the triumph of the newly landscaped formal gardens which complemented the beautiful house. This was England at its picture-perfect best.

In the top left corner, esteemed Japanese gardener Tatsuya Fujimoto had created a Japanese Zen garden, based on the Japanese principles of in and yo (or "emptiness" and "something"), which Lyric was sure was meant to be calming and relaxing, and which — though undoubtedly visually impressive — she found a little, well, spartan. And the Japanese principle that you should never create something that nature cannot had always seemed to her to be in stark contradiction to their enthusiasm for topiary and bonsai — such as the examples in the garden Fujimoto had created here.

On the diagonal was Yuan Ming Yuan — "The Garden of Perfect Brightness" — a miniature Chinese paradise complete with glazed-tile pagoda (using the rarest of tiles sourced from the Yuan Dynasty, bought and imported at huge cost), water feature and ornamental pond filled with brightly coloured exotic fish.

In between the two was "A Vision of Thinking" — the work of local conceptual sculptor Imelda King. A modernist vertical planting system played host to Imelda's wild and wonderful iron and stone sculptures, giving the effect of an eerie fantasy land — an otherworldly experience far removed from the traditional surrounds it had been created in.

Lyric could vaguely make out the Moschino-clad form of Treeva bending over and sniffing furtively at the leaves of the plants in the final showpiece, an earthy, rooty, wild English eco-garden designed by hot new celebrity gardener Philippe Chappeau. Lyric frowned in concern. She still hadn't spoken to Treeva since Monaco, but she'd spent a long time mulling over her friend's recent behaviour and had come to the firm conclusion that Treeva was definitely in the depths of drug addiction. Which was, sadly, borne out by today's evidence, as Treeva was clearly on the prowl for cannabis leaves. Lyric shook her head in disbelief. Unconventional he might be, but as if Laura's father would allow marijuana in his prized new gardens! Her irrationality seemed to Lyric to be another symptom of how far she had let herself be carried by her addiction. Her heart felt heavy when she thought about the long journey to sobriety Treeva had in front of her — the journey she had taken herself.

Chappeau's garden was Lyric's favourite — colourful even this late in the year, with shrubs and woodland plants, tangled roots among hellebores and ferns, autumn flames and golds, a truly natural garden, not theatre or art, but the sort of garden only a really talented artist and plantsman could create. Despite what the pack of pompous, pretentious critics were likely to say, this garden was *real*. It was perfectly imperfect: fragrant, natural and woody, and it represented everything she loved about the English countryside. That the plants had apparently been selected to provide food and shelter for a wide range of wildlife, not to mention the fact that the paths around the garden were raised to minimize impact on the ecosystem below, gave Lyric a warm, comforting feeling that made her want to gather the garden up in her arms and sprinkle it over the vast expanses of concrete jungle that scarred so many parts of the country she loved so dearly. She'd wanted to congratulate Monsieur Chappeau himself, to talk to him about his inspirations for the garden, but he was famously reclusive, and although Laura insisted he had been present at the start of the party, he had missed Lyric's official opening and, she assumed, had left as soon as he could.

She rubbed her ankle distractedly.

"Those look like the perfect shoes for an afternoon stroll," said a voice behind her. Lyric physically jumped, and squealed in agony as she jarred her injured foot. She looked up to see startlingly green eyes in a handsome tanned face beneath curly dark hair on a fit, rangy body. The face was perfectly symmetrical, except for a deep scar just below the right eye — which, though upsetting the delicate balance of his features, actually made them more attractive. The voice was soft and low, with a faint Mediterranean accent — French? Lyric felt herself melt a little at the sight of the man. If only Laura were here. Now *this* was more like her type. But that face — didn't she know it from somewhere?

She grimaced, pushing her thoughts to the back of her mind. Of course she'd never met this man before in her life — how would she ever have forgotten him?

"I should have taken them off before I set out, not afterwards," she said in answer to the stranger's question, trailing off as he knelt down and took her foot in his hands, gently massaging. She winced as he hit the spot, then relaxed as his strokes dulled the pain.

She stared at him, momentarily lost for words and loath to break the spell.

He looked up at her, his green eyes deep pools of promise. "You know, you can tell a lot from the soles of someone's feet," he murmured, still rhythmically massaging her foot. "They are like the bark of a tree."

"Really?" gasped Lyric, mouth suddenly dry. "And what can you tell from mine?"

The stranger smiled and gently placed her foot back on the floor. "They tell me there are layers and layers of this person in front of me to peel off before we reveal the real person underneath," he said, standing up. Lyric looked up at him, puzzled.

He reached over to her hair and pulled a stray twig out of it. "But what I see in front of me is a more genuine Lyric Charlton than the one I saw at the opening ceremony. More natural. More — real."

Lyric stared into his eyes. Those eyes . . . He felt so close. So familiar. So . . .

"Who . . . I'm sorry, have we met?" she stammered.

He laughed, not unkindly, but Lyric felt their sudden intimacy evaporate, and all at once, despite their physical closeness, she felt an ocean open up between them.

"We have, but of course you won't remember. Why would you?" His words were neutral, but the tone was edged with sarcasm, and Lyric frowned.

"I thought — I did think you looked familiar," she said lamely. "I — I feel like I know you already."

The man laughed again, this time more harshly. "Know me? I don't think so. But we have met before. Philippe Chappeau, garden designer to the rich and

103

famous now — but, as you might remember me, school gardener's son."

Lyric felt a surge of pleasure. Of course! Philippe! Monsieur Chappeau's son from boarding school! Philippe, who'd got her out of a hundred hideous scrapes, who'd helped her sneak out and back again for many an illicit night out. Philippe, who as he'd driven her off the school premises to a waiting taxi in his rackety tractor had talked to her with shining eyes about his father's talents and their plans for the school grounds. Philippe, the subject of her huge schoolgirl crush and a million and one schoolgirl dreams. And now celebrity gardener. Why hadn't she realized? Why hadn't Laura told her? Had Laura recognized him?

She reached out an apologetic hand. "Philippe! How wonderful to see you. I had no idea! I —"

Philippe smiled back at her, but the warmth had disappeared from his eyes and his voice was carefully neutral. "Of course. Why would you? I was just the gardener's son, after all — not part of the in crowd."

No, but you were part of every dream I had during every night at school — and so many since! Lyric wanted to scream. Instead, she reached out a timid hand. "It's good to see you, Philippe," she said sincerely. "And your garden — I love it. It's just perfect."

Philippe looked back at her searchingly, his eyes now warmer again. "Really?"

Sensing a bridging of the chasm between them, Lyric nodded eagerly. "Yes! It's just perfect. Perfectly imperfect. If you know what I mean?" She looked up at

104

him quizzically and his expression gave her hope. Not just for this conversation, but for something else. The future? Lyric shook herself. There she was, getting carried away again. They'd only just re-met, and here she was, reading things into his every move. She stood up to meet his gaze on the same level and stumbled into him as the pain shot through her foot once again.

Philippe put a strong, confident arm around her. "You're never going to make it back down there again on your own," he said in amusement. "May I?" Without waiting for an answer, he swept Lyric into his arms and started to walk down the path to the party.

Back at the party was the last place she wanted to be, but Lyric, arms gripping Philippe tightly around his neck, kept quiet. Because if going back to the party meant she got to spend a few more seconds in this man's arms, then it was worth it.

CHAPTER
EIGHT

Quentin mopped his heavily sweating brow with the towel around his neck and headed for the shower. Even after a deep-tissue massage, he felt strangely unsettled. His sense of unrest over Sergei's increasing demand for more, *more, MORE!* artwork had him feeling so unaccountably edgy that the masseuse's expert strokes had felt more irritating than relaxing to his bloated body. His Russian client, it seemed, had taken Quentin at his word and now had plans to fill each of the luxury properties on his island in the Palm, Dubai with the finest English artwork, making Quentin rich beyond his wildest dreams. Which was all very well, but Quentin's thus far unsuccessful attempt to grasp not just the Charltons' art collection but Broughton Hall meant that he had yet to get his hands on one single painting, let alone dozens of them.

He made a mental note to chase up the (very expensive) lawyer he had working on the case. Relations had lately soured slightly since Quentin had refused (for which read "been unable to come up with the funds") to pay for the fellow's astronomical first fee instalment. Luckily Quentin's silver tongue had brought the lawyer to see sense and he'd agreed to continue working on it for now, and so Quentin remained confident that the day he could see it through once and for all — if he could only come up with the necessary funds — was just around the corner.

Quentin stepped out of his robe and slapped the towel across the top of the glass door to the shower. Once inside, he turned the jets on full so the cubicle immediately filled up with steam. Today must be the first time in his long membership of the Wigmall Club that he hadn't taken advantage of the masseuse's many other more "intimate" services — and that thought made him even more tetchy. Once again, life had dealt him the cruellest blow. He was within touching distance of fantastic wealth, and yet he had been denied the chance to claim what was rightfully his.

As he reached for his towel, suddenly dizzy from the steam, Quentin shivered and felt uncharacteristically afraid. What if . . . what if he couldn't deliver the artwork, and he was exposed as a fake?

A fake. The thought plagued him as he pulled on his crumpled, stained, sweaty shirt and misshapen blazer. Running a hand through his still unwashed hair, he stumbled out of the dressing room and along the corridor into the bar.

"Large single malt, old boy," he barked at the bartender as he struggled on to the nearest bar stool. "And a Monte-cristo."

The bartender opened his mouth as if to object, then, noticing the steely look in Quentin's eye, shut it again abruptly. Quentin took a handful of peanuts from the bowl in front of him and threw them carelessly into his mouth. Half of them missed their target and scattered across his shoulders and on to the floor. Unaware, he chomped noisily and angrily. Clearly his credit rating was on the rocks here, too. Pah! Didn't these places have any idea about bloody loyalty? They'd soon change their tune once he was rolling in the millions Sergei had promised him. If only he could come up with a way to realize them.

A fake. The word kept ringing in his head, steadfastly refusing to go away. Quentin frowned and downed his whisky in one, impatiently motioning the bartender to refill his glass.

A *fake*! He bashed the heavy tumbler down triumphantly on the bar, startling the bartender and a couple of bespectacled customers at a corner table. Hallelujah. Why the devil hadn't he thought of it before? Sergei would never know. What he knew about art you could write on the back of a postage stamp. Quentin chuckled to himself and raised his glass to his fellow club members, blithely ignoring the fact that what *he* knew about art wouldn't take up much more than a second postage stamp. He knew enough to have come up with a genius plan — and frankly, right now that was all he needed to know.

He would commission an artist adept at fraudulent copies to recreate the entire collection of Charlton art. Then, somehow, he would replace the dusty heirlooms at Charlton with his artist's own work. How difficult could it be? There were wings of that house that hadn't been entered for decades. He had an inventory — his lawyer had managed to turn that up — so he knew exactly what works the family owned and where they were hung. It shouldn't be too much trouble to find a cat burglar who could swap them over for him.

"Quentin Charlton — thought that was you! How the devil?"

Quentin jumped at the slap on his shoulder and turned to find Henry Mogler, an old school chum and now a senior civil servant. Henry was a humourless, self-important man conservatively dressed in a blue pinstriped suit, white shirt and regimental tie. Slightly built, his face was heavily lined and the odd thread vein around his nose and cheeks gave away his penchant for a drink. Quentin beamed in delight — at finding someone to share his good humour with, and, more importantly, to land with the bill. He was in the mood to celebrate, and that, he knew, could be pricey.

"Henry — fancy seeing you here, old boy! Marvellous, marvellous — top hole! Whisky?" He shook his tumbler invitingly. Henry peered at it doubtfully and checked his watch.

"I don't know, old chap — bit early for me. Don't usually touch the hard stuff until the sun's passed the yardarm!"

"Only a couple of hours to go, then!" announced Quentin triumphantly. "Come on, Henry, rules are made to be broken. And I know you don't need much more persuasion than that! Another two," he said, nodding at the bartender.

Henry feigned reluctance but gave in happily and, half raising his glass to Quentin, settled into some social chit-chat.

"So, it's been a few years, hasn't it," he said and placed his whisky glass carefully back on the bar. "I've heard about your brother George, of course. Terrible business about his girl," said Henry, shaking his head. "I mean, a drug addict! It seems you just never know what's coming round the corner these days."

Quentin nodded in agreement, then immediately shook his head disapprovingly.

"So, how've you been?" continued Henry relentlessly.

"Oh, you know, old boy — can't complain!" lied Quentin. "A bit of business here and there. The old coffers overfloweth — just need to keep it that way."

Henry nodded approvingly. "Moved on myself in the past couple of years. Oversee the General Register Office now."

A distant bell started ringing in Quentin's mind. The General Register Office. Why was *that* so interesting to him?

"Oh, really?" he enquired in what he hoped was a casual, nonplussed manner. "So . . . passports and so on?"

"More births, marriages and deaths — life's little milestones, as I like to call them!" chortled Henry. "We see some stuff, let me tell you. At least, they do on the 'shop floor'. I tend to be rather further removed from the nitty-gritty up in my ivory tower and all that!"

Quentin was almost salivating now. The whisky fog had lifted a little and his mind was working overtime. Bulldog. Bulldog was trying to find out his origins, trying to worm his snivelling little working-class way

110

back into society, into the arms of his birth parents — the Charltons — and his twin sister, Lyric. Well, try as he might, Quentin had found a way to stop him. Thank the Lord for old school ties. If there was anyone you could trust, it was a fellow Etonian. Their word had always been their bond — hurrah for the alma mater.

"So you are the Fat Controller then?" said Quentin, trying to keep his voice light.

Henry gave him a self-satisfied smile. "Yes, Quentin, you could call it that."

Quentin gave an impressed smile. He looked Henry directly in the eye and tried to appear disingenuous. "And I expect you ultimately control requests for birth and death certificates?"

"Yes, that's right," said Henry proudly.

"Well, Henry, let's drink to that!" guffawed Quentin. "What a responsibility! One might say you're the keeper of the nation's family trees."

Henry laughed and raised his glass. "Spot on, Quentin."

Quentin paused, as if thinking hard. He turned solemnly to Henry and lowered his voice so that Henry had to crane his neck to hear him. "So, I would imagine, Henry, it's in your power to be a little — ah — creative with certain requests?"

Henry looked puzzled. "What on earth do you mean, old chap?"

Quentin laughed awkwardly and took another sip of his drink. "Well — and I'm talking hypothetically here, you understand?" He gave Henry a knowing look and Henry, puzzled, nodded back.

Quentin chose his words carefully. "Imagine someone were to come to you and suggest that somebody was seeking their true paternity. Their birthright, if you like. But were this person to find out, it would set in motion the most awful sequence of events, shaking an old and well-established family to the core — hurting existing children, affecting lineage, potentially changing the whole order as we know it . . ."

He let the end of his sentence dangle, and Henry, trying to keep up, drew his own conclusion. His eyes suddenly brightened and his face lit up with his own interpretation of what Quentin was getting at. He nudged Quentin in the ribs in a chummy fashion and slapped him on the back for a second time.

"Oh — so you . . . Quentin! I never realized, you sly old dog, you." He chuckled into his tumbler. "Well, I suppose that's par for the course for a love child. What's the name of this person you're trying to prevent re-entering your family?"

Quentin opened his mouth to correct Henry. It wasn't *his* love child, the stupid goat. Just as quickly, he shut it again. Maybe this was the best way — it would throw a further smokescreen over the awful truth. He moved closer to Henry and stage-whispered into his ear. "This must stay between you and me, Henry. You understand? No one must ever know." He paused again and sat back dramatically. "This person's name is Edward. Edward Charlton. But that is something he must never find out."

★   ★   ★

112

Hours later, Quentin waved goodbye to Henry and made his way uncertainly through to the restaurant. He should have felt elated, but strangely, he didn't. He felt it was a job only half done — just a start, so to speak. He had a strong niggling feeling it wasn't going to be nearly enough.

He felt in his pocket for a dog-eared, well-fingered card and looked at the number, Ali Hassan's smooth cosmopolitan tones reverberating around his fuddled head. *Any friend of Jacob's is a friend of ours*, he'd said, using the royal "we" as he slipped the card into Quentin's hand at Jacob's inaugural fundraiser. *And his father must enjoy all the privileges that we extend to our own family.* So if he, Quentin, was ever in need, here was his bodyguard's number. He would be happy to oblige with whatever it was Quentin needed, Hassan had assured him, whenever he needed it. *For us*, he'd said, *this is a matter of honour.*

Quentin had laughed and slapped Ali jovially on the back, inwardly crowing at his implied acceptance into this international power-player's inner circle, but trying to give the impression that it happened to him every day.

Now, Quentin blinked, his clogged-up arteries struggling with the sudden rush of blood activated by the adrenaline now coursing round his body.

Via Henry, Bulldog had been dealt with — for now. But for how long? How long before he reared his ugly head again, wanting to find out his real identity or, worse, having discovered it? What Quentin needed was a much more final situation.

He swept an irritable hand across his brow as beads of sweat sprang out again and ran in rivulets down his forehead and through the wiry grey hair on his temples. Pulling his phone out of his jacket pocket, he took a deep breath and punched in the number.

It was the perfect solution. A bodyguard like that would also be a trained killer. And he'd do it, Quentin was sure. Everyone had their price. Wasn't it a matter of honour, after all?

CHAPTER
NINE

November

Lyric and Crispin collapsed back on to the enormous king-size bed in their suite at Le Mélézin, giggling hysterically like schoolgirls. Through the panoramic window in front of them, Lyric caught a glimpse of the twinkling lights of Courchevel nestled in amongst the early, pillowy snow. Traditional, scenic and naturally pretty, it was a world away from the built-up concrete jungles elsewhere in the Alps. No wonder it was *the* hip and happening place on the ski map, a winter playground for the world's glitterati.

Her mind wandered to Philippe Chappeau — as it had done many times since the garden party. She had a feeling he would love the majestic beauty of the Alps and the natural beauty of Courchevel — its winding streets that gave out on to rugged mountain slopes. She shook the thoughts from her head. Philippe wasn't here, and what's more he had made no attempt to contact her. Really, it was immaterial whether he liked it or not — he wasn't here, was he?

"Darling! We forgot the cotton buds!"

Lyric looked over at Crispin mock seriously. "But weren't they on the dressing table with the cotton-wool pads?"

They stared at each other for a split second, then, as one, they leapt off the bed and raced each other through to the luxury bathroom. A free-standing bath with marble surround took centre stage, flanked by his-and-hers basins. It was lined up with the window to give bathers an uninterrupted view across the pistes to the mountains beyond, and sat directly under a glass pyramid roof that opened at the touch of a button to transform an average bathtime into a luxury starlit outdoor hot-tub experience. But now, both Lyric and Crispin went automatically to their respective vanity units and, pulling open the drawers, found what they were looking for.

"I got them first!" shrieked Lyric, pulling out the packet of complimentary cotton-wool buds. "Which means I win yours!"

She plucked Crispin's out of his hands and he glared at her dramatically. "You witch!"

Running out of the bathroom with Crispin in hot pursuit, Lyric dived at her half-unpacked Louis Vuitton luggage and threw both packets in. "Too late! I got them both!" she said, laughing breathlessly.

"Madam. May I remind you that it ain't over until it's over?" announced Crispin with a flourish. Bounding across the room with long strides, he disappeared through the door.

Still laughing, Lyric lay back on the pillows to catch her breath and looked out as the approach of night turned the grey sky deep blue before it became velvety black. The first thing she and Crispin always did in a hotel room was to steal everything. After unpacking their cases, they immediately refilled them with all the complimentary goodies. Writing paper, cotton buds, slippers — they all went in!

As the quiet in the room hit her, she had a sudden pang of loneliness, that all-too-familiar gnawing emptiness, and she hugged a cushion thoughtfully.

What a month it had turned out to be. First, the Monte Carlo drama. The Sheik and his wife, after their deplorable treatment of Lyric, were now estranged from the Charltons, but Lyric still hadn't addressed the situation with Treeva. Other, that is, than a few one-sided conversations with Laura, who, although clearly struggling to justify Treeva's actions, had reverted to her natural role as peacemaker and was desperately trying to reunite the two of them.

And then there had been her uncle's demands for Broughton Hall. After a shell-shocked dinner with her parents and some urgent discussions with the family lawyer, they had been advised to sit tight. Yes, Quentin had a case — but the repercussions of any kind of claim, not to mention the necessary investigations into his own dealings, meant the lawyer deemed any further action unlikely. Her father, she knew, doubted this — having jeopardized his position in the family by even raising the issue, he felt Quentin was bound to take it further — but now, two weeks on and with no further threat from her uncle, it seemed to have died down. Her father, of course, was still reeling — quietly, privately — but Lyric could tell from his subdued manner, the steely set of his jaw and the absence of his usual bounce that he was hurting. Lyric, for her part, had taken her cue from her mother and was determinedly "business as usual". So much so that, having dashed out to catch the year's first serious snowfall in the Alps, she and Crispin were due to hook up with Jacob and one of his friends for drinks that evening. It wasn't her cousin's fault he had a rotten father, and Jacob was the closest thing Lyric had to a brother. Anyway, contact with Jacob meant another opportunity to delve into her new suspicions and find out just why her uncle was suddenly showing his true colours so disagreeably.

And then finally, amazingly, there had been the meeting with Philippe. Lyric hugged a pillow to her as she allowed her mind to drift back to that gorgeous face, those crinkly eyes, those strong, muscular, suntanned arms —

"Da-daaaa!"

Lyric jumped and turned to see Crispin striking a pose at the bedroom door, wearing a plastic shower cap and holding a wicker basket.

"I win!"

Tipping it upside down, he scattered a shower of cotton buds across the plushly carpeted floor.

Lyric fell back on the bed laughing uncontrollably. "Where did you get all those from?"

"The housekeeping trolley, of course. And these, too." Turning out his pockets, Crispin revealed a stash of miniature bottles of bath foam and shampoo.

"OK, OK, you win!" Lyric said, still laughing. This time, Crispin had surpassed himself.

Now, however, he was looking crestfallen at the mess he'd created. "Oh dear," he mused. "I rather think I need to clear it all up." He looked up at Lyric with a comical look on his face. "After all, I've just had to take out a mortgage for room service," he said, nodding at the tray of pink champagne (for Crispin) and the mineral water (for Lyric). "The last thing I need is a second loan to tip the maid with."

"After you, darling."

Crispin stood back for Lyric as she stepped elegantly down the stairs before him, the high heels of her knee-length boots tapping rhythmically on the polished parquet floor. She smoothed her fine grey woollen jumper-dress along her curves and down over the matching grey tights.

Once in the bar, they made their way through the pine-panelled room to their table — a snug corner booth at the end of the bar, where soft yellow light cast by a rustic table lamp made the space feel even more intimate. Jacob and his friend Ali Hassan had made themselves comfortable on the richly upholstered banquette, and, as Lyric and Crispin approached, they quickly got to their feet. Lyric smiled inwardly. In smart designer jeans, cable-knit cashmere jumpers over open-necked Brooks Brothers shirts and leather loafers, the pair of them looked like an advertisement for Ralph Lauren: handsome, fragrant, cosmopolitan and cool, their clothes chosen for their "feel appeal" as much as their appearance. But their hastily chivalrous greeting had endearingly exposed the inner schoolboy in them both.

Jacob was the first to embrace Lyric, and he squirmed with embarrassment as they exchanged glances, secretly acknowledging their last meeting.

"Don't mention the Ritz," murmured Lyric in his ear as they hugged one another. "Just remember us all when we're homeless."

Jacob gave her a grateful squeeze in return. "It won't come to that, I promise," he whispered back. Lyric nodded in secret accord. They pulled apart as if nothing more than a customary salutation had passed between them.

"Hello, gorgeous," said Crispin, throwing a camp arm around Jacob's neck and puckering his lips. Jacob wriggled out from his grasp uncomfortably and managed a tight smile.

"Hi, Crispin."

Jacob sat down at one end of the banquette and crossed his legs pointedly away from Crispin, indicating that no more intimate banter was welcome.

"So, at last we meet!" said Ali Hassan, moving forward smoothly to take Lyric's hand. His mouth, as it brushed her skin, was warm and smooth, and she felt his soft breath on the back of her hand. "Miss Lyric Charlton, I presume?"

Lyric smiled at him in amusement. Ali was devilishly handsome, and no doubt his swarthy good looks, permatan and straight white teeth — plus the not inconsiderable matter of his enormous wealth —

usually had girls swooning in the aisles. But she'd grown up surrounded by boys blessed with his prowling, privileged kind of good looks, and although she appreciated their aesthetic, they did nothing for her physically. She preferred them a little less groomed, a little more rugged. Like Philippe. However, Philippe wasn't here, and there was nothing to prevent a little harmless flirtation.

"How lovely to meet you, Ali," she said warmly. "I've heard *sooo* much about you." She gave him a meaningful look and his eyes immediately sparked into life. It was true, too — she knew about his reputation as a player, his worldwide harem of beautiful girls, and how he was honing his killer business instinct to take over his father's oil empire. He was the type who judged a day by how many noughts he'd added to his fortune before breakfast — and, looking at him, it clearly agreed with him. And with Jacob. Lyric also knew that, having been best friends throughout their days at Eton, it was Ali who was now financing Jacob's political career. Heavily.

"Well, in that case, we'll have a lot to talk about," he said, beckoning to the waiter. "Martinis all round, please."

"Oh — something soft for me," said Lyric hurriedly.

"And a virgin Martini for the lady," Ali continued, hardly missing a beat and twinkling over at Lyric. "A first time for everything, eh?" he added suggestively.

Lyric blushed despite herself. Ali was clearly attracted to her, but this was forward, even by her flirtatious standards. She'd forgotten how direct his type could be.

"I really can't remember," she said, artfully leaning across and spearing an olive from the tray of canapés.

"Well, then it's time someone gave you something you won't forget," Ali returned with undisguised lust in his eyes.

"Over my dead body," she retorted swiftly.

Crispin touched her lightly on the arm and nodded over towards the bodyguard standing discreetly in the corner.

"Darling, I really wouldn't give him the option," he quipped. "You never know what his type has got up his — erm — sleeve."

Ali smiled neutrally at Crispin and turned back to Lyric, gazing directly into her eyes.

"If you sleep with me, I'll give you an oil rig," he said, straight-faced. "Refuse me, and I'll cut off the French oil supply."

Jacob leaned over, enjoying the exchange. "Lyric, you might want to know that Ali *has* actually done that before . . ."

Lyric covered her ears with her hands. "La-la-la-la-laaaaaa! I'm not listening to any of you! It's enough to drive a girl back to drink. Can we just change the subject, *please*?"

The waiter arrived with their cocktails, and Lyric took hers, grateful for the diversion. As the waiter handed her her drink, his fingers brushed hers, and she looked up, startled at the unexpected frisson that had run through her. The waiter was lightly tanned and had

122

thick, honey-coloured hair that hung to his shoulders. The skin around his brown eyes crinkled kindly as he smiled at her. He was attractive, very attractive. But oddly, the pull she felt towards him wasn't physical. It was — somehow — *meta*-physical. As though she'd met him somewhere before. But where — and how?

Whatever the answer was, the waiter didn't seem to feel it too — he withdrew his hand hurriedly and busied himself placing coasters and drinks on the table. Lyric took a sip of her drink to steady her suddenly racing pulse, and gently massaged around her left eye, which was threatening to twitch.

Regaining her courage, she looked up curiously as he placed a bowl of pistachios in front of her and caught his eye. There it was again, that incredible surge of chemistry! The waiter gazed at Lyric levelly, his eyes deep pools of Labrador brown, and gave her an unmistakeable, exaggerated wink.

Lyric gasped, heart racing, and stared into her glass with uncharacteristic embarrassment. She was sure she hadn't imagined it. He had just winked at her! Had she misread the chemistry? Had he been hitting on her? The barman spun the empty tray under his arm and glided away as if he couldn't wait to leave. The moment had passed.

"Nice pad," said Jacob, breaking into her thoughts and looking around the bar with approval. "I normally stay at Byblos," he said to Ali by way of explanation. "Though if you're talking to my constituents, I stay at the three-star pension at the lower end of the village. Paid for by my own means, natch."

They all laughed and Crispin leaned across the table and slapped Jacob's leg in mock reproach. Jacob jumped as if he'd been given an electric shock and moved his legs further away from Crispin.

"We're lucky to get a room here at all," pointed out Lyric. "Next week is half term and Abramovich has booked the whole place out."

"Abramovich doesn't stop Ali Hassan from doing anything," scowled Ali, bristling at the thought that someone else could get in his way. "In fact, I might just stay on a few extra days myself."

Lyric hid a smile. Ali was probably one of the few people in the universe who could match Roman's millions dollar for dollar — and it was more than his pride was worth to admit that his business rival had got something he hadn't. Even if it was a simple booking — albeit at one of the world's most exclusive hotels. Still, she thought, as she stole another glance at the waiter, now serving drinks to a booth further down the bar, it had taken Ali's attention away from trying to seduce her. And for that, she had to be truly grateful . . .

Later that night, a lone figure crunched through the snow along the frozen streets and out of the village, leaving yet another trail of footsteps on the well-trodden path. It climbed the steps of a villa apartment block and unlocked the door into a humble studio apartment.

Once inside, the figure discarded its snowboarding jacket, pulled off its snowy boots and, without stopping

124

to make a drink or snack, walked over to a small fold-up table and switched on the laptop placed on it.

Scrolling down the long list of favourite websites, the figure clicked on to one, entered a password and sat back expectantly. The screen came to life and the figure leaned forward eagerly, reading the message.

Dear Edward, aged 30

Thanks for your recent enquiry with iwasadopted.com

We have some exciting news about your birth family.

Please call us to discuss further.

Adoption Discovery Team

The figure ran his fingers through his honey-blond hair and rubbed his eyes as though he couldn't believe what he was seeing. Could this be it? The end of flitting around the world from one lonely seasonal job to the next, of seeing the globe's most glamorous places from the not-so-special position of "below stairs". Ski instructor, lifeguard, and presently bartender at Le Mélézin. But now — this. Could this be the start of what he'd craved ever since his adopted mother had told him he wasn't her blood son? Could this fill the gnawing chasm of emptiness he had always felt, but now experienced on a daily, if not hourly, basis?

CHAPTER
TEN

"Oh, I don't know, Crispin — I'm not sure," said Lyric, stretching her leg elegantly to appraise the sky-high pink ostrich-skin stiletto perched comfortably on her foot. She leaned back on the gilt-backed chair to get a better view. The subtle, low-level lighting cast a flattering glow around the boudoir-style store, making the calf extending from the bottom of Lyric's cigarette pants look even smoother and softer than usual.

"You don't know what you're talking about, darling — they are *fabulous*," said Crispin despairingly. "Where's your fashion mojo gone? You're beautiful single and *rich*, and you should be revelling in it — not trying to hide it like some dowdy old dowager. Just because you've fallen for a gardener doesn't mean you have to *dress* like one, darling," he finished tartly with a dismissive flick of his head.

Lyric sighed and turned her ankle left and right, still admiring the shoe. "I guess you're right," she said slowly. "I mean, it's not as if anything's going to happen with me and Philippe, is it? He hasn't exactly been ringing my phone off the hook."

Since the garden party, Lyric had thought of little else but Philippe Chappeau. And if her current level of

126

obsession was anything to go by, no wonder they had warned in rehab against falling straight into a new relationship — it had practically taken over her life! But despite what she was sure had been a major connection between them, and the fact that he could quite easily have found her number via Laura, he'd made no attempt to contact her. *She* had wheedled *his* number out of Laura the very next day, and had almost rung him herself countless times. But every time she had gone to dial his number, something — nerves? an outdated sense of what was "proper"? — had stopped her. Lyric sighed again. He obviously thought there was nothing more to her than her public It girl persona, and had dismissed their mutual attraction as simple nostalgia. She had to pull herself together — and quick.

"I'll take these," she said decisively, holding out the shoes she'd just tried on.

Crispin grabbed them from her and handed them to the sales assistant with a flourish. "In every colour," he added wickedly.

"Crispin!" Lyric gasped.

"Oh, come on, Lyric, what's the fun of a trust fund that doesn't come with a wardrobe full of Jimmy Choos?" he said, kissing the top of her head. "Buy in bulk, darling — it's better value. Anyhow, if you're wearing the pink, I might want to borrow the beige. They're a positive miracle of science when it comes to leg lengthening."

Once outside, Crispin put down the bags, pulled out his mobile and dialled. Lyric looked at him questioningly.

"The driver, darling," mouthed Crispin over the hand-piece by way of explanation.

Lyric frowned. "But I want to go to Chanel first," she said, pointing further down the wide, leafy, bustling length of Sloane Street with her head. She was due to accompany Truly Stunning on a promotional tour of the Far East in a couple of weeks, and she still didn't have anything suitable to accompany her impeccably groomed and stylishly dressed godmother on a trip to the bottom of the garden, let alone to a state reception in Beijing.

Crispin raised his eyes skywards in mock frustration. "Not for us, darling — for the bags!" he said, indicating the multiple designer bags hanging crowding round his legs.

With that, a blacked-out Mercedes pulled up smoothly beside them and, pulling open the door, Crispin flung the collection of smart shopping bags unceremoniously into the car and held out his arm for Lyric.

"We can't drag all that rubbish into Chanel, darling — what would they think of us?"

With that, he tucked his arm into Lyric's and sauntered off down the street, pulling her with him. Lyric giggled and skipped along with him. She'd always loved shopping, after all, especially with Crispin — she really needed to get over herself.

But as the doorman pushed open the heavy glass doors of the Chanel boutique for them, Lyric was suddenly filled with memories of another shopping trip several years previously. Early on in a relationship with her first "grown-up" boyfriend, he had taken her to Paris. They'd gone from designer store to designer store, and he had selected outfit after outfit for her to try on. Lyric, of course, had bought nothing — it was before she'd come into her trust fund and she was frugal by nature — but even with a generous allowance, most of the things were beyond her reach. She'd soon tired of having all these beautiful things paraded in front of her, but he had insisted on seeing her in everything that caught his eye.

Once back at the Georges V, he'd left her in the lobby to go for a swim. Dejected, she'd taken the lift to their suite — and discovered every item she'd tried on, still in their designer shopping bags, perfectly set out in a ring around the room. Lyric blushed as she remembered what, in her sheer surprise and delight, she'd done next. Instead of pulling out the items and trying them on again immediately, she'd rifled through for the receipts, added them all up and then phoned her mother to tell her what he'd spent. They had cost so much, he could have bought her a car! she'd gasped to Constance as she sat amongst the hoard. Lyric felt a pang of shame for the girl she'd been then. It had been a grotesque thing to do, but really, wouldn't anyone? Especially someone who, even at twenty-five, had still been relatively naïve.

That everything comes at a price had been her first lesson in love — the boyfriend had turned out to be controlling and aggressive. She shuddered as she thought about the harsh life lessons her drug addiction had taught her since, and gave Crispin a chaste kiss on the cheek. Dear Crispin — at least she could always rely on him!

She wandered through the store, thoughtfully fingering the clothes, feeling too lost in her memories to get fully immersed in shopping.

Then, she saw it. It was perfect. It wasn't exactly the show-stopping number she'd been looking for for Beijing — but it was just *her*. It was a white dress designed along simple planes, the silhouette cut in an A-line and tapering upwards to meet a cropped jacket with flat, squared-off shoulders and a stand-away collar. So far, so classic. Close up, though, the minutiae were mind-spinning. The classic Chanel braid was minimized to millimetres of hand-woven fluff, and the embroidered flowers modernized in weightless 3D montages of organza and cellophane. The palette was made up of microdots of matte plastic, and the lace shivered with tiny crystalline beads.

Lyric looked around for the sales assistant, immediately desperate to try it on. As the smart, bespectacled girl in a sharp Chanel suit came hurrying over, she held out the dress. "May I?" she asked.

"Madam, I think you'll find it is your size," murmured the assistant, sizing up Lyric expertly and searching down the back of the jacket for the size.

"Great," said Lyric, already on her way to the dressing room as the assistant hurried after her, carefully arranging the outfit alluringly on the hanger. Once inside, she stepped out of her clothes and into the dress. Buttoning up the jacket, she sighed in delight. The shimmering fabric reflected off her lightly tanned skin and gave it a peachy glow. The tailoring fitted her curvaceous figure perfectly, simultaneously emphasizing both her contours and her innocence, and the skirt grazed her kneecaps demurely, giving her the air of a modern-day Julie Christie. She loved it.

There was a swish, and she turned to see Crispin peering disdainfully around the curtain.

"Darling! You look ravishing. For a fifty-year-old," he said disapprovingly, pulling the cubicle curtain across and disappearing again.

Lyric turned back to the mirror to reappraise her appearance. What on earth was he talking about? It was chic and classy — what was his problem?

"You're mad, Crisp — it's perfect," she called confidently.

Without warning, the curtains were flung aside for a second time and Crispin reappeared, brandishing a huge pair of dress scissors. "It will be, darling," he said, bending down and cutting three inches off the bottom of the skirt.

"*Crispin!*" shrieked Lyric, as hundreds of pounds' worth of designer fabric fell to the floor.

But as she looked, through her shock she saw that he was right. It was still chic, it was still classy — but now the skirt sat mid-thigh, showing off her endless legs. It was flirty, cheeky and cool — much more her. The old, carefree her, anyway.

She clasped her hand to her mouth in horror and pulled the curtain tightly to hide both them and the carnage Crispin had created, giggling nervously.

"What are we going to do?" she whispered urgently. "That sales assistant is going to *freak*!"

"We're going to ask for their dressmaker," said Crispin loudly, also trying to conceal his laughter. "This is a couture house, isn't it? They'll be used to alterations."

An hour later, Lyric and Crispin were firmly ensconced at their favourite table in San Lorenzo, still laughing over Crispin's couture customizing. Their seats, right at the back of the restaurant, afforded them almost total privacy combined with not only a perfect view of the other VIPs lunching, but also an unrivalled vantage point over the street outside.

"We'll have two glasses of house champagne," said Crispin to the waiter, snapping the wine list shut decisively. "And two Caesar salads."

He gave Lyric a warning look as she opened her mouth to protest about the champagne he'd ordered for her. "I won't hear a word against it," he said firmly. "We always have Caesar salad on shopping trips."

Lyric grimaced. "Crisp, that's the kind of corny joke my father would come out with."

Crispin shrugged nonchalantly. "But seriously, Lyric, all this abstention — it's doing you harm, not good! You're forgetting who you are. It's not about getting drunk, it's about having fun. Loosening up. You had a drug problem, not a drink dependency — and if you can't jolly well toast a successful shopping trip with your best friend every now and then, frankly, I can't see what the point is."

Lyric raised a quizzical eyebrow. "The point of . . .?"

Crispin sighed huffily and broke a grissini stick in two, biting into one rebelliously. "Oh, I don't know, darling — anything!"

Lyric smiled into her water tumbler. Dear Crispin — he was right, of course. Since she'd left rehab, she'd taken their outpatient advice as gospel. No drugs, of course — but also no drink and no dabbling in relationships. Not through lack of wanting, though . . . Lyric pushed the thought of Philippe to one side and returned to considering Crispin's assessment. In her opinion, her treatment had definitely made her a better person, and, in taking away her dependency on drugs, had in many ways allowed her to be more of her own person. But there was an element of her new lifestyle that left her feeling a little — well — uptight. And if anyone was going to recognize that, it was Crispin. Especially because since she'd been back he'd practically moved in. They were — and ever since they'd met through their neighbouring boarding schools, always had been — carbon copies of each other. Both great performers but shy inside; both eternal optimists but with an inner melancholy; both sure of their feelings about other people but never a hundred per cent sure of themselves. And Lyric had learned in rehab that, in a narcissistic way, they probably loved one another for the very things they recognized in themselves. And, she suddenly realized with surprise, loved each other for the very things they actively *disliked* about themselves.

Maybe that was why he'd always looked out for her, just like she'd looked out for him — unlike more self-serving "friends" such as Treeva. It was funny. Most gays seemed to have a certain expiry date with women — inevitably jealousies or queeny bitchiness or simply the fact that they couldn't actually *be* you got in the way in the end — but this had never happened with Crispin.

The waiter arrived with their frosted flutes of champagne, and Lyric smiled as Crispin winked, clinking his glass with hers.

"Chin-chin, darling."

"Chin-chin, Crisp," she said, and inhaled deeply before taking a minute sip. It tasted good — and all at once, Lyric was overcome with confidence. She *could* do this — she *did* have the will power to have the odd glass now and again without becoming a slurring drunk.

Crispin put his glass down purposefully and leaned across the linen-covered table. "Now, darling, down to business."

Lyric laughed. "What business? The business of how I'm going to get Philippe Chappeau to call me?"

Now it was Crispin's turn to grimace. "No, darling, we've given that grubby little gardener far too much airtime already today. Nope, what we need to discuss is how we're going to get that cute-as-custard cousin of yours to take me on as his public relations officer."

Lyric stared at Crispin disbelievingly. The closest he'd ever come to getting a job was being paid to appear at the odd dreary society party or two. And now he wanted a round-the-clock role on the political circuit? With Jacob, of all people. Jacob had never disguised his dislike for Crispin, blaming it, when Lyric had questioned him, on a personality clash. Privately, Lyric thought it was something more; ever since she could remember, Jacob had been an open homophobe, and she could only imagine his reaction if she suggested he take Crispin on as a member of his campaign team.

"Think about it, darling," urged Crispin. "In this day and age, every political party — especially the Conservatives! — needs to represent every walk of life. And the pink vote is important — to make it, you need a reputation as a politician who not only accepts gays, but represents them, too. Jacob is currently very far from this point."

"So you don't want a job, as such, you want the notoriety!" said Lyric, spearing a piece of cos lettuce. Her tone was accusing, but secretly she was relieved to be able to justify Crispin's sudden interest in the world of work. "Crisp, do you have any idea what kind of hours you'd have to put in as a party spin doctor?"

"Do, delete, delegate — isn't that the phrase?" said Crispin, dodging the direct question. "It's all in the way you approach it and who you have working *for* you, darling. I think I'd be perfect — and anyhow, you owe me."

"Owe you?" spluttered Lyric through a mouthful of salad. "What for? Giving me a helping hand off the wagon?" With that, she picked up her glass and took another sip.

Crispin bought a few moments by taking a forkful of his own salad.

"No, for reminding you who you really are and preventing you from going out looking like an old granny," he said finally.

Lyric laughed. She couldn't argue with any of that. "OK, I'll speak to Jacob," she said. "But don't get your hopes up — I've never heard him say he needs any help on the PR front, and you're not exactly overqualified."

"I know everyone who's anyone, and understand how the rest of them tick. That's all the qualifications I need," retorted Crispin confidently. He nodded at her mobile lying on the table in between them. "Go on then, darling."

"What, *now*?" said Lyric, incredulously. Then, seeing he was deadly serious, she picked up her phone and dialled Jacob's number.

"Lyric?" Her cousin sounded breathless, busy — as well as surprised to hear from her in the middle of a weekday.

"Hi, Jacob," Lyric said warmly. "How's it going?"

"Fine, fine," said Jacob distractedly. "Look, is it urgent? I'm a bit . . ."

"No, it's not urgent — but it is important," said Lyric, feeling Crispin kick her sharply under the table. "I've had an idea that I want to put to you — no need to decide now, of course, just some food for thought." She was wittering now, she knew it, and she stopped herself and scowled back at Crispin. She hated having to do things like this under pressure. She took a deep breath. "Crispin and I were talking, and —"

"Crispin?" replied Jacob sharply. "As in raving queen Crispin?"

136

"Yes, that's the one," said Lyric, pressing the mobile closer to her ear so Crispin wouldn't hear. "Anyhow, you'd probably never guess this, but he has aspirations to get into politics — PR really — and we were talking about how fantastic he'd be for *you!*"

"For me?" said Jacob. "What do you mean, for me?"

"Well, for the party. You know — he knows everyone, would be able to put a fantastic spin on everything, and you really need to look gay-friendly these days," gabbled Lyric. Tired of playing the game, she let out a deep sigh. "Look, why don't you meet up and Crispin can brief you exactly on his vision?"

"And then I can *debrief* him afterwards," murmured Crispin wickedly, and it was Lyric's turn to kick out under the table.

There was silence on the other end of the phone. Lyric's heart sank. The last thing she needed at the moment was to alienate her cousin.

"Jacob?"

"Crispin — and me — we'd have to meet up in private," said Jacob slowly. "I don't want anything getting out. I mean, he might be totally unsuitable."

Lyric's jaw dropped. "So — you think it's a runner?" she said incredulously.

There was a pause at the other end of the line.

"I said I'll meet him, Lyric. No more than that."

Jacob hung up with a click, and Lyric took a sip of her champagne, staring at Crispin's triumphant face wonderingly. Well, well, well. Life never ceased to surprise her.

CHAPTER
ELEVEN

As the helicopter veered off to the right, Dubai's sunlit concrete skyline rose into view. Quentin sat forward on his leather bucketseat expectantly, mouth watering as the city's riches spread out before him as if for his very own personal delectation. He mopped his brow and blew out a long, sour, claretty breath as the veins in his temples bulged and strained repulsively. Luxury hotels, casinos, shopping malls — Dubai was Eldorado, and it could all be his for the taking.

He stroked the overstuffed arm of the seat in satisfaction. Sergei had put his fleet of cars, private jet and helicopter at Quentin's disposal in anticipation of some heavy-duty entertainment in the execution of his brief. It really did seem that the richer you were the more gullible you became, thought Quentin in self-congratulation. Or maybe you were just too rich to care. Either way, Quentin was the one who was going to benefit — and he planned to milk it for all it was worth.

The flight had already been an experience and a half. It was the first (but definitely not the last) time he'd travelled First Class with Emirates. He'd had his own personal plasma screen, a choice of vintage wine, a chair that massaged him in a thousand private places and a saucy little hostess. On landing, the helicopter had picked him up directly off the tarmac and was now flying him straight to his hotel — the plutocratic seven-star Burj Al Arab. Straight, that is, to the rarely used helipad on top of the dramatic sail-like tower, an architectural phenomenon that, like it or loathe it, had been the subject of impassioned debate the world over. As soon as Quentin had heard about it, he'd ignored the aeroplane pilot's warning about how windy it could be there and ordered Sergei's personal helicopter pilot to fly him in, as befitted his VIP status. Quentin slapped the arm of his seat in frustration. Who would build a helipad that was never used? It beggared belief. No sir — he, Quentin Charlton, was going to expose these namby-pamby Arabs as the spineless playboys they really were. He was *somebody*. Sergei and Ali Hassan realized it, and the rest of the world was about to realize it too.

The helicopter started to slow and Quentin looked out of the window eagerly. The hotel, on its own purpose-built island just off Dubai's main beach and linked to the mainland by a gentle curving causeway, was just below them. The pilot was clearly lining up the helicopter to land, and Quentin's chest puffed out at the thought of the VIP welcome that was no doubt awaiting him. Suddenly, the helicopter lurched to one side, buffetted off course by a gust of wind. They careered through the air, the helicopter rocking dramatically.

"Sorry for the turbulence, sir, conditions are as bad as always," said the pilot into Quentin's earpiece. "I strongly advise that we turn back and make the journey by road."

"Don't be ridiculous, man!" Quentin spat in disgust. He looked out again at the huge cross on the helipad. It seemed tantalizingly close. "I could land this thing on there myself!"

"But, sir . . ." protested the pilot, his voice filled with doubt.

"Just do it!"

He sat back in satisfaction, feeling the faint hint of an erection as the helicopter turned in again and prepared to land. Power, excitement. There really was nothing like it. And it might have come to him late in life, but how he was going to enjoy it now he finally had it.

The helicopter lurched alarmingly, this time spinning 360 degrees. It pitched downwards, once to the left and then to the right. Quentin felt the bottles of wine he'd consumed on the plane slosh around in his stomach and come terrifyingly close to appearing again.

"*Fuck!*"

Quentin jumped as the pilot's smooth tones turned to panic in his earpiece.

"Jesus, man, I'm taking us back to the airport. Your crazy ideas are going to have us fucking killed!"

Later that afternoon, Quentin chomped on a cigar as he nursed a single malt and gazed out over the spectacular views that the Club Suite afforded him: to his left, the endless blue of the Indian Ocean, and to his right, the gently undulating golds and ochres of the desert. Behind him, the luxurious living area stretched out

140

expansively, incorporating a sumptuous drawing room, full-sized snooker table, dining table for six, cocktail bar and even a guest washroom. Stairs led up to the suite's upper floor and the second sitting area, dressing room, bedroom with king-sized bed and luxury bathroom complete with full-sized Hermès bath products. Ah, yes. This was the life he'd been born for, that he should have been living for all of his sixty-seven years. Even the humiliation of the aborted helicopter ride had, in his head, morphed into a James Bond mission unaccomplished, and the effusive welcome he'd received from the hotel's senior management had dulled the indignity of the relatively mundane arrival in a chauffeur-driven car. The reception committee — including no less than the hotel's general manager — had been a grovelling group of sycophantic executives who, in his opinion, wouldn't know class or cleverness if it jumped up and grabbed them by the balls. What they did know, however, was money — and money, for once, was what Quentin was all about. Their desperation to indulge him with whatever material goods he desired was music to his ears. "Anything we can do for you, sir?" "Here's a coat for your son, sir," "Please, imagine that you are at home — nothing is too much trouble for our staff, nothing that you see cannot be yours." Quentin laughed out loud at the thought of it — and the case of Château Lafite 1971 he'd demanded they bring up to his suite.

Placing his cigar in the nearest ashtray, Quentin leaned over and rubbed his hands together gleefully. Silhouetted against the panoramic seascape, he had the appearance of a Quasimodo-style hunchback, an ugly character lost in his own narcissistic greed.

All of a sudden, Quentin's eye returned to the table. Retrieving his cigar in one hand, he picked up the ashtray with the other and held it up to the light, inspecting it closely. Ooooh — antique! He licked his lips in appreciation, then, furtively looking around him, tipped the ash into a plant pot and placed the priceless small saucer in his pocket. Nothing that he saw couldn't be his, eh? Well, he'd start with the priceless ashtray then, thank you very much.

The insistent ring of his mobile phone interrupted his reverie, and his eyes lit up as he saw his lawyer's number displayed on the LED screen. Finally, some progress! And how apt that he should officially become master of Broughton Hall whilst living it up like a lord in this seven-star palace.

"Charlton," he barked, as if this were any other run-of-the-mill business call.

There was a pause on the other end of the phone, as if the caller were counting to ten. "Charlton, it's de Brier here."

Quentin sucked his teeth and sat back on the sofa. "De Brier! One moment, old boy, just finishing off a business meeting." Quentin covered the mouthpiece and chuckled to himself as he took another swig of whisky. No harm keeping up appearances. And no matter that keeping this top legal eagle waiting even two minutes was going to cost him dear — when he was ensconced at Broughton Hall, this legal bill would be small change to him.

142

After an appropriate pause, he uncovered the mouthpiece.

"Sorry about that, old boy. Urgent business matter. Sure you understand. So, what progress?"

The lawyer cleared his throat.

"Mr Charlton, progress is slow. And . . . expensive. You have a case, certainly, but establishing character defects and behaviour serious enough to make such a case stand up — especially when the person in question is making all the necessary changes to redeem themselves — it takes time. And I'm sorry to be so blunt, but time is money, and we simply cannot continue with a case of this magnitude without some kind of financial commitment from you, sir."

There was a silence. Quentin felt his blood begin to boil. Every time! Every time in his life that he'd made one small step of progress, something happened to send him another two, three, even four steps backwards.

"This is preposterous!" he snapped. "You've said it yourself, man — we have a case. You are as aware as I am of the nature of the prize. Is this not commitment enough?"

There was another pause. "Mr Charlton, I am well aware of the 'prize', as you put it. But a legal battle of this nature is likely to take years. I'm afraid I cannot commit our services to such a fight without some interim funding from the client."

Quentin felt the ashtray digging into his side and pulled it out to reinspect it. That alone would make a dent in the legal bills, at least for the short term. And with his art scam well under way, he would soon be in a position to fund the case for Broughton Hall. But something was stopping him. Did his good name not stand for anything, goddammit? If George were to approach the same firm, would he be greeted with the same kind of mistrust, as if he were some kind of good-for-nothing pauper? No, he would not.

"Well, if that's the case, then I shall be taking my case — and the not inconsequential commission — elsewhere," he snarled into the phone. "Good-day to you."

"Good-day —" began the lawyer on the other end of the phone, before he was unceremoniously cut off.

Quentin hurled his phone across the room, striking a vase on a nearby table and smashing it into smithereens. Well, wouldn't you know it, he raged inwardly. That was probably worth a mint, too. Another small fortune just disappeared through his fingers. He stormed over to the window, staring unseeingly at the panorama in front of him as he seethed.

The suite intercom rang, startling him, and a tinny voice rang out across the room.

"Mr Charlton, sir, you have a guest here for you in the lobby. He won't give his name, but he says you're expecting him. Can I send him up?"

"Yes, yes, do send him up," said Quentin, composing himself. Onwards and upwards, Charlton, he reminded himself. And this business meeting was bound to be more fruitful, he thought, wiping his clammy hands down his trouser legs.

A few moments later, the private entrance to the suite opened and revealed two guests, rather than one.

144

First to enter the room was Richard Boxer, a shady London art dealer whose arrogant swagger belied his reputation for dodgy underground dealing. His greying curly hair grew long behind his ears, and his blue blazer, open-necked shirt and Lee jeans were teamed with tan Cuban-heeled boots. Behind him, the shrunken form of Hans Wavering, a nervy, bespectacled figure in a beige overcoat, insinuated itself apologetically into the room. No wonder the hotel receptionist hadn't noticed *him*, thought Quentin — given the chance, he'd probably miss his own reflection.

"Charlton," said Richard Boxer abruptly, nodding at him and shaking his hand briefly.

"Mr Charlton, erm, hello, erm, it's a pleasure to meet you," stammered Wavering, and Quentin felt himself grow several feet in stature at the feeling of power he had over these men. He was their meal ticket to a very large pay packet — probably the biggest they would ever receive in their lives — and he wasn't going to let them forget it.

"Gentlemen," he said, in what he hoped was a slick, confident, authoritative manner, but which was in practice boorish and bullying. "Come this way."

He led them across the drawing room, where Boxer accepted a large glass of Grey Goose on the rocks. Wavering refused any refreshment at all.

"I trust you both had pleasant journeys," he said, knowing full well they had both travelled Business Class, and whilst they might not have had the added extras he'd enjoyed in First, they would have been very royally treated.

Hans Wavering sat forward eagerly. "Oh, yes, well, marvellous — it was . . ."

"It was perfectly acceptable," interrupted Boxer brusquely. "Cut to the chase, Charlton. You haven't flown us halfway across the world to discuss our flights. What's the deal?"

Quentin inspected his fingers for an infuriatingly long time before finally looking across at his guests and smiling smugly.

"I want to sound you out on a little project I've got planned. I need to fake the entire Charlton art collection, slip the copies into Broughton Hall and ship the real ones over here. And I need it completed in a matter of weeks."

Hans Wavering gasped in shock. Richard Boxer, however, remained expressionless.

"Charlton, your family owns one of the finest collections of nineteenth-century art in the world," said Boxer evenly. "Millions of pounds' worth. Recreating it would take months, if not years."

Quentin looked him aggressively in the eye. "I don't have years, Boxer," he said uncompromisingly. "I have weeks. But I also have a handsome budget. Those involved will be rewarded generously, as will those they involve at the operational level. It goes without saying, however, that the bottom of the food chain must make no connection with those at the top."

"My word is my bond, as it is of those I select to work for me," said Boxer, his tone more slippery than an oil slick.

146

"I have a contact at Sotheby's on my payroll already," said Quentin, his chest swelling with self-importance. "A recent family event —" he cleared his throat at the memory of his unsuccessful attempt to assume ownership of Broughton Hall — "has caused my brother to have the entire collection revalued. Fortunately I was one step ahead. My man has advised him that to do so, every painting must be cleaned and restored. The fool has fallen for it and is ready to part with several paintings at a time."

"He would be well advised to," interrupted Hans Wavering, almost tripping over his words in his enthusiasm to show off his expertise. "Over the years lamplight, candles, cigar smoke — they can all contribute to a painting's deterioration."

Quentin and Boxer both glared at him.

"They won't be going for restoration, Wavering," said Boxer coldly. "They will be going to be copied."

"Oh yes, yes, of course — very good, very good," said Wavering hurriedly, shrinking back, trying to lose himself in the sofa.

"I can get the first paintings to you in a matter of days," said Quentin, turning to Boxer. "The point is, when can you get the forgeries back to me?"

Boxer thought fast. "Well, I'll need a generous advance, of course," he said. Quentin nodded his agreement. "And I'll need details of the dimensions of all the works in the collections — they will all be in the last Christie's inventory, whenever that was produced, so no problems there. But I'll need to pick up a few third — or fourth-rate works for the canvasses — all bigger than the actual works, of course, so we can cut them to size. And then, once we've removed the tacks and got the canvas off the stretcher, we'll need to treat the oils with nitromethane to take the canvas right back to the primer. That'll take three weeks for each, two at a push. Then it's over to the restorer — Hans? How quickly can you and your boys turn around old masters?"

Wavering pushed his glasses back up his nose nervously. "Well, you know, I'm not used to having to work that fast, and I would hate the quality of the work to be compromised," he gabbled, "especially for someone so discerning — it's not so much the painting, that can be done very quickly, you see, but it's the drying. Oils, you see, are very sticky and slow to dry out and —"

"How quickly, Hans?" growled Boxer threateningly.

"Well, I have heard of a method involving phenol formaldehyde," gabbled Wavering. "Combined with the heat of a fan or a hairdryer to speed up the drying process, we could have the works rock-hard in a few weeks."

Quentin did some quick arithmetic. The way they were talking, they needed a minimum of three months to complete the number of works he needed. He didn't have that much time.

"Two months," said Quentin decisively. "I want the lot in two months. You —" he nodded at Boxer — "need to cut your lead time by a week. And you —" he sneered at Hans — "need to put a rocket up your brush strokes and put two, three, ten fans on those paintings. I need them in two months' time."

"You've got a framer lined up, I presume?" asked Boxer smoothly. "As we'll need his details, naturally."

Quentin stopped dead. The frames! Of course. He cursed his sketchy knowledge of art. Why hadn't he thought about the bloody frames.

"And if the paintings are to be hung out here —" Boxer nodded out towards the shimmering Dubai heat — "you'll need to encase them in Teng glass to protect against the humidity. Heaven forbid the air con should fail." He cleared his throat. "Of course, if a framer wasn't on your original things-to-do list, I'm sure I can find one from my Cork Street contacts. Likewise, the *right* kind of shippers," continued Boxer, smiling humourlessly. "For a price, of course."

Quentin's mind was racing with cuts and percentages. At this rate, his own fee would be whittled down to nothing. He'd have to talk to Sergei about increasing his operational costs.

"Of course," said Quentin dangerously. "We all have our price, after all."

Quentin dragged himself out of his seat and away from his fifth gastronomic course at the celebrated Al Muntaha restaurant. He'd done justice to every delicacy placed before him, to say nothing of the vintage wines as well, but now he had to get to the gents, and fast. As he stumbled across the dining room, he tried desperately not to look out of the 360-degree windows. You couldn't fault the food or the wine here, but dining two hundred metres above sea level — a dizzying twenty-seven floors up — meant everything felt so, well, high. Of course, it didn't help that in his VIP position at one of the best tables in the room he had uninterrupted views of Dubai by night, none of which had helped his increasing sense of vertigo.

A sheik he'd played poker with the previous night was just leaving the bathroom, flanked by a pair of bodyguards, and they exchanged nods. Quentin looked at himself admiringly in the mirror as he stood at the urinal, inspecting his bloated appearance. Who would have thought it — Quentin Charlton, millionaire?

Suddenly a figure appeared behind him — a tall, menacing figure dressed all in black. Quentin started and, instinctively putting his manhood safely out of harm's way, closed his flies.

"Mr Charlton."

Quentin took a deep breath. "Yes, that's me."

"I am Ahmed, Ali Hassan's right-hand man. You phoned me. And I am here."

Quentin looked at him, almost unable to believe his luck. The bodyguard. Just as he'd hoped. It was all coming together. Everyone did indeed have their price. And this price meant that just as his new life was panning out so successfully, he could finally close a door on his old one.

He'd got his hit man. And Bulldog would finally get what he deserved.

CHAPTER
TWELVE

"Argh!" Lyric shook her hand impatiently, trying to flick the sticky, spiky curve of one false eyelash off the palm of her left hand without smudging the carefully applied glue on its sister lash which was delicately held between her right thumb and forefinger. With the final, overexuberant shake, she struck her elbow on her dresser, hitting her left funny bone. Instinctively she cried out and clutched at it with her right hand, forgetting about the eyelash, which immediately transferred to her arm, sticking in a straight line along her bicep.

Defeated, she sank on to her dressing-table chair and scrutinized herself in the mirror. Her soulful brown eyes stared back at her, huge pools of molten chocolate set deep in her beautifully sculpted face. Around them, her carefully applied make-up was showing signs of too much fussing — a heavily applied line of liquid eyeliner here, a stroke too far of blusher there. Underneath it all, her professionally applied "barely there" spray tan glowed a shade too orange, testament to the "extra layer" she'd applied herself before bed, worried that the initial job would be too pale.

Lyric sighed heavily and picked up her hairbrush, running it through her honey-blonde hair morosely. So much for "au naturel", the relaxed, earthy look she'd planned for the evening — she looked more like a middle-aged drag queen. She glanced at her favourite red crêpe Burberry shift dress — the one that never, ever let her down — hanging on the wardrobe door behind her. Even that wasn't going to get her out of this sartorial bomb site.

Suddenly, a toot from the street outside made her jump. Her car! She looked at her diamond-encrusted Cartier watch with a start. Her disastrous appearance was going to have to do. She had precisely five minutes to get her clothes on and get out of the house in order to make her date with Philippe on time. She hurriedly pulled on her dress, and a pair of Miu Miu flats, grabbed her quilted Chanel chain bag and ran helter-skelter down the stairs to the waiting Merc.

Her heart was still pounding as she settled back into the car's soft leather seats. Her stomach churned — whether from nerves or hunger (she hadn't eaten that day to prevent her stomach looking bloated) she wasn't sure. Her skirt had ridden up to her mid-thigh, and she tried ineffectually to pull it further down over her legs. She tutted at her own fussing. She was developing neuroses to rival those of her mother. Not to mention the fact that, since she'd left rehab, her self-confidence seemed to have totally deserted her. And whilst she'd found the paparazzi attention overwhelming and impossible to deal with, in a superficial kind of way she almost missed it now they'd moved on to this week's

152

story. Their focus had made her feel scared and intimidated but oddly alive at the same time.

Nothing, however, could match the jolt she'd got when, two days ago — totally out of the blue — Philippe had contacted her on her mobile and asked her out for dinner. He had been straightforward, direct — businesslike, even. There had been no chatty preamble, no flirting or skirting around the issue, just that simple question. Would she like to meet for dinner?

And she'd said yes. Of course she had! But once she'd hung up, the next forty-eight hours had been spent in a panicky whirl, culminating in tonight's could-do-better appearance.

By the time the car pulled up outside the restaurant — a quiet, nondescript but apparently excellent bistro — Lyric's heart was in her mouth. Her palms were hot, and she could feel the telltale prickle as beads of sweat appeared around her hairline and under her arms. She took a deep breath and stepped out of the car, relieved that there were no paparazzi waiting for her here either.

As she entered the restaurant, flustered and nervous, she subconsciously looked for a reflection of edgy panic in Philippe. But as she scanned the room, she saw him looking composed, laid-back — relaxed, even. He was studying the menu closely, his brow slightly furrowed over those penetrating green eyes and that rugged scar, his open-necked shirt showing a glimpse of tanned body, his jeans worn casually with trainers. As Lyric walked across the room, she was doubly glad she'd chosen flats — she was certain that heels wouldn't have supported her quaking legs.

"Lyric!" He stood up, delight written all over his face. "You look — amazing."

She cringed at his hesitation, saw it written all over his face that he'd noticed the orange tan, the botched make-up, the hours of effort culminating in total failure.

She smiled, accepting his compliment, but inside she wanted to correct him, make him see that, really, she knew she looked monstrous now, but she could look something close to beautiful. She looked up shyly.

"Thank you."

He leaned forward to kiss her hello, and she caught a faint whiff of his cologne. She'd expected him to smell musky, but this was fresh, woody — outdoorsy. She smiled. As if she should have expected anything else.

"So, what would you like to drink?" he asked in his lilting accent as they both sat back down.

Lyric's mind went blank. Drink? She hadn't . . . "I'll have a Bellini," she blurted out to the wine waiter who had appeared at the table. She bit her lip. Random! Normally she couldn't bear Bellinis. Too sweet.

Philippe raised an eyebrow at her questioningly. She got his meaning immediately — he was surprised she was drinking at all.

"I've stopped taking drugs, not enjoying myself," she said, instantly regretting her defensive tone.

"There's no need to explain yourself," said Philippe easily. "Drugs I have an issue with. But food and drink are some of life's greatest pleasures — and even better if you can enjoy them both in moderation. I'll just have a Perrier," he continued, turning back to the waiter.

154

Lyric could have kicked herself. Why had she ordered something she didn't even like for the sake of seeming sophisticated? And, even more annoyingly, when she would have preferred a mineral water?

Philippe looked up at her, mistaking her silence for surprise at his abstinence.

"I'm driving. I'll save myself for the wine," he explained, then picked up the wine list and studied it intently.

Lyric tried not to show her delight at the way he was taking control. She wasn't used to this. Her experience of dates, both social and romantic — ever since she'd come of age and inherited her trust fund, in fact — had been more or less the same. She would be expected to set the tone for the evening, choose the wine and, yes, pick up the bill too, whether it was with friends, boyfriends, or even Ralph towards the end. She'd got so used to it that it hadn't even occurred to her that someone else could do it. She sat back in her chair expectantly.

Philippe, unaware of her train of thought, looked across at her over the menu. "I thought we might have asparagus, and then the fish?" He waited for her nodded approval and then called the wine waiter over. "The Sancerre, *s'il vous plaît*," he said briskly, and handed over the list.

Lyric took a deep swig of her Bellini to try and steady her heart, which had started beating overtime again. She had a distinct sense of being swept off her feet. Old-fashioned it might be, but wow! — she had a feeling she was going to like it . . .

High on the great start to their date, she took another sip of her Bellini and felt the heat from the alcohol prickle the back of her neck as it entered her bloodstream. Her tolerance to alcohol wasn't what it had been, and the aperitif was going to her head.

Their entrée arrived. Asparagus had always been her bugbear, even after her refinement at finishing school. She simply found it impossible to eat with any kind of decorum. She knew it was correct to eat it in her fingers, but always ended up with butter running down her chin, all over her napkin and down her front as well. She glanced surreptitiously over at Philippe. Without any pomp or ceremony, he picked up a piece of asparagus with his fingers and bit into it, then put it back on the plate and licked his fingers with relish. He managed to make it look natural, fun and easy — and not in the slightest bit chaotic. Sensing her gazing at him, he looked up at her quizzically.

"Is everything OK?" he asked with a note of concern, spotting her untouched asparagus.

Lyric smiled back at him and felt herself relax properly for the first time that night. Forget the fact that Philippe was drop-dead gorgeous. She couldn't remember being with someone so lacking in airs and graces, but with such natural class. With someone so caring. So *real*.

Trying to steady her spinning head, she took a sip of water and then attacked her asparagus. Her wave of confidence took her successfully through the first couple of mouthfuls and, buoyed by a sip of wine, she went for the third.

156

As she looked up from her plate, she noticed Philippe looking at her with undisguised amusement.

"What's the matter?" she asked. "What are you laughing at?"

"I'm not laughing," said Philippe, his green eyes sparkling with unvoiced laughter. "I'm marvelling."

"Marvelling?" repeated Lyric stupidly.

"*Oui*," he grinned. "At how someone can look so beautiful with butter dripping down their chin." He leaned forward and stroked the corner of her mouth gently with his middle finger, then licked it. Lyric blushed deeply, then found herself smiling happily.

"I'm sorry . . ." she said falteringly.

He looked at her fondly. "Why apologize?" he said, eyes still dancing. "You can forgive anyone anything . . . once."

She stared at him, wondering at the remark, which seemed to be laced with meaning beyond the moment. But at the corner of her eye she caught sight of an older couple a few tables away looking at them fondly, and her heart leapt. She and Philippe obviously looked like a couple in love. So maybe . . .

"I was worried about how I look tonight," she confided, with a sudden need to maintain the new level of intimacy he'd created. "I was going for a natural look, but I kind of overdid it, and then it all went wrong."

Philippe smiled, his eyes like deep green wells of sensitivity, and Lyric felt like she could lose herself in them for ever.

He leaned across and tucked a stray strand of hair behind her ear.

"I think you look like a plant, a flower, that's been neglected and left to wilt," he said quietly. "But one that, when it is finally cared for the way it should be, will blossom." He touched her face softly. "I wasn't taken in by the Lyric I've seen in the newspapers for the past few years. The drugs, the all-night parties, the extravagances. And I'm not fooled by fake tan and make-up. I know the real Lyric — she's different from all the others. She's unique. I knew her many years ago. I saw her on the hill at the party that day, and I can see her now. And she's beautiful just the way she is."

Lyric stared at him, and for once was lost for words.

He reached out across the table and gently took her hand. "Less is more, Lyric. I've always lived that way — maybe you could learn to love that too?"

Lyric felt like she was flying. Everything she'd come to appreciate during her stint in rehab, everything she'd longed to find when she got out — Philippe was the living, breathing embodiment of it.

She looked up at him, hope spilling out of every pore. "I want to, Philippe, I so, so want to."

"It's the next left," said Lyric, sitting in the passenger seat of Philippe's battered Mini Cooper. She felt cocooned in happiness, excitement — and, yes, anticipation. It was years since she'd been on a proper date, especially one that felt this momentous. What should she do when they arrived outside her house? Invite him in and risk appearing too forward, or say goodnight and risk ending this gorgeous, fabulous dream of an evening all too early?

Following the established pattern of the evening, Philippe made the decision for her. Pulling on the handbrake, he turned to her and touched her face gently. He leaned in and Lyric closed her eyes, hardly daring to breathe. She felt his lips brush hers in the softest, most loving kiss she could ever remember. Every nerve ending was alive with longing, every part of her body crying out for his touch.

"This is the moment you're meant to invite me up for a coffee," he said, his voice low and husky with desire. "But it's also the moment I'm going to pledge good behaviour if I do. I haven't forgotten your definition of a lady, you know."

Lyric laughed softly. Her staunch belief that a lady never "put out" had led to vehement dismissal of those girls at school — "slags" — that did, and she, Laura and Treeva would passionately discuss their antics on their way out to their own illicit, but chaste, nights out. And for all her wild ways, Lyric had remained true to this belief — to this day, though she had more exes than she could count, she could list the men she'd actually slept with on one hand. But how funny that Philippe should remember all their silly school-girl chatter. He must have given her a lot of thought over the years . . .

"Well, rules are meant to be broken," she said teasingly, "And I can only offer decaf. I'm off drugs now, you know."

Philippe laughed and threw his arm around her shoulder as they walked up the path to her door. As Lyric fished in her bag for her key, she noticed light coming from the sitting room window and paused in confusion. Crispin had left that morning for a few days at his parents in the country, and she was sure she'd switched off all the lights before leaving that evening.

Noticing her hesitation, Philippe squeezed her shoulder. "Are you sure about this? I can go home, you know."

Lyric shook her head vehemently. "No, honestly — I don't want the evening to end . . . I was just thinking about something. Really, it's fine!"

"OK," said Philippe, sounding unconvinced. He pulled his arm away abruptly and Lyric cursed her suspicious nature.

She opened the door, and light and heat streamed out on to the street. "Wow — anyone would think we were in the Arctic," said Philippe. "You're a one-woman eco disaster!"

Lyric laughed uncertainly. "I don't normally . . . the timer must have come on by mistake," she said, turning from the hall into the living room, plumping cushions distractedly. Rehab had not only enhanced her appreciation of her environment and reinforced her parents' lifelong insistence on how lucky she was in life and how much care she should take of the world around her, but it had also cured her of her natural chaotic untidiness, and she'd become almost obsessive — compulsive in her attention to her home. To the untrained eye, her comfortably stylish sitting room still looked relatively ordered, but to her it bore all the hall-marks of a Crispin hit-and-run — the half-finished glass of red wine on the coffee table, the stereo flashing insistently, alerting her to the long-finished CD within it, the sweater discarded over the arm of the chair. She silently cursed her friend under her breath. Why did he have to be such a flake? The one time she really needed her space to be *her* space.

She shrugged helplessly at Philippe. "I'm sorry — this isn't my mess, honestly," she said. She looked around the room mock despairingly. "It's my best friend Crispin — he's been staying with me. Make yourself at home — I'll make us some coffee!" she finished brightly, eyes darting round for other signs of Crispin.

"OK, great," said Philippe slowly, sitting down on the leather sofa but looking anything but at home. Lyric's edginess had obviously not gone unnoticed, and his stiff, awkward position gave away his discomfort.

Once in the kitchen, Lyric pulled the door behind her and leaned against the cool of the tiled wall, heart beating. Why was it such a problem to her that Crispin had left a mess? They'd been on a date — it wasn't as if she was being assessed on her domestic skills, after all. *Because you desperately want Philippe to love you for who you are now, not who you have been,* whispered a voice inside her. But in that case, reasoned Lyric with herself, why couldn't she have just laughed it off and had done with it?

Lyric pulled herself up briskly. She was being an idiot. She would make the coffee, bounce back into the room and explain to Philippe why she'd been acting so strangely.

But as she approached the kettle, Lyric noticed a telltale wrap of paper on the worktop. Cocaine — and several grammes of it, by the looks of the packet. She felt anger rise up within her. How dare he! Crispin had promised never to bring drugs into her house again, and here was enough to put her into hospital, never mind rehab.

She picked up the wrap and was about to throw it into the bin when she noticed Philippe standing in the doorway, looking at her sadly.

"It's OK, Lyric — you don't need to hide it from me. I've already seen it for myself," he said, holding up a rolled-up twenty-pound note between thumb and fore-finger. He looked at it with disgust, as though it was releasing a particularly bad smell, and placed it on the breakfast bar. "Don't tell me this is Crispin's as well?"

Lyric looked at the note, and then back to the wrap in her hand in despair. "Yes! Of course it is!" Lyric protested. "You can't think . . .?"

"Oh, come on, Lyric," said Philippe disbelievingly. "It had fallen on the floor, just underneath the coffee table. You're not telling me that your friend — Crispin? — has been up to no good all on his own, are you? Without you having any knowledge of it?"

Lyric ran over to him. "Yes! No! I don't know! All I do know is it's not mine. None of it."

The words sounded hollow, even to her own ears. Philippe looked down at her, all warmth gone from his eyes, and Lyric felt the chill of rejection fall over her like a mantle.

"I guess you're not quite back to the old Lyric yet. Maybe you never will be. We can all get carried away with what could be, after all. Maybe I need to reconcile myself with what could have been. I'll see myself out."

Lyric stared at him, open-mouthed. Every bone in her body was crying out *You've got it wrong! It wasn't me!*, but the words wouldn't come out. Instead, she watched as Philippe left, slowly closing the door behind him, and then listened desperately as his trainers crunched down the front path.

She slumped to the floor, sobbing. Her mischievous, fun-loving nature meant that all her life she'd been accused of things she was innocent of. A school prank, a misquoted sound bite — even sleeping around. People just never seemed to believe her — even when, as was mostly the case, she was telling the truth. But this was something entirely different. This felt like torture. Tonight, she felt like she'd really found herself, her forever love and her future. And tonight, in just a matter of minutes, she'd lost it again. And nothing, simply nothing, was ever going to make it better.

CHAPTER
THIRTEEN

"Dear Lord!" exclaimed Lyric's glamorous godmother, Truly Stunning, from behind her brightly coloured oriental fan as the huge ceremonial dragon reared up in her face. "I certainly wasn't expecting *that*!"

Lyric stifled a giggle behind her own fan. Certainly, when Truly — an A-list actress of a certain age, currently enjoying an Indian summer in her career thanks to Hollywood's recent revival of period dramas — had insisted that, despite heartbreak, she keep her promise to accompany her on her promotional tour of China, Lyric hadn't expected *this*. Her adored godmother had a habit of making a huge, glittering impact wherever she went (it was an oft-observed similarity between her and Lyric), but this trip really had beaten all others. The Chinese administration were feting them wherever they went, but this reception in Beijing was the most overwhelming yet.

The climax of the celebrations amounted to what could only be described as a showcase of Chinese culture over the centuries. Dancers, soldiers, puppets and musicians had been parading in front of them for over an hour. It was a fantastical spectacle, and sitting with the winter sunshine on her face, Lyric was torn

164

between delight at the theatre playing out in front of her and regret that it would seem rude to put on her oversized Dior sunglasses.

In front of them sat a decorative tray of traditional moon cakes, eaten during the annual moon festival — historically made of sweet pastry with an egg yolk inside, but nowadays, Lyric had been pleased to hear, also filled with fruit, sweetmeat or chocolate — and she was determinedly trying to focus on them and the entertainment rather than the real meaning of the Moon Festival. Held each year on the day the full moon is said to be nearest the earth, it was a time for couples and families to look at the moon and think of one another. Distant though they were, her family were certainly in her thoughts, but the real focus of the occasion for Lyric was the disastrous end to her date with Philippe. Why hadn't she made him stay, so she could explain about Crispin? Why hadn't she made him believe her? She had simply let him walk out of her flat — and out of her life.

Lyric fanned herself a little harder, as if to banish any painful thoughts, and gazed dreamily beyond the celebrations over to where the Ming Tombs lay. She'd always found the idea of the mausoleums, of those celebrated lives perfectly preserved in all their ceremonial splendour, romantic rather than macabre, and she was itching to go and look around. They'd been promised an official tour after lunch, and as far as Lyric was concerned, this couldn't come quickly enough. She shifted on her seat. Talking of which, she was dying for the loo — when was she going to get a chance to go?

As if sensing her discomfort, Truly — belying her English roots and looking the epitome, after years living in the States, of WASP refinement in head-to-toe Ralph Lauren — placed an elegantly cool hand on top of Lyric's. "I think they're working up to a finale, darling. Just as well — I could murder a G and T."

With that, there was a final dramatic drum roll and all performers dropped to the ground, the pools of ceremonial robes creating a riot of colour across the concrete courtyard. Lyric suppressed a laugh at what her godmother had said and assumed her most gracious smile as she and Truly applauded enthusiastically.

As various bowing officials collected them from their seats and escorted them through the courtyard to the marquee in the ancient garden of the tombs for lunch, Lyric spotted a bathroom and excused herself. She knew that, once seated at the table, getting up again would be difficult — her exit would be made very public as each and every official had to stand up decorously as she left and again as she returned.

As she left the bathroom, she again caught sight of the Ming Tombs. They'd been opened especially for the occasion, and the tour later that day promised, as far as Lyric was concerned, to be the biggest draw of the visit. She felt an irresistible pull towards them — but something else attracted her, too. As she thought about her godmother's innate sense of humour, Lyric felt her own sense of mischief overcome her and a broad smile

166

spread across her face. She and Truly had always played practical jokes on each other. How perfect was this overwhelmingly kind but dull-as-dishwater event to spring one on her? Lyric hugged herself with glee and imagined her godmother's dismay when she realized, half-way through the ceremonial drinks reception, that Lyric had abandoned her to all the delegates for half an hour. And how much more fun it would be to explore the tombs on her own rather than as part of a group. Looking around her furtively, she took the path through the garden, past the marquee, and headed off towards the entrance.

As she walked, Lyric gathered what trivia she had learned about the tombs from the tourist brochure in her luxury hotel room that morning. The Ming Tombs was the general name given to the mausoleums of thirteen emperors of the Ming Dynasty which had ruled China from 1368 to 1644. The tombs, so she'd read, had been perfectly preserved, as had the necropolis of each of the many emperors. The first, and most impressive, was Changling, the tomb of Emperor Zhu Di and his empresses, a sprawling giant of a building housing a huge palace made of camphor wood, colourfully painted ceilings and a floor of gold bricks. The twelve other tombs of the succeeding twelve emperors had been built around Changling, and it was one of these in particular that she was keen to explore as she hurried past the main tomb's towering magnificence.

Despite her excitement, Lyric shivered involuntarily as she approached, the macabre significance of the tombs suddenly hitting home, and she cursed whatever it was inside her that was always drawn to the road less travelled, to the unknown. She looked over her shoulder at the dark silhouette of the Changling tomb, craving its more open appearance. In contrast, Dingling, the tomb she was headed for, was underground and had a more menacing feel to it. For some reason, she had the weird feeling someone was watching her, and she looked around her nervously. She took a deep breath. *God, Lyric,* she told herself firmly, *pull yourself together — that's what you get for mixing with the souls of the long dead!*

Her spirits tenuously revived, she continued on her path. The tower-like entrance was covered with yellow glazed tiles that shone gold in the sunshine but radiated an altogether more jaundiced, unpleasant hue in the shade. Beneath this roof, the eaves, archway, rafters and columns were all sculpted in colourfully painted stone, their cheerful appearance at odds with their solemn purpose.

Lyric slipped through the gap in the foot-thick stone door. It was dark and cool within — a welcome change from the harsh sunlight and heat outside. She tiptoed through the first hall to the second door, her footsteps echoing eerily around her until she reached the third. Here, she stopped and listened intently, heart beating with sudden fear. Were those her own footsteps she could hear, still bouncing off the stone walls? She took another even deeper breath and strained to listen to the layers of echoes, each merging into the last as they began to dull. *Of course they are,* she scolded herself.

168

Stop being paranoid. Now, concentrate on the job in hand.

She willed her eyes to focus through the gloom on the door in front of her. Although it was an interior door, it was as thick and heavy as the first. It was only open a tiny crack, and she stopped, biting her lip in anxiety. Every bone in her body was telling her to go back, to wait until she was with the others, to wait until it was officially *open* — but something else, much stronger, was pulling her on. She breathed in, trying to slim her washboard stomach even further, pressed her fulsome breasts as flat as she could and squeezed herself through it. As she did, she managed to move the door a fraction, leaving a bigger gap. Lyric started to advance into the front hall, but looked behind her anxiously. For some reason, moving that ancient artefact even a few inches had left her full of disquiet. It felt wrong to have disturbed it, and she had a sudden urge to return it to its original position. *You will close it again on the way out*, she said, making a mental note to herself. Happy at the thought of leaving the tomb, yet still drawn ever inwards by her curiosity, Lyric almost skipped off away from the door and further into the cool hall beyond.

As she turned, she let out an involuntary shriek — through the gloom she could make out the ghostly apparition of three white marble thrones. Before each of them, there were the glazed Five Offerings and a blue china jar that, if memory served her right, would have been filled with sesame oil to be used for lamps. Behind them, Lyric could make out the rear hall, which one of the delegates had told her only a short while before contained the coffins of Emperor Zhu Yijun and his two empresses. It was this palace that also contained the gold imperial crown, one of the world's rarest treasures.

God! Her resolve wavered again. There was a dead man and his two wives lying just through there! Lyric suppressed a sudden urge to go and say hi. She'd never seen a dead body before, let alone a mummified one, and she supposed now wasn't really the best time to make the acquaintance of one. She shivered again and jumpily looked over her shoulder. She could have sworn she'd heard something . . . Like the scraping of stone on stone and more footsteps, this time running away from her. Yes, definitely footsteps. She hadn't moved, so they couldn't have been hers . . .

Suddenly feeling the need to be outside in the afternoon light, to feel the pale winter sun on her face and see her godmother laugh, Lyric hurried back to the door. She stared at it dumbfounded. It was closed. *You idiot*, she scolded under her breath. How could she have been so stupid? She tugged on it half-heartedly, but it didn't move. Lyric thumped the cold, thick stone in frustration and then rubbed where it had hurt her fist. What on earth had made her close the door behind her?

But she hadn't closed the door. She went cold as the realization hit her. She'd squeezed through it and carried on into the tomb. Lyric's heart leapt into her mouth. If she hadn't shut it, then someone else had. Someone must have been following her, wanted to lock

170

her in here. Someone . . . who must want her *dead*? Overcome with panic, Lyric pulled at the door, the rough stone grazing the skin from her fingertips, the pain somehow compounding her panic till she started to sweat with fear. It wouldn't budge! She pulled and pulled, increasingly frantic as the realization set in that it was closed, and it wasn't going to open. She was trapped. Not only that, someone had wanted her trapped. Lyric chewed on a nail anxiously. What if . . . what if she was *stuck* here? For ever?

Her left eye started to twitch and she rubbed it irritably. Why, when she had more than enough to worry about, did her bloody eye always play up? Now was hardly the time to be worrying about impromptu winks. Not that she was in any danger of offending anyone in here. She looked around at her gloomy surroundings, trying not to let her desperation overcome her, and shook her head defiantly. She was in Beijing, on an official visit, surrounded by hundreds of delegates. She was one of the stars of the show. She would be missed. They would look for her soon. And she'd hardly gone off to climb the Great Wall of China — they'd know she had to be in the tombs somewhere. It was hardly rocket science.

But . . . someone had followed her in. And that someone could well still be in here. Who knew how far their murderous intent would take them? They might have locked her in here to perish and die a long, lonely death. Or they might still be in here, waiting to finish her off themselves. At the thought, Lyric shrank into the wall. She physically jumped as a rat scuttled out of

171

the shadows and across the tomb, shrieked in fear and immediately clamped a hand over her mouth. She mustn't let whoever was following hear her.

Using the deep-breathing techniques she'd learned in the daily yoga sessions in rehab, she tried to regain some of her self-control. *Calm down, Lyric Charlton,* she told herself. If whoever had been following was still in here, they'd know exactly where she was and what she was doing. They would hold every advantage, and, if they attacked, she was unlikely to be able to defend herself properly. The only way she was going to be able to leave here alive was if the person who'd locked her in here had indeed gone away and left her here to die, and if someone came to rescue her.

Her heart still pounding in her chest, Lyric stared at the stone door. She was deep in the belly of the tomb, and any would-be rescuers might not think to look beyond the first hall. She couldn't rely on chance. Her only way out was going to be by shouting.

"Heeeeeeeelp!"

The thick wall seemed to swallow up her voice, muffling even the shrillest shout. She called over and over, changing pitch and volume in a desperate attempt to be heard.

"Heeeeeeeelp!"

Two hours later, hoarse, cold and slumped in a crumpled heap against the stone door, Lyric began to cry. Her practical joke on Truly had completely backfired. Not only was the childish game of hide-and-seek she'd attempted to play on her godmother simply not funny any more, but she was stuck here, probably for eternity, with only a dusty old mummy and his crumbly wives for company. As if dying wasn't bad enough, she might have to endure the company of three people who for all she knew couldn't even speak English. The thought that there was a man in the tomb, just lying there, was really beginning to upset her. And what about the wives? What if they had never got on, and they decided to take out centuries of frustration on her? Or even worse, saw her as some kind of competition for their dead emperor and husband?

Her imagination ran riot, a childhood trait that, in times of distress, had always stopped her contemplating the real problem. Which was that she wasn't locked in here by accident. Someone had shut her in deliberately. Someone had followed her here — to the tombs, and maybe even to Beijing? — and had wanted her trapped. Was hoping she would never get out. Was hoping she would perish.

Lyric sat there for what seemed like two more hours, too exhausted now to cry any more, increasingly chilly, and starting to get hungry. The realization that she might never be rescued was growing with every passing second, and the sobering thought had dried her tears and replaced them with a dull ache of fear deep, deep inside her. Even the fact that the person who'd locked her in here didn't seem in a hurry to attack her didn't comfort her now. Either way, she was doomed.

With a start, Lyric felt an insistent buzz near her hip and jumped, her heart in her mouth. She put her hand to her heart, feeling it pulse wildly. What was that? She stood stock-still for several seconds. There it was again. Slowly, tentatively, she felt down her side with the palm of her hand. Reaching her bag, she flipped it open — and laughed out loud. Her phone! She'd totally forgotten she had it with her . . . and it was working! She whooped, then shut her mouth abruptly as her voice echoed eerily round and round the tomb. Pulling it open, she saw it was flashing a message from Crispin. Her brow furrowed. They hadn't spoken since she'd bawled him out over the mess — and the cocaine — he'd left in the flat. She opened the text guardedly. Typically for Crispin when he knew he'd been in the wrong, the tone of the text held no apology and showed no resentment or made any reference to their row.

Darling. I've sorted everything. You and the gardener are back on, you lucky, lucky girl.
C xoxo

Lyric's heart leapt, both her anger and her current predicament forgotten. Her and Philippe — back on? But how?

Another unexplained noise from deep in the tomb brought Lyric back to the present with a jolt. Urgently, she fumbled with the keypad and called her godmother's number. It rang. And rang. And rang. Lyric cried out in frustration. She could picture Truly's Chanel clutch clasped stylishly in her left hand as she said goodbye to her hosts. Why, oh why, couldn't she hear it? Why wasn't she answering?

Sobbing now, Lyric typed out a text.

174

HELP! TRAPPED IN DINGLING TOMB.
THINK SOMEONE TRYING TO KILL ME.
THIS IS NO JOKE. PLEASE HELP!
LYRIC XX.

As her phone indicated that the text had gone through, Lyric leaned back against the wall in relief. At least now someone would be on their way — whenever Truly next checked her phone, that was. Thank God she had remembered to bring it with her! Overcome with gratitude for Crispin, Lyric quickly typed out a second text.

You've probably saved my life babe. Love you xoxoxo

Her phone beeped again. Lyric looked at it in horror. It was low on battery! As she cursed herself and used the last of its energy to dial her godmother's phone again, she laughed hollowly at the irony. She couldn't wait to tell Crispin how he actually *had* saved her life. If only her would-be rescuers beat her enemy to it . . .

CHAPTER
FOURTEEN

Whichever way she looked, it was blue. In front, below, above, to the right and to the left — everywhere a glorious, sun-drenched, endless expanse of azure blue. The infinity pool, perched on its magnificent clifftop setting, merged seamlessly into the Balinese sea below, which itself morphed indistinguishably into the sky. It was like tiger balm for the gaze and a massage for the soul. Kandara, high up in the mountains of the Bukit peninsula, was probably her favourite place in the world. Not just the luxurious villa, with its silk furnishings, hardwood floors, bedrooms with en-suite swimming pools, personal butler and round-the-clock beauty technicians, but the very place itself. It was her very own wonder of the world — remote, naturally beautiful and somehow *Godly*.

But then the Ming Tombs had felt like that too, in a very different way — before someone had tried to kill her, that is. In spite of the searing heat of the sun, Lyric shivered and instinctively looked over her shoulder. The attempt on her life had shaken her to the very core, and even after leaving China she was finding it hard to sleep, or even relax. Unless, that is, she was with Philippe, who seemed to Lyric to be so physically, emotionally, morally strong that he was invincible. Everyone kept telling her that she'd fallen foul of some random nutter, that she should forget about it and move on, but something — call it sixth sense, gut instinct, whatever — was telling her there was more to it than that. And if someone could follow her to China to try to harm her — well, they could follow her anywhere, surely?

Lyric sighed and stretched her legs out in front of her, dabbling her toes under the surface. The dappled water enhanced her deep brown tan, and her long, lithe limbs looked even more svelte as the sun's rays danced on the ripples. She ducked her head backwards to drench her hair again. As she came back up she pushed it back from her face, wringing out the water that made her thick, honey-coloured hair look dark blonde.

"Penny for them." Philippe crept up behind her and from his position on the tiled poolside bent down and planted a kiss on her neck. With Philippe so close, she immediately felt some of the worry float away. Lyric giggled and turned to look at him reproachfully. He feigned hurt. *"Qu'est-ce qu'il y a?* What now?"

"Philippe, you really have to stop coming out with these twee little sayings," she said teasingly. "People seriously haven't said phrases like 'penny for them' since the 1950s! It's as if you learned to speak English by reading Enid Blyton."

He laughed. "Enid who?"

Without waiting for an answer, he pulled off his T-shirt and plopped into the pool beside her. Pulling her to him, he kissed her long and deeply before pulling her gently through the water with him, his face just millimetres away from hers.

Lyric gazed at him adoringly. How had she ever survived without this gorgeous, kind, funny, eccentric, goddamn sexy man? They'd been in Bali together for three days now, isolated not only by location but by Philippe's insistence that she turn off her mobile phone and surrender herself to total relaxation. She would have demanded the same thing of him, of course, if he'd actually owned a mobile phone — was there anyone else in the world who had achieved such success in his career with such an uncompromising attitude to modern communications? She doubted it. But it had worked, and their self-imposed bubble had made her more head over heels than she had ever thought possible. Her every thought was consumed by Philippe, and although he hadn't said so, his quiet attentiveness, caring playfulness and passionate loving certainly seemed to indicate that he felt the same.

Lyric bit her lip and felt a surge of longing as she thought of the intense lovemaking that rendered their nights almost entirely sleepless. Philippe was a skilled lover, considerate and masterful, at times bringing her to orgasm swiftly in a burning, heated frenzy, at others delaying the moment of delicious release and leaving her in lingering ecstasy — but it was their deep, almost otherworldly spiritual connection that took it all to another level entirely. She wrapped her legs around his waist and grinned as she felt him harden in response.

"*Alors*, what shall we do today?" Philippe muttered in her ear, kissing her neck repeatedly as they bobbed

178

around the pool, and letting out a low groan as she wrapped herself even tighter around him.

Lyric pulled back slightly and grinned at him. "Oh, I don't know. How about . . . we chill by the pool pretending to read our books but really just checking out how totally bloody gorgeous we both are. Then have a cheeky lychee Martini before a lazy lunch, and an even cheekier sexy siesta afterwards," she said, reciting their exact routine for the past few days. "Then it'll be time for another Martini, another lazy meal and more — and more and more — loving . . ."

Philippe swung her around in the water, and Lyric let out a delighted shriek.

"That sounds like a good idea to me," he growled. "But how about before all that we take a drive down to the beach? You can't improve on perfection, for sure — but I can't come to paradise without seeing at least one of its amazing beaches."

He lifted Lyric up and placed her on the poolside with her legs dangling in the water. Pulling himself up to sit beside her, he ran a finger along the dripping outline of her bikini top and reached behind her neck to undo it. "After, that is, I've had my wicked way with you all over again . . ."

Their beach buggy bounced along the dirt track as Lyric directed Philippe to a deserted stretch of glorious white sand later that afternoon. The scrubland was thick with overgrown trees and shrubs, and, though far from the rainforest, the humidity gave them the impression that they were driving through the middle of the jungle. It was also eerily quiet, the heavy silence punctuated only by the occasional squawk of a bird. Lyric was having as much trouble getting Philippe to keep his eyes off the multifarious flora and fauna as she was remembering the way.

Soon, though, the foresty footpath became increasingly sandy, and more and more sunlight found its way through the tree canopy until suddenly the scrub gave way to a perfect, paradisical beach: softly waving palm trees, icing-sugar sand and gently crested waves. Apart from the odd conch shell dotted along the sand, the stretch of coastline was completely and utterly deserted.

Philippe gave a low whistle. "Ooh, la-la — this really is something. *Quel rêve*." He swallowed and affected a carefully casual tone. "So you say you've been here before, huh?"

Lyric smiled slyly at his clumsy detective work. He was fishing to see if she'd been here with Ralph.

"Yes, I have. With Treeva, when we came out here a couple of years ago," she said pointedly. "She was desperate to get rid of her tan lines and wanted to sunbathe topless. Of course, it's really offensive to the Balinese — but we were advised that she'd be safe to do it here. So it was less of a romantic day with another man, and more about me playing gooseberry to the love-in between Treeva and her boobs."

Philippe laughed and Lyric smiled along with him, all of a sudden nostalgic for her scatty, self-obsessed but oh-so-unintentionally amusing friend. It was the first time she'd thought of the nice side of Treeva since the hideous situation in Monaco, and she was overcome with a sense of loss for their lifelong friendship. Subconsciously, she noted that her eye had started to twitch persistently.

Philippe pulled on the handbrake and touched Lyric's leg softly. "You know, it takes a lot more energy to stay angry than it does to forgive," he said lightly. "And if you miss Treeva, maybe you should find it in yourself to let all those negative feelings go."

Lyric looked at him in surprise. When she'd told Philippe about the incident, he had been apoplectic at Treeva's treatment of her.

"What — you mean make it up with her?" she said doubtfully.

Philippe's shrug was nonchalant. "Sure. Whatever makes you happiest. Everything happens for a reason. Maybe you finding out about her that way, and both you and Treeva being so miserable about it, is exactly what she needs to open her eyes to her problem. She's not herself at the moment, is she? She's a drug addict. I'm sure you took on a whole load of unwanted character traits when you were using. And hey, everyone deserves a second chance."

He winked at her knowingly, referring to their disastrous date. He kissed her on the lips and then swung his legs over the side of the buggy.

"Third chances, though, I'm not so sure about. So make sure she's not likely to mess up again. Come on, I'm dying to get in the water — race you! *On y va!*" Philippe ran off across the beach, his pounding feet throwing up small clouds of sand as he went. Lyric smiled and strolled slowly after him, waving as he dived into the water and turned back to her, gesturing to her to join him.

Make up with Treeva? After the past few weeks of turmoil, even the words sounded alien to Lyric. But the sentiment — well. Strangely, it gave her a warm, pleasant feeling, and the sense of a huge load being lifted from her shoulders. But how would she feel if she actually went ahead and did it? And how would she ensure that their friendship was indeed mended, and that she held no resentment for Treeva's deplorable behaviour?

Lyric chewed on a nail anxiously, then stopped to rub her eye. What on earth was it, this constant irritation in her left eye? It seemed to Lyric that it had been plaguing her on and off for ever, but it surely couldn't have been long. Months, rather than years. Or was it? Either way, she guessed she should get it checked out when she was back in England, and she made a mental note to book an opthalmologist appointment.

Lost in thought, she started to wander along the beach. It certainly wasn't the time for feuds — that was clear. And making up with Treeva felt like the right karma for right now. Philippe was right. With everything else going so well in her life for once, the last thing she needed was this bust-up hanging around like a dark cloud.

Lyric glanced over her shoulder to where Philippe was — swimming further out, now, to where the turquoise sea turned a darker blue and where she knew he would find cooler streams and shoals of brightly coloured fish for company.

How lucky she was to have found him. Over the past few days, she'd fallen even more deeply in love with him. There was so much she had discovered — and there was even more that she still didn't know — but she loved everything she'd learned so far, hard work though it was getting anything out of him. Philippe seemed loath to discuss his past, but she knew he was still close to his family and devoted to his country — a bond that had led him to sign up for extended national service and serve his country in Bosnia despite his abhorrence of violence and his passion for nature and the environment. She suspected this was where he had got his scar, but she had yet to get him to divulge the exact details. He was sharp, funny and caring, and, most importantly of all, he was his own person — almost uncompromisingly so. She knew, without a shadow of a doubt, that this was the man she had been waiting to meet all her life. He filled up her senses like no drug ever had, gave her a constant high unlike any artificial stimulant. And yet . . .

The beach was now arching around to the left and petering out into a little cove. Lyric followed it round till Philippe was almost out of view, dragging her toes through the soft, hot sand and relishing the feeling of the cooler sand underneath. A little shack caught her eye, and, curious as ever, she strolled towards it.

Lyric was so deep in contemplation that she was blind to the beauty of her surroundings, despite their impact. The thing was, there was still a part of her that

Philippe hadn't quite reached, that remained untouched. Deep, deep inside, there was still an unfulfilled longing — but for what? And how, if she ever discovered what it was, could she hope to resolve it?

As she approached the tiny, tumbledown construction of palm leaves and twigs, the unmistakeably sweet twang of incense hung heavy on the air. Lyric breathed in deeply, taking comfort from its soothing scent. She slowed her pace even further as she got closer to the makeshift shack, unwilling to disturb whoever lived here. Outside the shelter, she noticed a pair of battered sandals and a couple of handcrafted iron tools. As she looked closer at the building, she noticed palm leaves woven intricately between the sticks, and it became apparent that whoever had built this certainly knew what they were doing. It appeared to be years rather than months old, which meant it must have survived not only normal environmental wear and tear, but some of Bali's ferocious tropical storms too. A tattered orange curtain hung across the doorway, and Lyric could hear chanting from within. She cursed her innate curiosity — trust her to barge in on some poor reclusive monk's meditation time. Hardly daring to breathe, yet unable to tear her eyes away from the little house, she respectfully started back down the beach.

All at once, however, there was a shuffle and the curtain opened sharply. Lyric almost jumped out of her skin at the sight of a wizened old woman, shrunken within her once-colourful robes, her face the shade of polished teak, her skin a wrinkled map of her advancing years. Her eyes, tiny black marbles set deep into her skull, shone with inner peace and faith and revealed the life force still burning inside her.

"*Sell a mutt dull-tongue*," croaked the little figure. At least, that's how it sounded to Lyric. Then, in heavily accented English, "Welcome! I've been expecting you."

Lyric put her hand to her chest in surprise. "You've been expecting *me*?" she repeated.

"Yes, you," said the old woman impatiently, then turned and hobbled back into the shack. "Come."

Lyric stood rooted to the spot, uncertain of what to do next. She'd have to be insane to follow this woman, who was clearly a couple of peanuts short of a satay. After her disaster in Beijing, she'd promised herself she'd listen to common sense rather than her inquisitive side, but something was drawing her in, and, after a moment's hesitation, she followed her.

Compared with the bright noon sunshine outside, the shack was gloomy and full of smoke, and the pungent smell of incense caught the back of Lyric's throat, making her choke and feel momentarily light-headed. The old lady, bent almost double from age, was in the process of edging around a small table with cards on it. There was a stool on the other side.

"Sit," she said without turning round and waved impatiently at another stool to Lyric's left.

Without saying a word, Lyric did as she was bidden and crouched down on to the woven leather buffet stool. It was surprisingly comfortable, and as Lyric's eyes adjusted to the gloom, she began to relax a little.

The woman took a puff from what looked suspiciously like a bong before fixing Lyric with narrowed eyes.

"Give me your hands." Again Lyric did as the old woman requested and held them out. She took Lyric's right hand in her own wrinkled paws and inspected it closely.

"You have come into great wealth," she stated matter-of-factly. Lyric groaned inwardly. Why had she let herself get into this situation? This woman was more than likely a fake, a charlatan earning her living from gullible holiday-makers. After all, any Westerner staying in this part of Bali would have to be pretty well off — astronomically so in comparison to the poor indigenous people of Bali. Lyric sighed and prepared herself for some more amateur guesswork.

"But not just wealth of a material nature," continued the woman, her eyes now boring into Lyric's. "You feel great love. Your soul is gradually being restored."

"Restored?" questioned Lyric before she could stop herself.

"Yes, restored," repeated the woman with certainty. "Your body, it is in good health, but, until recently, your soul was not. It was starved, deprived — depraved."

Lyric stared at her, goose pimples appearing on her arms. Maybe she'd been too quick to judge her after all. How did she know all this? She had practically described the last five years of Lyric's life. She had a sudden urge to ask the old woman everything — about her uncle, about Treeva, about Philippe . . .

"But it is still too trusting," warned the old woman, frowning. "The yin and the yang — they are confused.

You have friends that are enemies, and enemies that may prove more worthy of your respect than those closest to you."

Lyric frowned, her mind racing. So she was being double-crossed — by someone close to her, it seemed. But who could that be? Maybe the woman was referring to Treeva and the way she'd behaved in Monaco. Or maybe . . .

The old woman studied her hands more closely, cooing and clucking to herself. Lyric became so wrapped up in working out who was out to get her that she almost missed the old woman's next statement.

"You seek something. Something important. This something, it is almost part of you. The second side of the coin, the missing link to the chain. But it is long gone, a long, long, long time ago lost."

Lyric stared at her, hardly daring to breathe. The longing. The inexplicable emptiness she'd felt all her life. Was this ancient Balinese lady the key to it all? Almost predictably, her left eye started to twitch. She rubbed it subtly, not wanting to disturb the old woman's train of thought.

The woman was almost in a trance now, her breathing shallow and irregular. She was muttering to herself, a half-chant that seemed to have no perceptible rhythm or repetition. Her eyes were half closed, and for several moments Lyric worried that she'd fallen asleep.

All of a sudden, the eyes opened, startling in their clarity. "This something," said the woman. "It is your twin brother."

★   ★   ★

187

Thousands of miles away, a dejected figure punched a number into his mobile phone and lay back on his bed, anxiously smoking the latest in a long line of cigarettes. After such initial promise, the adoption agency had drawn a blank. With no explanation, no reasons, the trail for his blood family had once again abruptly gone cold — as if Fate was trying to intercept his efforts to trace his real parents. The only person Edward could turn to, the only person who knew he was even trying to discover his true lineage, was his godfather — and so it was his godfather he was calling now.

"Edward! How are you?"

The doctor's tone was warm, welcoming but, as always, tinged with guilt. The anxious set of Edward's jaw softened. He knew his godfather felt unaccountably guilty for the poor — albeit loving — circumstances Edward had grown up in. And though the doctor had tried, with subtle financial gestures, to help him through his early years and education, Edward knew he felt restrained by his parents' fierce pride in their ability to provide for their only son. It was fear of denting this pride which had prevented Edward from investigating his birthright until recently, but although his love for his parents burned strongly, his need to know where he really came from — to fill the ever-gnawing emptiness inside him — burned brighter and brighter, until in the past year he had been unable to ignore it. With the doctor's reluctant help, he had started proceedings to trace his birth parents.

"Oh, you know — been better," said Edward, suddenly downcast again at the seemingly insurmountable task in front of him. "The agency has gone cold on me. They reckon that the lead was false, and they can't find anything."

There was a silence on the other end of the phone. The doctor, torn between guilt at his part in the twisted path of Edward's life and fear at the certain reprisals if Edward were to discover his birthright, remained silent.

"I mean, I just feel like this isn't meant to be. Like someone's trying to tell me it's going to hurt Mum and Dad so much, when I do find out who my real parents are, that it's not worth finding out in the first place. What do you reckon?"

The doctor sighed. "Edward, I've told you before — it's not a decision I can make on your behalf," he said guardedly. "It's really your call."

"Or maybe it's Fate trying to stop me finding out I'm the son of a mass murderer!" joked Edward darkly.

No, just the nephew of a madman, thought the doctor to himself. Out loud, he remained vague. "Edward, if the official channels can't help, then I really don't know what else you can do."

"That's just it, though, isn't it?" replied Edward, his godfather's non-committal responses all at once filling him with conviction. "That agency was just a middle man for the official channels. I've looked into it. I'm going straight to the General Register Office. They'll have to help me."

The rest of the conversation passed in a blur, and the doctor replaced the handset carefully. So this was it. The next stage of a predictable, interminable process was in progress. Play with Fate, he thought grimly, and Fate will play with you.

CHAPTER
FIFTEEN

December

It wasn't Disneyland on a desert island, decided Lyric as she watched yet another gondola float past along the purpose-built waterways that ferried Sin Island's guests from man-made beach to luxury villa and back again — it was more like Atlantis. Disneyland, for all its commercial tat, at least still held some of that childlike magic a leisure park should have, but this self-styled "Venice in the Seychelles" was like some kind of fairytale gone wrong, a grotesque fantasy land where OTT luxury took priority over taste at every turn. It had everything a modern fairytale needed but the stamp to say you were in.

But that was Treeva's dad all over. Anything for his princess. Throughout Treeva's life, her father had lavished whatever material goods he could on his only daughter, his gestures growing in tandem with her age and his escalating wealth. When Treeva had asked for a Barbie, he'd created her a scaled-down Barbieworld in their garden. When she'd wanted to ride, he'd bought her a string of polo ponies. When Treeva had had a fleeting penchant for carousels, he'd wanted to build her a rollercoaster in the paddock. The only thing that had stopped him was a furious neighbour who'd rejected his planning application and then — shock horror! — had refused to be bribed into submission. (The fact that by this time Treeva had already moved on to the next teen fancy had been totally lost on him.) But for all the cooing and the secret envy Lyric and Laura had had for Treeva's designer-stocked wardrobe, gadget-filled bedroom and exotic menagerie, Lyric knew neither of them would have swapped it for the warm, unconditional love their own families bestowed on them rather than gifts.

"Anyone for another pina colada?" asked Treeva from her padded gold lamé sunbed, listlessly lifting up her arm and half-heartedly trying to attract a waiter.

Remembering Treeva's blustering cover-ups and boastful competitiveness gave Lyric a surge of empathy for her friend, and made her doubly glad she'd forgiven her for her Monaco betrayal. Now, she shaded her eyes as she looked over at her. The sun's glare was bright enough, without factoring in the rays ricocheting off the Swarovski crystals decorating the frames of Treeva's Versace sunglasses.

"Roger, roger." A woman hurrying past, dressed in black Fred Perry T-shirt, shorts and box-fresh trainers, wearing a headset and self-importantly carrying a clipboard, pulled a walkie-talkie from her belt and spoke urgently into it, gesticulating wildly at Treeva's sunbed. "Drinks at post thirty-five. Platinum class. Over and out. Repeat, over and out," she hissed into the mouthpiece. Within seconds a harassed waiter in the same uniform — complete with compulsory

192

flowered lei garland hanging round his neck — appeared on the beach.

"I'll have another Perrier." Lyric waved her glass and Treeva tutted, shaking her head disapprovingly. Lyric hid a smile. Treeva would never get over Lyric's new subdued approach to partying — not until they could persuade her to go through rehab herself, at any rate.

"Oh, go on, twist my arm then," said Laura from further round the pool, waving the dregs of a vodka and tonic. Lyric turned to her in surprise. Laura had been drinking steadily all day. It was so unlike her!

"Well, it's our first weekend away without the kids, isn't it?" said Laura brightly, leaning over and patting the suntanned leg of her husband, Robert. He grunted from behind his *Financial Times* and shifted his leg away from her touch. "It's time to let loose and party!"

Her words hung shrilly in the sun-baked air, and Lyric tried to cover up her inner embarrassment. Laura was more than enough fun without having to put on some kind of *craaazy* act. Why was she feeling the need to act so out of character? She gazed thoughtfully at the pair of them side by side on their sunbeds, Laura fussing over her husband and him all but ignoring her, his body turned slightly away from her. Lyric was inwardly shocked. When Laura had met Robert at school all those years ago she had immediately become a beacon of hope to all in the sixth form. They had been gloriously, unashamedly, demonstratively in love, and their separate lives had morphed into a partnership so seamlessly that even the most die-hard cynics at school had begun to believe in romance.

But now . . . It had been so long since Lyric had spent any quality time with them that she hadn't appreciated the gulf that seemed to have opened up between them. Robert, once gregarious and chatty, seemed distant and withdrawn. His still-handsome face was lined and gaunt, and his swarthy body seemed to be a shell he was inhabiting rather than the lithe, tennis-honed power-pack it had once been. And Laura, usually so calm, collected and confident, seemed jittery and jumpy, a tinny-voiced bag of nerves. Laura had evidently not taken lightly the decision to leave the children with her mother for a long weekend, and Lyric had assumed the pair of them would hole themselves up in their luxury suite for at least some of the weekend, basking in the opportunity to rediscover each other without the constant interruption of their children. So why weren't they?

She compared their current froideur with the passionate euphoria she and Philippe had experienced in Bali. How she wished he was here with her now . . .

At that moment, another sweaty gondola bobbed past, rocking dangerously from its load of champagne-fuelled record executives tunelessly chanting "Sing Low, Sweet Chariot". Wherever on the island it was they were headed, they could have walked there quicker, observed Lyric drily. But then, she supposed, that wasn't really the point. On second thoughts . . . Lyric couldn't imagine how Philippe would cope with the purpose-built nature of the island — the beaches that had been created by shipping in fake sand from the other side of the world, the fish that had been imported to add colour to the rainbow that already existed in the coral reefs, the huge carbon footprint amassed purely from the energy needed for the thousands of fairy lights strung around the resort alone, never mind the travel energy used by its current inhabitants.

"Oh — look, girls!" trilled Treeva, pointing at an Arnold Schwarzenegger lookalike amongst the snorkellers on the reef just a few hundred yards beyond the shoreline. He was standing in the turquoise knee-deep waters, still wearing his mask and snorkel, proudly brandishing something sparkly. In his excitement at his find he had forgotten to remove his flippers, which were currently proving a trying obstacle to his swaggering return to shore. "He's found the diamond cuff!"

"I thought it was coral out there," observed Robert drily from behind his paper.

"It is, silly!" said Treeva, standing up and perching her sunglasses on her head, totally missing the joke in her eagerness to catch the action in the water. "I'm going to get my pinks!"

"Pinks?" questioned Laura.

"Pinks? As in pink slips? Ownership papers, you jerk," said Treeva in a bad American accent. Getting only blank looks in return, she tossed her hair in frustration and added, "Like, that's *so* an obvious *Grease* quote? Oh, honestly. Anyway, Daddy owns the island and he bought it for me. And Daddy was the one who bought all the goodies for the Underwater Lucky Dip. So technically, that makes the diamond bracelet *mine*!" She turned back to the sea and waved.

"Anyhow, the only thing missing from this weekend so far has been eye candy and that guy is *too* cute. Finders, keepers, ladies! Cooee! Carston!" Clasping her cosmetically-enhanced bikini bust with one hand and one side of her bikini thong in the other, Treeva jogged down to the water's edge.

Lyric laughed, shaking her head. It might be as naff as hell, but it was a fun kind of weekend, of course. Who wouldn't enjoy having their every need taken care of, basking in the tropical sun with every imaginable luxury for the asking? As much as this fell short of what she'd class as her dream weekend, she still had to pinch herself that she'd had the opportunity to be here at all. Not only that, but it was proving the perfect diversion from her mixed emotions and confusion over the "news" that she had a brother. Since Bali, she'd veered from a common-sense approach that told her an old woman who lived on a beach had no way of knowing anything about her life, particularly something so far-fetched, to feelings of anger and frustration at her parents and what might be one almighty cover-up. Something rang true about the woman's reading. She couldn't explain it, but it was the same something, she supposed, that was holding her back from confronting her parents about it.

"Oh God, it's going to be burger and chips for dinner." As if on cue, Lyric heard the unmistakeable tone of her mother's voice almost oozing disdain. "I can see it already — he's probably got Ronald McDonald to make a special appearance."

196

"Hi, Mummy, hi, Daddy," said Lyric, sitting up on her sunbed and retying her bikini strings around her neck. "So you've finally surfaced!" Her mother had a morbid fear of the sun's rays, and always insisted on staying indoors as much as possible in sunny climates. "Having fun?" She patted her seat invitingly.

"Hello, darling." Her father, wearing a pair of battered flip-flops, ancient shorts and a T-shirt with its collar standing up, kissed the top of her head and sat down next to her with a smile.

Her mother, fully made-up, coiffed and resplendent in a diaphanous Indian silk kaftan, declined her invitation with a sniff.

"Lyric, darling, you'll ruin your skin sitting out in this tropical sunshine." She moved her lacquered fringe out of her eyes with a wrinkled, manicured finger. Lyric ran a hand through her own hair, still damp from her last dip in the sea, and immediately felt that all-too-familiar feeling of inferiority.

"But, darling, it's all so delightfully tasteless, don't you think?" Constance looked around her with a face that said she was having anything but fun. She gave a scornful grimace as a short, squat, sunburnt German septuagenarian with a portly tummy and hairy toes walked past, hand on the pert bottom of his tall, willowy, twenty-something girlfriend. "All hip and hip replacements. Oh, hello, Treeva, darling — what simply fabulous sunnies you've got there."

"Hi, Lady C," said Treeva, plopping back down on to the sunbed, totally unfazed by Constance's obvious disgust at her surroundings. But then, with the bracelet

197

in hand and the snorkeller in tow, she had other things on her mind.

Lyric laughed and nudged her father in joint acknowledgement of her mother's crashing snobbery. "So, what are you up to?"

"We were on the hunt for some little snacks to have with our cocktails," said her father. "We thought about ringing room service, but I felt like a bit of a wander."

Lyric giggled again at the thought of her outdoorsy father being cooped up in a suite with air conditioning and her mother's neuroses all day.

"Haven't you got some in your mini-bar?"

Her father looked her meaningfully in the eyes. "Your mother has removed anything edible in favour of her face creams," he said, deadpan.

"Well, really, darling, what on earth is a fridge for if it's not for cosmetics and champagne?" asked Constance, genuinely perplexed. "We're in the tropics, not in the Third World, you know — there's no need to have them sweating away in the bathroom."

The loud roar from one of the constant succession of helicopters drowned out her final words, and Lyric looked around anxiously to see who might have heard. Really, for someone so fixed on good breeding, her mother could be terribly socially unaware at times. She frowned as the spectre of her Balinese medium returned. On her return to England, the fact that she might have a secret brother somewhere had started to feel a little like a dream, like something she'd have made up in an imaginary world when she was little. But all of a sudden, watching her mother take in their absurd surroundings through a Valium haze, it all seemed entirely feasible again. Lyric's eye twitched unbearably, and she blinked forcefully, as if trying to erase her inner turmoil.

Her father looked at his watch pointedly. "Constance, we really should be going. It's five-thirty already, the charity auction is due to start at seven, and if we're going to —"

"He wants to catch the racing," sighed Constance in a resigned way to no one in particular. "You can take the man out of Gloucestershire . . . Come on then, George, let's continue on our way through this freak-show."

Lyric watched them go thoughtfully, her unvoiced questions filling the air like the proverbial elephant in the room. She was going to have to get this off her chest. The question was, when? And how?

"Oh, *finally*," said Jed Sinclair, applauding with the rest of her table as his daughter, dazzling in skin-tight Giles Deacon T-shirt dress, six-inch ankle boots and the diver's diamond cuff, tottered over to her seat with Carston the snorkeller.

"Well, it's my party — I can be late if I want to," responded Treeva tartly, waving at a waiter to add another place for Carston. "We just had a lot of getting to know each other to do, that's all." With her back to Carston, she gave the table a theatrical wink. "And let's just say, he's a very *great* Dane."

Lyric and Laura shrieked with laughter, and next to Lyric, George tried to conceal a smirk.

"Oh, really, Treeva," scolded Constance, looking away from the table, but even she had the hint of a smile playing around her lips.

"Well, at least it's legal," retorted Treeva. "Daddy, I just walked past that dodgy Polish mate of yours trying to get a couple of call girls on to the island. Security wouldn't let them on. I mean, honestly!" She looked around the table, outraged. "I told them as long as they were high-class, they should let them pass. That's what you always say, isn't it?"

Jed roared with laughter and put a reassuring arm around his sequinned wife Pamela, a glamorous Essex girl with a heart of gold who, twenty years ago, would have been considered a trophy wife. These days, still dressing the same, she was now frequently outshone by the class of Essex girl she liked to think she'd moved away from. (The phrase mutton dressed as lamb could have been invented especially for her.) Unabashed, she squeezed his knee back happily. "What goes on on Sin Island stays on Sin Island, eh, Robert?" said Jed, displaying a flash of gold teeth. In an attempt to include Robert, who had so far remained silent throughout the gossipy preamble to dinner, Jed gave him a buddy wink. But instead of smiling back buddy fashion, Robert scowled and looked away.

"Your mother does have a point, Lyric," said Laura, downing her drink and accepting another. Next to her, Robert frowned and shook his head at the waiter. Laura tutted and told him to carry on regardless. "Everywhere you look there's a beautiful women in Hervé Léger on the arm of a walking heart attack."

200

Lyric was amused, but couldn't help noticing that Laura was slurring her words.

"And I see you've adhered to the theme of the weekend, dear," said Constance, giving Lyric's outfit a contemptuous look. Lyric looked down at her McQueen evening dress, suddenly feeling self-conscious. She'd picked the silky shift precisely because it *wasn't* figure-hugging or showy, but the cool pixilated print on the front made it feel fun and funky; perfect, she'd thought, for this evening. Now she wasn't so sure.

Unperturbed, Constance turned to a passing waitress and tapped the side of her glass with a fingernail. "I distinctly requested room-temperature water," she said. "That means water of twenty-two degrees exactly. This is more like twenty, or even nineteen. Kindly change it."

Blushing furiously, the waitress removed the glass and hurried off, looking even more scared at the thought of telling her maître d'hôtel that he needed to find some water to match Constance's exacting standards than she did at the prospect of facing Lyric's mother again.

Jed leaned forward and touched Constance's arm across the table. He might be crass, thought Lyric, and he might have no taste, but there was no denying Jed Sinclair's talent as a host — he succeeded in creating common ground between the most eclectic collection of people.

"So what do you think of my charity auction, Constance?" Jed asked as he gestured around the room, taking in the gaudy gilt decor, the oversized chandeliers, the practically topless hula waitresses sashaying their way around the tables and the giant illuminated pineapples. He'd even, finally, built Treeva that carousel she'd wanted once, and its fairy lights twinkled prettily above the pastel-painted horses from the far corner of the ballroom.

Lyric smiled. Jed was also a shameless social climber, and his undisguised admiration for her mother's tireless commitment to dinner parties, shooting weekends and charitable functions had led to the forging of an unexpected friendship between them over the years.

Constance looked around her at the colourful, flashily dressed crowd assembled around elaborately decorated tables the length of a state ballroom, lips pursed.

"Well, you've certainly got the raw material here," she said mildly. "I should think the collected wealth here would dwarf the gross national product of the Ukraine." She leaned forward combatively, placing her hands over Jed's. "But the proof of a charity auction is all in the pudding. Show me a seven-figure charitable donation at the end of it, and I'll tell you how successful you are."

Jed threw his head back and roared with laughter. "We'd better get on with it then!"

He waved over at the MC to begin proceedings, then he, too, leaned forward conspiratorially, drawing in the dinner guests around the table. "I know you're meant to do the bids after dinner when everyone's well oiled — but the way this weekend's going, we need to start while everyone's still compos mentis!" With that, the

202

table guests turned towards the stage expectantly as the evening's compère introduced the lots and invited bids for the first: drinks at Claridge's with Treeva.

Laura and Lyric giggled together as Treeva stood up to acknowledge the guests' applause with a little curtsey, and Jed and his wife Pamela sat back proudly, looking around the room to see who would make the first bid for their daughter.

"And so, my lords, ladies and gentlemen, I am starting the bids at £200,000," boomed the compère. "£200,000, am I bid £200,000?"

Treeva looked at Carston pointedly, and he put up his hand meekly. From across the room, a gnarled old cowboy who allegedly owned half of Texas bid £250,000. Treeva, staring in horror at her prospective date, nudged Carston, who, in return, obediently took the bid to £300,000.

At £450,000, however, Carston had obviously reached his limit and the cowboy won out at half a million. Treeva sat down grumpily and turned her back on Carston.

"That's one Dane who's failed to bring home the bacon," said George under his breath from across the table, giving Lyric a knowing look.

Lyric smiled fondly at him. She had noticed her father's unspoken surveillance of her from early on in the trip, and though she would never dream of acknowledging openly his awareness of how difficult this kind of hedonistic weekend was for her post-rehab, she was deeply touched by his sensitivity. Then, remembering the unspoken secret that she suspected

203

her father had been keeping from her all these years, her face clouded over and she turned back to the stage.

"And our next lot: a *private* ride around the Circle Line on London's underground!" proclaimed the compère. "£150,000, am I bid £150,000?"

Lyric stared at the stage in disbelief. "A private ride on the *tube*?" she whispered to Laura and Robert. "Going round and round on a smelly old train, seeing nothing — how romantic! Who on earth is going to bid for *that*?" Robert's lips twitched in amusement — the most Lyric had seen them move all evening — and shrugged in agreement. Laura, however, had other ideas.

"I am!" she squealed. "Lyric's right — how romantic! £200,000! Over here!"

"Laura!" hissed Robert, grabbing her hand in an attempt to restrain her. "You're making a show of yourself."

Laura shook him off. "You're always saying we need to shake things up a bit — maybe this is the way!" she hissed back loudly. Then, to the compère, "£300,000! I bid £300,000."

"£300,000, I am bid £300,000 for a ride around the Circle Line?" said the compère. "Going . . . going . . . Gone! To the lady in red over — um —" As the spotlight followed the auctioneer's gaze, it shone on nothing more than an empty seat and the figure of Robert angrily marching Laura upstairs to their room.

The table sat in uncomfortable silence as the rest of the lots were auctioned off. A week on the Gettys' boat, a golfing holiday in Augusta, the whole of Cliveden for

204

a shooting weekend — all went for astronomical amounts, with a place on Richard Branson's inaugural flight to the moon fetching the highest price of the night at £1.5 million.

But even Jed's relentless Tigger-style good humour could not resurrect the bonhomie of earlier in the evening, and, as the auction came to a close, Lyric shifted uncomfortably on her seat. For the second time since she'd left rehab, she was regretting the first glass of champagne, let alone the second. Her tolerance for alcohol seemed to be practically zero since she'd been out — her head was spinning, and the fevered atmosphere inside the ballroom was giving her a sense of rising panic deep inside her chest. As people flitted between tables, hungrily networking for the second consecutive day, it seemed the underlying frisson of power and riches that had defined day one of the weekend was giving rise to a desperate ambiance of uncontrolled greed — of people on the make looking for anything they could get their hands on from fellow freeloaders. The ugly menace of drugs seemed to lie round every corner, and, though resolutely hidden, to Lyric's eyes most of the party massive had been indulging. Everyone she saw, it seemed, hadn't slept — they were wasted, their skin pale beneath their tans, mechanically grinding jaws, eyes bigger than the pebbles on the beach, empty Ecstasy smiles pasted on their faces.

Even the carousel was starting to take on its own menace, reminding Lyric of a dream she'd had in rehab in which she'd been on a similar carousel: the lights

205

were bright, the horses painted and she'd got on it and clung to the pole. And it started going faster, and everyone else, all her friends, had got off, but she hadn't. It got faster and faster and the music louder and louder until she physically *couldn't* get off. And suddenly she was flung to the ground like a rag doll and she couldn't move. Waking in a cold sweat, unable to sleep again, she'd analysed the dream, trying to banish its demons, and had seen all the lights and the music and the adrenaline as a metaphor for the drugs. They, like the carousel, had swept her off her feet. They were fun and frightening and such a rush — but they had ultimately left her broken. And that was how she was feeling tonight — out of control, and in danger.

Even her parents, whose presence earlier in the weekend had provided her with so much comfort, were now starting to grate on her nerves. Instead of feeling spoilt by her father's thoughtful caring, she felt mollycoddled, and her mother's natural aloofness was beginning to smack of disinterest. The niggling thought that had been troubling her since Bali wouldn't go away — if anything, it was becoming more persistent. *What if* she'd had a brother? *What if* her parents had kept him secret from her all these years? What then?

The thought was almost too much to bear, and Lyric became fixated on a spot on the tablecloth in case her inner turmoil was radiating out through her eyes.

The waitresses came over with their mozzarella salad starters.

"You'll notice mine has five slices of mozzarella, not four," Constance said archly to the waitress. "And I ordered it to be served without dressing."

"So that's how you keep so trim," said Pamela admiringly, checking out Constance's size-eight figure encased in a sophisticated black Prada lace dress.

"Oh, no, that's another secret," said Constance jokingly.

"One of the many," said Lyric in a stinging aside. She bit her lip. That had been a cheap shot — unfair and unnecessary. Her mother turned to stare at her in shock, and as she met quizzical eyes around the table, Lyric suddenly felt as though she couldn't take it any more. She pushed back her chair and ran from the room, tears stinging her eyes and choking her throat.

Once outside, Lyric sat on a huge stone bench and breathed deeply, trying to steady her racing heart.

"Lyric?"

She heard her father's low voice behind her, her mother's clipped steps in her high-heeled courts behind him, and more tears welled up in her.

She swung round. "Why didn't you tell me? Why?"

George's brow furrowed and he looked at her in confusion. "Tell you what, Lyric?"

Lyric stared at them, hurt and rejection welling up in her like a volcano. "Oh, do me a favour, Daddy," she spat through her sobs. "You've lied to me all my life — you can do me the courtesy of telling me the truth now, surely?"

George took another step towards her. "Lyric, I'm not sure I know what you're talking about," he said tentatively. "What have we lied to you about?"

Lyric laughed hollowly. "Oh, don't tell me you've forgotten, Daddy? Surely not something this important?"

George looked over at Constance, who replied with a defeated, almost imperceptible shrug. He turned back to Lyric, mouth open to speak.

"*That I have a brother!*" Lyric screamed, before he had chance. "That I am a twin, and that there is part of me out there that I've never known about!"

Behind George there was a loud sob, and Constance fell to her knees in the sand, head in her hands.

"How do you know, darling?" she wept. "How?"

Her mother breaking down seemed to give Lyric the strength to compose herself, and she wiped her cheek angrily with the back of her hand.

"It hardly matters how I know, surely?" Lyric replied coldly as the realization that the clairvoyant had been right dawned on her. Her mother's words were all she needed to hear. It wasn't just the rants of an old woman. Out there, somewhere, she had a brother. A brother!

She looked down at her mother, devoid of her usual composure, and then across at her father, a broken figure trying helplessly to comfort his wife, and she felt her heart break at their betrayal at the same time that it soared at the knowledge that she was a twin. Her voice, when she spoke, wavered with the weight of the emotion it carried.

"I know *everything*. But why have I only found out now that I've got a brother? Why have you never told me yourselves? *Why?*"

Now there was silence, and George stood, head bowed, mouth opening and closing.

"I — I . . ."

"It's all right, George," said Constance, pulling herself up and placing a supportive hand on his shoulder. She then took another step towards Lyric, holding both hands out to her beseechingly.

"You don't have a twin brother, Lyric." Her voice caught on the word brother, and she cleared her throat, before continuing more slowly. "You *had* a twin brother. But he — he died. In childbirth." She closed her eyes, lost in a thirty-year-old sea of pain that time had clearly not dulled. "He was stillborn. We never even got to say hello, let alone goodbye. It's the most painful thing I've ever had to endure. To experience, still. I'm afraid I have never been able to bring myself to speak about it. And I still can't. So now, please, Lyric darling, please understand that we must never speak of it again." A sob rose up in her throat and she turned into her husband's arms. Lyric stared incredulously, wanting to join their embrace but loath to break the spell of their closeness.

Instead, she turned and walked slowly towards the beach, her mind and emotions a whirring tangle of confusion. This island was now making her feel claustrophobic, and she yearned to leave. There was no such thing as a free lunch, Lyric reminded herself —

and the greatest cost of being on this island, it seemed, was that you simply couldn't get off.

She rubbed her temples, trying to make sense of the turbulence in her head. Her twin. Dead. Lost as soon as he was found. The unexplained feelings of emptiness — they made sense now. But . . . it still didn't add up. The other feelings, of being incomplete, that there was something — someone — else out there.

The moonlight shone on to the sea, turning the ocean's inky blackness a midnight blue — still and cool and inviting. All at once, Lyric had the urge to be in it. Pulling off her dress, she ran into the water's velvety wetness, running against the tide until its weight slowed her limbs and was deep enough to dive into. She opened her eyes, steeling herself against the salty sting and marvelling at the shapes and shadows the moonlight shining through the water made of the fish swimming alongside her, above her and beneath her. Under here she felt weightless and peaceful and silent. It was a world devoid of ugliness and ghastliness — and she had a feeling she never, ever wanted to come up for air. Ever.

CHAPTER
SIXTEEN

Quentin sat back in his battered leather chair in the cluttered office of his Eaton Square house and gazed at the piece of paper in his hands with unadulterated glee. It was a long time since he'd been able to look at a bank statement without wanting to weep, let alone one that made him want to leap for joy. And this was only the start of things to come. Welcome to your future, Quentin Charlton! He smoothed out the sheet on his old-fashioned mahogany desk and leaned forward and kissed it. The cash advances from Sergei kept flooding in, and despite the unexpected rise in the expense of recreating the Charlton's art collection, Quentin's bank balance was stacking up pretty nicely in the black.

Quentin placed his hands behind his head and put his feet, clad in their usual ancient scuffed Tod's moccasins, up on the desk. Of course, he didn't just have Sergei to thank for his new prosperity. He had himself. Brilliant business minds such as his didn't rest on their laurels when presented with this kind of opportunity. Oh no. Nor did they wait for another one to come along. They sought out yet more opportunities within the existing one, scoured the possibilities until something, somewhere, clicked and they could double, treble — hell, even quadruple — their initial profit. Quentin chuckled to himself. The fact of the matter was that the sideline he'd created to Sergei's art contract could well end up dwarfing the initial deal altogether. Its potential stretched way beyond Sergei's interior decorations and home improvements, and with a little bit of investment, a little bit of TLC and a whole lot of Quentin's genius, it could turn him into one of the richest — and most powerful — men in Britain.

Bringing in Richard Boxer had been a stroke of genius, Quentin congratulated himself, taking a noisy gulp of now cold Nescafé from the chipped, stained mug on his desk. Subsequent conversations with his new business partner had unearthed a similar innate greed to his own — and a whole new network of underground contacts. Quentin rubbed his hands together in satisfaction. Together, they had hatched a plan to import the original canvases from abroad, using Sergei's private jet to transport them from A to B. In this case, fortune had most certainly favoured the brave. Sergei had not questioned Quentin's prolific adoption of his perks — nor the HM Revenue and Customs paperwork that detailed the number of paintings coming *in* to Britain rather than out. And fortunately, the same Customs and Excise had only questioned the contents of the bubble wrap surrounding the paintings, and not the bubbles themselves — for hidden within a second skin of each bubble was a perfectly manufactured Ecstasy tablet. The street value of the haul so far ran into millions, and Quentin felt they had only just uncovered the tip of the iceberg. Not content now with the wealth that Sergei had offered him, Quentin was already looking beyond their deal to when he'd have enough money to charter a jet of his own — buy one, even — facilitating more of his illicit imports. And then the world of the super-rich really was going to be his oyster at last.

Looking at his watch, Quentin reluctantly dragged his feet off the desk and sloped over to his computer in the corner of the room. Sergei had requested an audience with him over a webcam, for goodness' sake. Barely even in possession of a PC just over a week ago, let alone one of these confounded things, Quentin had been forced to ask Sergei to send someone to buy it, install it, and even show him how to use it, and it had sat blinking at him relentlessly ever since.

Now Quentin pressed a button tentatively and stared at it expectantly. Nothing happened. "Whitebotham!" he bellowed at his long-suffering secretary, a fifty-something spinster named Penny Whitebotham. Quentin preferred a fine young filly in a pencil skirt and stockings to this old dragon, of course, but they never seemed to last very long with him — and Whitebotham was not only efficient and reliable, she'd proven to be a dab hand at deflecting his army of debt collectors over the years. Right now, he was sure, she was about to prove her worth yet again by actually having listened to the instructions of the fellow who'd installed the thing in the first place, rather than daydreaming away, totting up his imminent wealth, as Quentin had done.

"You called, Mr Charlton?" said Penny Whitebotham from the doorway. A buxom woman, she wore a dark grey flannel skirt suit, fifty-denier American Tan tights and sturdy heels. Her hair was pulled back into a tight bun at the back of her head and could have been mistaken for the cause of her pained expression, had her repulsive boss not also been in the room.

"Come and help me with this bloody thing, will you," said Quentin in exasperation. "Old Sergio's due to come through on the camera-me-jig in five minutes and I can't get the damned thing to do anything."

Penny walked stiffly across the room, calmly cast her eye over the keyboard and pressed the On button. "It generally helps if you turn on the power before you try to use a computer, sir," she said evenly.

Quentin's face went an even deeper shade of puce than usual, and he laughed loudly. It rang falsely around the room.

"Isn't that just typical? I must have forgotten I'd switched it off last time I used it!"

Penny gave him a "look" over the top of her pince-nez-style glasses. "Humph," she responded, used to Quentin's bluster. "Well, if there's nothing else?"

"No, no, that'll be all for now, thank you," said Quentin rather too brightly, shifting from one foot to another nervously. He didn't like to admit that he had no idea what to do now.

Fortunately, the matter was resolved for him as Sergei's voice came booming out over the speakers and his image appeared on the monitor's screen.

"Charlton!" Sergei, back home in Moscow, was on some kind of godforsaken industrial estate, clad in full-length fur coat and wayfarers. A Russian *Minder*, if

214

you liked that sort of thing, thought Quentin, running a hand through his greasy hair and smoothing down his crumpled, faded old denim shirt and red jeans. "And so, my friend, how are things?"

"Well, since you ask, not bad, old friend, not bad," smirked Quentin, thinking of his ill-gotten gains. Suddenly remembering that the bank statement was in full view of the webcam, he moved backwards, feeling behind him on the table for it. Before he found it, he managed to dislodge a glass paperweight and an ink blotter, which fell to the floor with a crash.

"Charlton? What is that?" said Sergei as two burly minders rushed into view on the monitor.

"Nothing, Sergio, nothing!" said Quentin, feeling behind him desperately for the statement. "Just a paperweight!"

"Oh my God," said Sergei, dismissing his bodyguards. "I, Sergei, thought it was gunshot."

Quentin laughed overly loudly again. "Ha-ha — gunshot! You are a card, Sergio. No, no, just some junk on my desk."

Sergei looked left and right, and then leaned into the camera.

"Charlton. I, Sergei, have some news. It is good news. And it is news you must know."

"Oh, right?" said Quentin, unsure of how to respond.

"Yes. It concerns your reputation as an art dealer."

Quentin looked puzzled. He had no reputation as an art dealer. Then, remembering how he'd sold himself to Sergei in the first place, he nodded enthusiastically.

"Go on, Sergio. I'm all ears."

"Yes, Charlton, and so you should be. For I, Sergei, am about to enhance your reputation beyond your wildest dreams!"

"Oh, good!" replied Quentin doubtfully. "How's that then, old boy?"

Sergei smiled and opened his arms wide as if about to give Quentin a virtual embrace.

"I, Sergei, have decided to throw a party to celebrate my new home. And, more importantly, to celebrate my forthcoming gift to my darling wife." Off screen, someone passed him a lit cigar and he chomped on it cheerily. "I intend to invite every key member of the international art scene to this party. I will make them hungry for my new collection in its entirety! I will be accepted as one of the leading connoisseurs of eighteenth-century English art, and you, Charlton, will be recognized for what you are — the world's greatest art dealer."

Quentin stared at the screen, his mouth gaping open and shut in shock. This was akin to his worst nightmare! How was he going to cover up his huge-scale forgery if the evidence was being announced across the world and, even worse, paraded under the noses of some of the world's greatest experts?

"Um — right. Well, that's very flattering, old man. But are you sure it's wise?" He stroked his chin, hoping Sergei wouldn't notice his shaking hand.

"Wise?" Sergei's tone indicated it was a very brave man who suggested he was anything but.

216

"Well, you know — insurance and all that. Art thieves. I don't know — seems like a pretty rash move, advertising a collection like that to the world."

There was a silence, and then Sergei moved forward again, extending his arm as if to shake Quentin's hand.

"I, Sergei, thank you for your wisdom and loyalty. But do not concern yourself, my friend. I, Sergei, have the best security money can buy. What I need from you are the best paintings money can buy. In two weeks' time."

As if to underline his point, a bodyguard stepped back into view.

"I bid you farewell, Charlton — until the next time." Sergei's image disappeared from the screen, and Quentin turned off the monitor, mind racing. He wiped his brow of the streams of sweat that had suddenly appeared there. How the devil was he going to get out of this one? He needed to come up with a plausible reason for Sergei to change his mind, or he — and his dreams of untold wealth — were history.

Just then, Quentin's iPhone, another gift from Sergei, flashed and vibrated urgently. Quentin picked it up and studied the keypad, again unsure of how to work it. He worked from left to right, pressing random buttons until a voice boomed out.

"Hello?"

"Charlton here."

"Quentin. It's Macintosh."

As always when the doctor called, Quentin looked around him nervously — he even did it when he was in his own home. You could never be too careful, he told himself, especially when you were conducting the kind of high-powered business he was now engaged in.

"We agreed no calls," hissed Quentin. "Godammit, man, how many times do I have to remind you? Have you no common sense at all — or is it not a prerequisite for your profession these days?"

"There is a problem with Bulldog," said the doctor flatly. "Another one."

"Well, you don't say," spluttered Quentin. "I thought you were calling me to ask after my health."

The doctor paused, counting to ten before replying. "He has applied online for a copy of his birth certificate. Quentin, it is now only a matter of time. He is bound to discover the truth."

Quentin thumped the desk in anger. "It is not your job to predict what *will* happen," he raged. "It is your job to *prevent* it."

There was another silence.

"Quentin, with all due respect, there is very little one can do these days to prevent such enquiries. No interception, or even sabotage for that matter. With the Internet, it's not a case of how, but of how *long*. Unless you can think of a way out of this, I'm afraid the game is up." The doctor's voice wavered on the last sentence. He could feel the cold fingers of fear clutching him as he anticipated the inevitable reprisals for their years of subterfuge and the subsequent ruin.

"Very little? Pull yourself together, man. With that kind of defeatist attitude, you deserve your time to be up," shouted Quentin, the vein in his head throbbing in

218

fury. "Fortunately for you, I don't believe in the words 'very little'. I can see that, as usual, this is going to be left to me to sort out."

Quentin slammed the phone down on the desk in a rage, then, as the LED screen flashed, picked it up again hurriedly. What if he'd accidentally dialled someone's number? But a cursory examination indicated no one was being called. His panic immediately replaced with anger again, Quentin buzzed through to Penny on the intercom.

"Whitebotham? Send an email —" unused to the term, Quentin pronounced it "Eeeeemail" — "to Henry Mogler. Mark it urgent. Inform him that the matter we discussed is now imminent. His department will be receiving an online communication from an Edward Jones — he must act on it accordingly."

"Very well, Mr Charlton — consider it done," she said in a clipped, mechanical tone.

After pacing around his desk for a few moments, anxiously running his hand through his greasy hair, Quentin picked up his phone and flicked through his speed-dial options. With only three in his spanking new contacts list, this didn't take very long, and within seconds he was through to Ahmed the bodyguard. The dial tone was that of an overseas phone — so Ahmed wasn't in the UK, then. With any luck, Ahmed was hot on the trail of Bulldog in France, and the whole thing had been resolved before there was any need to worry about it.

"Yes, hello?" said Ahmed carefully.

"Charlton here, old boy. Wondered if you had any news for me? Must be looking forward to that pay day, after all . . ."

"I am in Libya, at the home of the esteemed Ali Hassan," said Ahmed carefully.

"Oh, so you're not in France, then," said Quentin in disappointment.

The line stayed silent. Quentin began to feel unnerved.

"So, old boy, any news?" he repeated tentatively. Again there was silence.

"The only news I have for you, Mr Charlton, is that there is no news."

With that, the line went dead. This time, as Quentin flung the phone down, he had no concerns about accidentally calling anyone. This time, he threw it to the floor, and stamped furiously up and down on it.

CHAPTER
SEVENTEEN

Lyric's footsteps pounded rhythmically on the path around Kensington Gardens as her feet crunched through the remaining piles of frost-covered red and gold leaves scattering the paths. Her heart rate rose, and as the crisp winter air rushed through her hair, she turned up her iPod joyously. Running was new to her — before rehab, the most exercise she took was tearing up the nearest dance floor — But after her counsellor in Arizona had suggested she take up running, she'd been surprised by how quickly she'd come to love it, relishing both the sweet release from real life and the adrenaline buzz it gave her.

Philippe, now an almost constant presence in her bed, was an early riser, and she loved having a reason to get up too, rather than be left alone with only the imprint of his head on the pillow for company. But as well as this, she found the little vignettes of other people's lives strangely calming — the lone dog-walkers strolling contentedly with their motley companions, the angst-ridden financiers buttoning up their overcoats against the chill morning as they hurried to work, the sleep-deprived mother pushing a pram in a desperate effort to persuade a fretful newborn to sleep, and the

Chelsea pensioners on an early-morning mission to feed the pigeons. Feeling part of this picture of normality gave Lyric great comfort and a sense of freedom which only strengthened her resolve never again to let her life spiral out of control into the drug-addled depths of the previous years.

On her return from the Seychelles, she'd found the time alone with her thoughts curiously therapeutic, helping her reconcile her feelings of hurt and rejection at her parent's lifelong lies with the pain and suffering they must have felt, and must still be feeling, at the loss of their son. She shivered when she thought back to all the loving family occasions over the years: the fun-filled birthdays, the joyful Christmases. What unadulterated fun they'd been for her — but what bittersweet occasions they must have been for her parents, aching underneath it all for the absent child, the silent voice, the never-to-be-heard laughter. All of a sudden, things began to make sense. Her father's faraway smile, so sad at times. Her mother's neurotic nature, her spiky responses, even her conspicuous intake of Valium, for goodness' sake — it all added up to grief over their lost son. Now that she'd had time for it all to sink in, she realized just how much they must love her to have wanted to spare her the same pain. Initially, she'd felt rejected by their secrecy — but now, with Philippe's help, she'd seen how hard even this path must have been for them, and how she was not in a position to judge how they'd dealt with it then, but only to shape how she dealt with it now. And however much her mother refused to talk about it, or her father felt duty-bound to support his wife and let her deal with her grief in her own particular way, Lyric was determined to recognize her dead brother and mark his short time in the world somehow — to make it up to him if she could. To show him he had not been forgotten and how much he mattered to her, his twin sister.

Now, as tears blurred her eyes, the thought spurred her onwards, and she picked up the pace until she was practically sprinting. She was going so fast that she almost missed the insistent buzz of her mobile. Slowing back down to a jog, she pulled it out and stared at the number showing with the slightest hint of recognition. She seemed to know it, but just couldn't put a name to it. She bit her lip nervously. She'd deleted so many numbers when she'd cut off all her "toxic" friends that her contacts book was half the size it had once been. But if this was a number she wasn't sure of, then it could only mean one thing — answering the phone would be bad news. She rejected the call and continued, her pace slowed by concern. She checked her phone every couple of minutes — no voice message showed up, and she felt herself relax. Maybe it had been nothing more than a wrong number, causing her paranoia about her past to play unwelcome tricks on her. With everything in her love life going so well, and with the secrets of her family's past unravelling to help her make sense of her present, it was typical that Lyric's inner pessimist should look for ways for it to go wrong again.

The path had narrowed now to be just wide enough for two runners. Lyric heard footsteps gaining on her, and she automatically slowed down and pulled into the side of the path to let the other runner pass. She was worn out after her sprint, and anyhow it would hardly be good manners to jostle for space.

As the footsteps overtook her, Lyric looked to her right in the spirit of sportsman-like comradeship to acknowledge the runner. Her eyes widened with shock as she took in the long-legged figure pacing beside her. Here was no track-suit-clad, red-faced early-morning runner. The man easily covering the ground alongside her wore a leather biker jacket, skinny black jeans and battered brown desert boots. His hair flew in wispy shoulder-length strands behind him, and he wore a misshapen trilby pulled down low over his eyes. Lyric gasped. Eyes or no eyes, there was no mistaking the runner's identity. Anatole Funk, celebrity cling-on, wannabe rich kid, sometime artist — and Lyric's former drug dealer.

She stopped short, panting, hands on hips.

"What do you want?"

There was no need for pleasantries. Funk was one of the many former associates she'd had no qualms about cutting off — he'd exploited her wealth, her connections and her desperate addiction for his own personal gain, and then, like so many others, hadn't so much as sent her an encouraging message while she was in rehab. Too scared he'd be rumbled, she'd concluded derisively. All she could think about when she looked at morally bankrupt people like Funk were the thousands, probably millions of people who had got themselves into a similar mess as Lyric but didn't have the financial wherewithal and emotional support to get themselves out of it. It was parasites like Funk who, in her opinion, had blood on their hands when these vulnerable people became the ultimate victim of their addiction through overdose, drug-related crime or infection.

"Lyyyyyric," he smarmed, bending over and holding his knees in an attempt to get his breath back. Clearly a nocturnal lifestyle and fifty-a-day nicotine habit did not a runner make. "That's no way to greet your old friend Anatole."

" 'Old friend' is hardly the way I'd describe you," she snapped back. There had been times when she'd sent a driver to bring Anatole miles across country, when she'd flown him by private jet across continents to bring her a wrap, a line, a smoke. Desperate acquaintance, yes. But "old friend"? Never.

"Are you stalking me, by any chance?" She looked over her shoulders nervously. Hemmed in by the avenue of trees, wisps of autumn mist hung over the path and Lyric suddenly felt exposed and alone. Not, she realized, looking at Anatole's unfit and flabby body, that she was in any danger of being outrun by him — but she guessed that he was probably stronger than he looked, and she would stand little chance should he decide to attack her.

Anatole smiled, revealing a set of spectacularly unclean teeth, stained brown from years of smoking and drinking and rotting away from lack of maintenance. "Lyric, Lyric, Lyric," he whined tune-lessly. "If you won't answer my calls, what else am I meant to do?"

"Your calls?" started Lyric, then realized. The number she'd rejected — of course. For years she'd have been able to recite that number at any time, day or night, when she'd needed drugs at short notice. It proved how far she'd come in such a short time that it had already been wiped from her memory.

"Well, my *call*. I was here, you see, in this neck of the woods and thought I'd look you up," Anatole said, standing up straight now. "What a pleasant coincidence to bump into you like this!"

Lyric stared at him, a feeling of fear and dread gnawing in the pit of her stomach. Whatever Funk wanted, it was nothing good.

"What do you want, Anatole?" she said in a monotone and started walking. She had an instinctive need to get further out into the open, away from this deserted area of the park.

"Oh, come now, Lyric, don't be like that!" said Anatole, stepping in beside her. He towered over her, and when he slung a thin arm around her shoulders, Lyric shrank away from him. "Tell me how you've been! What you've been up to! Long time no see and all that."

Lyric felt anger rise up inside her and she swung around to face him.

"Anatole, quit the long-lost friends act and tell me what you want. I'm in a very different place to last time I saw you. My life has moved on in the past few months, and I'm sure you'll forgive me for being blunt when I say that it no longer includes you."

Anatole stepped back, feigning hurt, then stroked his chin thoughtfully. "And there was I thinking we were friends for life. All that shared history and all that . . ." There was a hint of menace to his tone.

"What do you mean?" asked Lyric cagily. She moved her weight from one leg to the other, and as she moved her foot she heard the leaves crunch underneath it noisily. Only moments ago this noise had delighted her — now it seemed to be laced with warning.

"Well, I mean that you, maybe more than anyone, know how much my painting means to me. You've seen it, admired it — I think I even gave you a piece once."

Lyric cast her mind back to Anatole's nonsensical scrawls, grandly described by him as modern art. Yes, she remembered, he had given her a "piece" once, which, in her formerly superficial way, she'd announced was a masterpiece, then stuck on the fridge when he'd gone.

"That's right," she said carefully. "What of it?"

"Well, you see, you're not the only one going legit, Lyric. I want to turn my back on all this drugs business. Earn my living like a decent person, rather than running around breaking the law at every turn for people I don't really care about." His lip curled in disgust, and for a fleeting second Lyric felt sympathy for him — he was caught in a similar trap to the one she'd been in, desperate to get out. But then she remembered how he had found himself there in the first place, not out of spiralling addiction but out of a need to prey on people's weaknesses, to exploit them for all they were worth, and her heart hardened against him again.

"Is that right," she said deadpan. "And where do I fit into all this?"

"We-ell," said Anatole slowly. "I figure I've got two avenues open to me. First avenue, my art. All I need is a way in. And I figure, with all your contacts, that's you."

And all she needed, Lyric thought to herself with dismay, was to publicly back a dead-beat drug dealer with no talent. The press would sniff him out in seconds, and she'd be relegated to the ranks of back-on-it party Lyric, spoilt little rich girl who threw all the love, kindness and support of her family, friends, counsellors and, yes, the public, back in their faces. Not to mention the damage this would wreak on her relationship with Philippe.

"Is that right?" she said non-committally. "And, out of interest, what's the second?"

Anatole gave her another brown-toothed smile. "I need to know what your response is to my first option before I reveal my second," he said. "That being my preferred course of action and all."

Lyric took a deep breath. "I'm sorry, Anatole, but much as I wish you all the luck in the world launching yourself as a serious artist, I'm afraid I have no intention of being part of it. Whether I like it or not, I've had to turn my back on my old life — and everyone who was a part of it."

"And that would include Ralph Conway, would it?" enquired Anatole innocently. Too innocently.

Lyric jumped at the mention of her ex-boyfriend and in her shock missed the dark intent in Anatole's voice.

"Ralph didn't give me much of a choice in the matter, but since you ask, yes," she said, blushing furiously and inexplicably. The thought of her ill-fated relationship with Ralph made her shudder when she compared it with what she had with Philippe. How shameful that she could have fallen so hard — and for so long — for such a loser.

"Shame," said Anatole, shaking his head sadly. "You two made such a lovely couple. I recently found some pictures of you both, actually — want to see them? If they aren't going to make you feel too nostalgic, that is."

Lyric looked at him searchingly. What pictures could Anatole possibly have found that she would have any interest in? She racked her brains quickly for any social occasion he might have been at with them — with a camera. However wasted she'd been back then, she was sure there hadn't been any. Every bone in her body wanted to run away from him and never have to hear his oily voice again, but something kept her rooted to the spot.

"Go on, then," she said, her voice sounding oddly strangled with fearful anticipation. She had a feeling this wasn't going to be good.

Anatole's hand scrambled around in his inner pocket as he made a big deal of finding what he was looking for. Eventually, he pulled out his phone. Holding it up,

Anatole made a show of flicking through his folders, all the while keeping one eye on Lyric's face. Lyric's heart was in her mouth, and her eye was twitching over and over. Finally, unable to spin it out any longer, he handed it over.

"Here you go," he said with satisfaction.

Lyric looked blankly at the image filling the phone screen. At first glance, it looked like some kind of art-house porn — a man's profile, the soft curve of a woman's breast, the hot, heavy air of sexual potency. She frowned. Why . . .? Then, as she looked closer, she gave out a gasp of recognition. The man was Ralph. In his hand was a rolled-up fifty-pound note. And he wasn't just fondling the breast with sexual intent. Lying across it was the unmistakeable jagged white scar of a line of coke.

Lyric gasped and put her hand to her mouth, dropping the phone. She bent down to pick it up, breathing quickly to try and regain her composure. When she looked up, Anatole was gazing at her in undisguised triumph.

"Oh dear, Lyric, I didn't upset you, did I?" he said without a trace of concern in his voice. "Did it bring back old memories?"

Lyric looked at him, shaking with anger. She steeled herself to try and remain calm. Losing it wasn't going to help her in this situation.

"How did you get that picture, Anatole? When was it taken?" She cursed her voice as it shook tellingly. Showing weakness in front of Anatole would be fatal.

"You mean you can't remember?" he teased. "Oh dear. Well, let's just say it was very recently — more recently than the public would like to think. But, of course, they don't need to know if . . ."

"Who knows you've got it?" asked Lyric, back to bluntness again.

Anatole chuckled. "Oh dear, I've really rattled the Charlton cage, haven't I? I may have put in a call to the picture desk at the *News of the World* . . . I may not. But I happen to know they would pay a very high price for it . . . a very high price indeed. Not to mention the others in the same set . . ." Lyric rolled her eyes at what she hoped was a bluff — surely there couldn't be more? "But since you don't feel you can help me out with kindness, I thought maybe you'd like to help me out financially instead," Anatole continued. "Make me the right offer for the pictures, Lyric, and they will never see the light of day. Decide you won't, and let's just say we'll both be famous for modern art of a very different nature. Call me. But don't take too long."

Snatching back the phone, Anatole turned on his heel and strolled off in the opposite direction, whistling cheerily.

Lyric stared after him, shaking from shock and anger. She tried to follow him, but her legs buckled, and she crouched on the floor, head between her legs, breathing deeply.

That picture — or pictures — must never be allowed to be made public. They would not only reignite the media frenzy over her drug abuse, bringing shame on her and her family, they would, like any association with the drug-ridden world she'd left behind, rock the very foundations of the new life she had found — the new life she loved so much.

But there was another far greater betrayal behind her current state of shock. The man was definitely Ralph. But the perfect set of breasts in the pictures weren't her own. Of that she was certain. They were *too* perfect — the unmistakeable work of the world's most expensive cosmetic surgeon. Lyric hadn't had surgery. And nor did she sport a tiny, almost imperceptible star tattoo just above her left nipple.

But Treeva did.

Across town, Treeva tentatively opened one eye and then, wincing at the bright light, immediately shut it again. God, what was that noise? It felt like a pneumatic drill going off inside her head. She rubbed her temples and attempted to go back to sleep, despite her pumping heartbeat and a mouth that felt like a camel's armpit.

Suddenly aware of an arm hugging her, she brushed it off irritably and attempted to replace it with a duvet. She grabbed a corner of the musty, moth-eaten eiderdown and pulled it up around herself half-heartedly. How the bloody hell had she ended up with Carston again — and at his flat, come to that? Ever since Sin Island he'd been plaguing her with texts, and though no longer in the slightest bit interested (she was back home in London now, wasn't she, which meant she had bigger — richer, more glamorous — fish to fry?) she had finally given in to his requests to take her for a drink. And he'd been every bit as gorgeous — and boring — as she remembered. So much so that she'd demanded he take her to Chinawhite, where a DJ friend of hers was holding a night and where she knew she could easily lose him.

Eyes still tightly shut, Treeva frowned. Where she *had* lost Carston, surely? She willed her foggy mind to focus on the exact events of the night before. Yep, it was all coming back to her now. They'd bumped into a group of acquaintances in the VIP section — a music promoter she knew, his latest ex-girl-band star in the making, a sometime movie star from the States, who'd sacrificed her career for coke addiction, and her lesbian lover. Treeva rubbed her temples for a second time. She'd made it quite plain to Carston she hadn't wanted him around, and had got bang on it with the others. She flinched at the memory of how cruel she must have been, and a wave of self-loathing spread over her. Why did she always have to act like that after a couple of lines of cocaine? And if she hadn't ended up with Carston, where was she — and who with?

Just then, Treeva felt something scuttle across her arm, opened her eyes and shrieked out loud. A cockroach! Sitting bolt upright, she screamed again as it ran across her pillow and up along the wall, and pulled the threadbare duvet up to cover her bare breasts.

Around her was the scummiest room she had ever seen. A scrappy paisley scarf hung at the window, blowing in the breeze from the badly fitted panes of glass. The floorboards were bare and unpolished, and empty beer cans, a bottle of vodka and drug paraphernalia were scattered across them. The walls were also bare save for some peeling paint and — surely that wasn't a *blood* stain?

But the biggest shock was to come. As Treeva looked around her wildly, she took in the naked, entwined forms of not one, but two other people. In bed. With her.

Worse, neither of them was Carston. In fact, neither of them was male. Instead, it was the LA movie star and her girlfriend.

Stretching languidly, the actress sat up, long hair tumbling over one shoulder, strappy vest exposing her left breast.

"Welcome to paradise, baby," she said, artfully circling Treeva's nipple with her index finger. "Wanna go for round two?"

CHAPTER
EIGHTEEN

"I still think you're mad to have even thought of forgiving Treeva this time," said Philippe as he kissed Lyric goodbye. "It's one betrayal too many. I'm all for forgiveness, but that would be crazy. You'd be setting yourself up for a big fall, *chérie*."

Lyric frowned, unwilling to go over ground they'd already spent the previous night disagreeing on.

"Philippe, I agree — in principle. But Treeva and I go back so far. We were blood-sisters at school, for God's sake! She's lost, lonely and weak. She didn't have a family like mine. Her parents may have showered her with presents, but they were just never there for her! She's always been looking for it elsewhere. And fine, I didn't think she'd look for it in my boyfriend, but still . . ." She faltered, trying desperately to recall the textbook of forgiveness that she'd learned at rehab, and to which she'd been clinging hopelessly since she'd discovered Treeva's latest betrayal. "We still don't know one hundred per cent that it was her boob in the pictures. The tattoo — it was a bit blurred. It could have been a mole or anything. And I probably would have done the same," she finished. It sounded lame, even to her ears.

Philippe pulled back and studied her face intently. "*Franchement*, Lyric? In her position, would you really have done the same?" Lyric flinched under his close scrutiny. "Now that's what I would really like to know."

Lyric looked up at him, feeling inches tall. "Well, actually, no, I never would have done that," she admitted quietly. "But I *must* learn to forgive. It's the only way."

Lyric hugged him tightly. He responded, but she felt an unfamiliar coolness there, a distance she hadn't sensed before. She couldn't blame him, really — the shock of learning she'd spent nearly half a million pounds to prevent publication of a set of soft-porn pictures that claimed to show the love of his life with another man, followed by several days analysing them, trying to work out who the other woman was, was bound to affect him. She just hoped that this gulf was temporary.

She looked up at him. "But I know relationships are all about compromise. And you're more important to me than Treeva. If you really think making up with her is the wrong thing — then I'll leave it. For now." Even she wasn't convinced by this.

But Philippe smiled at her, more warmly this time, and she felt her heart lift optimistically.

"It's not about what I want. It's about you recognizing what's best for you. And not besmirching yourself — and your life — with so-called friendships with people who don't respect what you're about, who don't have the same values as you."

236

She smiled back brightly. "Well, I'm going to go shopping this morning. Take my mind off it!" She hugged him again, tightly, unable to look him in the eyes whilst lying so blatantly.

As he left, she closed the door behind her and looked at it longingly. If only she could stay behind it, remain for ever where she felt safe, in Philippe's embrace, and never have to face this cruel, hideous world again.

She shook herself. She wasn't going shopping at all. Today's real purpose was mission impossible — but after the searing hurt of Treeva's behaviour, after the realization that it was going to take more than a spell in rehab to erase all the negatives brought on by her own addiction, she'd become determined to confront Treeva rather than cut her off without giving her a chance to explain, whatever Philippe thought. To explain how, when Lyric had trusted Treeva to keep an eye on Ralph — her boyfriend of over two years — during her time in rehab, she'd betrayed her in the worst possible way. Ralph might be a thing of the past, but this had stung Lyric deeply — it was breaking the ultimate code of honour between friends. And though every inch of her wanted to cry out, to lash out at Treeva, to make her hurt in the way she'd made Lyric hurt, she was determined to take the higher moral ground and make a lasting peace. It was just a shame that the price of peace was lying to Philippe. Still, it was in the best interests of their future together, she told herself firmly.

Lyric tied her Louis Vuitton scarf tighter around her neck and stepped up the pace as she wandered across her courtyard garden, through a tiny gap in the fence and along the alleyway to Treeva's portered mansion block further down the road. It was hardly a short cut, since it took just as long and was more effort than going by the road, but it was their own secret private route between each other's houses. Today, it felt strange and somehow alien.

A couple of doors away, she stopped and took a deep breath. This was going to take every ounce of self-control she had within her — and some. *And it still might not be her*, a little voice inside reminded her. *You might have got it wrong.* She hoped against hope that she had.

She pressed the buzzer to Treeva's flat.

"Lyric! Come in," purred Treeva down the intercom, her tone as silky and sycophantic as ever.

She has no idea, thought Lyric. *No idea whatsoever.* She allowed herself one moment of rage before she attempted to quell the rising anger within her. How *dare* Treeva make such a fool of her?

Biting her lip, heart pounding, she pushed open the heavy front door and climbed the six steps to Treeva's flat. By the time she reached the front door, which had been left open for her as usual, she was so out of breath that she momentarily forgot her feelings of anxiety.

"Lyric!" squealed Treeva, appearing from her bedroom in shorter-than-short hot pants, white shirt tied at the waist to reveal her midriff, and over-the-knee socks. The effect was intended to be coquettish and sexy, but it was less Lolita, more tranny-at-school-disco, thought Lyric. And in comparison with her own jeans, white T-shirt and classic Joseph blazer, it looked *so* uncomfortable.

Treeva hugged her in an intoxicating cloud of Chloé perfume. "Glass of champ?" she called, skipping into the kitchen.

Lyric looked at her watch uneasily. Her worries over what she was going to say to Treeva had made her completely underestimate how difficult coming into this flat was going to be. It had been the hotbed of her partying days, and it was the first time she'd been back since rehab. Now, with only one foot through the door, she was being bombarded with what in rehab they called "triggers" — the smell, the photos in the collage frame inside the front door, even the *Sounds of Ibiza* CD Treeva was playing. She swallowed hard and reached for her composure.

"At ten a.m.?" she called after Treeva. "Not for me, thanks."

"Oh, right," said Treeva, appearing from the kitchen with two flutes of champagne and a crestfallen expression. "What, then? Um — a cup of tea?"

Her bemused expression made Lyric want to laugh out loud. She doubted Treeva owned any tea bags, let alone a mug to put one in.

"Don't worry, Tree, I've only just had coffee. I'll be fine."

"Okey-cokey," said Treeva. "Give me two minutes and I'll be right back."

Lyric settled into one of the overstuffed sofas and looked around at the familiar surroundings. *Shiny*, she thought — that was the right word to describe Treeva's flat. Shiny and modern with a touch of chintz — Pamela's telltale contribution. When Treeva had commissioned her mother to decorate it when she'd moved in five years ago, Lyric had put it down to laziness, but in her new spirit of benevolence decided it was more likely to have been a cry for attention from her parents. The flat was a combination of Pamela's new money and some half-hearted Treeva thrown in here and there. The result had been surprisingly effective, stunning even, but it now showed signs of Treeva's erratic and careless lifestyle. The carpet was patterned with cigarette burns, dirty footprints and red-wine stains. Not only did it have things living on it, it had the appearance of things living *in* it. On every surface there were relics of Treeva's constantly changing personas: a fat Buddha, a leather hip-hop Troop jacket, a half-empty bottle of Kabbalah water. One corner was dominated by a huge red neon sign flashing the words "Dirty Whore" above a pink quilted chaise longue — Treeva's personal, self-styled red-light district and the pride and joy of her apartment. As Lyric glanced over at it now, she spotted a half-empty bottle of Pouilly Fumé. Ralph's favourite wine . . .

Stop it!, she scolded herself. Just because she suspected they had been having an affair, didn't mean it was still going on. And what did she care if it was, anyhow? Good luck to them. It would be Treeva's loss in the end.

Impulsively, Lyric stood up and followed Treeva into the chaos that was her bedroom. Unwashed clothes were piled on top of new clothes still with their labels on, which were piled on top of bags containing impulse buys forgotten before they'd even arrived home. On the dressing table, open cosmetic bottles battled for space with half-drunk glasses of wine, ancient furry trolls and the odd used concert ticket. White towels were strewn everywhere bearing the ugly orange smudges of foundation and fake tan, and the satin pillowcases were smeared with mascara. Treeva's passport could be seen among a jumble of shoes. Lyric shuddered. Once upon a time, it could easily have been her bedroom. Now it was the exact opposite of her own newly-acquired OCD neatness.

"I'll be right with you," called Treeva from the bathroom.

Looking over at the clothes spilling out of the wardrobe, Lyric spotted Treeva's reflection in the open mirror door — bent over the loo seat, snorting a line. Lyric wrinkled her own nose instinctively. Treeva clearly thought she was hidden. But did she really have to be so insensitive to her supposed best friend, straight out of rehab?

Treeva appeared from the bathroom, conspicuously wiping her nose. Again, Lyric marvelled at her blatancy — but again, she kept it to herself.

"So, Tree, what's been going on?" she asked warmly, lying back on Treeva's unmade bed, the pink silk sheets crumpled underneath her. She tried not to think about who else had been in it recently. "It feels like for ever since I've seen you. I mean, I know I've seen you, but we haven't really had a chance to catch up *properly*.

What have you been up to? Tell me everything — right back from when I went to rehab."

Treeva jumped on the bed next to Lyric and leaned over for the packet of cigarettes on the other side of the bed. She offered Lyric one. Lyric shook her head. Marlboro Menthol, Lyric noted. Ralph's brand of choice. Since when had Treeva smoked menthol cigarettes? Unless . . .

"Oh, you know," said Treeva dismissively, reaching across again for some chewing gum. "Same old same old. What was rehab like, then?"

Lyric winced at the careless tone of her question. "Oh, you know. It was no picnic! Hard work, but I feel better for having done it. So, come on, then — you know all about me, and my meeting Philippe. Who have you got in your life? Must have been hard being single when you had to look after Ralph for me — poor old you. And to have spent all that time keeping your eye on him, and then to have me and Ralph split up regardless!"

Treeva, getting up to play with her hair in the mirror, seemed nonplussed. "Oh, you know, it was no trouble. Quite a laugh, really."

White-hot anger started to rise up in Lyric, and she silently forced herself to calm down. Not yet — she still couldn't be a hundred per cent sure. It might not have been Treeva.

"Well, there was no one else I would have trusted to look after him. No one," persisted Lyric, laying it on as thick as she could. "And there's still no one else in your life? Well, other than Carston, of course!" They both laughed at the recollection of Treeva's Sin Island fling, which had been over even before her (fake) tan had faded.

"No, no — no one else," said Treeva, unable to meet Lyric's gaze and fidgeting with her hair again. Lyric spotted a discarded Agent Provocateur bag on the floor and decided to change tack.

"Oh wow!" she said, picking up the bag and pulling out some black and pink underwear. "That is seriously gorgeous! I've been meaning to spice up my lingerie. It's the kind of thing you can't wait to do when you've got a new man, isn't it?"

"Oh, man, you're so right there," said Treeva enthusiastically. "Look at this baby."

She ripped open her shirt to display the peach and lime lace bra perfectly showcasing her rounded breasts — and the tiny star tattoo on the right one, just above the nipple, in exactly the same place as the one on Anatole's mobile phone. There was no trying to find excuses for her now. Treeva *was* the woman in the photograph — and Treeva was definitely the one who'd been playing around with Ralph behind Lyric's back.

Lyric was almost unable to breathe. She reached for her bag and pulled out a contact sheet of the picture she'd finally paid Anatole so much for — and all the others in the set. All the others he'd admitted to, anyway.

"What's that?" asked Treeva with immediate interest.

"I'll show you in a minute," said Lyric levelly. "Tree, look me in the eye a moment."

"What? You're freakin' me out, babe," Treeva tried to joke, laughing nervously and looking anywhere but straight into Lyric's eyes.

"Treeva!" Lyric said.

Treeva, shocked by her friend's tone, turned and looked at her guiltily.

"Game over, Treeva. Look me in the eye and tell me you didn't sleep with Ralph behind my back."

There was silence. Treeva, now staring at her dumbfounded, stood stock-still. Lyric, with a heavy heart, didn't need to go any further to find out the truth. Treeva's reaction told her all she needed to know. But as though she was wobbling an aching tooth, she had to press her friend harder — however much it hurt. She needed the truth — from Treeva's own mouth.

"Treeva, tell me it wasn't you."

Suddenly, Treeva crumpled to the ground and burst into tears. Great, heaving sobs that racked her body as she thumped the floor mercilessly.

Now it was Lyric's turn to stare. Crying on demand. The one thing Treeva had learned at the Lee Strasberg school in New York. The one thing *anyone* learned there. But Treeva had probably got more use out of it than the rest of the alumni put together. And now she cried big, fat, crocodile tears. For once, Lyric fought off the impulse to comfort her. Instead, she sat still and waited. And waited.

Finally, realizing that her crying fit was having no effect, Treeva looked up at Lyric through mascara-streaked eyes.

"I didn't mean to, Lyric — I really didn't mean to. It's just — it's just — you know . . ." she started to wail.

"No, I don't know," said Lyric patiently. "You'll have to tell me."

"Oh — you've no idea how — how — unhappy I am!" she sobbed between spitty, snotty tears. The crocodile tears were long gone, Lyric noted — either Treeva had worked herself up into a really good pretence, or she was genuinely unhappy. "You had gone away and left me, and Mummy and Daddy were doing their thing, and Laura was busy with the kids, and — oh, and I needed someone! I needed someone so badly, Lyric. And Ralph was there, and he was the closest thing I'd got to you, and . . . and I've never felt so guilty about anything in my life, and he's acting like such a shit anyway. Oh, it's all such a mess!"

Lyric hesitated for a split second, her instinct to comfort her friend momentarily eclipsed by doubt over her honesty. But the sight of Treeva's obvious misery made her reach out in spite of her feelings. She stood up and walked stiffly across the room to her friend, holding out her hand awkwardly, still torn between dismay for her friend and her own sense of betrayal. Lyric placed her hand on Treeva's shoulder. The action felt wooden and false, and she withdrew it quickly. "Oh, Tree, don't cry!" she said softly. "It's OK. It really is OK now . . ."

Much, much later, Lyric arrived back home. Philippe's keys were on the worktop and she could feel his presence in the house. But it felt different somehow. It felt cold.

She walked through to the sitting room where he was watching the news. She put her arms around him and kissed his cheek.

"Hi, baby," she said, nuzzling his neck.

"Hi," he said neutrally. "You've been a while. What did you buy?"

Lyric looked at her hands, empty of shopping bags, and her mouth opened and shut uncertainly. With all the emotional upheaval over Treeva, she'd completely forgotten about her cover story of going shopping. *Oh, what an evil web we weave*, she reprimanded herself. She wasn't used to lying, and this exposed what an inexperienced fibber she was.

She perched on the arm of his chair and traced his chin with her finger, turning his face to hers.

"I didn't go shopping," she said flatly. "I'm sorry, Philippe. I lied. I went to see Treeva after all."

"So I guessed," said Philippe, gazing at her neutrally. "And how did you find it?"

"Well, it was OK," she said carefully. "It was definitely Treeva in the picture, and we had a chat, and . . ."

". . . and you forgave her," Philippe finished for her, his tone flat and factual.

She pulled back and looked at him searchingly. "Yes. But you knew that's what I wanted to do. I figured —"

Philippe stood up. "I know what you figured," he said sadly. "We discussed it enough. But you also know what *I* figured. I wanted you to give Treeva a chance,

246

and you did. She blew it. And what I figure now is that if you want to let people like that into our life, then we haven't got a chance. They are toxic, they destroy all around them, and how can I protect you from them if you're going to let them back every time? They poison other people's relationships, Lyric, and she'll poison ours."

He walked to the door, leaving Lyric perched, speechless, on the arm of the sofa.

"But that's not the real problem." He opened the door and turned, his hand on the door handle. "You lied to me, Lyric. You did exactly what you promised not to do when you renounced your old life, when we met, when we started a new life together — you lied. And lies are not the foundation I intend building a new life upon. It's over, Lyric."

And with that, he left.

CHAPTER
NINETEEN

Quentin mopped his brow nervously. All efforts to persuade Sergei that his party plan was a bad one had failed, and he had insisted on having at least one painting to whet the appetites of the international art scene — and his other guests — at the party to celebrate the opening of his Dubai mansion. Since then, Quentin had had to double his costs to persuade his "restoration" team to produce the goods in time for the party. And they had done it — just. There was just one final problem. The copies had not been dry enough to send back to Broughton Hall in time to swap with the next batch of genuine paintings, so Quentin had been forced to send back the originals and, in due course, forward the frauds on to Sergei.

Fortunately, Sergei didn't seem too bothered about checking the Sotheby's stamp on the back of the canvases. The integrity of the first painting Quentin had sold him — his only original — was, it seemed, doing the talking for the rest. And so now Sergei was in possession of two perfectly forged — if not perfectly dry — Constables. At great additional cost, Quentin had paid for the paintings to be transported complete with attendants wielding hair-dryers, and they were now hung — admittedly still tacky to the touch — in pride of place at either end of the mansion's grand ceremonial dining room. Fortunately, Sergei's people had bought Quentin's claptrap that centuries-old paintings rehung in the Gulf Stream needed dehumidifiers to acclimatize them, and both works had had enormous fans blowing on them to finish the job off properly.

Quentin scoffed inwardly at the thought of the paintings hanging incongruously in this mock marble palace on the beach — all gold leaf and Grecian pillars. Money-grabbing and mercenary he might be, but even he could appreciate how ill-placed the two Constable copies were. Paintings like these looked out of place more or less anywhere but in the rambling English country houses they'd been painted for. A Matisse, yes — that would work here, or something more contemporary — but a heavy oiled Constable, or a Stubbs, or a Turner, really didn't fit the exotic Dubai setting. They were at their best filling a neglected corner in a stately home, or beautifully lit above a Chelsea fireplace, not taking pride of place in some blinging Middle Eastern mansion. But with Sergei, it didn't seem to be about the art. It was all about having the one and only "this", the biggest "that", the most expensive "other". It was about being so saturated in wealth that you didn't know where to look next, let alone how best to appreciate it. Still, Quentin reminded himself smugly, if this was the new order, then who was he to complain? Anyone willing to pay the eye-watering sums that Sergei was currently trumping up was, as far as Quentin was concerned, allowed to hang a Picasso upside down in a downstairs loo if they wanted to. And they probably wouldn't even realize they'd done it!

Quentin chuckled at his own joke. As he stood by the (free) bar watching Sergei's glitterati party guests mingle, he could seriously not believe his luck. This was the biggest game of Russian roulette that he'd ever played, the greatest chess game of his life — and he was approaching checkmate. But the high stakes were taking it out of him!

He chuckled again at his clever analogies. Oh, Quentin Charlton, he congratulated himself, you are *on fire*! He mopped his brow again. This confounded heat! Despite the air conditioning everywhere he went, the humidity of Dubai, combined with his own nervous energy, he had noticed, were making him sweat constantly and prolifically. So much so that tonight, for the first time ever, he'd applied talcum powder under his armpits.

However, so far so good. Sergei and his wife Olga had been desperate to show off their new assets to the colourful collection of guests — an international melange of princes, sheiks, oil barons and mega-rich business executives. In amongst the sober suits and the United Arab Emirates national dress were more ostentatious jewellery, fake tan and shiny clothes than in the players' lounge at a premiership football match. But every time he'd heard Olga say to a guest "you simply *must* come and see our new paintings", Quentin had done his best to divert said guests away from them. In the event, it seemed unnecessary. Of the international somebodies and their glamorous wives who'd slipped the net and been given the grand tour — most of whom had names longer than most normal sentences — all had seemed politely impressed with the artwork but not overly interested in it. And with each glass of vintage champagne, he was feeling the initial tension of the evening slipping gently away.

"Oh, Mr Charlton, how wonderful to meet you!" gushed a cut-glass voice behind him, and he turned to see Lady Danbury, the chic, attractive middle-aged wife of the charismatic Lord Danbury, well known Master of Foxhounds from Lincolnshire, beaming up at him. "I've met your brother George, of course, through our horse racing connections. I hear you're the genius behind Sergei's recent acquisition of these *maaahvellous* paintings. So let's go through and have a look at them!"

Quentin mentally ran through the guest list, and the notes that Whitebotham had attached for him from her research on the Internet, and inwardly groaned. Lord Danbury, he knew, was from an old-established and respected family who could probably trace their ancestry to Magna Carta — and a huge Constable enthusiast to boot. He had just the kind of background to persuade Sergei, the social astronaut, that, by getting him to his party, he, Sergei, had arrived. Moreover, he most likely knew the Charlton collection inside out. "Oh, there's one very like that at Broughton Hall" was something Quentin did not want to hear tonight, neither from him nor his lady-wife.

"Delighted to meet you, Lady Danbury — or may I call you Helene?" he greased. "But there's plenty of time to see the paintings later. How about another drink — and one for your enchanting friend?"

Her friend, Ina Infanti, wife of an Italian politician of dubious integrity, smiled prettily and giggled.

"God, it's like a WAG hell on earth, isn't it?" observed Lady Danbury, looking around her with a twinkle in her eye.

"Well, as everyone knows, there are more princes than dentists in Dubai," said Ina wickedly in perfect English. "And with so much competition for wealth and glamour, it's up to their wives to prove it!"

Helene leaned in towards both Ina and Quentin. "But what I want to know, then, is, if money and time are no object, why do all these WAGGIES end up looking exactly the same?"

They all laughed conspiratorially and Quentin's chest puffed with pride at being drawn into the confidence of these beautiful, cultured, *educated* women. In more ways than one, it seemed, he was destined, at long last, to be recognized as *someone*. Now, all he had to do was prevent Lady Danbury asking to see the paintings again. He looked around him, desperate for something to distract her. The huge dimensions of the mansion's rooms suddenly felt smaller, as if its cavernous walls were closing in around him. Only now did he realize how claustrophobic it had begun to feel.

"Charlton, old boy, been looking for you everywhere. See you've been collared by the wife — marvellous filly, isn't she?" The booming tones of Lord Danbury rang out around the ballroom, and Quentin's heart shot from its self-propelled position somewhere on the ceiling to the very bottom of his dress shoes. Lord Danbury, the art expert. Arm in arm with Sergei. Just what he needed. He pasted what he hoped was a jovial smile on his face.

"Charming, absolutely charming," he muttered, wiping his brow as he felt the trickles of sweat run down his temples again.

"So, I've been checking out this art of yours, and I have to admit to being damned suspicious," boomed Danbury.

The room around them went eerily quiet, and when Ina coughed delicately it sounded like a clap of thunder.

"Suspicious, Danbury? How so?" replied Quentin, his face looking like it was about to spontaneously combust.

"Well, I'm sure I've seen these paintings somewhere before," started Danbury. "I just can't put my finger on where." Behind him, Sergei's face was a studied picture of angry confusion. Quentin felt a sticky, cloying sensation as the dam of talcum powder breached and his armpits started to sweat profusely.

Quentin's mouth opened and shut like a goldfish. "I — I can assure you, Danbury, that it —"

"I mean, I only bother with the very finest art collections, so it must be somewhere worth its salt," continued Danbury, talking over Quentin as if he hadn't even opened his mouth. "So what I want to know is — where the devil did you source such beauties for this rogue of a Russian crook?" He roared with laughter at his own bonhomie, slapping Sergei on the back repeatedly until he joined in and the guests around them also started to titter nervously.

However, no one laughed louder than Quentin. He'd thought his goose was cooked there for a moment. But it seemed he'd got away with it — again. For now . . .

Later, as Quentin took the golf buggy along the short path to his room in the guest house further along the beach, he took in a deep breath of air and leaned back, taking in the clear, starry night sky above him. Across the water, the lights from a dozen other identical purpose-built mansions on a dozen other identical purpose-built islands twinkled and reflected on the still, inky sea. It felt good to have escaped from the party. The tension of the whole evening had been overwhelming, culminating in the near-miss with Lord Danbury. He barely allowed himself to consider what the consequences would have been if Danbury had really been suspicious.

He turned to the bodyguard driving the buggy. "Good bash, that, old boy."

The bodyguard remained expressionless, simply raising a questioning eyebrow at him.

"Bash?"

Quentin laughed nervously. "Party, old boy, party. Yes, it was a good night — one of the best."

"Mr Alexandrov knows how to treat his friends," said the bodyguard, resolutely staring ahead. There was a pause. "And he knows how to deal with his enemies."

Quentin cleared his throat, scared his voice would come out several octaves higher than usual. "And how would that be?"

The bodyguard fixed him with a steely gaze. "How would what be?"

Quentin laughed again. "Well, say, for example, Mr Alexandrov wasn't very happy with someone. Let's say someone in Dubai made him very angry. What might he do to show them how furious he really was?"

The bodyguard stared in front of him again. "Then he would give them a one-way ticket to Atlantis."

Quentin stared at him for a split second and patted him on the shoulder, chuckling. "Oh, come on," he said, gesturing across to the Dubai hotel and theme park. "Just across the water there?"

As they pulled up outside the guest house, the bodyguard brushed Quentin's hand from his shoulder unceremoniously. "No, not Atlantis Dubai," he said brusquely, his voice still expressionless, his face conveying his disgust at Quentin's perceived stupidity. "Atlantis *under the sea.*"

Quentin hurriedly hopped out of the buggy and scurried up the path, loath to look back over his shoulder at the glowering bodyguard.

It was time to regroup his restoration team and plan for delivery of the remainder of the paintings.

He mustn't allow anything to upset Sergei. Anything at all.

CHAPTER
TWENTY

"So this is what you would put into a box of treasures, is it, Maxy?" asked Lyric, fondly ruffling her godson's hair and surveying the pile of precious belongings that he'd deposited on the kitchen table in front of her. There was a marble, a couple of toffees, one of his ancient cuddle blankets (not his very favourite one, she noticed in amusement, but one that she guessed ranked pretty highly in his affections), and a picture he'd drawn of Mummy, Daddy, Kitty and Aunt Lyric.

"It's not just what you *would* deposit, is it, darling?" said Laura, giving Lyric a knowing look from where she was arranging flowers at the other end of the huge wooden table. A stream of pale winter sunshine flooded in through the Victorian bay window of Laura's Chelsea home, dispersing around Laura in refracted rays that resembled an aura, and creating a textbook picture of timeless domestic tranquillity. "It's what you *are* going to put into Aunt Lyric's memory box."

"For your lost-long brother, Aunt Lyric," said Max with the self-important lisp of a toddler, pushing the pile closer towards her. Lyric felt a lump appear in her throat and she looked up at Laura for confirmation.

"It's all right, he knows they'll be gone for ever," said Laura. "But I explained that you'd lost your version of Kitty when he was even littler than Kitty is now, and that you were creating a box of lovely things for him. He went off, collected all those things, and said he wants your brother to have them. Sweet, isn't it?"

Lyric nodded, lost for words. "Edward," she said quietly.

"I'm sorry?"

"Edward. Dad told me that's what they called my brother. Before they had him cremated."

Laura stopped what she was doing and smiled over at her friend. "It's a lovely name, and I'm sure he would have been a lovely brother, Lyric. And I think what you're doing is wonderful. I'm sure that wherever he is, whatever he's doing, Edward's spirit is looking down on you and feeling very touched by that gesture. Ouch — dammit!" Laura grabbed her finger irritably where she'd stabbed it with a rose thorn.

Lyric's brow wrinkled with concern. Laura had never been the most dextrous of women, but these days she was downright clumsy. It seemed to be one minor incident after another. Only a few days before she'd tripped on the stairs and sprained her ankle. It had been sheer fluke that she hadn't been carrying Kitty.

Lyric's frown deepened as she turned back to the letter she was attempting to write. "God, Laura, there's so much that I want to say — but I can't seem to find the words. I mean, how do you sum up thirty-odd years in one single letter?"

"Well, you don't have to write *everything* that's happened!" reasoned Laura, picking up the roses again, this time more tentatively. "Just write what you feel."

"I don't know how I feel," moaned Lyric. "I mean, I feel sad, but I feel weirdly happy too. I feel that I want him to know all the good stuff, but how can I put that in without the bad? Argh!"

Laura walked round the table and hugged her. "Maybe this is all too soon?" she suggested gently. "I mean, it's a big thing to get your head round. Maybe you should wait until it's all sunk in a bit more."

"No," said Lyric, shaking her head firmly. "It's not too soon. And you know what, it doesn't feel like such a big thing to get my head round. I mean, obviously it's a shock, but it kind of makes sense, you know? All those strange feelings I've had over the years, the unexplainable sense of loneliness I've often had — I know you thought I was a fruit loop at the time, but now it makes sense. All — well nearly all — the loose ends are tied up. Don't you see?"

Laura squeezed her shoulder and walked back round to her flower arranging, kicking a stray toy car out of her way with her foot en route. "What do you mean, *nearly* all the loose ends?"

"Oh, nothing," said Lyric, almost to herself. She had a feeling even Laura wouldn't understand her new theory — that her frequently twitchy eye was somehow connected to her twin brother. It always seemed to start when something bad was about to happen, after all — almost like a warning. It was as if she had a guardian angel looking over her. But it was her little secret —

hers and Edward's. And she had no intention of sharing it with anyone.

Suddenly, she perked up. *That* was what she wanted to talk about in her letter. Let the objects she was storing in the memory box do the talking about her life and the life Edward might have had — what she wanted to tell him about was the bond she still felt, even though he was long passed. Feeling encouraged, she put the unfinished letter to one side for later on, and instead turned her attention to the collection of treasures in front of her.

A shell from the beach in Bali. Her much-loved, threadbare Paddington Bear. A photo from every year of her life. Finding these, of course, had proved another matter entirely — Lyric's carefree approach to life meant she had previously had few sentimentalities and kept few souvenirs. And as she was having to keep everything secret from her mother and father so as not to upset them any more, she'd come a bit unstuck. Which was what had brought her here, to Laura's house. In complete contrast to Lyric, her friend was the most accomplished hoarder in the Northern Hemisphere, and Lyric had been sure she'd be able to fill the gaps in her birthday pictures. She'd been right, and they'd spent a riotous few hours this afternoon going through old photo albums and reminiscing.

"God, I really needed this afternoon, you know," said Laura, admiring her handiwork and carrying the vase of flowers over to the window. "What a laugh!"

Lyric couldn't help but notice Laura's hands shake slightly as she picked the vase up, but she decided not to mention it. Her friend had looked pinched and drawn when Lyric had arrived just after lunch, her bright eyes lacking their normal lustre. But now, three hours later, the spring was back in her step and there was colour in her cheeks, and Lyric had no intention of seeing it disappear again.

"Me too," said Lyric, thinking forlornly of Philippe, due to collect his things from her house this afternoon. She glanced at her watch. In fact, he'd probably already moved them out by now. She tried to push away the hollow feeling in the pit of her stomach and turned round to Laura, who was now busy tidying up the toys strewn across the stone-tiled floor.

"Why is it that nothing ever goes right all at once? I meet Ralph, I get messed up on drugs. I get off drugs, I lose my career anyway, I lose Ralph too."

"Hey!" said Laura warningly.

Lyric shook her head reassuringly. "Don't worry, I'm not about to start pining for Ralph. I came to my senses long ago about him. So then I fall out with Treeva — and I meet Philippe. I make up with Tree. I lose Philippe again. I find my brother. I lose my brother. It's just never-ending! Why can't life be plain sailing, at least for a week or so?!"

She looked across at Laura, expecting to see her smiling wryly. Instead, her friend was looking out of the window with a look of such sadness that Lyric jumped to her feet to hug her.

"Laura! Whatever's the matter with you?"

Laura turned to her, her eyes glassy with unshed tears. "Oh, nothing, Lyric — I was just thinking how right you are! Life is a bitch — and then you die." She nudged Lyric and they both burst out laughing, the melancholy of the past few moments dispelled. "Now, it's about time I was making the children's tea. Have you got everything you need for this memory box of yours?"

"Yes, I think so," said Lyric, taking the hint and gathering everything together. "Although it feels like I need something else to take it full circle. I mean, I took a copy of his birth certificate from Daddy's safe, so it feels like —" she gulped. "It feels like I should have the death certificate, too."

Laura nodded sagely. "Yes, I can see that. But how are you going to get that without asking your father?"

Lyric placed the lid on the Jimmy Choo boot box and looked up hesitantly. "Well. I did have one idea. I'm sure Jacob has a friend in the Home Office. The son of that hideous old lech Henry Mogler. What's his name now — Gideon? I'm sure I overheard Daddy saying Gideon got his father a job there recently, so he must still be there somewhere. I'll have to ask Jacob. Maybe, just maybe, he can help."

She tossed her wavy, honey-blonde hair off her shoulders, crossed her fingers and held them up in the air, the mischievous twinkle firmly back in her eyes.

Laura laughed. "As if anyone could refuse you anything, Lyric Charlton."

Lyric blew her nose and moved the sheet of paper to one side to let the ink dry. When she was a girl she'd loved writing letters, and had adopted little rituals: her favourite ink pen, some gorgeous writing paper, a crunchy apple. She'd done the same to write the letter to Edward and found it strangely comforting, and now, several hours after she'd first started, she had a neat, handwritten letter three pages long to place in the top of the box. Tears had smudged the ink in a couple of places, but other than that she was proud of what it contained: her deepest, innermost thoughts, hopes and dreams. The kinds of things she and Edward, she liked to think, would have talked about as children. The things that would have shaped their lives and their reactions to what happened to each other, the things that would have compounded their instinctive understanding of each other and made them truly two sides of a coin. But she'd also added her adult perspective on her life so far: what she'd hoped for and what fate had actually dealt her; her passions, her successes, her regrets. If, by any chance, Edward — wherever he was — didn't know her before, he'd sure as hell know her now, she thought as she placed the lid firmly back on the pen.

A coat hanging over the back of the chair caught her eye and made her stomach flip over. It was Philippe's. He must have forgotten it. She'd been so focused on writing her letter when she arrived back from Laura's, so equally focused on *not* noticing how empty the house felt without his things in it, that she hadn't seen it then. Lyric felt a hand close around her heart as she thought of Philippe leaving her life almost as soon as he'd entered it. Losing him was almost more than she could bear — especially tonight, after the emotional strains of the day.

She stretched and rubbed her eyes. It was only just nine o'clock, but she felt exhausted. Once upon a time she'd have dealt with the monumental turn of events of the past few days by going out and getting blotto. Now all she wanted to do was take a sleeping tablet and block out the world in the unconscious safety of sleep.

It felt as though she'd only been asleep for a matter of moments when she woke with a start. She sat bolt upright in bed, her sleeping tablet making the normally sharp edges of her mind foggy. What had woken her? There must have been a noise . . .

She pulled the duvet around her, her tiny silk négligée no match for the night chill. There it was again! A click, and then a rustle. Someone was downstairs . . .

Heart thumping loudly in her chest, Lyric felt on her bedside table for her mobile phone. It wasn't there. She racked her brains for where she'd last had it, and then remembered. At the dining room table, writing her letter. She'd probably left it under the memory box or something.

There was another thump from downstairs, and suddenly Lyric felt a wave of anger rise up inside her. How dare anyone break into her house! What right did they have to enter her space, her haven — her *home?* Pulling on a robe, she climbed out of bed and tiptoed out on to the landing and down the stairs. A step creaked underneath her weight and she flinched, expecting someone to rush up and grab her. She stood stock-still for over a minute, but there was nothing. She swallowed hard and berated herself for her quaking limbs. She was sure the intruder would be able to hear her beating heart, even if he couldn't hear her footsteps.

At the bottom of the stairs, Lyric stopped and listened hard. It had all gone quiet. She crept down the hall and spotted a chink of light escaping under the dining room door. The bloody cheek! Not only had someone broken in, but they had even used her electricity to light their way in and out! Angry again, Lyric sidled up to the door, grabbing the pole for the hall skylight as she went.

As she got closer, however, she felt some of her bravado desert her. Exactly what was she going to do, dressed in a silk négligée and robe, holding a wooden pole, if when she opened the door there was a band of robbers behind it?

She heard another noise and stiffened. Was that — was that a man *sobbing?* There was another loud sniff and what sounded like a muffled wail. Yep, she had definitely heard right . . .

Gaining courage, Lyric tiptoed forward and opened the door a crack. Her mouth fell open in surprise as she peered around it. There, sitting surrounded by the contents of Edward's memory box and reading her letter to him, was Philippe. Philippe, with tears streaming down his face.

"Philippe?"

Philippe looked up in surprise and an expression of guilt spread over his face. "Lyric!" He looked down at the memory box spread out all around him and shrugged helplessly. *"J'en suis désolé.* I meant only to glance at it, but your words — the things — they are so beautiful. I got lost in them."

Lyric stepped gingerly into the room and closed the door softly behind her.

"They were — they are — kind of private . . ."

Philippe's face closed up and he hurriedly replaced everything where he'd found it.

"I know. And I am sorry. It is none of my business."

Lyric put up a hand to stop him. "It's OK, Philippe. Until a couple of days ago, I shared everything with you. Planned to share everything with you for the rest of my life. I don't mind at all."

"No, but snooping around, reading things in secret — this is unforgivable," said Philippe, clearly ashamed of himself. "Again, I am sorry. I came to get my coat — I didn't want to wake you. I left my keys . . ."

They both turned as one to the occasional table where Philippe had left the spare key. Lyric felt a dull thud in her stomach. So this really was final.

"But Lyric?"

She turned back to Philippe and saw his big green eyes full of pain. Although his athletic frame towered above her, tonight he looked vulnerable and frailer than normal. Lyric wanted to reach out and hug him, but she steeled herself and held herself back. Philippe had said goodbye and meant it. It wasn't her right any more.

"Lyric, I'm also sorry for the way I behaved. For the way I have judged you, tried to enforce my opinions on

265

you. Reading your letter, I was reminded of how strong the real you is, how your soul is as beautiful as your face, as your body . . ." Philippe's voice caught on the last word and Lyric bit her lip, willing him not to start crying again. Once was very touching, admittedly, but she wasn't used to this Gallic outpouring of emotion and she wasn't absolutely sure she could handle another outburst.

"Lyric, do you still want me? Forgive me," he implored, grabbing her close to him. Lyric thought she was going to be lost for ever in the endless green oceans of his eyes. Her heart soared.

"Yes!" she sobbed into his chest, overcome with emotion.

Philippe pulled back and tipped her chin up so she was looking into his eyes again.

"Lyric Charlton, will you take me back?"

Lyric pushed him backwards on to the table and leapt on top of him, straddling his muscular torso. "I'll do more than that," she said, hair toppling sexily over one shoulder as she slipped her robe off. "I'll take you on the table, *mon cher*."

CHAPTER
TWENTY-ONE

"*'Tis the season to be jolly, fa la la la la, la la la laaaaaaaa!*"

At the keyboard, Lyric sang with the full force of her lungs as she led the family through yet another Christmas carol, joyously making out Philippe's tone-deaf drone amongst the more familiar — and more tuneful — voices of her mother and father and the dogs barking as they and various members of the estate staff clustered around the grand piano in the drawing room for their annual Boxing Day singsong. "Deck the Halls" had been her beloved grandfather's favourite. There was perhaps no time that Lyric missed her Pops more than at Christmas, and she always made sure they finished with this one in his memory.

It had been a bittersweet Christmas so far. As her first with Philippe, of course it had had been undeniably special — they had arrived at Broughton Hall on Christmas Eve, just in time for carols around the huge Christmas tree in the centre of the village. From then on, from the Charltons' traditional Christmas Eve dinner to the frosty walk to church yesterday morning and the table groaning with a lavish Christmas lunch in the afternoon, it had been a picture-perfect couple of days. It was also her first Christmas since rehab, and she was relishing how guilt-free the occasion was, the feeling of being at home, embracing her childlike enthusiasm for her family's long-held traditions — she'd left out a mince pie and brandy for Father Christmas and a carrot for Rudolph, and had been rewarded with a stocking by the fireplace on Christmas morning — and not wishing she was somewhere else, some*one* else.

The biggest surprise of the day had been when her father had presented her with an overwhelming gift to celebrate her sobriety and mark this new stage in her life — a racehorse! Lyric had been *almost* speechless at his generosity. "Is this a present to me, or to you?" she had quipped in response, well aware of her father's racing obsession.

Doppelganger was a sleek six-year-old bay gelding with a velvety nose and a warrior's heart, and Lyric had fallen in love at first sight as he clattered down the ramp of the horse box. Her father's trainer, Roger Skelton, had driven him over specially to meet his new mistress, and now he'd been returned to his new home at their yard near Aintree, Lyric was already looking forward to meeting him again.

But despite all the warmth, love and excitement, Lyric couldn't shake off the melancholy sense of "what if" that hung over every oh-so-familiar Christmas ritual. *What if* Edward was still here? *What if* he'd been at every Christmas celebration throughout her life? *What if* they'd been a family of four not three. She wouldn't have been an only child — how would things

268

have been then? All these thoughts and more, she realized, must have haunted her parents every Christmas throughout her life. And though this realization made her feel closer to her mother and father, the inability to share it with them made her feel disconnected from them, and the battle between the two conflicting emotions was affecting every moment now she was at home.

The carol came to an end, and Constance busied herself with refilling everyone's glasses. "Philippe — more mulled wine?" she called from the drinks cabinet as she fixed George another whisky. She'd spent the last few days trying to overfeed and overlubricate everyone whilst simultaneously avoiding touching anything herself — a classic feeder, Lyric had explained under her breath to Philippe on Christmas morning as Constance had insisted he have yet another glass of champagne before they began to open their presents.

"*Non, merci*, Constance — I've had more than enough," Philippe replied, strolling over to her. "But here, let me help you with those."

As he took the glasses from her and brought them over, Lyric thought her heart would burst with pride. Her parents had taken to Philippe instantly, and he to them. Not only that, he seemed totally at home at Broughton Hall. In fact, this was the first place she'd seen him where he didn't seem too tall! He was so suited to the countryside, with his love of horticulture, of the outdoors, and with his easy, relaxed manner, he slipped naturally into his surroundings.

Just then, there was a furious pounding at the door. Lyric, idly improvising on the piano, looked around her in surprise. Her mother, still fussing over the drinks cabinet, looked up, hand still hovering over the crystal whisky decanter, ready to replace the stopper. Her father, swilling his whisky around the tumbler, looked up in surprise.

"If that's Santa Claus, he's late," observed Philippe drily, and they all laughed, breaking the tension of the moment. But it was short-lived. The drawing room door opened and Jeffries appeared, looking uncharacteristically out of sorts.

"It's Master Jacob Charlton, sir," he said, addressing Lyric's father. "In a state of some distress."

He moved to one side and Jacob appeared. He was almost unrecognizable. His normally immaculate appearance was crumpled and dishevelled — his hair uncombed, his shirt creased and his face pale and wan.

Constance stepped forward in concern.

"Jacob, dear! Whatever is the matter?"

"It's all over, Aunt Constance," Jacob said, breaking into heaving sobs that racked his entire body. "I'm finished." He looked around the room wildly. "Finished!"

SEASON'S MEETINGS!
MORE STUFFING ANYONE?
DEEP IN CRISPIN NIELSON!
CHARLTON GETS A PINK CHRISTMAS
RISING TORY STAR IN GAY ROMP

270

The headlines were lurid and unforgiving, but they were as nothing compared with the editorials they led into. Tabloid, broadsheet and morning freebie — the nation's newspapers were, for once, agreed on the story of the day. Or, in all likelihood, the story for the next fortnight. To the newspapers stuck in the middle of the festive silly season, this scandal was nothing short of a gift-wrapped Christmas present with oversized bow on top.

Lyric, leaning forward on the sofa, looked in dismay at the front pages strewn across the coffee table in Broughton Hall's cosy sitting room. And they hadn't limited it to a cover-splash, either. The story had everything — sex, secrecy, politics, wealth, homosexuality — and each and every national had totally gone to town with it, scrapping their usual half-hearted coverage of Christmas lottery winners, abandoned kittens and central-heating deprived pensioners for pages and pages analysing the political scandal of the year and anyone remotely connected with it.

Lyric looked over at Jacob, sitting miserably in an armchair next to the fireplace gazing blindly into the roaring flames. Behind him, the Christmas tree that yesterday had sparkled with excitement and seasonal promise now looked flat and tatty. How had she not guessed? How had none of them worked it out? The fanatically conservative politics. The angry homophobia. The finicky metrosexuality. And the "perfect" girlfriends with the textbook Tory backgrounds and society connections that ticked every box apart from

271

personality and charisma. It was all a front for Jacob's own closeted gay sexuality.

But Crispin, of all people. Flamboyant, flighty, fabulously indiscreet — they say opposites attract, but this really did take the biscuit. Lyric tried to reject the thought that Crispin, with his omnipresent lust for self-publicity, might have somehow engineered this. Crispin, who had fled the country that morning to the convenient refuge of the superluxe St Tropez villa of Sir Malcolm Donahoe, legendary music producer and multibillionaire. Any excuse for a luxury holiday. But this was Crispin, Lyric reminded herself, her dear, dear, flaky friend Crispin. He was no Treeva. There was no malice in him. Forget Jacob for a moment — Crispin would never want to harm her or the Charlton name even inadvertently. She had to believe he was as innocent as Jacob in this.

Sensing her gaze, Jacob looked up at Lyric and smiled bitterly. "Guess it's my turn to bring shame on the family, eh? Good job there isn't any more of our generation in the family — I'm not sure the Charlton name could take it."

Lyric flinched at his outburst and bit her lip as she silently thought of Edward. *If only there was another one*, she thought to herself.

"Oh, come on, Jacob," said George, trying to sound matter-of-fact from his own armchair on the opposite side of the fireplace, where he was reading the *Daily Telegraph* sports section as if it were any normal day and the life and political aspirations of his only nephew hadn't just come crashing around his ears. The

272

Labrador lying over his feet sighed at the disturbance as George crossed his legs, then flopped back down on the remaining foot. He tried to make it sound light.

"It's not as if you've killed anyone. So you've had a bit of a fling with another chap. So what? I'll put in a few calls and your position will be restored, mark my words. I know just who to speak to, and it'll only be a matter of time before you're leading the back benches again. It'll all come out in the wash, as they say. Which is more —" he added ruefully, almost to himself — "than can be said for my Boxing Day shoot." A fox had wrought havoc in the woods and scattered all the game before the first drive of the morning, virtually ruining the day.

Jacob put his head in his hands. "It's going to take a hell of a lot longer than just 'time'," he groaned. "They not only caught Crispin leaving my flat three nights running, they've apparently got 'intimate' pictures of us *inside* the flat."

"Well, the privacy laws will stop those ever being printed, won't they?" Lyric pointed out, moving from the table to the floor to lean against Philippe's legs. "So don't waste precious energy worrying about that."

"That doesn't stop them appearing on the Internet," moaned Jacob, oblivious to her reasoning. "I want to die."

"Right, that's enough," said Constance, busying herself in true Blitz spirit by handing out slices of Christmas cake and cups of tea from the tray the maid had quietly brought in. "No talk of topping yourself on Boxing Day, please. Now, fruit cake or chocolate log,

Jacob?" Constance had always believed that food was the ultimate panacea in a family crisis.

The silence that followed was suddenly shattered by a clattering from the hall, followed by a loud shout.

"Where is he, then? I want to see my son. Take me to my boy, Jeffries!"

There was a collective sigh from Lyric, Constance and George at Quentin's familiar boorish tones. Jacob looked up fearfully as Quentin's heavy footsteps approached along the corridor.

"Jacob! What the hell is going on?" he boomed from the doorway, face redder than usual and greasy hair standing straight up in affront.

George sprang into action, walking across the room to his brother, arms outstretched appeasingly, but eyes hard and cold. *He'll never forgive Uncle Quentin for that verbal assault on me and Broughton Hall*, thought Lyric in surprise. She'd been so wrapped up in all the things going on in her own world — not to mention her conspiracy theories about what had driven Uncle Quentin's attempted coup — that she'd barely given a second thought to how her father was feeling about the whole matter. A naturally steadfast, unimpressionable character, her father's pride in his family and his heritage was absolute — it was his sole *raison d'être* — and any threat to this, especially from his own flesh and blood, must have rocked him to the very core. Yet still, here he was, outwardly welcoming his wayward brother back into the family home. Where did one develop that magnanimity and strength of character? Lyric wondered.

274

"Quentin, just calm down. Anger isn't going to solve anything," George said soothingly.

"Anger?" bellowed Quentin disbelievingly, pushing his arm out of the way irritably. "I find out at the same time as the rest of the world that my son is a raving queer, and you talk to me about *anger?*"

Jacob, cowering into his armchair, hid his head under his arms in the face of his father's fury.

"Now, now, dear, there's no need for that," said Constance matter-of-factly, walking over to Quentin and leading him to a chair set further back from the rest of the gathered family. "It could be worse. Imagine that!" But even Constance was at a loss to elaborate on what could possibly have been worse, so she brushed down her Margaret Howell slacks and smoothed a hand over her perfectly-coiffed bob. "Anyhow, Quentin, it's probably only a phase — most boys get it out of their systems at boarding school. Jacob's just left if for later. It'll pass, I'm sure."

There was a stunned silence from around the room. Quentin, for a moment, anyhow, seemed at a loss for words. He accepted the whisky Constance offered him and stared into it, his anger silently simmering.

"I'm sorry, Father," piped up Jacob, breaking the silence and making everyone jump.

As if remembering where he was and why, Quentin leapt up again, whisky sloshing over the side of his tumbler.

"Sorry? *SORRY?* Have you thought about the repercussions of this, boy?"

He paced over to his son and glowered at him. Jacob flinched and covered his head again, letting out what sounded suspiciously like a whimper.

George held out a restraining hand again, but Quentin would not be checked and continued his rant unheeded.

"Cowering out here like Lord Muck in the middle of nowhere!" he stormed. (Quentin seemed to have conveniently forgotten that the middle of nowhere was the place he had recently put up a significant fight to get his hands on.) "They're calling for your resignation, all those right-wing constituents you've spent the past few months wooing — that's when you've not been sniffing around those bloody shirt-lifters, that is!"

"Quentin, that's enough!" admonished George from across the room. But Quentin carried on heedlessly, lost in his own fury.

"This is going to point yet another unfavourable spotlight on the Charlton family. First a drug addict, and now a poofter! The papers will be muckraking for months — and not just here! Oh no," raged Quentin, warming to his theme. "It'll be headline news all over the world. It'll be 'the Charlton family, owners of Broughton Hall, multimillion-pound landowners this, landed gentry art collectors that . . .'" The thought seemed to spin Quentin even further out of control, and, spluttering, he stalked over to the bay window overlooking the drive, clearly so apoplectic he was lost for words.

Everyone in the room remained still and silent, unsure of what was coming next.

276

After a couple of moments, Quentin turned round. Lyric felt herself physically recoil from him and slid up on the sofa into the comfort of Philippe's arms. Quentin's features were twisted into something resembling a grotesque gargoyle. Amongst the emotions flashing across his face she recognized anger, disgust and — something else — fear?

He looked down at Jacob and spoke, his voice now low and laced with danger. "And have you thought about how your little friend Ali Hassan is going to feel about this?" he snarled. Jacob shrank as far into the chair as he could go. "How your best buddy, biggest investor and Muslim prince is going to react when he discovers his protégé is a . . . *fairy*?" He spat out the word.

Through her horror, Quentin's rant triggered a flicker of something in the back of Lyric's mind. Why was he so worried about Ali Hassan? Clearly, from his reaction to Jacob's predicament, the welfare of his only son was of little concern to Quentin. Uppermost in his list of priorities was his own selfish agenda. So what possible reason could he have for fearing Ali's reaction to Jacob's affair with Crispin?

Lyric thought back momentarily to his desperate bid for Broughton Hall, and his clear — and, from what she could work out, recent — dislike for her. There was more to Uncle Quentin than met the eye. He was up to something, she was sure of it. But what? And why did she have the nasty feeling that it was going to involve her?

CHAPTER
TWENTY-TWO

New Year

Lyric's eyes opened with a start. A chink of early-morning light was sneaking through a gap in the curtains, but the soft orange glow of a street lamp told her it was still early. Cosily wrapped in both the duvet and Philippe's burly arms, she had no desire to leave the safety of her snug cocoon. It was New Year's Eve — still officially Christmas week, a holiday after all — and she wasn't planning to get up any time soon. Yet something had woken her . . .

Then she heard the door buzzer, the insistent buzz of a second or even third attempt to get a response. She sighed resignedly and slipped out of bed, pulled on a thick towelling robe and her slippers, and padded downstairs, still bleary-eyed. She flinched as it buzzed again. She'd always been torn between not wanting to be rudely woken by her strident door bell and not wanting to miss out on whatever excitement might await her on the other side of the door, but it didn't make it any easier to take.

As she reached the door, the buzzer went again.

"Delivery for Miss Charlton!" called a voice on the other side.

278

"OK, OK, I'm coming!" she called.

As she opened the door, she just had time to take in an average-looking man wearing a Royal Mail uniform and holding an A4 package before her eyes were blinded by a succession of bright flashes. Panicking, she backed into the house and tried to slam the door.

"It's OK, Lyric, it's the *Sun*," said the man, swiftly placing a hard-booted foot into the doorway. As her eyes recovered, she realized the package was actually the type of hard-backed envelope used for sending pictures. "We just want to ask you about these photographs, Lyric. Is this you with your ex-lover Ralph Conway, Lyric? When was it taken, Lyric?"

Heart racing, Lyric slammed the door behind her, wrestling with the reporter's foot until the Yale lock clicked shut. She didn't need to look to know which photographs he was referring to. It had to be what she and Philippe, in an attempt to lighten the whole incident, now referred to as "Treeva's tit pics". She instantly felt that all-too familiar sense of being hunted. In a matter of seconds, she'd gone from being Lyric Charlton, contented girlfriend of Philippe Chappeau, back to Lyric Charlton, ex-drug addict and party animal. She leaned her whole body against the door, eyes shut, as if to barricade herself against that overwhelming sensation of fear.

When she opened them, Philippe was standing on the stairs in dressing gown and slippers, looking at her with undisguised amusement.

"Something wrong, *chérie?*"

At the sight of his innocent happiness, Lyric felt herself start to shake. Not again. Please, God, don't let anything upset their happiness again. She should have known. Ever since the papers had revealed Jacob and Crispin's affair, the knives had been out for their friends and family, and there had probably been a high value on anything they could make stick to fill column inches and shift papers.

Her voice wavered as she replied.

"The papers. They've got the pictures. Treeva's tit pics. They think they're me." The words sounded ridiculous, alien even — but Lyric knew their impact was about to become very, very real.

She looked up at Philippe nervously. Philippe blew out his cheeks and let out a long, long breath. He moved forward and enveloped her in his arms. Lyric felt she never wanted to escape their warmth and safety.

"Well, *chérie*, this was always going to happen," he said softly. "But this time, we deal with it together. *Oui?*" He detached himself so he could look at her properly, and tilted her chin up to him with his big, strong, powerful hands.

Lyric felt herself go weak with relief. "*Oui*, Philippe," she said quietly.

He drew her close and spoke over her head. "What you have to remember is that these pictures, they are not you, *non?*"

Lyric pulled away from him, anger making her strong again. "No — they're my so-called friend. And this is one time in my life I am not going to take the blame for her stupidity. Honestly, I can't believe she's even put

280

me in this position! It's been the same since we were little. What happens when the shit hits the fan? Lyric is too honest for her own good and sticks her neck on the line. Treeva is miraculously nowhere to be seen and Lyric has to take the flak!"

Philippe grimaced. "*Exactement*. And Treeva is a big girl now. Did she consider you when she took up with Ralph? *Non*. Did she for one minute think of the risk to you when those photographs were taken? *Non*. So, if they find out it is her, then it is up to her to deal with it herself. What you need to do is stop acting like the guilty party and show that you are offended. This is something Lyric Charlton would never demean herself by doing — and so it is something she will not demean herself by even considering. You understand? You must — how do you say — rise above it. There is no shame in denial, there is only shame in lying. And you and I, we have no secrets. There is nothing that the papers could possibly say that I don't know or that would make me doubt you. So, as long as you tell the truth, there is no problem."

Lyric's eyes stung with tears. He was right. And he was amazing. What had she done to deserve him? She kissed him passionately.

Then the door buzzer sounded again. Now, more than ever before, Lyric wished she hadn't resisted the installation of CCTV at her door. When she'd been using drugs, she had feared it would pick up the number of visits Anatole Funk and other unsavoury characters paid to her and the unsociable hours that they paid them. Now, however, she really could do with

281

having some warning as to who was at the door. She looked up at Philippe desperately.

He put a finger to his lips. "Don't answer," he whispered, ushering her up the stairs. "Go. Have a bath, get yourself dressed, and answer it when you feel ready. They won't be going anywhere. *Malheureusement!*"

Lyric peeled herself away from him reluctantly. She knew he was right. Blowing him a kiss she skipped up the stairs. "Make me a coffee though, babe!"

He grinned, nodded and ambled into the kitchen.

Twenty minutes later, Lyric bounded back down the stairs wearing a pair of midriff-baring sweat pants, strappy vest and bed socks. She hated wrapping up, and always had the thermostat at a piping-hot twenty-eight degrees. Consequently when it came to lounge-wear it was always summer. Her hair, still damp, hung around her shoulders in a heavy mane and her shower-fresh skin radiated happiness. A slick of tinted lip balm was the only make-up she wore. She was determined the papers were not going to get the better of her. Not only that, she was going to present to them the real Lyric Charlton, not the drug-addled Lyric Charlton they were hoping to find.

"I don't know if you've heard, but the door has been going non-stop," said Philippe through a mouthful of croissant. Lyric leaned across the granite breakfast bar and pinched the last piece from his hand. "I give it approximately two minutes —"

Before he could even finish his sentence, the buzzer sounded. Grabbing the cup of coffee he handed to her, Lyric took a gulp before backing out of the kitchen.

"Wish me luck," she said, holding up two sets of crossed fingers.

Out in the corridor, she suddenly felt scared. She wished she had the safety net of a manager to do all this kind of thing for her, but for some reason, inexplicable even to herself, she'd always shied away from that particular trapping of fame.

She took a deep breath before opening the door, then pasted on her most engaging, open smile. She wasn't going to let these turkeys get her down.

This time, a weaselly-looking man in wire-rimmed glasses, anorak and Hush Puppies was standing on her top step, his face only inches away from hers. Behind him, Kensington was starting to wake up, and the leafy Regency street was now alive with the hum of cars navigating the speed bumps and commuters bracing themselves against the early morning chill on their way to the bus stop or tube station.

The reporter's proximity jarred with the familiar scene and made Lyric feel edgy again.

"Lyric!" he said, addressing her with the familiarity of a good friend. "Dennis Patterson, *News International*. I wondered if you'd like to comment on some pictures which have surfaced overnight."

Lyric feigned surprise. "Well, yes, of course — but why do you think I'm going to be any help?"

The reporter produced the same envelope she'd seen earlier and pulled out the photographs. He studied her face for reaction, and Lyric steeled herself to remain expressionless.

"Is this you?" he asked bluntly. Lyric studied the black and white images with careful distaste. Finally, she laughed. To her ear, it sounded brittle and false — she just hoped it was enough to fool the reporter.

"Do you mean, is that my breast?"

The reporter ignored her attempt at a joke. "Is this you?" he repeated doggedly.

"Well, no, sadly — but I'd like to meet the cosmetic surgeon responsible," Lyric said pleasantly. She handed back the pictures more confidently than she felt. "He's done a good job. I've only got Mother Nature to thank for mine."

"But this *is* your ex-boyfriend, Ralph Conway," stated the reporter in a deadly monotone.

Lyric started to feel rattled. His direct approach was making her feel nervous. Why had she just not said "no comment" and had done with it?

"Well, yes, I suppose it could be," she stuttered. "But I couldn't possibly comment on who that is with him."

"So you do *know* who this is with him?" persisted the reporter, picking up on something in her tone.

Lyric began to feel claustrophobic, almost on the brink of a panic attack. "Look, I do not do drugs, these are not my breasts, I don't have silicone implants," she gabbled. "I'm not responsible for what my friends do."

"So this is one of your friends?" said the reporter, arching one eyebrow in interest.

Lyric narrowed her eyes at him. He was like a dog with a bone — but she was certainly not about to throw it in Treeva's direction. If anyone was to find out it was her friend in the pictures, it certainly wasn't going to be because of something she'd said. Think strategically, Lyric, she told herself. Get him back on your side. She smiled at him artfully. "Look, I might have made mistakes, but being a porn star isn't one of them. I've been a drug addict, but I'm not a soft-porn star!"

He looked at her, glasses blinking as they caught the light. There was a momentary pause, and then he smiled back at her.

"OK, Lyric, well, thanks for your time. Happy New Year!" With that, he backed off down the path, still smiling.

"Happy New Year!" she returned, puzzled. With all the drama, she'd forgotten it was New Year's Eve. And she couldn't believe she'd got rid of him that quickly. Buoyed by her success, she waved happily at the growing corps of photographers camped outside her door. There would be more attempts to incriminate her, she was sure, but if they were all as easy to get round as that one, then maybe it wasn't going to be so bad after all.

As she shut the door behind her, she found Philippe camped out on the stairs. She squeezed on to the step next to him and he kissed her softly on the lips.

"Well done, brave girl," he said. "Think that's done it?"

"Oh, for the next ten minutes," said Lyric lightly. "But I'm going to call Treeva. I know their kind. It won't be long before they work it out, and forewarned is forearmed, after all."

* * *

Just over an hour later, Lyric's phone sounded with a text alert from Treeva. *On way*, it said.

Come back route, responded Lyric, typing quickly, then dashed to the kitchen window to let Treeva in. She peered out into the grey morning light. There were no paps out here yet by the looks of it, but you could never be too sure. Good job she'd told Treeva to come in disguise.

But she groaned inwardly as her friend appeared through the gap in the fence. When she'd said "disguise", she'd imagined Treeva might choose some kind of old-lady get-up, or at least a long coat and baggy trousers — something inconspicuous. But no. Granted, Treeva had managed to completely cover up her face by virtue of a Michael Jackson-style hat-and-scarf combo. But underneath she was wearing a brightly coloured skin-tight Moschino jumper-dress, over-the-knee boots and a tiny cropped fluoro Puffa jacket. From the neck down, she looked like a reject from the *Pretty Woman* audition.

"Hi, Lyric," she panted, out of breath from her sprint across the garden. "Got here as soon as I could." She leaned over for an air kiss and Lyric recoiled at the smell of stale smoke and alcohol that enveloped her. Either she hadn't cleaned her teeth that morning or Treeva had been bang at it since dawn.

It got worse. As Treeva peeled off her scarf, Lyric tried not to react. Because of Christmas, it was now a few weeks since their last encounter, but from Treeva's appearance it could have been several years. Her skin was orange from too much fake tan — what you could see of it under her foundation. Her make-up was caked on so heavily that Lyric could almost see it crack as Treeva changed expression, and her hair was overly bleached and brittle. Her face was puffy and she looked, Lyric decided, like a transvestite. But, more worryingly, on the brink of a meltdown.

"Do you want something to drink?" asked Lyric, all at once feeling awkward. There was still so much unspoken between them that in a way it felt like having a stranger in the house. And Treeva's nervous disposition wasn't helping matters.

"Ooh, yes, I'll have a voddy," said Treeva automatically, walking through to the sitting room and sprawling on the sofa. "Neat, no ice."

Lyric quietly put down the coffee jug she'd picked up and searched in the cupboard for the Grey Goose instead. Hearing Treeva rummage around for a cigarette and spark up, she picked up an ashtray on her way out of the kitchen.

"So, what's the deal?" said Treeva, looking around her jumpily.

"It's OK, Tree, you can relax — Philippe has popped out," said Lyric, sensing her friend wasn't really in the mood for an introduction. She perched on the piano stool across the room from Treeva, watching her as if she were a particularly rare species on a wildlife programme. Treeva sat up and fidgeted with the zip on her left boot, smoking furiously. She looked like a Jack-in-the-box, ready to spring up at the slightest disturbance.

"Oh, OK," said Treeva absently. She stood up and squinted through the blind at the gathered press corps and then sat down again. "I can't believe the number of paps out there!" she said. Then she seemed to relax. "Jeez, I'm really sorry, Lyric. For everything."

She looked up at Lyric, then leaned across and stubbed out her cigarette, reaching automatically into the packet for another. An Embassy, Lyric noted privately. Treeva had obviously grown tired of Ralph's brand of cigarette — or he had grown tired of her. Lyric sat quietly, not knowing how to respond.

Treeva inhaled sharply. "Listen, you know I'm not with Ralph any more, don't you?" Lyric shrugged in response. Treeva smiled sheepishly, blowing smoke rings as she exhaled the smoke. "I dunno — I just wanted you to know that."

There was a long silence. Treeva studied the air around her and Lyric studied her hands. Neither seemed to know how to continue.

"He's broke now, you know, anyway," Treeva blurted out unnecessarily. "And anyway, he's crap in bed. In fact, he's a total shit."

"But wasn't that the appeal?" said Lyric innocently. She caught Treeva's eye momentarily, and they both inexplicably collapsed into giggles.

"Let's have another look at the pictures, then," said Treeva.

Lyric pulled out the contact sheet from a drawer. Treeva studied them thoughtfully.

"Wow, that was a great fake tan," she said finally. "Fake Bake, if memory serves . . ."

There was another silence as Lyric, stumped, wondered how best to respond. In the end, Treeva broke the heavy silence.

"Look, Lyric, I think I'm gonna have to own up to this," she said, lighting the umpteenth cigarette since she had arrived and nodding towards the pile. "This isn't gonna go away."

Lyric tried to console her. "But, Tree, you never know — they might not find out . . ." It sounded lame even to her ears.

"They will," stated Treeva matter-of-factly, taking a long pull on her cigarette and inhaling deeply. "And frankly, it's the least I can do."

Lyric looked at her in shock. "But — your career . . ."

"To hell with my 'career'. What career, anyway?" Treeva said. She looked away, and, despite her surprise, Lyric had a random and inappropriate urge to laugh out loud. Treeva had never been comfortable with deep-and-meaningfuls, and it seemed she wasn't going to change now.

Treeva cleared her throat uncomfortably and took another drag on her cigarette.

"My friendship with you is the most important thing I've ever had. I had a family and a friend and a sister all wrapped into one. No Ralph, no amount of cocaine, no amount of modelling jobs are ever going to make up for that. I fucked up, Lyric, and I want to make it better. OK?"

Her tone was harsh, but Lyric detected the admission of guilt — and profound apology — that she knew it was.

"OK," Lyric said slowly. "Well, as long as you know that I don't need you to do this for me. And as long as you're clear on what impact this could have on you. Take it from me, I know what it's like to be on the wrong side of the press!"

They smiled sadly at one another. Lyric looked closely at Treeva. *You never know*, she thought to herself. Like Lyric's own exposure, this admission might just end up being Treeva's saving grace. God knew something needed to happen to save her from the narcotic-fuelled hell she was drowning in. But Lyric's had been carefully and lovingly stage-managed by her family. Treeva was doing this off the cuff and flying solo. Who knew what the outcome would be?

"So," said Treeva, standing up and taking a deep breath. "I'm going out there now."

Lyric looked at her wide-eyed. "You're crazy!"

Treeva turned to her, something in her eyes willing Lyric to understand. And Lyric thought maybe she did — she wanted to get this over and done with. Now. It was the ultimate call for help.

But as she watched Treeva walk slowly to the front door and open it theatrically, striking a pose to the blaze of flashes, the scene was reminiscent of Butch Cassidy and the Sundance Kid walking out into a hail of bullets. She hoped against hope that Treeva came out of it a bit better than they had.

Then, Lyric heard the back window crash. She cried out in fright, expecting to see a rogue paparazzo, then relaxed as she saw Philippe clamber through, carrying a bag of supermarket groceries in one hand and the *Evening Standard* in the other.

"I couldn't get up the path because of that braying mob," he said grimly, throwing the paper down on the coffee table and sinking into the sofa. He looked up at her, green eyes despairing. "Looks like we have a whole new problem, *chérie*."

Lyric looked at it and gasped.

IT GIRL DENIES PORN-STAR PAST! screamed the front page, accompanied by a censored image of the most incriminating picture.

Lyric sank on to the floor in defeat. What a fool she'd been to think she'd got one over on the press. But in trying to maintain a good relationship with the reporters who were hunting her down, she'd made the classic mistake. She had denied something she had never even been accused of. She'd linked herself to the very thing she was trying to distance herself from. And opened a whole new can of worms in the process.

CHAPTER
TWENTY-THREE

"I'm off, *chérie*. Are you sure you're going to be OK doing this on your own?"

Lyric, curled up in one of her battered leather armchairs, looked up from the Welcome Pack she was reading as Philippe came into the sitting room to kiss her goodbye, and covered it secretly with her hand.

"Yes, yes — I think so. In a way, I feel like it's something I need to do on my own."

He nodded in understanding. "OK. Well, I'm only going to be in Muswell Hill if you need me. What's that?"

Lyric shook her head. "Nothing."

Philippe smiled and moved over as if to tickle her. "Oh, come on — you can tell me!" he teased.

"You tell me how you got your scar and I'll tell you what this is," said Lyric, smiling in spite of herself.

"Oh, I think you can do better than that," laughed Philippe, tickling her mercilessly till she squealed and moved her hand away from the pack.

"It's an information pack on Sunny Street hospital," she said catching her breath, suddenly guarded again. She was referring to the famous children's hospital that specialized in paediatric cancer care.

Philippe smiled at her patiently and she could tell she hadn't got away with it. "I can see that. But what's that got to do with you?"

Lyric looked up at him nervously. "Well, I'm trying to think what I can do with my life. I mean, since I've left rehab, it's been so mad — trying to get the media off my back, all that business with Uncle Quentin, falling out with Treeva, meeting you, and then the Jacob and Crispin scandal — that I haven't really thought about a job. I mean, it's not that I need the money, but I do need something to *do*. I'll never be a lady who lunches — well, not a very good one, anyway." They both smiled in agreement. "And I've got no intention of returning to It-dom. I'm probably past it anyway."

Philippe laughed and ruffled her hair fondly.

Lyric took a deep breath and pointed to the huge pile of fan mail spread out along the cushioned window seat that had arrived that week, supporting her after Porngate.

"I figure there must be some way of harnessing all that and doing something with it. So I think I'm going to get involved with a charity or two."

Philippe nodded encouragingly.

"But I mean *really* get involved — behind the scenes, not simply a celebrity patron," Lyric continued earnestly. "There must be lots that I can do as a normal person as well as someone famous — or should I say infamous," she added, smiling. "And, well, I love children, as you know. And Laura is always saying I have a way with Max and Kitty. So I thought I'd start off by doing some research into children's charities before I approach any of them. They used to call me a national treasure. Well, it's about time I put it to some use."

Philippe picked Lyric up in his strong, muscly gardener's arms and swung her round. "I think that's a wonderful idea, *chérie*," he said, hugging her to him.

"I want life to be more simple," Lyric said into Philippe's neck. "I want it to be about you and me and about people and work that we care about. Not about the press or gold-diggers or people trying to make a name on the back of our names."

"You are a wonderful woman, Lyric Charlton," said Philippe, letting her go and ushering her back to her seat. "But I am late for my appointment." He kissed her on the lips and left, winking at her before he closed the door behind him. "And again, *bonne chance!*"

Lyric sat down again, tying her thick honey-blonde hair away from her face, and reached for her pen and notebook. Good luck indeed. Today was the beginning of the rest of her life in more ways than one. The day she put her New Year's resolutions into action — and, for once, stuck to them. Not only had she promised herself that she would find an occupation, she had also decided to banish all the negatives, once and for all. And that meant finding out who had leaked Treeva's tit pics to the press.

With hindsight, she should have gone to the police over Anatole's amateur attempt to blackmail her, but at the time, she had honestly believed that he would be happy with the half a million she'd paid him, that he would stand by his word, had given her all existing copies and would disappear back into the world he'd come from. She had been so naive.

Moreover, she had forgotten how greed could be all-consuming. How once someone had more than a little, they would so often want a lot, lot more. And it seemed that Anatole was one of these people. But something in her told her it wasn't him who was behind the sale of the images to the papers. Anatole might be low-life, but she believed he had a shred of honour, and if he'd promised specifically not to do something, something told her he wouldn't have done it. Found a way around it, yes, but not done it himself. So, there was someone else involved — some*thing* else? — and her gut instinct told her it was something bigger than she or Philippe could handle on their own. So today Lyric was going to hand over the responsibility to someone else: to find a professional to discover exactly who was out to get her. And why.

Lyric doodled idly on her Smythson notepad as she considered how she'd made her next move. She'd contacted José, a guy from rehab, and son of the most powerful mafia don in Mexico, to ask him to recommend someone. (One of the plusses of her incarceration, she supposed, would be these random characters she would now take through life with her.) José had been sent to rehab because he'd slept with his father's maid, a beautiful local girl named Teresa. In time-honoured tradition, she had become pregnant with his child. They were in love, and she refused to give up the baby. She and José had both pleaded to be allowed to keep their child, but José's father had not

295

only denied them that right, he had extinguished their future entirely by having Teresa unceremoniously shot dead. Just like that. The death of his lover and his unborn baby had sent José, a lovely guy with a soft-as-butter heart, into a tailspin. He had found his salvation in drugs and had messed up his life. Eventually, he had been sent away to rehab. He and Lyric had arrived and left rehab on the same day, and via this odd bond, he'd told her emphatically to contact him if she ever needed help. She'd agreed, happy to stay in touch, privately unable to think of anything urgent she might need José for in the future. But sooner than she could have believed possible, a reason had presented itself. Money was no object, after all, and this was too important to throw just anyone at. José was her man, and it appeared José had indeed delivered.

And wow, José was good. Rehab seemed a world away to Lyric already, but it appeared their briefest of encounters and shared journey to sobriety were all it had taken to spur José into action. Or was it his mob upbringing? Lyric couldn't be sure. All she knew was that within a few hours of knowing that Lyric was somehow in trouble and needed to find out who was behind it, José had sent her the name, number and résumé of a man in the UK who owed him. On reading it, Lyric had allowed herself to relax slightly. The candidate was ex-secret service, highly experienced in all areas of spying and detective work. He was also highly trained in both combat and martial arts. And, what's more, this guy, she knew, wasn't even in it just for the money — he was already a billionaire from having worked as a bodyguard for some of the most powerful men in the world, and, at some point or other, nearly every famous person in the world as well. Nope, this man wasn't in it for the cash — he was up for the *challenge*. And that was what Lyric knew was going to get her the results she was after.

So this morning, finally, she was due to meet him. But, as she sat tensely chewing on the end of her Mont Blanc pen, she realized there was a big difference between finding a private investigator and actually briefing one. What the hell was she going to say to him? "I think someone's out to get me, sir, but I don't know who they are or why they're after me." How was that going to get him the leads he needed? He might not even believe her — or, worse still, he'd laugh at her, take the commission and fob her off about what he was doing and the progress he was making.

There was a noise as the door buzzer sounded. Lyric wiped her suddenly clammy hands down the sides of her jogging bottoms. Come on, Lyric Charlton, this is the biggest step you could possibly take in bringing some peace to your life, she told herself. *Or you're going to make things even worse for yourself*, whispered another little voice inside her. She shrugged off her doubts. Whoever it was who was after her, whatever it was they wanted, she was better off knowing and dealing with it. Whatever the consequences.

She opened the door, and her heart sank in disappointment. In front of her stood a nondescript man of about five foot nine inches — stocky, with crinkly laugh lines and a five o'clock shadow of stubble

297

across his jaw. The gas man. He was wearing a boiler suit — the archetypal service bloke, in fact. Of all the times! Showing his ID badge efficiently, the man smiled confidently.

"Come to read your gas meter, madam."

Lyric stared at him in dismay. She couldn't brief a PI when there was a gas man in the house! She had to get rid of him, and quick.

"Erm — I'm sorry. Could you come back another time?" she said hesitantly. "It's just — erm — right now isn't so great for me . . ."

The man held out his hand politely as if to ask Lyric to move aside for him. "It won't take a minute, madam," he said firmly, and walked past her into the house.

Open-mouthed with shock, Lyric stood stock-still, watching as he walked through the hall and turned, indicating that she should shut the door. She did so speechlessly.

"It's — it's through there," she stammered eventually, indicating the kitchen.

As she watched, the gas man put down his clipboard and briefcase on the seagrass-covered floor and peeled off his boiler suit to reveal a smart dark grey suit underneath. Now, the five o'clock shadow was less harassed service man and more "business man on the tube". If James Bond travelled on the tube, that is.

Lyric was aware she was gaping at him, but somehow she couldn't pull herself together and close her mouth.

"Your PI, Miss Charlton. We had an appointment."

298

Lyric's shoulders sank with relief and she wanted to clap for joy. The private investigator. He'd managed to fool even her — and she had been expecting him! He was perfect. He looked like no one, but, she was aware from his CV, knew everyone. And from his credentials, she knew that this nondescript appearance hid a brain like a chess board, the mind of a computer-geek genius and the stealth tactics of a ninja.

She smiled, a wide, infectious, joyous smile. She was safe. He would find her pursuers. And he would know how to deal with them. She had no doubt of that.

Much later, Lyric and Philippe were wrapped up together on the sofa, watching a rerun of *Die Hard*. One of Lyric's all-time favourite films, she'd been outraged to discover Philippe had never seen any of the series of action movies, and was now revelling in observing his reaction as he watched it for the first time. Philippe, for his part, seemed unimpressed — bored, even — and was using the opportunity to question Lyric more about the PI.

"So, did he look like that?" said Philippe, pointing at the film's baddie.

"No!" said Lyric, laughing in spite of herself. "I've told you, he was very nondescript. Very everyman. Now watch!"

"I just want to know what he looks like in case I come across him on the corner of the street," said Philippe, eyes twinkling. "Doing surveillance or whatever it is they do."

"So what — if you did, you'd stop and have a chat, would you?" replied Lyric, laughing at Philippe's *Boy's Own* inquisitiveness. "That would certainly blow his cover."

"Or did he look like *that?*" persisted Philippe, pointing now at Bruce Willis on the TV screen.

"Philippe!" said Lyric in mock exasperation. "If he'd looked like Bruce Willis in *Die Hard*, I'd have said 'he looks like Bruce Willis in *Die Hard*'. For the fifteenth time, will you please watch — or shall we turn it off?"

"Let's turn it off," said Philippe, unbuttoning her jersey top and nuzzling into her cleavage. "You're turning me on!"

Lyric giggled as he rolled on top of her and gave up her struggle to get Philippe to concentrate on the film. He might be fascinated by the machinations of her private investigator, but 1980s action films were clearly not his thing. She kissed him back, long and hard. This certainly beat a movie rerun . . .

All of a sudden, the door buzzer sounded insistently. Lyric pulled away from Philippe and frowned at him. "You didn't order a takeaway, did you?"

Philippe shook his head, unconcerned. "*Non, chérie.* It's probably another newspaper. What have you been up to today in my absence, Lyric Charlton?" He kissed her neck and moved down towards her breasts again. The door sounded a second time. Reluctantly, Lyric pushed him away.

"I'm sorry, babe, I'm going to have to find out who it is," she said softly. "I won't be able to relax if I think

300

there's another scoop about to hit the headlines — although God knows what it might be . . ."

Adjusting her top, Lyric hurried along to the front door. Putting the chain across, she opened the door a crack. Her heart sank as she saw a pizza delivery man standing there, peaked cap pulled down over his eyes. Classic tabloid doorstepping, she thought — but what on earth could they have on her this time?

"Hello," she said nervously, careful not to show her face around the door for fear there were photographers lurking there. "Can I help?"

"Pizza!" said the delivery man brightly, not looking up at her.

By now, Lyric was on red alert. Unsure whether to call Philippe or shut the door on this man altogether, she hesitated a moment.

"Pizza delivery . . . ordered by José," said the man, lifting his cap slightly. Under the peak, Lyric could make out the features of the PI she'd only said goodbye to a few hours earlier. She gasped. Lyric's heart started to race now — what on earth could have brought him back so quickly?

Hurriedly, she unhooked the chain and let him in.

"I'm sorry to intrude, Miss Charlton, but I have some news I felt could not wait," he said, placing his delivery bag on the floor and, turning it inside out, converting it into a briefcase.

She stared at him, open-mouthed. "Already? But . . . I'll call my boyfriend."

The PI put up a cautionary hand. "No. If you please — the fewer people who know of me, the better."

Lyric shook her head firmly. "I'm sorry, but I must share this with one person — and that person is my boyfriend." She tipped her chin up and raised her voice slightly. "Philippe!"

After a moment, Philippe loped into the hall, looking the PI up and down with undisguised interest.

"Pizza?" Philippe said questioningly.

"No, Philippe — this is the PI," explained Lyric, seeing his eyes light up as he took a second, more curious look at the man. "He says he has turned up something — already!" She turned to the PI, who had now removed his cap and was pulling some papers from his case.

"So what do you have?"

The PI spread out a series of papers on the hall table, some of them phone bills, and others covered with lines of closely written type that looked like transcripts of conversation.

"Well, Miss Charlton, I have no concrete answers for you — yet," he said haltingly.

Lyric gave a nervous, hiccupy laugh. "I only briefed you a matter of hours ago — I'd be surprised if you did!" she exclaimed.

The PI looked at her kindly. "But what I do have is a hot lead. And as your employee, it is my duty to keep you informed of these leads — especially when the persons involved are known to you — so you, in turn, can keep your wits about you where the suspect is concerned."

"Known to me?" said Lyric fearfully, clutching hold of Philippe's arm. "You mean . . . ?"

302

The PI nodded gravely. "Yes. This lead . . . Let me explain. I have, today, investigated all of Anatole Funk's known cohorts, and some of those less well known." He indicated the phone bills and the transcripts and paused, waiting for Lyric's go-ahead to continue. She nodded silently.

"It seems, Miss Charlton, that Anatole is known to your uncle — a Mr Quentin Charlton."

Lyric's mouth dropped open in shock. "Uncle Quentin?"

The PI nodded again. "Yes, Miss Charlton. I'm sorry, but it seems Mr Charlton has been dabbling in some form of drug deal with Mr Funk." He held his hand up to silence Lyric's questions before she had time to pose them. "Of this, I will know more later. But as far as the wider matter is concerned, it seems your uncle is somehow involved. I suspect he may have been the one who fed the offending pictures to the press." He held up a cautionary hand. "But I have no evidence for this — it is more of a hunch. I do, however, Miss Charlton, advise caution where your uncle is concerned. I will report back as soon as my investigations progress further."

With that, the PI closed up his briefcase, turned it back into a pizza delivery bag and was gone.

Lyric turned and looked at Philippe, shocked into silence. He squeezed her hand reassuringly.

"*Zut alors!*" he said quietly.

"I knew it!" said Lyric, startled out of her shock by anger. "I knew Uncle Quentin had it in for me! All that fuss about my drug addiction — and feeding the tabloids those pictures — he's just trying to discredit me so he can get his hands on Broughton Hall. No wonder he was so pissed off when Jacob ended up in the press instead of me! We'll see how he feels when it's his name plastered all over the papers as a drug dealer!"

"Woah, woah, woah," said Philippe, grabbing both Lyric's shoulders and looking directly into her eyes. "*Arrête!* Just hold on a minute. This is getting too big for you to deal with — too big for *either* of us to deal with. From what it sounds like, your uncle isn't just some crazy relative trying to discredit you in some kind of amateur way. So he's involved in the drug world too? This could run much deeper than either of us thinks. We need to speak to your father, and then maybe the police."

Lyric's big, soulful brown eyes looked up at him balefully through stray wisps of honey-coloured hair. "Philippe, you don't understand. Where my father and Uncle Quentin are concerned, it's so complicated . . ."

She sighed deeply, unwilling to rake over old family history, but needing him to understand why it was necessary — imperative — that she do this on her own.

"My father has always felt some unexplainable guilt over inheriting Broughton Hall. Despite the fact that Quentin was left pretty wealthy himself and simply frittered it all away, he's always felt like he has to look after him, make it up to him. And he's always been pretty blind to all his faults, too. In fact, we all have," she added wonderingly.

She paused a moment, thinking back over years of family get-togethers. Uncle Quentin had always been odd, but they'd put it down to good old English eccentricity. How much of Uncle Quentin's so-called eccentricities were actually clever cover-ups for his inherent evil? She pulled away from Philippe, hugging her arms around herself tightly.

"There's no point going to Daddy — or the police, for that matter — until we have concrete evidence of what Uncle Quentin has done, and how. Until then, let's leave it to the PI. That's what I'm paying him for, after all." She looked at Philippe again, willing him to understand. "I'll just have to keep my wits about me."

Philippe shook his head slowly, half in disbelief, half in reluctant admiration.

"You worry me, Lyric Charlton," he said. "What have I let myself in for? It was only this morning you were planning your new, quiet life. And now here we are, planning a life of subterfuge and second-guessing until we can safely accuse your uncle of plotting your public downfall and the redistribution of the family fortune."

He gazed at her wonderingly for what seemed like hours. Finally, he held his hand out.

"Come on, we've got work to do."

Lyric, idly flicking through the phone bills on the table, frowned. "Work?"

"The film," said Philippe, eyes dancing, walking backwards towards the living room and pulling her with him. "The film. I think we'd better rewind and make notes. We sleuths might need some of Bruce's tips in the days to come."

CHAPTER
TWENTY-FOUR

"Yoo-hoo! Huey!"

Treeva's straight-out-of-the-bottle golden tan shimmered in the Californian winter sunshine as her pneumatic body modelled a new purple D&G cut-out swimming costume. She sashayed around the kidney-shaped pool, stirring her vivid tequila sunrise coquettishly with a twirly pink straw, looking cool and cheekily sexy.

At least, that's how she imagined the effect to be. The reality was more Pamela Anderson on acid as she tottered around unsteadily on her vertiginous heels, full-on make-up sweating slightly in the sun, too-small swimming costume cutting into her cosmetically enhanced curves unattractively. Her body, ravaged from drink and drug abuse, looked like a bag of bones in comparison with her previous sporty curves, and her skin was also lumpy and swollen after her recent booster course of surgery.

Almost the first thing Treeva had done when she'd set down in LA — after employing the services of an agent, of course — was to drive her 4×4 across town to Frederick's. On the advice of her agent, of course. Frederick's was an Aladdin's Cave of sexy gear where the hookers from the Strip went for their stilettos, and she'd splurged on the highest, pointiest, most outlandish pairs she could find. The perfect foil for showcasing her endless legs, she'd thought, ignoring the fact that most normal Californians spent every waking hour in flip-flops. The fact was, Treeva wasn't here to mix with normal people. She was here to *make it big*. And as far as she was concerned, *making it big* started and ended with *the right look*.

"Hey, Treeva!" Hugh Lovett, her new agent, bounded around the corner, a silver fox in Diadora T-shirt, denim shorts and trainers with white sports socks pulled up to mid-calf. He carried a weekend bag slung over one shoulder and clutched a holdall in the other. He stopped and saluted Treeva deferentially with his free hand.

"Huey, that's not much luggage!" she cooed. "You can't have brought much more than a clean pair of pants!"

"There isn't much call for pants in LA," said Huey, air-kissing her elaborately. "It's too warm."

Treeva took off her oversized sunglasses and stared at him, puzzled. "Huey?"

He looked back, perplexed at her confusion. Then, as realization dawned, they broke into simultaneous laughter.

"Oh, you mean trousers!" roared Treeva. She laughed shrilly at their mutual misunderstanding. "Oh, Huey, how funny."

They both trailed off, and Treeva took a noisy slurp of her drink, sniffing loudly. There was a moment's uncomfortable silence before Huey picked up his bags again.

"Well then, I'll just . . ."

"Oh, yes, Huey, I almost forgot," babbled Treeva, remembering her self-imposed role as hostess. "Do take them in. Make yourself at home!"

Huey smiled gratefully and bounced through the open door of the pool house.

Treeva plopped down on the sunbed next to an oversized palm tree and gazed around her as she waited for Hugh to reappear. Who'd have thought it? Only a couple of weeks ago, she'd been staring down the barrel of national humiliation as the tit pics had been made public and she'd decided to fess up. The press had, predictably, gone to town. Like Lyric, who had been dropped from all her campaigns and ripped apart in the papers when the story that she was using cocaine had broken last year, Treeva had been publicly lambasted, mocked for her spoilt lifestyle and hung out to dry by the nation's columnists for her lavish lifestyle. But unlike Lyric, her coverage had contained none of the warmth, the undertone of forgiveness, that had softened the edges of her friend's column inches. Instead, Treeva had been turned into a national hate figure, pilloried at every turn. And despite her impressive and influential contacts, she'd been dropped from her VJ job. Treeva's future in her home country, let alone her career in the public eye, looked doomed.

That was before, she thought, almost clapping in delighted excitement, she'd come up with her latest fabulous idea. Daddy had given her a clear choice —

rehab or spiritual enlightenment (anything to get her out of the country) — and, desperate to avoid any kind of deprivation treatment, she'd racked her brains for an alternative.

And there, aimlessly flicking through some late-night satellite shows in her flat one night, she'd found it. Right there, in between *Girls of the Playboy Mansion* reruns and the latest, seemingly never-ending series of *Dog the Bounty Hunter*. At least, it hadn't *been* there exactly — but that was the point. It was something that *should* have been there. The answer to all her woes. Treeva Sinclair's own reality TV show.

The following few days had been a blur. Of course, striking while the iron was hot had been key, and her father's people had leapt into action behind the scenes to find her somewhere to live out here and support her plans. Meanwhile, Treeva had done a 180-degree turnaround on the way she dealt with her public confession. Instead of hiding away, she'd emerged into the spotlight to greet the press and to maximize every single second of her new-found notoriety. Z-list film premieres, product launches, photo calls — she embraced them all, ready with a revealing outfit and a saucy sound bite whenever the press were present.

Daddy had gone for it, of course, and he'd found her a pretty Spanish hacienda in the Hollywood Hills. (Privately, she'd have preferred a condo closer to Sunset Boulevard, but Daddy was paying and he thought she'd be safer up here.) They'd had to do a few renovations before she could move in, of course — like plastering over the Moorish-style frescos in the courtyard (they'd given Treeva a headache every time she'd looked at them), knocking down the original exposed brick fireplace in order to fit in the 32-inch plasma screen, and pulling up the terracotta-tiled patio to accommodate a full-sized hot tub. But now she was here, in her brand-new LA home, with a brand-new agent and — soon — a brand-new career to boot!

"Well, there we go — all pretty much shipshape," said Hugh from behind her as he came out of the pool house. "You know, it really shouldn't be for much more than a week or two . . ."

"Oh, hush, Huey," trilled Treeva, holding out her glass to him. "You're welcome to stay for as long as you want. Now fill mine up, and make yourself one too."

As Hugh trotted obediently over to the poolside bar to fix more cocktails, Treeva settled back contentedly. It was all serendipity, really. Huey was the perfect agent for the perfect career direction at the perfect time. His client list was made up of glamorous, high-maintenance, good-time girls — just like her! The only difference was that they all had the kind of high profile she enjoyed in the UK, only in the States. There was Bunty Schiffer, the Playboy Bunny who had never actually slept with Hugh Hefner. There was Lindy Grant, the underwear model who'd landed a six-figure deal with a bra manufacturer who promptly went bust. Treeva got endless mileage from that pun. (Lindy had famously never collected her fee — but Huey had hinted that the publicity he had managed to squeeze out of the situation had made up her shortfall several times over since.) And finally there was Heather

Chubb, the reality TV star who had got voted off her sorority show because her acting was too bad. All of them had faced extenuating circumstances in their career, but now all of them were a firm fixture on the party scene and often featured in America's weekly gossip magazines. Heather had even starred in a "What was she thinking?" fashion slot, which was a sure sign of *making it big*, wasn't it?

And to Treeva it seemed that dear Huey had been there for her almost from the moment she'd landed — just when she'd needed him most. It was almost as though he'd been waiting for her! So she'd paid Huey the advance he'd demanded for her membership to what he called "his girls" (Daddy had said he was in the wrong business when she'd told him how much it was), and Huey had promised her fame and fortune. With a twenty-five per cent commission fee, naturally. And sure enough, karma had ensured that when he'd needed Treeva, she'd been able to return the favour. Huey's landlord, a disagreeable fellow by the sounds of it, had reneged on their tenancy deal and had evicted him. Poor Huey had had to take up residency at the Chateau Marmont, but had hated the lack of privacy — so Treeva had stepped in and offered the use of her spacious pool house for as long as he needed it.

"So, you ready for your close-up?" grinned Hugh with a flash of gold tooth as he returned with their drinks.

Treeva giggled. "As ready as I'll ever be!" she trilled. "When is the first one arriving?"

Hugh looked at his Rolex, glittering ostentatiously on his wrist. "Well, honey, I reckon we've just got enough time to sink these drinks and pour ourselves another two before we have to get down to business," he said, settling down on the sunbed next to her and taking off his shirt.

Treeva sat up expectantly. "Do I look all right?"

"You look beautiful, honey."

Treeva nodded happily and rearranged her newly enhanced breasts, protecting their modesty from the frequent slippage of her minimal swimming costume. Then, she touched her face gently. The Botox and fillers she'd spent all of last week having hadn't been strictly necessary, but you only got one shot to *make it big*, and so she'd thrown everything she could at it. Subsequently her face was still tender, and, underneath the caked-on foundation, red raw — but she was hoping the TV people they were meeting today could see past her current state of repair to the all-natural, wholesome Treeva underneath.

"Good — because today is the most important day of the rest of my life!" she said brightly, her inflated lips giving her smile a slightly *Thriller* video-esque air. "I'm going to make it, aren't I, Huey?"

"Sure you are, honey," Hugh said, oozing insincerity. "One whiff of that cute-as-a-button English accent, and they'll be putty in our hands."

Treeva sat back, satisfied with his response. "And the rest!" she squealed excitedly. "My breeding, my background, my looks — I've got it all going for me, haven't I, Huey?"

"Yes, honey, you sure have," he agreed, smiling, and leaned over to give her knee a squeeze.

"So with my talent and your contacts, we can't help but succeed, can we, Huey?" she continued, repeating parrot fashion the spiel that he'd first seduced her with.

"That's right, honey," he said with a smile.

Treeva leaned forward again. These days, she had trouble sitting still for a matter of seconds on a boring day, let alone on the day she was going to be presenting her wares to a succession of eager-beaver production companies.

"Tell me again, Huey, who we're meeting with," she urged. "I can barely contain myself!"

Huey smiled indulgently.

"Well, honey, we're hitting the majorest players in the market today," he said proudly. "We've got an audition with a production company doing a new poker game for Challenge TV — they need a co-presenter — and we're meeting a couple of directors. Not sure that you'd have seen anything they've done, but they've got some stuff in the pipeline that would give you great, ahem, exposure . . ."

"And tell me again who our first meeting is with," breathed Treeva restlessly. It was this one she was most excited about.

"Well, it's with a production company called 'Under Radar'," said Hugh reverently. "They are the team behind *Deadbeat, Downtown* and *Reality Shockers*. They have mooted the idea for a reality TV show — of which you would be the star, of course — called *One*

Brit Wonder. It sounds like it would essentially be following you around as you hit the LA dating scene. *An Englishwoman in LA*, that kind of thing."

"It sounds ama-azing," breathed Treeva.

"In fact, that sounds like them now!" said Huey, jumping up from his sunbed as a car horn sounded loudly on the street outside.

Five minutes later, Pete, a twenty-something guy in Kangol cap, oversized Nike high-tops and baseball jacket, and Jeff, an old man in grimy white T-shirt, leather biker jacket, stonewashed tapered jeans and Cuban heels, were positioned on one side of the pool dining table shaded by an oversized parasol. Hugh and Treeva sat on the other, blinking as they soaked up the sunshine.

"So, we loved your show reel," said biker-jacket Jeff to Treeva with a leering smile.

"Well, she's had a lot of experience," said Hugh with a knowing look.

"And, of course, we know all about your latest adventures, you naughty girl," put in Kangol-cap Pete with an even seedier leer.

Treeva recrossed her legs nervously. "That won't stand against me, will it?" she said worriedly.

Hugh patted her knee reassuringly. "I'm sure it won't," he said.

"No, no," put in Jeff smoothly. "In fact, as far as we're concerned, it's a bonus."

"Because of the profile it's given you," put in Hugh hurriedly, smiling at Treeva paternally.

314

"So, really we just wanted to meet you and take a few shots ourselves," interjected Pete, producing a camera. "May we?"

"Sure," said Treeva happily. This was her moment. "Where do you want me?"

"It's not where, so much as how!" said Pete, laughing. Then, seeing Treeva's dismay, "I'm only joking. How about you lie over there on that sunbed?"

Treeva tottered over to her sunbed and affected a series of increasingly provocative poses as Pete snapped away.

"Gorgeous, baby, gorgeous," he crooned. "And just spread those lovely legs a bit more — yeah, baby, work it — and there — and maybe a few without your bikini top?"

There was an instant silence, as if a needle had been dragged across a record, and Treeva sat up as if she'd been shot. She was prepared for sexy, yes, but this wasn't what she'd had in mind! She looked over at her agent, who was cracking into his third cocktail with Jeff at the table.

"Huey? Is that really necessary?"

Hugh bounded over. "Heyyyy, Treeva, honey! There's no problem here!"

He looked over at Pete, who was frowning crossly on the other side of the sunbed. "They do things a little differently over in England," he said.

Turning back to Treeva, he squeezed her shoulder.

"Treeva, honey, I thought I'd explained. If you want to get on in this town, you'll need to lose

315

those   inhibitions. They've all been there, you know
— Paris Hilton, Lindsay Lohan. It's all out there!
We're gonna make you a star. Trust me!"

CHAPTER
TWENTY-FIVE

"Bring me my papers. And Ahmed — where is he? It is time for my morning briefing."

Ali Hassan walked out of his private spinning class, platinum water bottle in hand, wiping a stray bead of sweat away from his forehead with the Egyptian cotton sports towel hung around his tanned neck. He was flanked, as always, by two ex-SAS bodyguards dressed all in black, rifles permanently cocked. As he marched purposefully along the palace corridor like some Middle Eastern Pied Piper, aides dashed one after the other out of rooms along the way and joined the animated throng behind him.

Ali's palace was a sprawling mini-kingdom deluxe and it looked as if everything in it had been brought by the three wise men and then double-dipped in gold. Its luxurious decor glittered under the layers of gold leaf — the sumptuous silk lining the walls, the velvets and satins covering banquettes, daybeds and chaises longues, the finest Persian rugs scattered over the highly polished floors all reflected the precious metal's warm, yellow hue. It contrasted starkly with the reigning yellows outside the palace — the dusty ochre of the poverty-stricken desert city beyond the palace gates; the dirty yellow of the scruffy camels lined up outside the palace walls; even the haunted faces of the beggar children roaming the ramshackle slums.

Not that any of this concerned Ali Hassan as he strode purposefully into his morning office. The room, shaded from the harsh glare of the January sun by gentle silken drapes hanging over every window, and ventilated by enormous fans on the ceiling, felt cool and airy. At various posts around the room exotic-looking women lay dressed from head to toe in brightly coloured flowing silk gowns and headdresses. Their beauty was such that they looked like bright jewels glowing softly until Ali's attentions lit their inner sparkle and they glittered brilliantly. As Ali entered they all stood, heads bowed, in acknowledgement of their boss and leader.

Ali ignored them all, stalking masterfully past and taking a seat instead on the biggest daybed in the centre of the room. Immediately the two women closest to him positioned themselves at his side, one stroking his head, the other his right hand.

Ali clicked his fingers and his entourage of aides retreated respectfully to the sides of the room. There was a click, and all heads turned to see Ahmed the bodyguard standing to attention in the doorway.

Ali held out his arms to his friend and protector.

"Ahmed! My friend. Come, come — tell me all the news of those crazy English and their bizarre little lives. How, for example, is my dear friend Jacob?"

318

Ahmed moved forward and stood to attention in front of Ali, then relaxed at ease. "Sir, I have grave news of your friend Jacob Charlton," he said seriously.

Ali leaned forward in concern. "Grave news? What of it, Ahmed? Speak! Is he ill? Injured? *Dead?*"

Ahmed moved backwards almost imperceptibly, as if to move further out of his boss's range. "No, sir. It is much worse. He is *gay.*"

There was a stunned silence as Ali stared at Ahmed in shock. The aides and Ali's women sat tensely around the room, waiting for his reaction.

"Gay?" repeated Ali quietly. Then, louder: "GAY?"

"Yes, sir," said Ahmed. "It transpires he has been having a relationship with one of his cousin's cohorts. One of his cousin's *male* cohorts. It is something of a scandal in England at the moment. His constituents are calling for him to stand down. As you can imagine, sir, it has brought immense shame on the Charlton family."

"Shame? *SHAME?*" shouted Ali, his eyes almost popping out of his head with anger. "They know nothing of shame, these loose-living Brits. Shame is what Jacob Charlton has cast on Ali Hassan and his family, his business, his country. Shame is what Ali Hassan shall feel through his association with this — with this — creature! OLAF!"

Olaf, Ali's chief advisor, dressed in traditional white Libyan robes, ran over to him and knelt at his feet.

"Yes, sir?"

"My national and international reputation has been insulted by association with this heretic. Deal with it!"

Olaf nodded his bowed head, and stood as if to leave.

"And Olaf!"

Olaf, head still bowed, now busy shuffling backwards out of the room, stopped short at the sound of his name again.

"Yes, sir?"

"Someone has to pay for this. Do you hear? Ali Hassan will not be insulted in this way without someone having to pay. I want retribution. Do you hear, Olaf? *I WANT RETRIBUTION!*"

It was murky and joyless on the deserted bank of the River Thames, where the grey of the winter morning seemed endemic. The monochrome sky merged into the concrete that in turn merged into the dull, opaque water, and wisps of grey fog hung eerily low over the riverscape.

From the plush leather interior of his blacked-out Mercedes, it seemed to Quentin that the bleakness outside permeated everything it touched, as if he too would turn the same shade of grey when he got out of the car. He shivered at the prospect. Either he was early or Ahmed was late — but one thing was certain. If the bodyguard didn't turn up soon, Quentin was doing a runner, progress report or no progress report. Even during the short-lived heyday of the Millennium Dome, Quentin had found it a curiously unnerving place — bleak, depressing and somehow dangerous. Everything was so *big* here. It made you realize your insignificance as a human being.

Well, relative insignificance, that was. These days, with Quentin's position as one of the world's great players firmly in place, it would take more than a couple of overpowering riverside building sites to dwarf his high opinion of himself. The thought gave him a surge of confidence and he checked his watch irritably. Ahmed was working for him, not the other way round. And not only that — Ahmed was the one who had requested the meeting, and therefore he should have the decency at least to turn up on time.

At that moment, a second blacked-out Mercedes rolled into view and parked at a ninety-degree angle to Quentin's. There was a short pause, during which Quentin felt his pulse unaccountably begin to race. Then, finally, the rear door opened and Ahmed's familiar bulk — enhanced by his bullet-proof vest, Schott jacket and gun-filled holster — appeared. He didn't move, however. He stood by the closed door, staring steadily at Quentin's car.

No briefcase, thought Quentin immediately. No briefcase, no progress?

He pushed the unwelcome thought to the back of his mind, determined to remain positive, and, taking his cue from Ahmed — but careful not to look overkeen — Quentin also got out of his driver's seat. Trying to recreate the drama and suspense of Ahmed's studied exit, however, was futile — in comparison he looked like a shabby tramp being kicked out of his overnight shelter. But to Quentin, as he approached Ahmed, arm outstretched in greeting, it didn't feel like that. He was, in his opinion, the king of all he surveyed — including Ahmed.

"Ahmed, old boy, good to see you," said Quentin, shaking Ahmed's hand up and down effusively.

Ahmed looked at Quentin impassively as he pumped his arm, then withdrew it.

"Mr Charlton." His tone was neutral, flat — disinterested?

There was a silence, punctuated only by a steady dripping noise from the dry dock behind them. Quentin started to feel unnerved. This wasn't really going the way he'd hoped.

"Yes. So, Ahmed, I —" He left his sentence hanging, waiting for Ahmed to take the initiative and report his progress on the Bulldog commission.

Ahmed gazed at Quentin, his expression inscrutable. "Yes?"

Quentin laughed suddenly. The noise unsettled a lone raven that had roosted in the rafters, and it flew away in a flapping cloud of feathers. As both Ahmed and Quentin watched it fly, the echo of Quentin's laughter came back to them, ringing mockingly around their ears. As it died down, it was replaced by the steady drip, drip, drip behind them.

With cowardly, quivering lips, Quentin attempted another smile. He knew Ahmed was a man of fewer words and more action — that was one of his attractions as a hit man, after all — but this was bordering on unacceptable. His smile, when it finally appeared, seemed more like a sneer.

"So, Ahmed, I was wondering how it was all coming along. You know, the commission — Bulldog? Do we have a deal?"

Ahmed moved without warning, shifting his weight and crossing his arms. Quentin jumped and eyed Ahmed's gun uneasily, and the full weight of what he was here to discuss with Ahmed suddenly struck him. Ahmed had agreed to kill someone for him. In cold blood. He was a murderer. By trade. Quentin had the sudden, uncomfortable thought that maybe, just maybe, he was in too deep. Out of his depth. Totally, hopelessly.

"I know Bulldog," said Ahmed slowly, ignoring Quentin's question.

Quentin glanced at the gun again. Was that the only one Ahmed carried? Or did he have others hidden about his person, in his sock, or maybe —

With a quick movement, Ahmed reached inside his jacket pocket. Quentin stared, eyes bulging with fear. Ahmed paused, as if in momentary reflection, and then lowered his eyes decisively. His hand moved deliberately inside his jacket, then he found what he was looking for. Swiftly, he pulled it out.

A cigarette. Quentin nearly jumped out of his skin. A cigarette! His nerves were shot already and they hadn't even got past the pleasantries stage. He realized now why he'd always hated this place. It was the kind of place you might never come back from. And no one would ever know.

Lighting his Marlboro Red, Ahmed studied Quentin carefully. Despite the cold and his threadbare old overcoat, Quentin felt himself begin to sweat under Ahmed's scrutiny. And still there was that confounded drip, drip, drip.

"I know Bulldog. My question to you is, do you know these?" said Ahmed in a dangerous monotone. Slipping his hand into his jacket pocket once more, he pulled out an A4 envelope, the type used to carry photographs. Quentin, edgier than ever after this last close shave, eyed them with trepidation.

"What are they?" he said in what he hoped was an off-hand, confident manner.

In response, Ahmed put his cigarette between his teeth, pulled out a pile of black and white photographs and handed them silently to Quentin. They were grainy, monochrome Tarantino-style shots, blown up way beyond their original resolution. Looking at them, Quentin got the feeling the photos were going to get increasingly seedy. The first was of a man's bare bottom, raised as if in the middle of lovemaking.

Quentin looked at Ahmed as if this was a joke. Ahmed looked back at him, still impassive.

Drip, drip, drip.

"Who's that?" Quentin asked, coughing uncomfortably.

Ahmed stared at him as if trying to find some answers in his face.

"That is your son," he replied without emotion.

Quentin's smile disappeared as quickly as it had appeared, and was replaced with a look of unadulterated horror. As he flicked through the photographs, each more incriminating than the last, he saw that Ahmed was right, and felt a gnawing sense of fear deep in the pit of his stomach. There was no mistaking them. Jacob and Crispin. Crispin and Jacob. Together. Naked.

Naked, and — He could hardly bring himself to think the words. Thinking them, let alone saying them, would make it even more real than the black and white evidence in front of him.

He looked up at Ahmed, his expression now raw panic. Ahmed's emotions remained as imperceptible as ever.

"And he, Mr Charlton, has broken the code of honour. The code on which Ali Hassan and all his associates judge themselves and pride themselves on doing business. This, Mr Charlton, is one of the worst atrocities he could commit. A grave insult."

Shit, thought Quentin. As if the risk of his entire scam being exposed wasn't enough, now it looked like he was losing Hassan too. Bloody Jacob — why couldn't he keep his trousers on, or at least have them pulled down by a woman instead of a man?

Quentin thought fast and pasted a thunderous look on his face. "My son?" he raged. "I'll kill him! How dare he? This is not only against Ali Hassan's code of honour, it is against mine! No son of mine behaves like this and gets away with it. I'm disowning him, Ahmed — as of this minute!"

Ahmed looked at him again, his expression still impassive, even at Quentin's immediate, unthinking betrayal of his only son.

Drip, drip, drip, *drip*.

"But you have not disowned him, Mr Charlton. We have been watching since this news became public. You have not disowned him at all. And we cannot do business with a heretic."

Quentin felt rising panic in his chest. He wasn't just going to lose Hassan. He was going to lose his hit man, too.

Ahmed stubbed his cigarette out beneath his foot and looked up at Quentin. In his eyes there was no apology, only pride at his decision.

"My duty is to my master," he said decisively. "My master is Ali Hassan. Anyone who offends Ali Hassan offends me. And this is why we, Mr Charlton, do not have a deal. Not now, not ever. You will have to find another way to deal with your Bulldog. Goodbye."

Quentin watched as Ali got back into the car and it drove off, bumping across the rough terrain, splashing through grey murky puddles and then pulling off across the tarmac. He limped back to his own car and leaned on it, suddenly short of breath. He unfastened his collar, gasping, grabbing desperately for air. He felt as though Ahmed had tried to strangle him. He didn't know whether to be relieved that he was still alive or utterly petrified of what the future held as public enemy number one of international mover and shaker Ali Hassan.

When his breathing was almost back to normal, Quentin got back into the car. Though his nerves were run ragged and his pulse was still racing, his ego was firmly back in place. Completely oblivious to the predicament his own uncontrollable greed and ambition had got him into, he chose instead to blame his former allies. He kicked himself for ever getting involved in Ali Hassan's business in the first place. *If only I'd just gone down to Camden Lock with a few hundred notes*, he thought, *it could be all over*. But no, these people had wooed him, flattered him, made up to him until he'd had no choice but to go with them. And now look where it had got him. A big fat nowhere — and on the wrong side of one of the most powerful men on the planet.

There was only one thing for it. Quentin had exhausted all other options, and only one remained. In tune with his heartbeat, his pulse quickened yet again at the thought, his breathing now short and shallow. If you wanted something done, you had to do it yourself. There was no other solution. Finish off Bulldog before Bulldog finished *him* off. It was the natural order, really — almost self-defence, if you thought about it long enough.

Quentin wiped his profusely sweating brow with the back of his hand and started up the engine. He again had the feeling of being suffocated by the grey stillness outside. Oddly, instead of dispersing as the morning progressed, the fog now seemed to have closed in on him, steaming up the windscreen and covering the glass in condensation. Quentin switched on the wipers, put the dehumidifiers on full blast and waited a moment. But they did nothing. The fog remained.

And it was only then that Quentin realized the mist outside the car was different from that inside the car. The suffocating, overpowering fog in the Mercedes wasn't a by-product of the weather. It was the fog of his own, all-consuming, inescapable fear.

CHAPTER
TWENTY-SIX

The photograph, sitting innocently in its antique silver frame on the mantelpiece and radiating sheer happiness, all at once seemed incongruous and inappropriate. Laura, Robert and Max, all bundled together with baby Kitty in the middle, laughing on her christening day just over a year ago as if they hadn't a care in the world. That, Lyric realized now, must have been the last time she'd seen them all happy together. Or even together full stop. Lyric stared at it as if she could expect it to give her answers about the predicament the family now found themselves in.

She looked across at Laura, busy in the wintry bright, airy sitting room of her chocolate-box cottage deep in the Somerset countryside, helping Max lay out a train set on the floor whilst Kitty chewed happily on a wooden brick next to them.

It just went to prove, thought Lyric grimly, that you could never tell what cards life was going to deal you next. One minute Laura was a carefree mother of two with her financial and emotional future taken care of, and the next it had all come crashing down around her. Not that you'd ever know from the apparently light-hearted way she was playing with Max and Kitty now. How her friend was keeping it together Lyric simply had no idea.

"Choo-choo!" sang Max happily, pushing a train in a wobbly line over her hand as Laura tried to build the track underneath it. Laura stopped, gazing at him lovingly.

"The kids don't deserve this kind of upset," she said suddenly, as if she'd read Lyric's mind. "I've got to keep going as if everything's normal. I'd never forgive myself if they picked up on any of this trauma from me."

Lyric nodded understandingly. From her vantage point on the sofa she appraised Laura critically. Her appearance was showing even more signs of neglect than it had when Lyric had last seen her at home in London. Her jeans and striped Breton top were crumpled and obviously a couple of wears shy of a wash. Wiry grey roots were showing along her hairline, her upper lip was covered in a soft down of dark hair, and she probably hadn't been near a leg wax for months. Beneath the show of strength, Laura was clearly feeling very far removed from the persona of the flawless, fun, high-society wife that she usually liked to exude.

"So have you heard from Robert today?" asked Lyric softly. At the mention of her husband's name, Laura visibly flinched.

"No," she said shortly. "Not much to say, is there, really? Until we're evicted, it's all a waiting game." She turned from her to fix a fiddly bit of track.

Lyric bit her lip and looked at her friend pityingly.

"And don't look at me like that, Lyric," said Laura with her back still turned.

"Like what?" said Lyric, genuinely perplexed.

"All big eyes and sympathy — like someone's just run over my puppy. Robert has messed up, full stop," said Laura, still not looking round. "We have to deal with it. So we don't get to keep the house in Cheyne Walk, the villa in Tuscany, or — or —" her voice caught on the last words. "Or this, our dream cottage." From behind her, Lyric recognized the characteristic stoic shake of her head as she tried to convince herself. "So what? Millions of other people get along fine without luxuries like these."

Lyric looked around sadly at the uneven walls and the dark, jagged beams of the sixteenth-century cottage. Laura's defensive front didn't fool her one little bit. She and Robert had bought this five-bedroomed rural bolthole as a picturesque wreck full of 1970s atrocities when they'd returned from honeymoon, and had lovingly overseen its restoration room by room, painstakingly following the guidelines of Grade One listed buildings in their plans, until it had become the cosy, family home it was today. Even without the photographs that covered every available surface — their wedding, exotic holidays before Max and Kitty came along, idyllic English holidays since — their personalities were visible in every carefully chosen brush of paint, every length of curtain fabric, every cherished pot plant. Even more than their London home, this was the reflection of their hopes, their dreams, and how they had planned their future to be —

330

all of which, like their chances of keeping the house, was now lying in ruins.

There was a silence between them, broken only by the persistent hooting of Max's "choo-choo" trains.

"You know, it's not that I'm scared of living without the trappings of wealth," said Laura. "So I stop delivering my dry-cleaning in my Birkin bag and I start going to the launderette. So what? Like I said, millions of other people get by that way. It's just that once you have them — the cars, the private nursery, the staff — how *do* you let them go? Of course we'll be able to afford a modest home somewhere, but the children will be uprooted and upset, the cars will have to go, I expect, the staff will have to lose their jobs." She paused. Lyric held her breath as she watched her friend fight to maintain her composure. She cared about her small household staff as if they were family, and Lyric knew that Laura would be fearing for their future almost as much as her own. Laura shook her head as if to physically pull herself together, and smiled bravely at Lyric. "Still, I know that compared with the people being made redundant all over the country we still have a lot, but from where I'm standing, it feels like we've lost an awful lot too."

"Oh, Lau," said Lyric, wanting to give her friend a hug but afraid to give the children any reason to suspect that anything was the matter with their mummy. "Is it really going to come to that?"

Head held high against her shame, Laura looked straight at Lyric, eyes shining with unshed tears.

"Robert is being investigated by the Serious Fraud Office," she said, bitterly. "How many people do you know who get into that position and come out of it OK? From my experience, it has got to be something pretty serious to even attract their attention in the first place."

Lyric hung her head. Laura came from a banking family, and her father, Tiny Goldstein, was one of its most respected figures. He was a blunt, direct man who believed that understanding the opposition inside out was key to winning the battle, and he would not have left Laura under any illusions as to his opinion of the situation his darling daughter — and his grandchildren — now found themselves in. And it was true. When you put it like Laura just had, there seemed very little hope for a positive resolution to this. After the exposé of Jacob and Crispin's affair and Porngate, the media, like a pack of dogs on the scent of a fox, had been intent on muckraking their way through every single one of Lyric's friends' and family's interests. And it seemed that Robert, via some highly suspect transactions at work, had provided them with their long-awaited hat-trick. The embezzlement scandal that had subsequently unfolded had implicated him almost without a shadow of a doubt as an accomplished fraudster, who had added to his already impressive portfolio with the proceeds of a string of illegal deals.

"Do you have a hanky," asked Laura quietly. Realizing the last thing Laura wanted was to break down in front of her children, Lyric quickly handed her one from her bag.

With her back turned to Lyric once more, Laura resumed her position on the floor and pushed Max's train around the track. When she spoke, it was so quietly that at first Lyric didn't even realize it was directed at her.

"You know, I should have guessed something was going on. Things — things haven't been good between Robert and me for a while," she said hesitantly.

Lyric frowned. Laura had never mentioned anything about this before. She remained quiet, waiting for her friend to continue.

"Ever since Maxy was born — well. It all started that very minute. That idyllic scene where Mummy is screaming and grabbing Daddy's hand, and he mops her brow with his shirt sleeve? That's a bloody joke, Lyric. Literally. I mean, you pay them enough, but what do those doctors know really?" Laura's speech was gaining speed as if a dam was bursting, as if she was finally getting something off her chest that had been bothering her for a long time. "There was me waist-deep in the birthing pool, and they let Robert go down the sharp end. From then on, Lyric, I swear to you, he was so put off — what happened must have repelled him so deeply — that he's barely been back there since."

Lyric winced at the raw rejection in Laura's voice. Max looked up at his mother and ran the train over her face, unaware of the turmoil she was going through. Behind them, Kitty, now bored of her brick, started to grizzle. Not wanting to interrupt Laura mid-flow, Lyric picked the baby up and bounced her on her knee as a diversion.

"And then, you know, we didn't agree on his upbringing at all. Robert wanted me to have nannies," Laura continued, sitting up now in indignation as she warmed to her theme. "Not just a nanny. Nannies. Plural. One for the daytime, one for night-time and one — oh, I don't know. He just didn't understand about getting up in the night to look after your baby yourself — about breastfeeding, about *mothering*." Laura threw a piece of train track down in despair and Max looked up at her in surprise. She stroked his head reassuringly and cooed at him.

Lyric took the opportunity to interrupt. "But — Kitty?" she asked, now very confused.

"Oh, Kitty happened during a little interlude," replied Laura bitterly. "I mean, I could understand Robert might go off sex for a while — I certainly did! I found Max's whole first year so exhausting, such a huge, *huge* learning curve. I didn't even notice to begin with. But then, it took so long for me to get my body back, and I started to lose confidence, and then I realized that Robert hadn't so much as tried to touch me for months! And that made me feel even worse, and so I started to eat even more, for comfort, you see and — oh, how did I get on to this tangent?"

Lyric smiled encouragingly. "How Kitty came about," she prompted gently.

Laura sighed deeply. "Oh, yes. Well, all of a sudden, Robert seemed to get his mojo back. Suddenly wanted sex, all of the time. I mean! Obviously, I was delighted.

334

And so — well. There's the result. Gorgeous, delightful, loveable Kitty-Kat."

Her face softened as she looked at her baby girl, who was chewing on Lyric's gold Breitling watch, plump cheeks pink from an imminent tooth.

"Well then, maybe Robert was going through some kind of post-natal depression himself," said Lyric, desperately scrabbling around in the dark for an explanation. "Maybe he's experiencing it again now, since Kitty was born. You know, maybe once he's over that you can both go back to normal and fight this fraud thing together . . ." She trailed off at Laura's expression. She was looking at Lyric as if she was deluded.

"He's been using *prostitutes*," Laura spat, as if the word had a particularly nasty taste. "High-class call girls, I believe they call themselves. Hah! What's high-class about taking a husband and father away from his family to play sordid sex games?"

"Laura," interjected Lyric, holding out a hand helplessly. "You don't know . . ."

Laura's face was contorted with pain, humiliation and shame. When she spoke, her voice was uncharacteristically harsh and brittle.

"Oh, but I do, Lyric. I know everything. I know about his suite on the sixth floor at the Dorchester. I know about the pornography he keeps there. I know about the sex toys. I even know what kind of girls he invites to his sex den and when!" Her laugh was hollow as a sob welled up in her throat. "The Serious Fraud Office, you see, Lyric — they're very helpful in bringing certain — shall we call them 'matters'? — to light. They provide you with totally transparent accounts, bank statements, receipts — the lot. And so, Lyric, when I tell you that my husband is addicted to hookers, I know only too well what I am talking about."

Laura's pitch was rising, her voice getting shriller and shriller, and she clapped a hand over her mouth to stop herself from wailing out loud. Max had now stopped playing and was staring at his mother with a look of perplexed bewilderment on his face.

Laura cleared her throat and tried to start talking again.

"All that time, Lyric. All that time I was keeping the ship running, trying to be the perfect wife and mother, thinking everything wasn't great, but would be OK. All that time, and Robert was not only frittering away our future on God knows what, but taking comfort with a bunch of whores instead of his family!"

With that, Laura ran out of the room, sobbing wildly. Kitty, going through her separation anxiety stage, immediately started to cry at her mother's swift departure. Seeing his sister cry, an already unnerved Max started to whimper too.

"There, there, Kitty-Kat," Lyric soothed, standing up and jigging Kitty around comfortingly, bending down to stroke Max's head as he clutched her leg. All the while, her mind tried to make sense of Laura's predicament, and how little she'd known of her friend's unhappiness for so, so long. Her horror and concern were tinged with guilt. How had she been so wrapped up in her own world that this had all been unravelling under her nose without her realizing? She couldn't even blame being away in rehab. Since then, she'd picked up on so many things between Laura and Robert that hadn't quite added up — the apparent gulf between them, Robert's black moods, Laura's jittery demeanour and over-the-top gregariousness — but she'd been too carried away with her own life to give them due attention. Now Lyric found her own tears welling up on behalf of her friend. Laura's perfect life, which she and so many others had held up as a shining example of what they all aspired to, was nothing more than a sham. How wretched she must feel — and how wretched Lyric felt on her behalf.

As Kitty cheered up and started leaning out for her toys on the floor, Lyric put her down and turned her attentions to Max.

"Where's Mummy, Aunt Lyric?" he whined, lisping even more in his distress. "Why has she left us all alone?"

"Your mummy's just gone to the loo, Maxy — nothing to worry about!" said Lyric brightly, looking around for something to divert him. She spotted a glass of Ribena Laura had been drinking throughout the afternoon.

"I tell you what, Maxy — why don't we share some juice?" she said conspiratorially. "Pass me your little cup, and I'll pour you some."

With wide, excited eyes, Max reached out for his beaker and handed it to Lyric reverently. She poured in the purple liquid and gave it back to him.

"Now, carefully does it, Max — don't drop any on the floor!" She smiled as, unused to sweet drinks except as a special treat, he gulped down the drink. "Yum-yum!" he said as he finished, showing her the empty cup. "Now you, Aunt Lyric!"

Lyric smiled at him over her glass. It was years since she'd had Ribena, she thought, as she took a sip. The prospect made her almost nostalgic for her own nursery years.

But as the liquid hit the back of her throat, it burned slightly as she swallowed it, and another, horrific, thought immediately replaced it. This wasn't Ribena as she remembered it. This was —

At that moment, Laura came back into the room, her expression of abject misery immediately replaced by horror as she saw Lyric with the glass to her lips.

"Lyric — no! I mean . . ." She immediately turned to Max and, seeing the Ribena smile around his lips, ran over to him in panic. "Maxy!"

"Mummy, I don't feel very well," he said, his joyful smile turning downwards as he rubbed his tummy pitifully. "My tummy hurts." With that, he threw up dramatically, a projectile purple river that splattered all over the carpet in an angry, berry-coloured splash.

As she rushed to fetch Max some water, leaving Laura cuddling him tightly, Lyric was inwardly horrified. Now, suddenly, something else added up. Laura's jittery demeanour and over-the-top gregarious-ness weren't just down to her domestic situation. They had something to do with Laura's uncharacteristic clumsiness, her penchant for an afternoon drink, her lack of self-control on Sin Island . . .

As Lyric returned to the sitting room and bent down to give the water to the tearful Max, Laura looked up at her, reflecting Lyric's horror in her own expression. Their eyes met for a nanosecond before Laura looked away, ashamed. The look told Lyric all she needed to know. Immediately, she reached out for Laura's hand.

"That wasn't just Ribena, was it?" she said quietly as Laura hugged Max to her tightly.

Laura shook her head miserably.

"It was laced with vodka, wasn't it?"

Laura looked up at her, desperation and self-loathing written all over her face. She sobbed loudly, rocking Max to and fro vehemently. "Yes!" she spluttered. "Oh, Lyric — I'm in a terrible mess. A terrible, terrible mess . . ."

Lyric gazed at her compassionately. Laura, the secret alcoholic. Who'd have guessed. Did anybody know? Dependency, it seemed, really could happen to anyone. But this was different. This time, there was something she could do. And she knew that, whatever it took, she was going to do all she could to get her friend through this and out the other side stronger, better, than before.

CHAPTER
TWENTY-SEVEN

Edward wiped his hands down his black tabard and ran them through his hair impatiently as he surveyed the empty bar of Le Mélézin. The rush of the festive period made this low-season lull seem even quieter, even in an uber-luxurious hotel such as this. He could almost hear the ghosts of Christmas revellers reverberate around the bar. But the Christmas and New Year holiday was well and truly over. There had been ample time for the letter to arrive, and ample time for him to fret over its non-appearance. The British civil service and all its departments had, he knew, been closed for a two-week break, but now that had come to an end, and so had all his excuses for the continued delay over news about his birthright. Fate, it seemed, was planning to continue the role it had played in his past and his present into his future.

Edward bit his lip anxiously and rubbed his right eye absently. The continued delays were beginning to exacerbate his bad feeling over what revelations might await him with the discovery of his true-blood family. But he'd got this far. He sure as hell wasn't going to give up now — or halt the opportunity to fill that gnawing emptiness he knew was caused by not knowing where he came from or from whom.

It was his one chance to silence his inner demons. The question was, what new demons would it uncover?

Lyric, on the phone to Truly, almost dropped the handset at the familiar knock on her door. She'd been lost in the fantastical world that her godmother inhabited, agog at her latest instalment of insider Hollywood gossip. She could have imagined anything. Except *that*.

"Truly — just a moment." She remained stock-still, her head cocked as she listened for a few more seconds.

Rat-a-tat-tat.

Nope, it was definitely a knock, not simply a figment of her imagination. *That* knock. There was no mistaking it. But still Lyric sat, unwilling to make the commitment to opening the door. Opening it meant trouble. She was better off ignoring it.

However, despite the feeling of dread deep in the pit of her stomach, her innate curiosity was piqued. She had no idea what could have led to this moment. What was behind the knock? What would really happen if she opened the door?

"Truly, can I call you back later?" said Lyric into the receiver. Her godmother, accustomed to their frequent calls being interrupted at one end of the line or the other, was unfazed.

"Of course, darling. Adieu!"

Lyric hung up and, unable to resist the lure of "what if" any longer, she stood up, flicking her mane of hair

341

back from her face and over her shoulders, and gave her appearance a fleeting glance in the mirror. *Lyric!* she warned herself. *Stop that right now. What does it matter how you look?*

Walking to the front door gave her an odd sensation — whether it was a sense of nerves or something else, she wasn't sure. She swallowed hard and sternly tried to calm herself. She should have no feelings about this whatsoever. She needed to get a grip. Her reaction would be measured, calm — and cold.

A rush of crisp, chilly air hit her as she opened the door to the arctic January afternoon, and she blinked, her eyes watering.

"Hi, Lyric." He moved on to the top step as if to greet her with a kiss. She moved backwards sharply.

He stood, as he had so many times before, gazing up at her with those hooded aquamarine eyes. Except this time he was clutching a wilting bunch of flowers that, if she wasn't very much mistaken, he'd picked up from the garage at the end of the road. She gazed at him impassively, numb to the sight of him — a sight that would once have reduced her to a quivering pool of desire. For some reason, she couldn't take her eyes off the flowers. She drove past that garage every day, bought her petrol there — did he not think she would recognize the identikit bunches they had sitting in buckets on the forecourt every morning?

"Hello, Ralph."

Flowers aside, it was the same, drop-dead gorgeous Ralph. Well, almost the same. The same slight build, the same floppy hair, the same dishevelled cool, the same

342

louche air. And those eyes — those eyes! — still burned out of his face arrestingly. But it seemed to Lyric that all the gloss had gone from him. The once sharply defined features were less acute, as if someone had rubbed an eraser around his profile. And even on the doorstep, with at least three feet and the frosty air between them, she detected a whiff of damp mustiness about him, as if he'd put his clothes on before they were properly aired. And his *je ne sais quoi* — well, she really didn't know where, let alone what, it was any more.

He handed her the flowers sheepishly. "Peace offering." His nose was red from the cold, and his breath made frosty clouds that lingered like cigarette smoke.

She gazed at him, speechless for a moment. After all he'd done, after all he *hadn't* done, he thought a measly bunch of flowers was all it would take to make peace? She should be enraged. She should be hurt, humiliated. But instead of flaring with outrage and anger, Lyric found herself wanting to laugh. What a joke!

"Thanks, Ralph," she said, taking them from him solemnly. "They're — um —"

"A bit pathetic?" he finished for her with a rakish grin. "Well, you know me — romance has never been my strong point."

Now, Lyric was too stunned to even laugh. He hadn't even got his foot through the door and he was talking about *romance*?

"What do you want, Ralph?" she said, casting the drooping flowers aside on to the hall table. She glanced at her watch as if she were pressed for time.

"Well, I was rather hoping you'd invite me in," he said meekly. "At least through the front door." He looked past her as if trying to gauge an imaginary opponent.

"There's no one else here at the moment," said Lyric, pointedly referring to the fact that yes, someone else did practically live here. "But that's not why I'm not letting you in. I just want to know what you could possibly think we've got to say to one another."

Ralph took a step up on to the top stair so that he was nose to nose with Lyric. She felt suddenly unnerved by his proximity. It felt — intimate.

"Well, let me in and you might find out," he said in a low, sexy voice, the hint of a smile playing around the corner of his lips. Flustered, Lyric stood back, leaving a gap that Ralph immediately slipped through. She turned, about to protest, and then slumped her shoulders in defeat. He was already in. And anyway, part of her was intrigued to hear what he had come for — intrigued to get some kind of closure. But she was glad he'd taken the decision out of her hands. There was some kind of strange comfort in this being out of her control.

She followed Ralph as he strolled casually through to the sitting room — *she* was following *him*, she raged inwardly, annoyed, as if this were his house! — and watched as he made himself comfortable on the sofa, arms spread across the back, legs stretched out confidently on her coffee table. He was wearing the tan Tod's boots she'd bought him a couple of years before, she noticed absently. Then, hardening her heart again, she stood facing him, arms crossed, determined not to crumble under his charm offensive.

"Ralph, what exactly do you want?" she repeated through gritted teeth.

He was drumming his fingers on the sofa. "Well, I figured I've got a lot of explaining to do," he smiled, as if she'd just asked him what he'd had for breakfast.

"Really? I'm surprised you didn't work that out while I was in rehab. Or when I got out. Or any time in the seven months since," said Lyric levelly.

She cast her mind back, allowing a fleeting thought of the pain she'd felt in rehab when, all alone and facing the hardest battle of her life, she'd realized the extent of Ralph's selfishness, that he really didn't care about her at all, that she'd haemorrhaged not only time and money but her health and her reputation — goddammit, her life! — on this waster. There had been so many times when she'd ached to hear his voice, when she'd physically prayed that he'd send word that he still loved her. Lyric, of course, had been banned from contacting him at all during her incarceration. And since then? Well, there had been Philippe. And before that? Her pride. Her self-respect.

Lyric took a deep breath and pulled herself up tall. Her self-*worth*.

"Lyric, Lyric, Lyric!" Ralph soothed, pulling his feet off the table and sitting up straight, suddenly looking serious. "As if that would have been appropriate!"

Lyric couldn't believe her ears. "Appropriate?" she repeated, stunned. "Appropriate? Your girlfriend of over two years goes into meltdown, then into rehab, and you're telling me that being there for her seemed *inappropriate?*"

Ralph adopted a wounded expression and stood up, holding his arms out to embrace her. Lyric backed off, keeping her own arms crossed.

"Lyric! I was keeping out of your way. Giving you some space. I figured the last person you needed clouding your recovery was the person you did the drugs with in the first place!" His tone was pleading, for all the world as though he'd had her best interests at heart.

She frowned. "Ralph, I think I would have been the best judge of that," she mumbled, trying to make sense of the turbulence inside her. Sensing her weakness, Ralph moved a step closer.

"You weren't in a fit state to make a decision about anything," he said softly. Then he changed the subject abruptly. "I see you're still wearing that underwear I bought you," he murmured, touching the black lace La Perla bra strap peeking out from under her vest top.

Lyric pulled it up irritably, the momentary spell broken. There he went again, trying to push her buttons.

"I still don't understand what you're doing here," she said, trying to regain the upper hand. "There's been a lot of water under the bridge since then. What could you possibly have to say to me that would make any difference to how I feel about you now?"

346

Ralph gave one of his lopsided smiles. "Who said anything about *changing* the way you feel about me?" he said smoothly. "For all I know nothing's changed between us except that we're seven months older. And wiser."

There it was again, that lopsided grin. The one that once upon a time could have turned Lyric's world on its axis. She remained silent, unable to think of a suitable response, and turned away to fiddle with the collection of Diptyque candles on the mantelpiece.

"So why don't you hear me out and then decide how you feel?" he said softly. His tone was gently persuasive, the kind you'd use to convince a toddler to finish his tea. As Lyric looked at his reflection in the mirror, she noticed his smile had turned more confident — cocky even. All at once, Lyric felt patronized, suffocated, and she swung round to face him again.

"You've mistaken me for someone who gives a shit," she said quietly. It sounded hollow, even to her ears, and hung on the air unconvincingly — it was the kind of thing Treeva would say. Treeva, whom Ralph had . . . At the thought of her friend and Ralph as lovers, Lyric felt the familiar lurch of revulsion, of rejection. Ralph, interpreting her hesitation as uncertainty, ploughed onwards, clutching both her elbows and attempting to draw her to him.

"Really?" he said softly. "I didn't think I was ever mistaken about how you felt — or how to make you feel." He looked at her meaningfully and the reference to their passionate love life wasn't lost on her. But coming directly after the mental image of him and

Treeva in bed together, it had the opposite effect. Rather than making Lyric feel nostalgic, it made her feel nauseous. She shook Ralph's hands off her arms.

"And this attempt at reconciliation, it wouldn't have anything to do with the fact that you're skint, and, I would imagine, probably homeless, too, would it?" she ventured, hurt making her lash out.

He stepped back from her as though she'd slapped him. His face tensed in apprehension as he tried to bluff his way out of her accusations.

His laugh was hollow. "Wherever did you get that idea from?"

She could see it now — the absence of aftershave, the clothes that hadn't been updated for months when he'd always been such a dandy, the desperation behind the eyes. He'd drunk, sniffed and partied his trust fund away — and he was left with nothing. She should feel sorry for him. But she had more wounds to heal first. She turned and looked him directly in the eye.

"From Treeva."

Again, that conflict of emotions, from bluster to shock to bluster again. "Treeva? Fake-tanned, fake-boobed, fake-personality Treeva?" Ralph looked at her with what she felt he hoped was derision. "What's she got to do with all of this?"

Now it was Lyric's turn to laugh. But she couldn't even bring herself to act amused at his blatantly spineless and cruel response.

"That's a fine way to talk about the person you've been sleeping with for the past seven months," she said calmly, trying to disguise her racing heart. "What was she — your meal ticket while I was out of circulation? And now she's sussed you out you've come crawling back to me?"

Ralph's jaw dropped, gaping open and shut like a stranded fish.

"She was — I was — I was . . . lonely," he finally managed. "I missed you," he added.

Lyric stared at him, shaking her head in disbelief.

"Funnily enough, she said the same thing about you. Did you cook that one up between you? Or was that one of the things you bonded over — the cruel desertion that Lyric foisted upon you?" She tried — and failed — to keep the bitterness out of her voice. How *dare* he?

"It's true!" protested Ralph. He kicked the coffee table in frustration. "Well, as if I could expect you to understand. Nobody ever understands me. Ever."

He walked over to the window. Abruptly, as if changing tack, he turned and walked slowly back over to Lyric, dropping to his knees in front of her. He clutched at her hands and she turned away, unable to watch his sheer desperation.

"We're one and the same, you and me — misunderstood," he said, his tone pleading. "We always have been. That's what made us such a great team. Always on the same page. You and me against the world. And you think you can stand here and say, hand on heart, that you really don't feel anything for me?"

Lyric felt something give within her. *He's playing you like a cheap piano*, she told herself. *Anyhow, you're not alone against the world any more — you've got Philippe.*

But whilst there was a sense of satisfaction in being able to say no to him, at the same time Lyric had a nostalgic pang for the naively deep feelings she'd once had for him. That overpowering, overriding teenage kind of love that transcended reason — and real life. The romantic in her wanted to love him still, but the realist knew he was beyond love — and beyond loving anyone other than himself. The attraction to him in the first place had always been that he was a bit of a shit — that in the face of all the women lusting after him at any one time in any one room, he was hers, all hers. But now he was lost, crumpled. The more she looked, the more pitiful he became. And the closer he got, the more she couldn't bear the smell of defeat, of despair, that engulfed him.

"Oh, I feel something for you all right," said Lyric, finally gaining strength. "Pity! Disappointment! Concern! But physical attraction? Adoration? *Love?*" Her voice broke on the last word as she thought of Philippe. *Her* Philippe. "You wouldn't know the meaning of the word, Ralph. And neither did I until you did me the favour of sodding off and leaving me all on my own. Because now I've met someone who has taught me exactly what love is — what it can be. And I would never, ever, ever trade that in to take a punt on you again. Ever."

The realization that she meant every word slowly dawned on Ralph. And at the mention of someone else, at the spoken admission that his power over her was no longer, his lip curled and rejection turned his faded beauty into unparalleled ugliness.

"Oh, I did you a favour all right," he spat. "In fact, setting up that exposé on you was the biggest favour anyone's ever done you."

There was a stunned silence. Lyric's mouth went dry and she had the strange sensation that her heart was beating inside her head. Time seemed to stand still. Opposite her Ralph, too, was standing as if frozen. He had the crushed look of a man truly finished etched indelibly over his features.

Lyric stared at him, marvelling at how things could change even within a couple of seconds. For a while there, if Ralph had once said, "I've never stopped wanting you, loving you," she might have been moved. She might even have succumbed. Honestly. And she didn't like to think what else might have happened. But he hadn't. He'd forged ahead, talking about himself. Forget "Lyric and Ralph". Forget soulmates. With Ralph, it was "me-me-me". That's all it had ever been. And all it would ever be. And now, in his total self-absorption, he'd revealed himself for exactly what he was — not just a boyfriend who'd abandoned her when she'd needed him most, but one who'd never really been there for her *ever*. One who'd done everything he could to look after number one. And this realization was more devastating than she could ever have thought possible. She'd been duped all along. Cheated.

It was absolute. Intolerable. Lyric felt herself physically reeling, spinning, as she felt the full impact of his words. Ralph was worse than skint. He was worse than heartless. He was soulless — a morally bankrupt reject from life. What had she ever seen in him? Now she could barely bring herself to look at him, let alone consider how much of her life she'd wasted on him.

Lyric felt a lurch of nausea overcome her and rushed through to the tiny downstairs loo, where she was violently sick. Sitting on the closed loo seat afterwards, she leaned her head against the cool of the painted wall. She felt weak, defeated — and overwhelmed. She ran the tap and splashed water on her face and inside her mouth. She had to pull herself together. She had to go back and face him one last time, to find out why he had done it.

When Lyric returned, Ralph was leaning against the sitting room door frame, his face transformed by concern. *For himself*, Lyric said to herself, hardening her heart against the tsunami of excuses he'd have prepared while she was in the loo. Ralph was the only person Ralph cared about. He had never cared about her.

"Lyric . . ." he started sheepishly.

Lyric held her hand up to silence him, barely able to look him in the eye.

"Don't, Ralph," she said dully. "There's no point even trying to get round me. But you owe me."

He looked up at her, suddenly hopeful. Lyric shook her head.

"You owe me an explanation, Ralph."

Ralph sighed and patted the door frame awkwardly.

352

"Well, you know. Things were a bit tight. I'd made a couple of dodgy investments, spent a lot of money on — erm — living expenses."

Once upon a time, that was the kind of Ralph understatement that would have made Lyric laugh out loud. Now she looked at him pityingly. Even with a situation this serious, he couldn't bring himself to be a hundred per cent serious.

"So you sold me down the river," she interjected bitterly.

"No!" he protested. Lyric raised her eyebrows at him. "I never intended to. Well, not immediately, anyway."

"Well, thanks, darling — I'm touched," Lyric muttered sarcastically under her breath. Ralph either didn't hear or ignored her and carried on.

"So I was in the Wigmall one afternoon . . ."

Lyric let out a snort of disdain. The Wigmall! She'd always thought it was a knocking shop for sad old men, but her boyfriend had been a regular too! Perhaps if Ralph had spent more afternoons in gainful employment and fewer on the massage table, he might not be in the jam he found himself now. Was there any other surprise Ralph could spring on her in the next few minutes?

It didn't take long to find out.

"So I'm in the Wigmall," repeated Ralph in a bid to regain her attention, "and who should I bump into but your Uncle Quentin!" Ralph's voice reflected the surprise he clearly felt Lyric should be feeling at this latest revelation. But she felt nothing — nothing but the stone-cold dread that mention of her uncle gave her these days.

Clearly not getting the response he expected, Ralph looked at Lyric quizzically.

"Go on," she said coldly.

He took a deep breath. "Well, we had a couple of bottles of wine together. Followed by a few whiskies. I had a sniff, and he wanted to know all about it."

"Uncle Quentin did cocaine with you?" squealed Lyric, eyes wide open with shock.

"No, no," said Ralph, smiling to himself. "He didn't do it. Just wanted to know about how I got it, who I did it with, how often — all that kind of thing."

"So you sold me down the river," repeated Lyric.

Ralph looked at her desperately. "Lyric, you don't understand. I was off my face! And he was your uncle. He was being all pally and matey with me and acted like he already knew everything that you and I got up to. So it didn't feel like I was giving anything away."

Lyric stared at him. It was like listening to a stranger.

"Ralph, you know my family. We spent two years together, during which time you were a guest of Mummy and Daddy more times than I care to remember. You know how they felt about drugs. And you know the lengths I went to to keep my addiction from them. Why on earth did you think it was going to do either of us any good to confide in my bonkers old uncle, who none of us much liked, let alone trusted?"

Ralph hung his head. "Oh, I don't know," he mumbled. "He didn't come across as that bad that afternoon."

"I'm sure he didn't if he was bankrolling an afternoon booze-up with you," scoffed Lyric.

Ralph looked at her sheepishly. "Well, that's just it. It turned out he wasn't. I ended up with the bill."

This time, Lyric did laugh. Ralph had finally met his match, it seemed. How ironic that it should be her nemesis.

"Get to the point, Ralph," she said in a bored voice.

He took a deep breath. "Well, I was well and truly slaughtered. And I'd not only told him about you and me, I'd dropped Anatole in it and everything. He's a clever old fox, that Quentin."

"Hmm," said Lyric. This wasn't making her feel any better.

"So when the bill arrived, he made as if to leave and I had to admit to him that I couldn't pay it. And then he got nasty."

That was no surprise, thought Lyric. She'd never known Uncle Quentin put his hand in his pocket voluntarily.

"He paid up, but he wasn't happy about it," continued Ralph. "And not only did I have to thank him for the afternoon, I then had to ask him not to mention to anyone what we'd talked about. What goes on tour, stays on tour, and all that . . ."

Lyric shook her head in disgust. Some old boys' network. She'd always had her doubts.

"And that's when he offered me the deal," continued Ralph hesitantly.

Lyric's heart stopped. "What deal?" she said.

Ralph cleared his throat. "He offered me what seemed like a fortune and the promise he'd keep everything I'd told him quiet — if I took the pictures. The ones of you snorting coke off the loo seat."

Lyric looked at Ralph through misty eyes. His voice seemed distant, as if he was talking to her underwater. It had all been a set-up after all. Masterminded by the last person she'd have suspected — her partner in crime. Her boyfriend.

"Did he say why?" she asked, clenching her hands together in tight fists.

Ralph shook his head. "No. And I was too wasted to ask him." He chuckled mirthlessly, expecting Lyric to laugh along with him. "I just got the impression he was sick of you pulling the family name through the mud and wanted to stop you somehow."

Lyric bit her lip. The exact opposite, in her mind, was true. Her Uncle Quentin had clearly wanted to drag the family's name through the mud in order to discredit her father and get Broughton Hall for himself. Stupid, gullible Ralph — he couldn't see the truth even when it was staring him in his drugged-up face.

But the irony. Quentin had tried to bring shame on her via Ralph, but all he'd really done was sort out her addiction and set her life back in the right direction. The only person who'd really come out of it shamefully badly, it seemed, was Ralph. Poor, self-centred Ralph.

Ralph held out his arms to her and moved in for a hug. "Lyric, if you only knew how I've regretted it since. How it's haunted my every move. How —"

Lyric took a step backwards to keep the distance between them. Shock had made her practical, and her head was cool. Now all she wanted was her own space back so she could come to terms with Ralph's revelations.

"Get out, Ralph," she said in a steely voice. "Get out."

Ralph gave her a hangdog look. "But — Lyric. The consequences of Quentin talking . . . He could have brought us both down. He could have —"

"So you figured destroying just me was preferable, did you?" she said calmly. "Well, I can't say I'm very impressed. But now you've said your piece, really, I think it's time you left."

"But . . ."

"*NOW*, Ralph. I'm not interested in anything else you have to say," said Lyric, holding on to the banister for support. Her voice was clear and steady, but she could feel her entire body shaking, and she was worried her legs would buckle and give way. There was time for that in a minute. All she wanted right now was for Ralph to get out of her house.

Ralph slowly made his way past her, dragging his heels as might a small child. As he passed Lyric, he turned towards her.

"Lyric . . ." he started slowly.

With her back to him, she closed her eyes and held her breath. *Count to ten, Lyric, and he'll be gone*, she told herself. *Count to ten.*

She gritted her teeth. "What?"

"You won't . . . you won't mention to your uncle that I told you all this, will you? It's just that . . . well, you can imagine he wouldn't be too pleased . . ."

Not for the first time that afternoon, Lyric was dumbfounded. She turned and stared at Ralph incredulously.

"Yes, Ralph, of course I'm going to tell my Uncle Quentin that I know he set up the entire sting that cost me my job, my pride and my family's name. Of course I'm going to tell him that I know he paid my ex-boyfriend to do it. Of course I'm going to tell him I know that he's probably still after my hide, and that I'm aware that I'm in mortal danger from his every move."

Ralph stared at her as if it had never occurred to him that Quentin could have had a deeper, more sinister motive.

"Lyric, I never —"

"Like I said — get out."

Ralph hung his head and took another couple of steps towards the door. Lyric was just about to let out a breath of relief when he turned again. She could hardly contain her irritation. Why wouldn't he just give up?

"Ummmm — Lyric?"

"*What?*" she almost screamed.

Ralph put his hands in his jacket pockets and turned them inside out. "I don't suppose you've got a tenner for a taxi, have you? I spent the last cash I had on the flowers."

When the door was finally shut, locked and bolted behind Ralph, Lyric collapsed on to the sofa and cried.

358

She felt exhausted, wrung out, spent — she simply had nothing left to give.

But as the torrents of tears died down to hiccup-filled sobs, she sat up to reflect on the past couple of hours. Despite the turmoil within her, she realized she was glad. Glad she'd known before he'd revealed the extent of his treachery that she was well and truly over him. Glad that once she'd realized the levels to which he would stoop, he was out of her life for ever. And glad beyond all previous levels of gladness that she now had Philippe in her life.

After all, she thought, clutching on to the beautiful truth of the present — when you know, you know. And what she knew, beyond anything, was that Ralph Conway was so far in her past he was history. And that Philippe was not only her present but her future too.

She was glad, too, that he'd told her about the set-up. Yes, it hurt. In fact, it was only now, as she played Ralph's words over and over in her mind, that the full magnitude of Ralph's confession hit her. The PI's hunch had been right. Lyric had been right. Uncle Quentin was somehow, for some reason, spearheading an almighty smear campaign against her. But even she hadn't realized how deep his hatred of her ran, how ingrained in him this evil was. Part of her couldn't believe her uncle was capable of such evil, nor could she fathom why.

But as she sat back, alternately chewing her nails and gently rubbing at her eye, part of her realized that there was much, much more to Uncle Quentin than one saw, and that she had only just scratched the surface in finding out the true extent of his evil.

One thing was certain, though. If Quentin was capable of this, then he was capable of anything. And that really scared her.

CHAPTER
TWENTY-EIGHT

Treeva squealed with delight as the 4×4 taking her to LAX airport pulled up at Departures. There, ringfencing the entrance to the lounge, was the biggest collection of paparazzi she had ever seen. Then she remembered why. She was taking a charter flight home rather than her customary private jet. There was more chance of maxing out her publicity on a regular airline, and anyhow, when she'd flown out here Customs had made her wait for seven hours whilst they practically pulled her private plane apart looking for drugs. Her fast-living reputation and increasingly high profile, it seemed, didn't open doors for her in *every* industry. Plus, she was in America, where the stiflingly restrictive privacy laws of the UK simply didn't exist. Out here, the press could hound a celebrity until they got their picture, even if it meant making that person's existence a living nightmare. Look at what had happened to Britney, to Michael Jackson. That would never have happened in Britain. Treeva shook her head wonderingly. She'd never understood it, frankly. Why would anyone try to *avoid* being photographed? Why would anyone *not* want to be in the papers?

So now, she blotted her lips with a length of loo roll and slicked another layer of cherry lip gloss on her plumped-up lips, fluffed up her hair and prepared herself to meet their lenses. No bowing her head bashfully or trying to cover her face with a scarf for Treeva Sinclair. Oh no. She was going to give the paps the time of their lives. She wasn't going to make them work for it. Instead, she was going to work *it* for *them*!

Pulling her child's T-shirt down to reveal more cleavage, and up to reveal more midriff, Treeva stepped boldly out of the car, voguing for all her life as if she was on a stadium stage with Madonna rather than alone on a tarmac concourse in the LA sunshine. The paps went wild. With the sun's rays magnifying their flash lenses, Treeva was momentarily blinded, but she worked it to her advantage, closing her eyes and blowing seductive kisses to the photographers. *Wow!* she thought to herself. Huey was better than she could ever have expected. He must have tipped this bunch off, and Treeva Sinclair was a star before she'd even filmed her first episode!

Dear Huey. Not only was he a fantastic agent and friend, but with him taking up residence in the pool house, she could leave LA for a few days, as she was being forced to now (to answer indecency charges regarding her tit pics), safe in the knowledge that he was there to keep an eye on her hacienda.

"Jaymi!"

"Over here, Jaymi!"

"J! Give us some leg, honey!"

Treeva frowned. (At least, tried to. Fortunately her frozen forehead failed to show any visible reaction and remained smoothly impassive.) She couldn't believe it. They'd got her name wrong! Regaining her composure swiftly, she pasted the smile back on her face and blinked hard, trying to get her vision back.

"Hey, boys — it's Treeva! Treeva Sinclair!"

As her eyes adjusted to the glare, Treeva was pleased to see the cameras still click-clicking away. There was just one problem. They weren't clicking at *her*. Looking over her shoulder, Treeva's face fell. (At least, tried to. Her "chintox" had restricted nearly all movement in the jaw area.) Behind her stood an Amazonian vision, all false lashes, peroxide nylon hair extensions, pneumatic boobs and endless legs in perilous hooker-style platform mules. It was the unmistakeably statuesque form of controversial trannie and sometime chat-show guest Jaymi Lee, whose notoriety stemmed from a public indiscretion with a married politician on the Strip. He was determinedly Z-list. And he was Treeva's alter ego — in drag.

Treeva stamped her feet angrily and put her hands on her hips in outrage. She'd been upstaged by a drag queen! But the worst wasn't over yet. Spotting her opportunity, Jaymi leaned over and blew Treeva a theatrical kiss.

"Sorry, sweetie — guess they prefer the real thing!"

The cameras went wild.

Treeva felt her face burn with humiliation. Bloody Americans! What did they know anyway? Picking up the handle of her Louis Vuitton overnight wheelie case, she stomped through into Departures. Thank God she'd only got hand luggage with her and could exit that hideous situation with some dignity!

As she searched about for her check-in desk, she felt a tap on the shoulder.

"Excuse me!"

She looked down and saw a Japanese tourist smiling at her politely.

"Madam, you have something stuck to your shoe."

Treeva inspected her heel, and, sure enough, there was the length of loo roll that she'd used to blot her lips with earlier, trailing behind her. She must have dragged it all the way from the car — past the photographers and everybody. Huffily, she pulled it off. Today really wasn't going her way. At least, she consoled herself, she'd soon be in the safe confines of First Class and could blot out this hideous town and everyone in it.

As always, the queue at check-in was non-existent and it was only a matter of moments before she was heading for the reassuring comfort of the executive VIP lounge and the free champagne — she needed it to still her jangling nerves. The line of coke she'd done before leaving home was already wearing off, and she wasn't quite sure how she was going to cope for another twelve or so hours until the next one.

Spurred on by the prospect of alcohol, Treeva deposited her small face-case on to the conveyor belt and smiled brightly at the stern-looking customs official on the other side of the electronic barrier. The woman — short and stout with no make-up and cropped, fuss-free hair — stared back at her crossly. Lesbian,

364

thought Treeva immediately. And the kind of person who really took pleasure in making her life a misery. (Ever since the night with the movie star and her girlfriend, Treeva had been convinced all lesbians were out to get her.) And sure enough, as Treeva tottered through, the security alarm sounded loudly.

"Please remove your belt and your jewellery," said the official.

Treeva sighed and started the interminable process of removing everything that might activate the buzzer again — belt, watch, bracelets, necklaces, earrings, tummy stud, nipple ring . . . Finally, free of bling, she walked successfully past the stony-faced officials.

But her ordeal wasn't over yet. As Treeva looked for her case, she saw with a sinking heart that another customs officer had taken it to one side and was patiently waiting to search it. With, she noted dismally, an expression of expectant intent.

"Is this your case, ma'am?"

Treeva gave him what she hoped was a winning smile.

"Why, yes it is!"

"Then I'd like you to accompany me through here," he said, indicating a room to the side of the lounge.

Treeva looked at him, puzzled.

"But why?"

"We have reason to believe you are carrying prohibited items," the official said sternly.

Treeva's mind raced in panic as she desperately tried to remember if there might be any old evidence of drugs in there. A stray wrap of coke, or even a cheeky bag of grass. But after a thorough mental search, she relaxed slightly. She was sure there wasn't. This must be some mistake.

"Contraband goods?" she said brightly. "What on earth do you think is in there?" She gave a tinny laugh.

The official cleared his throat. "That's what we need to investigate, ma'am."

At the thought of even more time passing between now and her next drink, Treeva felt the beginning of panic.

"This is preposterous!" she squealed. "Don't you know who I am?"

The official looked back at her impassively.

"You could be the Queen of England, for all I care," said the official humourlessly. "With all due respect, who you are makes no difference to us, ma'am, when we're investigating a possible firearms offence."

Five hours later, Treeva was broken, sitting slumped over the small square table in front of her. She was tired and thirsty, and being in this stressful environment had made her even more desperate for her next line. The fluorescent strip lighting and three bare walls of the incident room were making her dizzy, and through the glass door she'd watched the customs team check so many people through, she was sure she could now qualify to do the job herself.

That was if they ever let her go. Bloody Americans! Couldn't they tell the difference between a designer shoe and a handgun when it was staring them in the face?

The door opened and she turned her gaze defeatedly to yet another official (if the size of his epaulettes was anything to go by, he was much more senior than the succession of previous customs officers) who was carrying her prized Chanel shoes with the pistol heels in an exhibit bag. She sighed as she stared at them. No wonder they were limited edition — they were *beautiful*. And not available in the UK. Which was why she sure as hell wasn't getting on a flight without them. And if she had to stay here all night — which, judging by the current rate of progress, was quite likely — she would do. She wasn't going anywhere until these idiots handed back her prized new shoes.

Although clearly higher-ranking, this new guy was smaller than the other burly customs guards — a slightly built, bookish fellow who couldn't be more than five feet tall. Treeva pulled herself up in her seat, suddenly feeling more optimistic. Maybe he was actually the admin guy, sent to do the paperwork to release her, and she could get straight on the next flight home.

The official took a seat opposite her and placed the bag containing the shoes on the table between them. He pulled a notebook from his holster and looked at something written on it.

"So, Miss Sinclair. Can I check some details." It was a statement from someone not used to asking the kinds of questions anyone wanted to answer, not a question.

Treeva sighed audibly and slumped on her side of the table.

"What is your mother's maiden name?"

Treeva sighed in irritation. She'd answered this question about a hundred times already, to a hundred different people.

"Jenkins," she said in a bored voice.

"Where were you born?"

"Dagenham," she replied in the same bored voice.

The official self-importantly pulled on some white gloves, placed a pair of pince-nez glasses on the end of his nose, and tipped the shoes out on to the table. Treeva winced as one of the heels caught on the edge. If he scuffed them, she'd get Daddy to sue him.

"And these are your — um — shoes?" He picked one up delicately by the toe, as if it were emanating a particularly bad smell.

"Yes," sighed Treeva.

The official inspected one of the shoes all round and attempted to unscrew the heel. Treeva looked at him in astonishment.

"What are you looking for in there?"

The man looked at her over the top of his glasses. "If I said cocaine, what would your response be, Miss Sinclair?"

Treeva snorted. "Oh yeah," she said sarcastically to no one in particular. "I'm really gonna hide my drugs in my gun . . ."

The man looked at her again, unamused. "How much were these shoes, Miss Sinclair?"

Irritated again, Treeva raised her finely plucked eyebrows skywards. "Oh God, I don't know. Two thousand pounds? Three thousand? Who knows? It's all small change to me."

Now it was the official's turn to raise an eyebrow. Just one, disdainful, unimpressed eyebrow. But it was enough. Tired of his patronizing, jobsworth attitude, and frazzled by the pressure of her ordeal, Treeva snapped.

"I'm sure that's the first time you've been that close to a Chanel shoe. Maybe you'd like to try them on? I'm sure they'd suit you."

She smiled in spite of herself. Good one. Even under pressure, she never lost it. Must remember that one for the TV show.

The official fixed Treeva with a disapproving, almost nasty look. She felt the atmosphere in the room freeze and take a distinct turn for the worse.

"Well, Miss Sinclair, at this point I am obliged to tell you that you have the right to make one phone call. I suggest you might like to call a family member." He paused. "Or your lawyer."

Treeva looked at him blankly. It was the middle of the night at home — Daddy would simply *kill* her if she called him now. But she'd never had to deal directly with problems like this. Who could she call to help her out?

Then, as if a light bulb had turned on, she thought of Huey. Huey would know what to do. She tapped his number into the phone the official gave her and waited for him to pick up, heart beating wildly.

"Yell-o!" Huey shouted his customary phone greeting into the phone above some loudly pumping background music. Odd, thought Treeva absently. Where could there be a party going on this early in the evening? She pushed the thought to the back of her mind.

"Huey! Huey, it's me, Treeva!" she said, the sound of a familiar voice making her want to cry.

"Who? Who's that? Sorry, can't hear you — can you turn the music down? Guys?" Huey's voice moved away from the receiver. "Hey — what's that they've just launched into the pool? Hey!"

There was a pause filled with shrieking, laughing and a pounding bass line, and then the ruckus muffled and died down a little. Eventually, Huey's voice came back on to the line.

"Hey, sorry about that. I'm house-sitting for someone and we've got a *major* party going on. It's kinda getting out of hand! Who did you say this is?"

Treeva stared at the phone miserably. So much for trustworthy Huey looking after her house. And so much for her only call. It looked like she was going home without her shoes, after all. That was if, after her behaviour, Customs ever let her go.

CHAPTER
TWENTY-NINE

The picturesque, tree-lined streets of Le Marais slipped by in a colourful, well-tended blur as Lyric's taxi negotiated the traffic through the bustling Jewish *quartier*. She snuggled further down inside her coat and let her mind drift back to Philippe, still in bed in their plush, amber-scented suite at the Plaza Athénée. As she'd kissed him goodbye, Philippe had looked like an advertisement for the hotel, she thought longingly, lounging back on his lavender pillow in their king-size bed, with his smouldering good looks all wrapped up in a fluffy white bath robe and matching slippers complete with the Athénée logo. The scene had been repeated on both mornings since they'd arrived in Paris forty-eight hours ago. The day's papers were spread all around Philippe, and room service sat on a tray next to him on the bed, the curtains drawn to let in the winter sunshine and the view of the chestnut trees outside. The only difference today was that Lyric had had no time to laze around with him or luxuriate in a romantic breakfast and late-morning love-in, and, despite the fun ahead of her, she had found it a wrench to leave the luxurious Regency-style surroundings for the cold January morning outside.

But as the taxi turned off down the side street and pulled up at the unassuming front door of her destination, Lyric perked up. Never mind where she'd come from, she was lucky, lucky, *lucky* to be heading where she was this morning. And anyway, after her appointment, and then a long lunch with Truly, at which she could finally introduce her two favourite people in the world to one another, it wouldn't be long before she and Philippe were back in the hotel and back in each other's arms . . .

A text message sounded and she jumped at the sight of Sheik Haddad de Sattamin's private number. She bit her lip nervously. Although the Sheik and Carola had apologized profusely for their deplorable treatment of Lyric in Monaco, and had tentatively been forgiven by both her and her family, the hurt was still raw and Lyric was still keeping them at arm's length.

Dear Lyric, we would love to meet Philippe.
How does a spot of winter sunshine appeal?
We look forward to welcoming you both at the palace sometime soon.

Lyric closed the text quickly. A lovely offer, most genuinely made, she was sure — but it still felt too soon. She was still too raw. The taxi pulled over, bringing Lyric abruptly back to the present.
"Merci bien. Au revoir!"
As Lyric collected her change, she shut the taxi door behind her firmly, and knocked at the front door of the smart townhouse. The door opened, and Lyric followed

the smart assistant through to the studio. The door was already open to greet her, and another, more harried assistant with pins in her mouth scurried over to greet her.

"*Mademoiselle Charlton, bonjour, bonjour. Comment allez-vous?*"

"*Très bien, merci.*" said Lyric, smiling broadly as she looked around at the familiar chaos of Azzedine Alaïa's studio. Compared with the fine decor *à la Parisienne* at the Plaza Athénée, this place looked positively home-made. Rails of dresses were lined up behind huge dressmaking tables scattered with oversized scissors, clothes patterns, rolls of fabric and designer drawings. Mannequins wearing toiles, half-finished dresses, dotted the room, and the walls were crammed with framed photos of the designer both at home and here with his muses. Also on display were doodles and notes from supermodels, and Polaroids of jovial past gatherings at the studio when Azzedine had accommodated fledgling models — too broke even to stay in a hostel — on his studio floor during the Paris shows. Naomi Campbell, Stephanie Seymour, Tatjana Patitz — they all starred on these walls, their careers profiled in this most fashionable of scrapbook displays. No wonder his name on its own was enough to warm the heart of even the most hardened industry players, let alone his fabulous figure-sculpting designs. It was, Lyric decided, so shabby as to be the very *epitome* of glamour.

"Lyric! *Ma chérie!* How are you, darling, *darling?*"

Lyric turned in delight to see the designer, dressed in his customary baggy black trousers and black

373

turtleneck, hurrying over to her, arms outstretched, a broad smile on his beaming face. She felt his trademark black hair, combed back into a kind of quiff, brush her cheek as she bent down to embrace him. She had barely said hello, she thought, yet she was already feeling a million dollars after his effusive greeting. He might only come up to her knees, but Azzedine's aura was greater than any other she'd ever come across.

"I'm all the better for seeing you!" she laughed. "It's so wonderful to be here!"

Azzedine stepped back and looked her up and down appraisingly. "You look wonderful, darling, simply wonderful!" he proclaimed. "So you've ditched the drugs and now you have a new addiction, huh? A man, if I am not mistaken?"

Lyric smiled. There was no hiding things from some people. "I might have . . ." she ventured. Then, seeing Azzedine's reproachful expression, dissolved into giggles. "Oh, OK then — yes, I have! And if you're very lucky, you might meet him later."

Azzedine hugged her appreciatively and then clapped loudly in a businesslike fashion. "Come, darling, *darling*, come," he said, leading her through the studio. "Elise! Champagne for Mademoiselle Lyric! Patricia! A pen, a notebook. And girls, girls, girls," he called, clapping on every syllable. "Off we go!"

Ushering Lyric into her seat, Azzedine brought order to the room, and as his assistants plied her with refreshments, an order form and a pencil, she could see his models congregating behind a screen and swiftly changing into their first outfits for her private viewing of his latest collection. She suddenly felt overwhelmingly spoilt. It was a privilege to be here. She was the sole audience for one of the world's most exclusive theatre shows, and the lack of pandemonium amongst the organized chaos and the uniqueness of the occasion made her feel luxuriously exhilarated, excited — and *alive*.

As the models paraded in front of her, Lyric had the sense of being completely and utterly transported to another world, a world in which everything was gorgeous, and groomed, and glamorous. A world in which nothing was unflattering, no one was flustered, and nothing, but nothing, was anything but fabulous. This was one of her favourite collections to date. The designer's signature knits and leathers had been woven into bouncy skirts featuring open-work decoration and intricate embellishment. Cutout feather effects were hand-painted with streaks of white, while white cotton blouses freshened up the tough side of black leather. Coats were cinched at the waist and tiny jackets were fashioned from fake crocodile hide or faux pony skin treated to look like miniature leopard spots. A succession of bias-cut velvet evening gowns in black or brown added some show-stopping va-va-voom. And all of it was underpinned by Azzedine's trademark tailoring, which could sculpt even the most shapeless of forms into a curvaceous bombshell.

Lyric's pencil almost developed a life of its own as it flew in a breathless frenzy across the order form, marking outfit after outfit until the show ended and, she realized almost dizzy with excitement, that it was going to cost an *obscene* amount of money.

She chewed the end of her pencil guiltily, mentally totting up the extent of her extravagance and wondering how many families it might feed instead.

There was an insistent buzzing from her bag, and Lyric pulled out her phone, glad for the distraction from the dreaded mathematics on her notepad. She checked the LED screen — caller's number withheld. But as she was in France, this could be anyone calling from the UK who wasn't already programmed into her phone.

"Hello!" she trilled happily, shaking her head at the second glass of champagne being offered to her by one of Azzedine's many assistants.

"Lyric?" The clipped public-school tones on the other end of the phone were familiar, but the voice itself wasn't. Although, it did ring faint bells . . .

"Yes, speaking," she said hesitantly. She still couldn't shake her instinctive distrust of anyone she didn't instantly know.

"George, here. George Mogler. That is — you'd know me better as *Gideon* Mogler, before I changed my name. We spoke a few weeks ago."

"Oh, Gideon — I mean, George!" Lyric breathed out in relief. It wasn't a journalist with more bad news, after all — Gideon-George was Jacob's friend at the Home Office who'd promised to find her a copy of Edward's death certificate. That was over a month ago now, and so much had happened since then, she'd almost forgotten about it. And even if she had remembered, she'd have been loath to call him, what with the scandal over Jacob and Crispin and everything. After all, most of Jacob's friends and associates had disowned Jacob over it, or at the very least distanced themselves from him. Why should Gideon Mogler, son of spineless snake Henry Mogler, be any different?

But he had rung her, so maybe he wasn't cut from the same cloth as the rest of them.

"I didn't recognize your voice!" she said apologetically.

"How's Jacob?" asked Gideon awkwardly. "I've tried to ring him, but . . ."

"Well, he's still got the same number," snapped Lyric sharply, feeling defensive. "Maybe he didn't recognize you. Which name did you leave for him — Gideon or George? Or is there another moniker you go by too?"

Platitudes were all very well, but what Jacob needed right now was concrete support. Since the collapse of not only his political career but his entire life as he knew it, Jacob had been keeping a low profile in various boltholes around the world, and his mental state was fragile, at best. He needed the physical presence of friends and family, not people paying lip service to his well-being.

"No, really, Lyric — I have tried to contact him," continued Gideon-George quietly. "But I didn't want to pester him."

Lyric chastized herself inwardly. Really, she had to stop acting like a terrier whenever Jacob's name was mentioned. And anyway, for all she knew, Gideon-George was ringing to tell her he'd spent the last few weeks trying to help her.

"I'm sorry," she said. "It's just been a very difficult time for us all."

"Please, don't apologize," said Gideon-George earnestly. Lyric relaxed. Her gut instinct was telling her this was one of life's few good guys. "But I was genuinely calling you to ask after Jacob — and that, erm, other family matter you asked me to look into."

Lyric breathed in sharply. "George, when you say 'family' matter, you haven't mentioned this to anyone, have you?"

"Of course not!" said Gideon-George, sounding offended that she'd even felt the need to ask. "I promised it would stay between you and me. But I'm not sure there's anything to tell."

"What do you mean?" asked Lyric, bewildered.

Gideon-George hesitated. "Well, nothing you want to hear, anyway."

"Go on," said Lyric carefully, as a familiar and unwelcome sense of impending doom crept over her.

"What I thought was going to be a straightforward archive case has proved rather more difficult," said Gideon-George. "And I wanted to look into it as far as I possibly could before coming back to you."

"Go on," said Lyric slowly.

"As soon as I looked up your brother's records, another — very recent — request came up. For his birth certificate."

"From whom?" wailed Lyric, perplexed. Who else would want proof of her brother's existence?

378

"Well, this is where the mystery deepens," said Gideon-George hesitantly. "I couldn't find out. The information was classified."

"Classified?" repeated Lyric, now beyond confused. "But why?"

"Without going to the very top, I can't find out," continued Gideon-George. "And I didn't want to involve anyone else before I spoke to you again. I'm not sure if you are aware, but my father is now head honcho at the very top of the food chain at the General Register Office. I could ask him."

"No, not yet," interrupted Lyric. Something told her the last person she wanted involved in all this was Henry Mogler. "It's too weird. I need to think about it first."

She paused, still trying to rack her brains for the answer. Who on earth could want a copy of Edward's birth certificate — and why would it be so secret it was classified? Almost subconsciously, she rubbed her twitchy eye.

Lyric's pulse was racing now, and she felt hot, clammy, and dizzy. She got up and paced up and down, not knowing what else to do with the nervous energy racing around her body. Someone else was seeking information on her brother — but who? And why? It couldn't be her mother and father. They'd got their own copy in her father's safe. Lyric tried to pinpoint someone — anyone — who might have a vested interest, but her head was spinning.

Then she had a moment of clarity. Of course. The PI. Perhaps, for whatever reason, his search had uncovered the death of a twin brother and, for whatever reason, led him to request a copy of the birth certificate. She racked her brains to try and remember if she'd mentioned Edward at all in her briefing. She should be able to remember something so significant, but with everything else she'd had going on, she couldn't be quite sure . . .

On the other end of the phone, Gideon-George cleared his throat. "There is one other thing, Lyric," he said quietly.

"Oh — go on?" said Lyric. At the tone of his voice, she felt another knot of dread rise in her chest.

"The death certificate you requested."

"Oh, of course," said Lyric, mentally kicking herself. "Thanks for reminding me. With the other matter, I'd completely forgotten. Should I give you an address to send it to?"

"Well, that's just it," continued Gideon-George. "I can't send it to you."

"Why?" responded Lyric. "Don't tell me that's classified, too?"

"No, the death certificate isn't classified," he replied. "The death certificate isn't there."

"What do you mean? Where is it then?"

There was a pause on the other end of the phone.

"The death certificate isn't there, Lyric, because it doesn't exist. There is no death certificate."

"Oh my God," cried Lyric, sitting down as the full force of the revelation hit her. Then she leapt up again with a shriek. "Oh my God. So — does that mean —?"

Again, Gideon cleared his throat. "Well, it can mean only one thing," he said sombrely. "If there is no death certificate, there was no death."

She waited.

"And if there was no death, then your brother must still be alive."

CHAPTER
THIRTY

"Miss Charlton."

Lyric pulled herself out of her now semi-permanent reverie over the possibility that her brother might still be alive, and the questions that had been filling every harrowing day and sleepless night since Gideon-George had called her, and stepped out of the club's chauffeur-driven car and up to the hallowed town-house entrance of Aspinalls. The liveried doorman nodded reverently and opened the door for her.

"Mr Hassan is waiting for you inside, Miss Charlton."

Lyric had been coming to the Mayfair club, in an elegant street just off Berkeley Square, with her father since she was a small child. Now, so many years later, she still marvelled at the service. It was several months since she'd been here and she didn't recognize the doorman, but still he knew instantly who she was, who she was meeting, and, probably, what she'd be drinking.

"Thank you," she murmured, shrugging off her Burberry trench once she was inside the elegant lobby and handing it to the concierge.

A waitress appeared at her elbow. "Mr Hassan is in the Club Room," she said, smiling, and led Lyric through to the warm, intimate room where Ali Hassan was waiting for her.

As they made their way down the corridor, Lyric caught glimpses of foreigners and dishevelled old toffs busily squandering away their fortunes in the gaming rooms and conducting illicit whispered meetings in others. She was hit, as always, by the overwhelming history of the place. Imagine the affairs, deals and scandals that had begun, been played out and ended in this establishment! Even as a child, when she'd asked loudly who everyone else in the room was, the waiter had bent to tell her that he couldn't possibly comment because everyone there was with someone they shouldn't be. Since then, the club had held a fascination for her, and tonight, with all the dramas taking place in her own life making anything possible, it seemed to hold an even greater sense of mystery than ever before. She shrugged off the unwelcome thought that, in many people's eyes, going to meet a notorious philanderer and womanizer could initiate a scandal of her own. But the reason she was here was not sex, and she had no desire to add to the romantic liaisons of the club's history.

Lyric attempted to quell the mounting butterflies in her stomach. After their previous highly-charged meeting in Courchevel, she'd turned down repeated invitations for drinks with Ali Hassan. She wasn't flattered into thinking that he thought she was anything special, but she also knew he was not used to being turned down by women, and was sure that until he managed to add her to his impressive list of conquests he would persist in trying to seduce her. So even though he'd assured her it was an "innocent" drink between friends, she'd refused point-blank. Then, since the scandal over Jacob and Crispin's affair had broken, Ali's phone calls had ceased, and Lyric had figured she was off the hook. Every cloud had a silver lining, after all. Maybe in wanting to distance himself from Jacob, Ali had lost interest in Lyric, too.

But Ali's most recent call, just two days ago, had seemed different. And though she had initially politely declined, something in his tone had changed her mind. Call it instinct, but with all the upheavals life had presented her with recently, Lyric was getting used to not just listening to her instincts, but acting on them.

She followed the waitress into the bright and cosy Club Room. The cream walls were framed by Georgian-style coving and picture rails and decorated with wildlife paintings from the late John Aspinall's private collection. Sofas and armchairs were dotted around the room, arranged around tables holding oversized backgammon boards with pieces the size of Babybel cheeses. Rare *objets d'art* were casually scattered on mantelpieces and occasional tables. It had the elegance of an old English stately home, and was a million miles away from other gaming clubs in the city.

So here she was. And here, she thought, as she saw Ali stand up by his table in the corner, was he — "feel appeal" personified, as Crispin would say. Ali must have a three-ply cashmere sweater in every pastel colour of

384

the rainbow, she thought to herself as she took in his peppermint V-neck sweater and noted the small curl of black chest hair escaping out of the top. Ali's anthracite eyes flashed dangerously under his shock of dark hair. Such similar features to Philippe, thought Lyric with a jolt of recognition — but how differently put together! How odd it was that people could share such strong characteristics yet look so completely unalike.

"Lyric — you look beautiful, as always," said Ali, taking in her beige thigh-length Phillip Lim 3.1 dress, black opaque tights and YSL Tributes appreciatively. He brushed her hand with a kiss and gave her a devilish smile. He just can't help himself, thought Lyric, amused. And though she had no intention of giving in to his charms, it was nice to be admired.

"And you're looking well, Ali," she replied, sitting down gracefully and crossing her legs demurely.

As the waitress brought her a Perrier, Lyric smiled in gratitude. As she had predicted, they had got her order spot on. How did they do that?

Ali raised his glass to Lyric. "So, you have finally succumbed," he teased, a victorious smile playing on his lips.

"Yes, I have finally succumbed to a drink with you," corrected Lyric sternly, but smiled in spite of herself. "Because something told me there was more to this rendezvous than just another attempt to get me into your bed."

Ali shook his head, admiring her chutzpah. "Say it like it is, why don't you? You really are something, Lyric Charlton," he marvelled.

"Yes, well, my boyfriend thinks so too," said Lyric deliberately, and then returned to the point of their meeting. "So to what do I owe this pleasure? It's nothing to do with Jacob, is it?" she asked, suddenly anxious.

"No," said Ali, his face darkening. "I have no business with your cousin now."

At the mention of Jacob, the bodyguard hovering behind the table moved forward slightly, and Ali held up his hand to signal him back to his post.

"Well, I do," said Lyric firmly, determined not to get involved in any of Ali's macho nonsense. "So we're probably best avoiding the subject altogether."

Ali sat back, swirling the liquid in his glass around slowly and considering Lyric carefully.

"Well, perhaps not altogether," he said after a few moments' pause.

"Oh, really?" said Lyric, intrigued but determined not to show it. "And why not 'altogether'?"

"Well, because your cousin —" Ali seemed uncomfortable even speaking Jacob's name, thought Lyric in surprise — "is partly the reason we are here tonight."

He leaned forward, the sexy spark back in his eyes. "And because I wanted to set eyes on your beautiful face again, of course."

He couldn't help himself. But there it was again, that crackle of sexual chemistry. Lyric shifted awkwardly in her seat. She had an uncomfortable sense of her life running away with her again, of fate playing a hand in building up the events surrounding her until they met in some explosive finale.

"Get to the point, Ali," she said, not unkindly. "I'm a busy woman."

Ali bent his head closer to hers. "And one who could be in grave danger," he said urgently, covering her hand with his. "Things have come to light, Lyric, since your cousin so disgraced your family and mine. You must know it is a matter of honour that I demand retribution. Therefore, in the name of friendship, I intend to safeguard you and your next of kin."

Lyric stared at him, chilled to the bone at what he was implying, yet at the same time totally confused. What was it Ali knew that would repay the so-called shame Jacob's sexuality had placed on the Hassan family, and what on earth did he mean by "safeguard" her?

Ali looked right, looked left, and finally leaned still further forward. In unison, both bodyguards stepped forward to flank him closer.

"It concerns your cousin's father," said Ali in hushed tones.

Lyric's mouth went dry, and she took a long sip of water to steady her nerves. She, too, swirled the liquid drink around, staring into the clear bubbles intently, scared to lift her eyes to meet Ali's, afraid that he would see the raw fear in them. Uncle Quentin. Again. With every move, it seemed her uncle was several steps ahead of her, leading her deeper and deeper into a mystery she neither understood nor felt qualified to unravel.

And, if she was honest, she was almost too scared to want to solve it.

"What, you mean Uncle Quentin?" she said lightly. "What of him?"

Ali leaned in further, searching for eye contact with her.

"He is a dangerous man, Lyric."

Finally, fear nearly bursting out of her, Lyric raised her eyes to Ali's. "I know," she whispered. "But how do *you* know?"

Again, Ali looked left, looked right, and then leaned in to Lyric. His bodyguards shuffled an extra few inches closer. They were now so close that Lyric could almost feel their body heat.

"He engaged the services of one of my men," said Ali, quietly but urgently. "He asked him to kill someone."

Lyric gasped. "He took out a contract?" she shrieked. Then, remembering where she was, she lowered her voice. "But *who?* And more to the point, *how?* That kind of thing costs a lot of money, doesn't it?" She bit her lip — she sounded like a gauche schoolgirl. She lowered her voice several octaves. "I mean, Uncle Quentin is not a rich man."

Ali Hassan sucked his teeth in disagreement. "On the contrary, dear Lyric. Your uncle is currently a *very* rich man. And he has a very big problem with an English bartender in France. A *BIG* problem. For it is this bartender that your uncle paid a considerable advance to my man to find. And it is this bartender for whom your uncle would have paid my man another, even

388

bigger fee —" he paused and lowered his voice — "to eliminate."

Lyric stared unseeingly at Ali. "Uncle Quentin . . . a killer?" she said softly. And the intended victim an apparently random bartender in France, at that. It just didn't add up. Then she rounded on him, a desperate need to return to normality making her accusatory. "Don't be ridiculous," she snapped. "Uncle Quentin couldn't organize a piss-up in a brewery. He's a bumbling fool, everyone knows that. And no, I agree, he's not the nicest person in the universe, but *murder*? Never." She shook her head, willing it to be untrue.

Ali took her hand again, gently this time.

"Lyric, I only tell you because retribution is due," he said, repeating his earlier point. "Your cousin has shamed my family. Therefore I vowed retribution on your cousin's family. It is not vindictive. It is honour. By alerting you to this, I get satisfaction."

Lyric nodded in reluctant understanding. "But . . . earlier you said you also wanted to safeguard me . . . and my next of kin?" she stammered, as if trying to make sense of the words simply by speaking them. "How can Uncle Quentin's vendetta against some barman possibly harm me and my family?"

Ali looked at her meaningfully. "Lyric, if I knew, I would tell you. But what I do know is that your uncle, in briefing my man, made many mentions of you. You and this barman, somehow you are linked. And whoever this barman is, however you are linked to him, it is not good news. Because your Uncle Quentin . . ." Ali paused. "If your Uncle Quentin wants him dead,

389

there is only one possible conclusion to draw. He wants you dead too."

Lyric's hands were now visibly shaking. She tried to pick up her glass to take a steadying sip of water and dropped it, spilling the remainder of her drink over herself and the table. Lyric was totally unaware of the waitress hurrying over to clear it up and mop up her dripping dress.

"I still don't quite understand," Lyric said, her voice catching as she spoke. "Quentin has no reason to want anybody dead. The only thing he's ever wanted is Broughton Hall —"

She trailed off. Broughton Hall. Could all this be somehow linked to his bid for ownership of her parents' home? Was Uncle Quentin's desperation for the estate so great that he would *kill* for it? Kill his own *niece*? Lyric could feel the blood pounding round her head. The connection she'd felt with the barman at Le Mélézin that night. It had been strong, but not sexual. Instead, almost *fraternal*. Looking at his face, in fact, had almost been like looking in a mirror. Could the barman be not just a passing stranger, but a blood relative?

Lyric looked at Ali and spoke haltingly, almost wonderingly.

"There is a covenant. In our family. It dictates that the first-born son in any generation of Charltons will be the one to inherit Broughton Hall. In my father's generation, it was him. In my generation, it will be Jacob. Unless . . . unless . . ."

390

She didn't notice Ali supportively clasping her hand as the breeze block of realization hit her.

The only possible reason Uncle Quentin could have for wanting to kill anyone, let alone some humble bartender, would be that that person stood between him and Broughton Hall.

"My father — he had a son. I had a brother," stammered Lyric clumsily. "He's dead. At least, we thought he was dead . . ."

Gideon-George was right. There was no death certificate, because there had been no death.

Which meant that, in all certainty, the humble bartender was her father's son and heir.

He was her long-lost twin brother. And he was alive. For now.

She looked at Ali with growing dread. Somehow, some way, Uncle Quentin knew of his existence. He knew her brother was still alive. How was almost immaterial at this moment. What mattered was that Uncle Quentin wanted him gone again. And Lyric too, for that matter.

"How can I find him?" she asked Ali desperately. "The bartender — how can I get to him?" She swallowed. "Before my Uncle Quentin does?"

1st February

CHAPTER
THIRTY-ONE

Trying not to flinch as the ice-cold metal of the gun barrel bored into her temple, Lyric took a sideways look to her right, and with her elbow tried to nudge Philippe's limp body into action. His arm moved in response to her touch and fell limply on to her lap. Helplessly, she tried to grab hold of his hand in some kind of futile attempt to reassure — who? Both of them? At the movement the attendant shoved the gun harder into the side of her head.

"Don't move, *Miss Charlton*, or I will blow your brains out."

Lyric's mouth fell open with shock. Behind her, she saw their co-pilot creep up behind the air stewardess. She tried not to react, and slowly placed her glass on the tray in front of her.

"I — I . . ."

"*And don't speak!*" the girl said shrilly in a heavy Russian accent. "This is not a toy, Miss Charlton! And I am trained to use it. Do not test me!" With that, she spun round and with a ninja-style karate kick caught the co-pilot clean in the jaw and knocked him cold to the ground.

A tall, blond young man with cold good looks wearing a steward's uniform and a blank expression appeared from the cockpit. He was another crew member Lyric had never seen before — certainly not one of the jet's regular team — and his piercing blue eyes seemed to stare right through her. He looked down at the prostrate co-pilot with no emotion, and, kicking his head softly as he passed, approached the air stewardess. Without meeting her eye, he spoke in low and urgent tones into her ear. She, in turn, never took her eyes off Lyric. The air stewardess nodded crisply.

"Everyone is dispensable," she said curtly in English, still staring intently at Lyric.

Lyric gripped the arms of her leather chair tightly and swallowed hard. Her throat was dry and tight, and when she spoke, her voice sounded strained and foreign.

"Might — might I ask what's going on?"

The stewardess nudged her head again with the barrel of the gun.

"Your pilot is dead," she snapped. Lyric gasped. "Your boyfriend could well be too. And if you don't want to go the same way, keep quiet."

"But . . ." protested Lyric, stunned.

"Do you not understand your mother tongue, Miss Charlton? This is not a film. Your pilot was no hero. And we are no amateurs. We are SAS-trained professionals — and you are under our orders. Only when we reach our destination may you begin to understand our purpose."

396

Lyric stared at her in disbelief. Her stomach lurched as the plane changed course abruptly, and she looked out of the window helplessly. There was, it seemed, no way out of this nightmare. Lyric had desperately been through everything in her mind in the few terrifying moments since they'd been hijacked. And those few moments, tinged with the threat of almost certain death, had seemed like a lifetime. A trickle of sweat appeared at her hairline and made its way slowly down her temple.

It seemed, Lyric thought, trying to edge away from the pressure of the gun, as though the pistol was surgically attached to her head. She switched her gaze and watched the blond steward as he urgently barked something into a walkie-talkie. He spoke almost like a robot, she thought absently. As if he'd been electronically programmed to do whatever it was they were going to do.

The problem she had, reasoned Lyric — other than being hijacked at fifty-thousand feet by a bunch of Russian nutters who would probably see killing both her and Philippe as the easiest solution — was that they were well and truly outnumbered. Even if Philippe came round and they managed to somehow overpower the steward and the stewardess, there had to be at least one other member of their team on board, otherwise who was currently flying the plane in place of poor Jean-Jacques? And even if, between her and Philippe, they managed to overpower the new pilot too, the pair of them would still have to fly and land the plane safely. Lyric felt the hairs on the back of her neck stand up and her throat close up in fear — a dull, creeping, cold kind of fear that she'd never felt in her life before — as she came to terms with the facts. She was never going to find Edward. She was never going to see her parents or her friends again. And she and Philippe were as good as dead — destined for either a watery grave or a snowy end somewhere between here and Siberia.

Which meant, of course, that her long-lost brother Edward was also on course for certain death. It was Lyric's PI who, just hours earlier, had alerted Lyric to her Uncle Quentin's latest plan — to travel to Courchevel to seek out Edward somewhere on the snowy slopes and kill him with his own hands. Her uncle, it seemed, was already heading over to France — overland, by train, so as to better cover his tracks. It had taken Lyric only seconds to decide what to do next, and, shortly after a call to the recently reconciled Sheik, she and Philippe had been on his private jet en route to Geneva, hot on the trail of her uncle. How exhilarated she'd been at the time — scared, yet buoyed by her ability to play an active part in the single most important event of her life. What she and Philippe were going to do when they got there Lyric had no idea. All she knew was that she had to get to Courchevel, and to Edward, before her uncle.

But what a fat lot of good it had done them. Now, not only was Edward destined to have his tragic life cut short before it had really begun, but she and Philippe seemed to be heading for the same destiny.

A sob rose up in Lyric's throat and she reached out blindly for Philippe's hand. The stewardess put her finger on the trigger and jerked the gun harder into the side of her head.

"Don't move, Miss Charlton!" she spat. "You know the consequences!"

"For God's sake!" Lyric snapped back, hysteria beginning to overwhelm her. "You threaten us with our lives, and then you tell me I can't spend my last minutes holding my boyfriend's hand? If you have any heart whatsoever, grant me that much, at least!"

Lyric sighed miserably and sank bank as far into her seat as the gun would let her. Suddenly, she felt Philippe's fingers tighten around hers. She started, and immediately felt him give her hand a warning squeeze. Her heart soared. Philippe was conscious! He was alive, and he was — She bit her lip. She must stay calm. She mustn't, simply mustn't, give any of this away. She steeled herself against the temptation to turn and look at him, to catch a glimpse of those warm, twinkling, *reassuring* brown eyes. Philippe pressed her palm and she squeezed back. He pressed again, and again. She frowned. Once was comforting, twice was doubly so, but if Philippe kept squeezing her then the stewardess was bound to notice — and object. She gave him another sidelong glance, telepathically trying to transmit her thoughts to him.

He squeezed again, this time another sequence of short and long presses. Lyric instinctively turned to look at him in surprise, then tried to make it look natural as the stewardess warningly rammed the gun harder against her temple.

399

There it was again. Two short squeezes and a long one. Lyric felt another surge of emotion, but this time it was more akin to an excited laugh than misery. Unless she was very much mistaken, that was the beginning of a message in Morse code. She was sure Philippe had spelt out "understand". Was Philippe attempting to communicate with her — and trying to work out if she'd get what he was talking about?

Silently thanking her father — a decorated code breaker in the Second World War — for all the hours he'd spent entertaining her with wartime stories and teaching her the code she'd found so fascinating as a child, Lyric pressed on the top of Philippe's hand with her little finger. "Yes," she spelt back in Morse.

She stole a surreptitious glance at the stewardess. Though her physical stance was unwavering, it seemed the Russian woman's attention was more focused on the steward, busy arranging a veritable arsenal of weapons in the passageway to the cockpit.

Philippe started to press the palm of her hand again, and Lyric turned her attention back to him, trying desperately to decipher his message. It took several attempts, but finally Lyric thought she understood what he was trying to say. On a count of three, he would push sideways into the stewardess at the same time as Lyric pushed herself forwards into her stomach, catching her unawares and dislodging the gun. Lyric guessed Philippe planned to take the pistol from her as he pushed, and then somehow overcome the steward — but she couldn't be sure how. All she knew was what her part in the initial attempted coup was to be, and she had to trust that her boyfriend had a plan for the rest.

Philippe pressed her hand again. After three. Lyric took a deep breath. It was now or never.

One, two . . .

There was an almighty roar, and Lyric watched as, in a blur, Philippe sprang from his seat and hurled himself clumsily at the stewardess. Lyric felt herself freeze in fear. However much she willed her body into action, it simply wouldn't move. She was rooted to the spot. Around her, events unfolded at breakneck speed. By some kind of fluke, it seemed to Lyric, Philippe caught the stewardess in the face with his outstretched fist and she crumpled to the floor. As the force made Philippe's body richochet off her, he lurched with his full weight into the stunned form of the steward. The steward keeled over with a cry, hitting his head on the glass-topped coffee table with a thwack. Philippe, seizing the opportunity, grabbed the pistol the stewardess had dropped. Training it on the stewardess, he kicked the machine gun beyond the reach of the unconscious steward.

"Lyric, get it!"

At last Lyric felt her limbs come back to life and she swiftly picked it up. No stranger to guns after a lifetime loading for the shooting guests at Broughton Hall, Lyric fixed it on the slumped form of the steward. Breathless, she and Philippe — still groggy from his spell of unconsciousness — looked at one another in shock.

"Oh my God!" Lyric shrieked. "What on —"

Philippe pressed a finger to his lips urgently and pointed at the cockpit with his free hand. Lyric immediately understood. Their hijackers might be down for the moment, but her own and Philippe's lives were still in the hands of one of the aggressors — the new pilot. Anger ripped through her as she thought of poor Jean-Jacques lying there in the cockpit lifeless and cold, and she clenched her fists and bit her lips determinedly. She would do anything Philippe told her to do — as long as it got them to safety, and allowed them to avenge Jean-Jacques' death.

The stewardess twitched and tried to lift her head, and Philippe pushed his foot roughly into her face. Motioning towards Lyric's cashmere in-flight blanket, he moved the direction of his gun obsessively between the stewardess and her accomplice.

"Gag her," he mouthed urgently to Lyric. Lyric grabbed the fine wool blanket and tied it tightly around the woman's mouth, trying to ignore her rolling eyes and bared teeth, and the spittle which ran down over the scarf and on to Lyric's hands.

Just then, there was a loud, urgent shout from the cockpit in Russian. The stewardess struggled violently, desperately trying to make herself heard despite her improvised gag. Lyric moved forward, pointing the gun directly at her head. The woman couldn't speak, but her eyes said it all. Outrage, discomfort, and raw, primeval fear. Lyric couldn't help but give the woman a look of victory. Ha! How did it feel now, to be the one being restrained? Not nice at all — she could vouch for that herself.

Philippe shouted something back in what sounded like Russian. Lyric's eyes nearly popped out of her head. What else was there about Philippe that she didn't know? He'd never seemed keen to talk about his military past — but what depths of character had he kept from her all these months? Immediately, she shook the thoughts from her head. Time enough for these questions when — if — they got out of here alive. Whatever Philippe said, it seemed to satisfy the pilot, who muttered something in response and then went quiet. Panicking that her remaining comrade had deserted her, the stewardess kicked out violently, dealing a painful blow to Lyric's shin. It seemed to make something in her snap, and with a red mist of anger, Lyric turned and lashed out with the hand that was holding the gun.

With a sickening crack, the woman slumped back down on the floor like a rag doll, all struggle gone from her. Philippe stretched his toe out gingerly and nudged her. She gave out a low moan and then seemed to descend fully into unconsciousness.

"It's OK, *chérie*," said Philippe in a low voice. "She is unconscious."

Lyric breathed a sigh of relief and, making the most of their moment out of immediate danger, ran over to hug Philippe. She couldn't stop trembling.

Philippe gave her a brief hug, then pushed her away in a businesslike fashion. "So, now to the pilot," he murmured, nodding towards the cockpit.

"But what . . . ?" whispered Lyric questioningly, then shut her mouth abruptly as Philippe frowned and pressed his gun to his lips to indicate silence. He waved it towards the unconscious stewards, indicating to her to keep her gun trained on them.

Lyric stood her ground, trembling, as she heard a scuffle in the cockpit followed by a deep, gruff voice shouting in Russian. There was a loud bang and the unmistakeable sound of gunfire. Then there was an ominous silence, broken only by Lyric's huge rasping gulps as she tried to breathe through her fear. Who had been shot? Was it the pilot — or was it . . .?

"Lyric! *Chérie! Viens ici.*" Lyric held back a sob as Philippe called out to her urgently. He was alive!

Backing up into the cockpit, a sudden lurch sent Lyric careering through the partition and on to the floor, eye to eye with the dead Russian pilot. She scrambled to regain her feet, sobbing hysterically and trying not to look beyond him at the similarly slumped form of Jean-Jacques. The air was filled with the screech of dying engines, and she stumbled as the plane started a speedy descent. She stared wildly at Philippe, who was in the pilot's seat, studiously inspecting the controls.

"Philippe," she almost screamed. "What is going on? We're going to crash!"

Philippe looked up at her testily. "We are not going to crash, *chérie*. But I need you to make sure that our friends through there —" he nodded back at the unconscious stewards — "do not interrupt us during the next few minutes."

"During the next few minutes of what?" screamed back Lyric as the plane took another lurching nosedive. "Of us hurtling towards our deaths?"

Philippe gazed at her impenetrably. "We are currently on course for St Petersburg, *chérie*. I need to get us back on course for Europe." He gave Lyric a meaningful look. "And there is still time to reach your brother before your uncle does. If we are quick."

There was a silence, broken after a few seconds by Lyric's hesitant voice.

"But, Philippe — how are we going to land safely anywhere?" Her voice caught in desperation. "We're not going to make it, are we?"

"*Au contraire*," said Philippe proudly, reaching for the radio to contact ground control. "We are not going to die. We are in *my* hands, *chérie*. I am a qualified pilot. I did my national service in the French Air Force." He glanced out of the plane window. "We are still over France, where I have many contacts high up in the military. We will shut down the engines and glide. If I can get clearance to land in classified airspace, I think we can reach a restricted airbase in a matter of minutes. It's closer to Courchevel than Geneva. And once there, we will be among people who can deal with this — this — bunch of punks —" his eyes flashed angrily as he took in the pilot and his two colleagues behind him — "and who will be able to give us safe passage through customs, no questions asked."

Lyric looked at him in shock. He cleared his throat uncomfortably.

"Well, *chérie*, no questions until later." He smiled at her as he corrected himself, eyes twinkling again for a brief second. "But by then, your brother will be safe and these three will be under lock and key."

Lyric stared at him, pride and relief in her eyes. Now there really could be no surprises left in the world. Philippe, it seemed, was not just the man of her dreams, but her bone fide action hero, too.

He smiled grimly at her and nodded at the slumped forms of the stewards beyond the cockpit. "Don't lose concentration for a second, *chérie*. We might be safe for the moment, but your brother is not. There is no time to lose."

CHAPTER
THIRTY-TWO

Lyric sat forward tensely as the chauffeur-driven Lexus slushed its way slowly along the winding mountain roads, twisting through the pine trees and making tracks in the steadily falling snow. Although still only two in the afternoon, the sky, grey and heavy, announced impending nightfall. The car's headlights caught the fat, flurrying snowflakes as they fell persistently on to the windscreen. "Come on," she urged.

Philippe placed a restraining hand on her arm. "He is going as fast as he can, *chérie*," he said in a low voice. "Remember, if we can only achieve a certain speed, then so too can your uncle."

Lyric sank back into the leather upholstery, looking out at the weather miserably. The fact that he was right didn't make it any easier to cope with. They'd got this far — through a hijacking, an emergency landing, and, thanks to ex-air stewardess Carola's ground-staff contacts, a secret escape from the airport to avoid police questioning — and she simply couldn't bear it if they missed their moment now because of a few snowflakes. Plus, the slow journey was giving her the opportunity to think some unwelcome thoughts. How, even if they did all survive this, would Edward react to the news that he had a twin sister and had been deprived of his birthright for thirty years? What if he was angry or — even worse — not in the slightest bit interested?

"And remember, *chérie*, we have the PI on our side, too," said Philippe, breaking into her thoughts. "We have to trust he will do everything to reach Quentin before he finds Edward."

Lyric felt herself relax a little at the thought of the PI, currently travelling separately to Courchevel, hot on the heels of her uncle. How, she didn't know. She hadn't dared to ask. But how much more than a simple detective he had turned out to be, she thought — not just in solving the case, but in ensuring Lyric got out of this particular tangle alive.

You're not there yet, she reminded herself with trepidation. Her eye, which had been twitching on and off for the past twenty-four hours, was now simply unbearable and she rubbed it worriedly. If it signified anything, could it be that not just she, but Edward too, was already in danger? And was his wink in the bar at Le Mélézin all those months ago a sign that he, too, had her rare affliction — an affliction shared only by the closest kinship?

Finally, in the distance she could make out the twinkling lights of Courchevel against the backdrop of the pine-covered mountainside, which the snow was covering with yet another deep layer of powder, and the car accelerated along the clearer, wider road. The driver turned off into Le Mélézin's car park and Lyric leapt out of the car, with Philippe following close behind. Running her fastest, with no thought to manners or decorum, Lyric burst through the lobby and raced down the steep stairs to the bar, where she'd first — unbeknown to her at the time — set eyes on Edward.

The bar was almost empty, save for a septuagenarian couple having an afternoon Verveine and a uniformed bar attendant, idly polishing glasses. Lyric knew at a glance that it wasn't Edward.

"Edward! Your colleague! Is he here?" she shouted in French. The barman looked up in surprise at the commotion.

"*C'est urgent!*" shouted Philippe behind her. "Where is Edward?"

The barman shrugged non-committally. "*Il a un jour de congé,*" he said, addressing Philippe. "*Pourquoi?*"

Jour de congé. A day off. Lyric sank on to the nearest bar stool in defeat. They'd wasted vital minutes by coming straight here. It had never occurred to her that Edward might not be at work. And now she might be too late.

"Do you know where he lives?" she asked in a small voice.

The bar attendant shook his head, then stood up to attention as another man, clearly his senior, entered the bar.

"*Est-ce que vous cherchez Edward?*" he asked Lyric interestedly. "I was on a break — but I couldn't help but overhear."

Lyric perked up immediately. "Yes!" she exclaimed, leaping to her feet. "We're looking for Edward! Do you know where we can find him?"

"As a matter of fact, I do," said the manager, smiling. "I saw him only a few moments ago, on the street, heading up the mountain. He had received a letter — he said he had some news. Serious news, I guess, from the look on his face."

Lyric practically jumped over the bar in her haste to know more. "Where was he going?" she shrieked. "Where is he now? Can we get to him?"

The barman grinned. "I should think, *mademoiselle*, that you can even *see* him. Come."

He gestured to both her and Philippe, and they followed him out of the bar and back up the wooden staircase to a panoramic window in the lobby. It displayed the whole mountainside — the softly undulating lower slopes and the steeper ones above. And sure enough, there, through the gloomy afternoon light and the steadily falling snow, they could make out a lone figure hunched on a wooden bench. Her brother! He must be freezing, thought Lyric, instinctively concerned as she looked out at him. Then, remembering their urgent mission, she grabbed Philippe's arm.

"Come on! We have to be quick!"

At the pinnacle of the mountain, a lone figure slipped off the top of an otherwise empty chairlift and adjusted his ancient ski goggles. Unaccustomed to any kind of physical exertion, Quentin Charlton huffed and took a deep breath of icy, snowy air to revive him. Pulling a hip flask from his backpack, he took a deep swig to enhance the effect and surveyed the mountainscape in front of him. Or rather, the snowscape. For, beyond the tips of his skis, the view amounted to a complete whiteout.

"Just my bloody luck," mused Quentin. But although it was years since he'd so much as taken a sniff of alpine air, he did not feel swayed from his purpose, or any blow to his confidence. For the first time in his life, he felt born to his mission, and buoyed by destiny. Like all the Charltons, he'd been an expert skier in his youth — once a skier, always a skier, he reminded himself — and anyway, Fate would see him through where expertise might let him down.

Fate. It had got him this far — it wouldn't let him down now. Not now, after everything. Not after he'd been so cruelly cheated by it all through his early years. Through the death of his newborn son, just days before his brother George was due to become a father himself. What cruel blow had made Quentin's son — the firstborn male Charlton of the next generation — die so unexpectedly, while George became a father to not one but two healthy babies? Quentin's grip on his poles tightened in anger — anger that the years had never dulled. Twins. Ha! Well, not for long, Georgie boy! Twisted by grief and greed, Quentin had used the death of his own baby to blackmail the family doctor into pretending the boy twin had also died, soon after his birth. Exhausted by the delivery and overcome with despair, George and Constance had suspected nothing as Quentin had spirited the baby away — not, as he'd initially planned, to an early grave, but to childless acquaintances of the doctor's. With Doctor Macintosh's spotless reputation it was an easy matter to forge back-papers on the pregnancy, and the couple, overjoyed at their good fortune, had never questioned the respectable doctor's story of a gymslip mother who'd been unable to keep her child. They'd welcomed the baby boy with unconditional love. The kind of love he, Quentin, should have been able to shower upon his first son and heir. Swallowing his decades-old grief, Quentin took one final swig of whisky and replaced the hip flask, and, double-checking his specially adapted ski pole, began to swoop expertly down the mountain. This was the only way. Swish, swish, swish. Dead, dead, dead. Adieu, Edward Charlton. Adieu, Lyric Charlton. With every turn, Quentin's murderous intent grew along with his speed, until the exhilaration made him shout out loud in joy.

"*Adieuuuuuuuuuuuuuuuu!*"

Pulling her quilted Chanel jacket around her, Lyric ran out into the snow, veering right and left like a cornered mouse until she found the correct route across the hotel's terrace. Once on the slope, she started to run uphill.

The snow was falling harder now, and progress through the virgin powder was tough going. It wasn't long before Lyric's Ugg boots were soaked through and weighed down with melted snow. The slope was steeper than it looked from the hotel, and her throat was burning with the exertion and the cold air. Worse, a slight wind had got up and was muffling her cries of "Edward" before they had so much as left her mouth. She turned back towards the hotel and looked down the slope. Philippe was way behind her — desperation was obviously making her move faster. Buoyed by the progress she'd made, she turned uphill again and carried on climbing. Edward's silhouette was still frustratingly distant. It was like running in a bad dream.

After another couple of minutes, Lyric stopped for a second to catch her breath and looked up the slope. Off piste, she could see a solo skier hurtling down the mountainside. She frowned. Something about the figure of the skier — the speed, the intent — made her double-take. A cold hand seemed to grab her around the heart. It looked all too familiar. Could it be . . . could it be Uncle Quentin? She watched as it forged an expert and unmistakeable path in the direction of the hotel. She gasped. The route the skier was taking, she knew from experience, was full of trees, icy patches and hidden hazards. In this visibility there was no way you would take that path for pleasure unless you were a total lunatic — or you had some alternative sinister purpose. Desperation spurred Lyric on, though her chest was bursting. She dragged her feet doggedly through the snow. She had to reach Edward. *Had* to.

"Edward!" she cried as she got closer and closer. *"Edward!"*

Finally, Edward seemed to hear her, and turned, shielding his eyes to try and make her out through the

413

snow. As if in a race against the skier, Lyric looked up at the slope. The figure had disappeared, but she could make out his tracks through the pine trees, and then — yes! There he was — closer, much closer. And there — she squinted. No, she wasn't mistaken — there was another skier now, too, racing in hot pursuit at a close but discreet distance from him. Could that be the PI?

Her heart beating overtime now, Lyric looked determinedly back at Edward. She couldn't take any chances. He was still staring at her quizzically, and she started to run, pulling off her coat and discarding it on the snow behind her as the sweat from running started to pour off her. Feeling the cold air whistle through her jeans and her fine-knit top seemed to drive Lyric on, and she ran even faster.

She was so close now she could make out his face, those features that she'd found so curiously familiar, that aura that she'd been so curiously drawn to that first night in the bar of Le Mélézin. Of course she'd recognized them! The big brown eyes, the thick, dark blond hair, the chiselled cheekbones. She'd seen those same features every day of her life — every time she'd looked in a mirror. They were her features and his — twin features. Twin brother and sister.

"Edward!"

He stared intently at her, first as if she was some kind of madwoman, and then with a look of dawning realization. Lyric stretched out her arms to him as she ran, wanting the wind to pick her up and spirit her over to him. As she approached him, she felt all the years of unexplained loneliness melt away, those countless times

414

she'd felt her happiness tarnished with a permanent feeling of emptiness just disappear. It was all about him — her twin brother — and now he was here, almost within touching distance.

Almost. At that moment, the world went into slow motion. A rhythmic swishing filled the air, and Lyric and Edward both turned to see their uncle round the corner of the slope just five hundred yards away, his figure hunched over his speeding skis with murderous purpose. Seeing them both, Quentin let out a blood-curdling yell and lifted his ski pole up, pointing it directly at the pair of them.

Lyric screamed. The ski pole must be a gun! *"Get down!"* she screamed at Edward.

As she leapt forward, a series of shots rang out around the valley, and Lyric felt a ton weight throw her on to the snow. She felt punched, as though winded, as the bullet penetrated the skin just underneath her shoulder-blade. Her back felt first warm, then cold, as the blood running down it hit the freezing air. But then there was nothing, only numbness, and had it not been for the blur of the snow turning pink around her, she might have thought she had simply tripped. Lyric struggled to pull herself forward, but as the lifeblood ran from her body, she was helpless to move.

In front of her, she saw Edward crumple into a heap on the ground too. Next, her uncle hurtled past, still at breakneck speed. Hot on his heels, the second figure — the PI, she saw now — raced past, and the shots continued further down the slope. Philippe! Lyric thought in a dreamlike panic. Edward! Philippe! Neither must be hurt. Please, let neither be hurt . . .

She let her head sink back into the snow for a few moments, until the voice — or the cold, she wasn't sure which — revived her a little. She lifted her head to see Edward crawling across the snow to her, the crumpled letter still in hand.

"Who are you?" he said in confusion. "Do I know you?"

Lyric weakly lifted her head and pointed to the letter. "I'm guessing that letter tells you who you are. That you are Edward Charlton."

Edward frowned. "Yes. I was adopted — but yes. The letter confirms that's my real name. How do you know?"

Lyric smiled softly. "Because I'm Lyric Charlton. Your sister." She reached out a limp hand towards him. Despite being only inches away from him, she was by now too weak to stretch out to him. Feeling the life-energy ebbing out of her, she smiled again, then let her hand drop into the snow. "Your *twin* sister."

Adrenaline coursing through his clogged-up veins, Quentin turned sharply off the slope and into the bordering woods, skis scraping noisily on the exposed ice covering trees, roots and pine cones. Swearing loudly, he pushed doggedly on along the bumpy woodland tracks. After a few fruitless moments, he acknowledged defeat and cast aside his skis and boots, pulling on instead the walking shoes he'd stashed in his backpack.

416

Curses! He'd banked on being able to reach the foot of the slopes — and the safety of his getaway car — whilst still on skis, and whilst the *gendarmerie* were still dealing with the fallout from Lyric and Edward's injuries. Lyric and Edward's fatal injuries, Quentin corrected himself — or at least, so he hoped. He'd shot enough bullets at them.

Huffing and puffing, face bright red from the unaccustomed exertion, Quentin stopped to lean against a tree to catch his breath. He mopped his brow irritably. Why did everything always have to go so bloody wrong for him? Resuming his sprint, if you could call it that, Quentin squinted his eyes to try and make out the way. The gloom of the afternoon was now making way for nightfall, but finally he spotted lights through the trees. At last! Once in his little car, zooming along the autoroute to the border, he was convinced he'd be safe — en route back to Dubai, where, tucked away in Sergei's safe house, he planned to continue delivery of the fraudulent paintings. And if word of this little upset ever reached Sergei's ears, Quentin was sure it wouldn't faze him — he'd no doubt be happy to welcome Quentin as one of his own. Much happier than if he ever discovered Quentin's art deception. In fact, if Quentin had to choose between the two, he'd much rather give himself up to the French police than face the wrath of Sergei. The problem was, one rather led to the other. If he were caught by the police now, he'd be unable to continue his art fraud, which would mean certain discovery by Sergei. It was yet another reason to keep on running . . .

Just then, he heard faint shouts behind him. Goddammit! It had to be police. The shouts grew louder, and he realized they were gaining on him. Quentin's heart grew heavy. His feet just simply wouldn't move fast enough and his chest felt like it was going to explode. But there was no choice. He had to make it. *Had* to!

It was then that he heard the barks. Not one, not two, but three dogs. And they had his scent. Panic gave Quentin a final burst of speed, but as he stumbled over frozen roots, he knew it was too late.

He felt a thud on his shoulder as one of the dogs floored him, and teeth nipping at his ankles as another took hold of his trouser leg. A third growled in his ear — Quentin could smell its breath as it let out occasional loud barks to alert its masters to its find.

The shouts grew louder, joined now by myriad footsteps crunching swiftly through the snow. Quentin felt his upper body being lifted off the snow as a hefty pair of hands heaved him by the shoulders. Stale cigar breath replaced the Alsatian's meaty fumes as a police officer snarled in his ear.

"*Monsieur Charlton!*" said the *gendarme*. "*Vous allez en vacances quelque part?*"

On holiday. Some hope. Quentin cursed his bad luck yet again. He had a horrible feeling it would be a long time before he'd be going anywhere . . .

Epilogue

Treeva twiddled her pink sparkly pen thoughtfully, and tickled the end of her nose with the fluffy end. What on earth should she write this week?

She adjusted the zip on her Juicy Couture tracksuit top to reveal more of her now even more voluptuous cleavage, and smoothed the lace camisole underneath. After all, writing was like acting, right? You had to look the part to *feel* the part.

She picked a handful of Haribo out of the bowl in front of her and resumed her thoughtful pose, looking out of the window at the rolling Berkshire fields beyond. Maybe the view wasn't inspiring enough. After all, when Carrie Bradshaw wrote her column in *Sex and the City*, she'd had the dynamic streets of Manhattan as her inspiration. Rural England wasn't quite cutting-edge enough. Treeva sighed. When she'd landed the weekly column at *OK!* just three weeks ago, she'd insisted on writing it herself. The editor had been horrified — simply no celebs wrote their own exclusive columns, apparently — and he'd urged Treeva to reconsider. But Treeva had been adamant. This was the new her — and she was going to start as she meant to go on.

Treeva suddenly squealed with delight. Of course! You didn't see Carrie Bradshaw writing *by hand*. She wrote on a laptop!

Grabbing her Swarovski-customized pink computer, Treeva leapt onto her bed excitedly, then chastized herself. She had to take more care now — no leaping around like that in her condition. Now, what on earth was she going to write?

The last two weeks' columns had been more straight-forward. In the first one, Treeva had told the readers the exclusive and shocking story of how she'd discovered she was pregnant (she'd fainted in customs whilst being held for the gun shoes), of her confusion over who the father might be (Treeva was a hundred per cent certain the father was Ralph. Or a second-division footballer father-of-three. Or any one of the scumbags she'd come across on her more, erm, hedonistic nights out), and of why she would never set foot in LA again (Huey's pool party had been busted by narcotics police, and now, annoyingly, her father, as official tenant of the hacienda, was facing charges). But more importantly, Treeva had come to terms with the fact that, whilst her trailer-trash tart-with-a-heart reality TV persona might well have appealed to middle America, the unmarried single-mom-to-be aspect most certainly would not have. It was her laboured weekly monologues cataloguing every stage of her pregnancy, waxing lyrical about the challenges facing single mums all over the country (trust fund and multimillionaire father notwithstanding, natu-rally) and fast capturing the nation's consciousness that seemed destined to make her name.

And it seemed to be making her happy. For since she'd discovered the little life growing inside her, Treeva had felt joy and excitement like she'd never known before. Without even a day at rehab, she'd not touched drink, drugs or even Botox since she'd found out, and here, installed in the sprawling family home, she felt calmer than she could ever remember.

The intercom buzzed and the soft burr of the family housekeeper sounded from the foyer.

"Miss Sinclair, you have a visitor."

Glad of the distraction, Treeva jumped up excitedly. Visitors this far out of town were few and far between. "Who is it, Maddy?"

"It's a young man, Miss Sinclair," said Maddy, sounding uncharacteristically sniffy. "Calls himself Ralph something or other." There was a murmur from the intercom. "Mr Ralph Conway," she said sulkily.

Treeva grinned in satisfaction. She'd been expecting this. But even she hadn't guessed how quickly. She slicked on some lip gloss and pressed the intercom lightly. "I just need to make a quick call."

Within a couple of moments she'd hung up. Heart beating, she pressed the intercom again.

"Send him up, Maddy."

She could almost feel the woman's disapproval down the intercom, and Treeva grinned. So what if it wasn't proper to entertain in her bedroom? What was the worst that could happen? She was already up the duff, after all!

Treeva took off her tracksuit top and pulled down the camisole to show maximum cleavage, then arranged herself alluringly across the pink satin duvet on her bed.

There was a knock at the door, and Ralph appeared with a rakish grin.

"I see you're waiting for me then, babe?"

Treeva bit her lip. He was thin, dishevelled and looked as though he hadn't slept in a week — but he was still bloody sexy. Immediately, though, his presence made her long for a cigarette, a glass of wine, a line . . . Was this what Lyric said they referred to as a "trigger" in rehab?

She shifted uncomfortably as he leaned in to kiss her on the cheek, then sat beside her on the bed.

"Of course I'm waiting for you. You've come to visit, idiot."

Ralph grinned and looked around her at the elaborately decorated room — the four-poster bed, the walk-in wardrobe, the marble en suite bathroom.

"I see Daddy's supporting you through this, then?" he said casually.

Treeva frowned. "Of course he's supporting me! It's not the Middle Ages, you know, Ralph. We're not going to hunt you down and force you up the aisle."

Ralph let out an audible sigh of relief.

"Anyhow, he's thrilled at the thought of being a granddad," Treeva continued. "And you know what? I can't wait to be a mum."

Ralph nodded cautiously. "That's good, that's good. And so what's the plan — you going to stay here when it's born, or is he going to set you up in your own place somewhere?"

Treeva laughed. "Don't worry, Ralph. I'm sure Daddy will make sure we're both very comfortable. You won't need to worry at all."

Ralph cleared his throat awkwardly. "So it's definitely mine?"

Treeva looked at him searchingly. He was really concerned. She sat up on the bed and hugged her knees.

"Well, the DNA test will tell us everything we need to know."

Ralph frowned. "The DNA test?"

Treeva laughed again. "Yes, Daddy made me promise to have one done to make sure we wouldn't get any false paternity suits against us that might endanger his millions. It'll take place as soon as possible after the birth."

Ralph shifted edgily on the bed. "Well, who else's could it be?"

Treeva looked at him, seeing him clearly for the first time — his suavity obliterated by nerves, his louche air eaten away by excess. Throughout the whole episode of their betrayal of Lyric, Ralph had never worried about them being exclusive to one another — or afterwards, for that matter. Was he seeing the DNA test as a slight against his masculinity — or a prospective payday running through his fingers? After all, if he was the baby's father, and he and Treeva were together, it could mean he'd never want for anything financially ever again. If, however, it transpired that someone else was the father — well, that was another opportunity down the pan, wasn't it?

Treeva wanted to laugh out loud. Strange how she'd hung on to his every word for so long. Now, clean and with a whole new future ahead of her, he suddenly meant very little to her. If he were the baby's father, of course she would have to work something out. But as a lover? Give her a break.

"Ralph, in all honesty, I don't know. In many ways, I don't care. Don't tell me that you do?"

Ralph stood up and searched in his jacket pockets, finally pulling out what appeared to be a scrappy bit of loo paper. He looked down at Treeva as though he wanted to throw up, then fell to his knees dramatically in front of her.

"I do care, Treeva. In fact, I care so much, I'm asking you to marry me."

From within the tissue he produced a gold ring with a pretty ruby set inside tiny diamonds.

"It was my grandmother's engagement ring," he said, holding it out to Treeva. "I'd like you to have it."

She stared at him, not sure whether to laugh or cry at the botched attempt at romance. A few weeks ago she'd have leapt at the chance to snaffle Ralph from under Lyric's nose. What a bitch she'd been. Looking at him now, she couldn't imagine what it was she'd ever seen in him — apart from the fact that he was Lyric's.

She held out her hand and closed his fingers back over the ring.

"Oh, Ralph," she said, shaking her head. "Save it for someone your grandmother would like to have it. For someone you *love*, not someone you think you should marry. I'm sorry, but I'm not interested."

The intercom buzzed and Maddy's voice, concerned now, rang out.

"Miss Sinclair! The police are here. They say they're after Mr Conway. They say they have a warrant for his arrest!"

Ralph stared at her, open-mouthed in shock, and stood up, fumbling with the ring as he walked backwards towards the door.

"The police? How do they know I'm here?"

Treeva shrugged apologetically.

"Ralph, we all know you told Quentin Charlton that Lyric knew all about his part in her drug exposé. That he paid you! You, in essence, blew Quentin's cover and set in motion everything that happened in Courchevel. Don't you see, Ralph? You, in many ways, are culpable for what happened to Lyric. And with Quentin now implicating you in the drug-smuggling ring — well. You're bang to rights, aren't you, Ralph? I've done enough damage to Lyric myself over the past few months. Let's just say alerting the police is my way of saying sorry to Lyric. You never know, you might just thank me for this too, one day . . ."

Treeva hugged herself inwardly as she watched him retreat in shock — and shame. He had never expected that she'd turn him down. *She* had never expected that she'd turn him down.

But more than that, he'd never expected that she'd betray him in the way he'd betrayed each and every one of them. Baby daddy or no baby daddy, she couldn't let Ralph get away with what amounted to attempted murder. It would be interesting to see if the silver tongue that had talked its way out of so many near-misses throughout his thirty-something years could now extricate him from drug-smuggling charges.

She sat up, grabbing a congratulatory handful of Haribo, and munched on them satisfactorily. It seemed a baby wasn't the only thing she'd discovered in the past few weeks. She'd found some self-respect too.

And, finally, something to write about in this week's *OK!* column.

Lyric opened her eyes, and immediately they were filled with an all-consuming white, almost celestial light. Ice? Or snow? It glittered, bright and hard, blinding her to everything but its cold intensity.

She was still lying on her hospital bed — she could tell from the cool, starched sheets. But at the same time, she had an odd sensation of floating above it, hovering in some half-conscious hinterland, somewhere between this world and the next.

This world. How it had changed in the days — weeks? — that Lyric had been lying here. She had pieced together the low murmurings of friends and family as they talked self-consciously to her, wanting to believe — but not totally convinced — that they were reaching her as she slipped in and out of consciousness. Then, reassured by her fleeting moments of lucidity that, yes, she could hear them, could make sense of their mumblings, their monologues had become more detailed, more animated, and Lyric had benefited from the regular updates from those she loved so much.

Well, *nearly* all of them. Laura, for one, had been conspicuous by her absence for some time. Shocked into a searing re-evaluation of herself by Lyric's discovery of her alcoholism, and brought up short by the treachery Lyric had experienced in her own family, Laura had left Max and Kitty with her mother and packed herself off to rehab. Discreetly, naturally. There (as Constance had related to Lyric in the resigned tones of a martyred matriarch), Laura had decided that it was most definitely better to stick with the devil you know, and had decided to stand by Robert — with a few caveats. The first was that, whilst he was under investigation by the Serious Fraud Office and unable to work, Robert should seek treatment for his sex addiction at a neighbouring rehabilitation centre. Anonymously, of course. The second was that he should agree to an intense (and hush-hush) course of marriage guidance. For though Laura had sworn that even if Robert received a custodial sentence she would be waiting for him when he left prison, she was under no illusion that it was going to be easy to rebuild their lives. And the third was that Robert would unswervingly support Laura's future commitment to Alcoholics Anonymous. AA, Constance confidently predicted, would soon be added to Laura's list of charity patronages.

Much less discreet had been Jacob. After years of covering up his sexuality — and who knew what else? — at the hands of his father's bully-boy tactics and bigoted views, Jacob had officially come out, admitting to his sexuality live on You Tube and then in an in-depth interview on the story behind his father's betrayal (in his own words, with exclusive *new* photographs) in *Hello!* magazine. With the six-figure fee from the interview he'd bought a modest country house close to Milton Keynes — lavish enough to support his still-burning political aspirations, but low-key enough to allow "ordinary" people to relate to him (and not too far from the shopping centre, either). Jacob had also used his high-profile platform to announce that, in line with his recent treatment, he'd switched allegiance to the Liberal Democrats. His raw honesty and new-found humility had proved a hit with the British electorate, and now tabloids and broadsheet papers alike were hailing him as the new future of politics.

But if humility had been key to Jacob's reinvention, it had been almost non-existent in the new direction life was taking his paramour Crispin. Crispin's arrival into the public's consciousness had coincided with a dire national shortage of loveable queens with a natty sense of style and a talent for a quick, bitchy turn of phrase. Subsequently, Crispin's brief flirtation with the tabloids had turned into a full-blown love affair with the British public. After just a few weeks as a household name, doing the rounds of day-time TV sofas and weekend chat shows, he'd filled the (ample) seat of one of the country's foremost morning television hosts as she went on maternity leave, and was proving a huge hit. In fact, he was already well on the way to upgrading his status to fully-fledged national treasure — even, he'd confided confidently to Lyric on a pre-recorded bedside message, surpassing her own unique place in the hearts of the Brits. So much so, in fact, that

American stations were clamouring for him to join them and throwing all kinds of offers at him. But, as he'd confided in the same message, he wasn't too fussed about going to America for the time being. Bad food, bad cars — and it was full of Americans, after all.

In fact, the only one of Lyric's inner circle who remained in the States for the time being was her godmother, Truly Stunning. On a whirlwind stop-over to visit Lyric with her new beau — Swedish actor, international playboy and Hollywood heart-throb Jeorg Swooney — Truly had been forced to enter the hospital via the back door for fear of fuelling the press hysteria that surrounded her new relationship. Despite a string of young and beautiful A-list girlfriends, serial monogamist Jeorg had been unable to shake persistent rumours over his sexuality. Surely he was too beautiful to be straight? Too fragrantly alluring to be anything but (at the very least) a bit bi? However, his obvious adoration for renowned cougar and man-bewitcher Truly meant he had to be one hundred per cent straight. If he was man enough for Truly Stunning, who could question his sexuality?

In complete contrast, the Sheik and Carola had made several flamboyant visits to the hospital, showing their concern by means of endless fuss and an elaborately gift-laden entourage. The overflowing fruit baskets, luxury hampers and boxes of handmade chocolates would have fed an army, let alone one semi-conscious Lyric, but had nevertheless been graciously accepted on her behalf by Constance and George — only to be swiftly and discreetly distributed amongst the staff and local homeless charities. But the Sheik's genuine support of the Charltons throughout their troubles seemed to have touched even Ali Hassan, who, despite the fact that taking out his own retribution on Quentin had meant drawing a line under his connection with the Charltons, had sent an elaborate bouquet of flowers weekly to Lyric's bedside.

Lyric blinked, the thought of her nemesis awakening something inside her. The intensity of the white light seemed to ebb for a moment, then returned with increased vigour. The problem was that, after he had been arrested for her attempted murder then charged with not only drug smuggling but the art fraud too, no one was sure what had happened to Quentin. During a routine transfer between custody and the magistrate's court, it seemed that Quentin had been spirited away from his high-security prison transport. A super-skilled group of armed men, reportedly speaking Russian, had held up the van and disappeared into the night with him. Not even the Foreign Office could furnish them with any more details beyond his certain abduction. But after a sighting of him apparently unwillingly boarding a certain Sergei Alexandrov's private jet, the last whereabouts of Quentin, it seemed, were somewhere over the depths of the Indian Ocean . . .

Lyric shivered and turned her confused thoughts to more heart-warming matters. To Lyric's semi-conscious delight, a frequent visitor to her bedside had been her brother Edward. The injuries he'd sustained from the shoot-out on the slopes had turned out to be superficial, and, with Philippe, he'd accompanied

Lyric's stretcher on to the flight back from France. There, it seemed, he'd had an emotional reunion with his long-lost mother and father. At the joy of finding their son, both George and Constance seemed to have lost twenty years between them, and even Constance had a jubilant spring in her step and a twinkle in her eye. Edward was now permanently based at Charlton Hall, where, as well as getting to know his parents, he was learning about estate management, keen to know how to maintain his inheritance for the future. It was his populist vision that had persuaded George to share the living history that Broughton Hall represented and open up most of the house to the public, using the proceeds to fund the newly-established Charlton Charitable Foundation. Constance, for her part, was spending her time away from Lyric's bedside in tireless lunching, gala dining and auctioning in order to raise the profile of the charity, which aimed to reunite families torn apart by war, poverty and circumstance.

Philippe, in the few moments he hadn't been at Lyric's side, had also been throwing himself into Charlton family life. In his detailed daily updates, Philippe had told her with relief how he'd sold his business, retiring at last from the public life he detested to help Edward and George restore Broughton Hall's grounds to their rightful magnificence. With renewed vigour and intensity, he channelled the desperation he felt for Lyric to regain consciousness and full health into energy for his new projects. He was full of ideas, too, about their future together — his vision for Broughton Hall's grounds, for Lyric's continued commitment to Sunny Street Hospital and her other charities — and, most important, his plans for marriage, and children, too . . .

At the thought of a future with Philippe, Lyric gasped and choked, and slowly her eyes regained their focus. The bright light developed edges, and facets, and spectral colours, glowing with a curiously familiar lustre. And as the glow it gave off seemed not only to be reflected on Lyric, but to radiate out from within her, suddenly, instead of blinding her, it seemed, with new clarity, to light up the path of her future. With a start, Lyric realized she was holding her hand up in front of her. And the light was not some otherworldly aura, but a paragon sparkling in her engagement ring — the gorgeous, glittering engagement ring that glowed on the third finger of her left hand. It seemed to reflect all the life, love and hope that lay in wait for her. And as she looked beyond it, she saw with delight an array of faces — her mother's, stern and disapproving as always, but softer, somehow more beautiful in her distress, without the carefully constructed society face in place. Then there was her father's, crinkly eyes screwed up with concern, face more gaunt than she could remember ever seeing it. Beside his the new — but oh-so-familiar — face of Edward, her twin. And then Philippe's, as he paced up and down, glowering, unable to sit still, the scar on his face making it even more handsome in its imperfection. As one, their faces lit up and transformed into beacons of hope as Lyric's arm moved and her eyes opened.

434

"*Lyric!*" shrieked her mother, leaning forward excitedly. At once, it seemed, Philippe was by her side, holding her hand and murmuring "*chérie*" with unadulterated love and hope in his eyes.

Never before had Lyric felt so happy — so *content*. What was that saying? No pain, no gain? Now she really understood it. Because without all the terrible things that she had suffered over the past few months, none of the amazing things could have happened either. It wasn't all going to be plain sailing — that was certain. But as she looked up into Philippe's eyes, she knew that her life — an even better one than she could ever have hoped for — really was about to begin.

Acknowledgements

Wrapped in my cashmere wrap in my chalet in Switzerland, it occurs to me there are some people I'd rather like to bring to your attention.

Firstly, as a writer drawing on personal experience, it's customary to give oneself something of a disclaimer. I should point out, therefore, that any similarities between the characters of *Inheritance* and any living individuals are, of course, entirely coincidental.

And so, on to the acknowledgements, and the people without whom *Inheritance* simply wouldn't have been possible. Thank you, Gordon at Curtis Brown. Wise by name, and wise by nature — not only does he make the best deals, he also makes the perfect escort at all the best parties.

Thanks also to Jeremy Trevathan at Pan Macmillan for believing in me, and giving me the opportunity to write this book. (And he knows what I'm *really* like!)

Thank you to Wayne for your hard work and patience editing this story, to Katie for handling the press and to Antonia for her work in marketing it. We wouldn't have been able to get it out there without you.

And to my partner in crime, Claire. (Come on, everyone needs some help . . . It might be my voice, my story and my feelings — but I can't type!) I'm not exactly the maternal type, and I thought a brand-new mum was exactly the last person I wanted to work with

— but it seems some mothers do have 'em (martinis, that is), and our girly evenings cooking up *Inheritance* were a fabulously leaky-boob-free zone.

Behind every Swiss watch is a fantastically talented craftsman — Becca Barr is mine! Thanks also to Carly at Becca Barr Management. Carly, every candle I've lit this year has had your name on it.

Thanks to John Spence for the good karma you gave me during those sunset evenings in Bali, and to John Myatt for giving us the inside story on the art world.

And thanks to Rene, my trusted make-up artist, for so fabulously helping me look the part!

Finally I would like to thank my lucky stars, who shine so brightly every day in my life. My family — my father and mother, Santa and Sebag, James and Sos. I would never have been able to do half the things I've done in my life if it wasn't for your continued love and support.

This book is dedicated to my Mother. Thank you for all the hours you put in reading and editing *Inheritance* and your truly unique words of wisdom.

Also available in ISIS Large Print:

Scandalous

Martel Maxwell

Max is a gorgeous showbiz reporter whose life is a whirlwind of celebrity parties, glamorous bars and gorgeous men; Lucy, a beautiful, elegant fashion writer, has always been the sensible one, taking care of her little sister and never seeking the limelight. But that all changes when she starts dating Hartley, Britain's most eligible bachelor, and her love life becomes front-page news. And with Hartley's ex-girlfriend, a scheming socialite, determined to get her man back and destroy Lucy in the process, she's horrified to see her private life splashed across the tabloids.

Meanwhile Max, tired of the non-stop partying that her job entails, has finally met the perfect man, but Lucy is convinced that he is Mr Totally Wrong. Will Max be forced to choose between him and her sister? And can Lucy's relationship with Hartley survive the cruel intentions of his bitter ex-girlfriend?

ISBN 978-0-7531-8814-9 (hb)
ISBN 978-0-7531-8815-6 (pb)

Living La Vida Loca

Belinda Jones

Carmen has been feeling the need to break free for too darn long!

So when her equally frustrated friend Beth suggests the ultimate escape — dancing their way through a series of scorchingly-hot countries — she can't resist. There's just one catch . . . they can only go on this adventure if they participate in a reality TV show, one intent on teaching them the mournful tango in Argentina, the feisty flamenco in Spain and the sassy, celebratory salsa in Cuba.

As they travel from Buenos Aires to Seville and ultimately steamy Havana, each dance has a profound effect on the girls — as indeed do the sexy gauchos, matadors and dirty dancers who partner them . . . But when the sun goes down, will Beth and Carmen have what it takes to go beyond the steps and free their hearts for love?

ISBN 978-0-7531-8800-2 (hb)
ISBN 978-0-7531-8801-9 (pb)

A Reluctant Cinderella

Alison Bond

Samantha Sharp turned 17, left her old life behind and moved to London, determined to make her fortune. Ten years later and she's super-agent to the stars, with her name in the papers, millions in the bank and one success after another. Love has taken a back seat because her past has put her off relationships for good.

Everyone's got a history but Samantha's is particularly murky. What's more, she hasn't got to the top of her game without collecting a few enemies along the way. So when she meets a man who might be a little bit dangerous, someone she's finally close to loving, is there anyone to tell her what a terrible mistake she's making?

ISBN 978-0-7531-8796-8 (hb)
ISBN 978-0-7531-8797-5 (pb)

My Single Friend

Jane Costello

Four bad dates. Three sassy women. Two inseperable friends. And one way too successful makeover . . .

Lucy Tyler and Henry Fox have been best friends since primary school. So when he enlists her help to embark on an image makeover, she and her friends Dominique and Erin approach the project with relish. As well as the haircut and fashion overhaul, there are master classes in flirting and seduction.

But none of the girls imagine at the start of "Project Henry" quite how successful it's going to be. Henry's transformation from Lucy's terminally single friend to irresistible sex god takes on a life of its own. And Lucy isn't at all sure she likes it. It would help if her own dates were more promising. Only, between breaking someone's arm and an errant chopstick, they're anything but. With a dating history like that, Lucy starts to despair when she finds herself living with the man of everyone else's dreams!

ISBN 978-0-7531-8772-2 (hb)
ISBN 978-0-7531-8773-9 (pb)